SOWLS.

C000174832

About the author

Frank Westworth shares several characteristics with JJ Stoner: they both play mean blues guitar and ride Harley-Davidson motor-cycles. Unlike Stoner, Frank hasn't deliberately killed anyone. Instead, he edits *RealClassic* magazine and has written exten-sively for the UK motoring press. Frank lives in Cornwall with his guitars, motorcycles, partner and cat.

1 3 1676815 6

A LAST ACT
OF CHARITY

Killing Sisters

Book I

Frank Westworth

Book Guild Publishing

Sussex, England

First published in Great Britain in 2014 by
The Book Guild Ltd
The Werks
45 Church Road
Hove
East Sussex
BN3 2BE

Typesetting in Cambria by Ellipsis Digital Limited, Glasgow

Printed in Great Britain by CPI Group (UK) Ltd, Croydon, CR0 4YY

A catalogue record for this book is available from
The British Library.

ISBN 978 1 909984 42 4

Many, many cooks . . .

Lots of people, friends mostly, and they mostly still are, helped with this attempt at a novel. Thanks are due and are duly offered. Charity's book would have been impossible without painfully heavy advice, subtle threats, very loud guitars, powerful music and dread whiskeys from RJ Ellory. Meanwhile, Rowena Hoseason has read the drafts so many times and suffered so noisily for so long that she can now recite entire passages from memory. Without her; no book. It has been a blast.

1

ONE IS ONE

Dangerous days, these. All of them. Trying too hard can be dangerous. If in doubt . . . do not try; simply do it. If you've done it, and if you are still in doubt . . . do it again, but this time do it harder. Then once more . . . with feeling. With conviction. On dangerous days, it is always best to do it hardest the first time. On dangerous days, there might be no second chance, no second attempt, no never-mind-must-try-harder moment for the slow of thinking, the slow in action. On dangerous days . . . there is always the chance that holding back a little in reserve could prove fatal.

Which is only a problem if the fatality is yours, and not that of your target.

Charity knew all the signs of dangerous days. She recognised the signs of her own dangerous days best of all, and the signs she recognised the most after those were the trails, the tracks, the trash left by her sister. And her sister had definitely been here; the signs were entirely clear on that. Her sister's days were deadly dangerous. Extreme. Always.

There was blood everywhere. That was the first sign. Blood everywhere was a trademark of Charity's sister. And where there was blood, there too was a body. There was usually a body. Most often, there was a body. Or more than one. Bodies were her sister's speciality, her most valuable skill. She could transform some stranger's life into something entirely different. Into not-life. Into death. Death. Such a tidy word. Death. Short and sweet. The word, that is; death itself, death the condition, death the state-of-not-living . . . that tended to be quite the opposite. Death tended to be infinitely long . . . and infinitely bitter.

Charity gazed at the blood. As all fans of televisual crime scene investigations know, blood lies in patterns, it tells tales. It lies . . . most often it lies and lies and lies, and the only truth it shares is that the twisted sisters of discomfort and death are nearby. And where there is death, so there is a body. The body is the thing. The body is the result of her sister's calling, and her contract. Because Charity's sister killed people. It was her speciality, her most valuable skill. Charity's sister made her living from others' dying. And she lived a comfortable and rewarding life built upon the deaths of others. And dying is never comfortable. Reward lies only in the killing.

The tale told by the lying blood was a familiar one. You did not need to be a detective, televisual or terrestrial, to work that out. It told a tale of violence, of sudden, tight-beam aggression. Aggression with a fine focus reduces the chances of failure, which is important if you're a contracted killer, not least because career enhancement follows successful contract fulfilment. Failure to fulfil the contract could be . . . well . . . fatal. Fatal for the wrong person. That rather depended on the identity of the contractual victim, but we'll get back to that.

In this case, the blood was lying, as blood does when spilled in a great quantity, all around the body. The body was crumpled in the furthest corner of the room. It was defended by a moat of blood. The cheap carpet was a mess. The body was a mess, as bodies tend to be, but the carpet was worse.

Charity sighed. What is it with blood and carpets?

She pulled the door gently closed behind her. And wondered why she was being so quiet, so careful. Her sister would have been entirely uncaring about the sound of a closing door. Her sister would have been more concerned with the sound of a closing life; closing doors tended not to attract attention of the lawful kind, of the vengeful kind, which possibly made silence the virtue it so often is; the taking of life should be silent. Slamming doors rarely suggest that a life has ended, even though the ending of a life reflects the closing of all doors. Forever.

Charity cleaned up. If anything was likely to irritate Charity, it could have been the suggestion that she was a cleaner, that her peculiar speciality was to follow in her sister's bloody footsteps and to clean up after her. But in this case, that was precisely what she was doing. Cleaning up. Cleaning up the mess was as important as the business of creating, causing, that mess in the first place. It was the subject of considerable if occasional debate between the sisters. Because cleaning up properly should deflect the almost inevitable police investigation. It is almost impossible to disguise, to hide, a violent killing. It is always important that a professional killer disguises the scene of their professional activity. Obviously. The scene of the crime must not be surrounded by a trail which would track back to the killer. There are many ways of achieving this, and Charity could have written the manual, had she wished to be an author.

Today's bloody mess was spectacular. Blood was all over the place, not just settling into the carpet; it disfigured the furniture, the walls, even, remarkably, the ceiling. Charity's sister had been in an energetic mood, unmistakeably passionate. She had plainly carried some issues of her own with her this time. But that was probably unavoidable; everyone carries issues, personal issues, especially those whose chosen profession involves the taking of life. A grand phrase, the taking of life; a

3

politically sensitive phrase; killing is the only game, whatever the name for it.

Blood stained the dark screen and pooled between the keys of the laptop computer sitting on the floor facing the victim. Charity was interested in this. Had the victim been surfing the net, seeking solutions for his woes? Watching a slasher movie, maybe, for a little final entertainment? Updating his Facebook page with breaking news of his demise? She closed the screen and kicked the device away from the body. Its days were as done as his own were; neither had need of the other any more.

Crime scenes tell tales. This one told a tale which was increasingly, uncomfortably, familiar to Charity; a tale of a partner deviating, not for the first time, from the agreed plan. The plan had suggested that the victim's final evening should have been a convivial experience. It is always easier to kill someone who is happy, cheerful and relaxed than someone who is angry, fearful and cautious. Some professional killers preferred their victims to be angry, to put up a fight. Maybe they needed to pretend some justification for the killing. Charity's sister killed for money. No other justification needed. She was incapable of caring sufficiently to need a big excuse.

However, the scene of this crime told no tale of a relaxed victim, of someone who had pegged out after an evening of delight, of intellectual enjoyment ... or in fact of enjoyment of any kind. The scene which Charity had expected to massage gently into a misleading maze of confusing and conflicting clues was instead a clearly defined tale of anger. Where there should have been a body in a bed, tucked up as though sleeping off an evening of entertainment and enjoyment, there was instead a crumpled, bloody corpse and a chaotic, bloody carpet. And bloody walls. And even, remarkably, that bloody ceiling. Charity's challenge.

The killing plan had been that the victim should be found dead in bed. The cause of death should have been plain. It would have involved paid-for sex; hard rope and silken twine. The hard rope would have restrained the limbs; the silken twine would have been providing sensual constriction at throat and groin. The latter would have been the cause of death. It's easy to get your knots in a twist at a moment of passion. How many evening companions are experts in naughty knotting? Really? Should one utilise the delights of the bowline? The round turn and two half-hitches? How tight should one pull the silken twine before the reef knot turned into the grief knot? One can imagine the drawing room debate . . . almost.

Charity had expected to add a little misdirection to the scene. She had brought a small assortment of underwear, trusting that her sister would have taken her own with her when she left. Charity had expected to mop the body with the underwear, adding appropriate bodily fluids to feminine frillery to provide proof positive that man and woman had shared dark delights prior to a sadly fatal misadventure. The original owner of the underwear might even have been implicated, depending upon the efficiency of the clothes' last washing prior to Charity's launderette appropriation and whether that anonymous owner had supplied DNA to the police at some point, but she presumed that if that was the case, the owner would be able to provide an alibi. And if not; so what? A little confusion goes a long way, and police resources are not infinite. The interests of the press are both avoidable and fickle; adding evidential confusion would never hurt.

But all of that careful thinking had been rendered pointless by the actual scene of the crime. Charity leaned on a clean wall and pondered. She flicked open her cell phone and dialled her sister. There was no reply. There almost never was. She dialled her other sister. There was no reply, which was less usual. Perhaps they were off together, enjoying a great time while she did the dirty work. It seemed unlikely, but it was possible.

It would not be possible to present this mess as a night of

passion gone wrong. This was a fight scene. At least two individuals had fought, and the victim had lost that fight. Terminally. Conventional thinking implied that the corpse was that of the intended victim, whether that was the fact of the matter, or not. Reasonable doubt; only a little confusion would be needed to introduce doubt into the minds of the inevitable investigators.

Charity pondered some more, and looked carefully around her. A life had been ended. How? The killing weapon appeared to be a wine bottle, one of three she could see. Presumably the broken one. She felt a fast flurry of worry. Did all of the blood come from the victim? She dialled her sister's cell again. There was no reply. Was her sister even now languishing bloodied somewhere, needing or receiving medical assistance?

No time to worry about that at the moment. Plenty of time to worry later. Charity needed to massage the scene and leave it. And fast. She returned to the door, moved her carrier bag to one side and laid it flat. She stripped off her clothes, all of them, revealing herself in her startling and unique nakedness to the unseeing eyes of the victim. His treat, she reflected, although exactly what he would have made of her entirely hairless, athlete-thin, wire-muscled body would be forever a mystery. She removed her wig, shivering as her shining bald scalp reacted to the air-conditioned chill. Her skin goosed; the stressed patches which had once been the sites of her nipples tightened. She rubbed them, distracted, and smiled at her inappropriate behaviour. Shouldn't she show respect for the dead?

Her hands ran away down her belly. All the way down. Both hands. She held herself, expecting and experiencing the familiar wet heat. What was it about death? Ungently, with both hands, she parted her lips, leaned back against the clean wall and pressed far into herself. She snapped upright, clapped her hands and walked into the pooled blood. Charity needed to meet the victim. The briefest of encounters.

Blood on the carpet, then. A strange expression. Blood pools into the carpet; it does not lie on top of it. Charity smiled; a strange sight, white skin, rouge-red lips, white teeth. She smiled at the thought of fictional blood on fictional carpets; how the latter could somehow be cleaned of the former. She smiled at the memory of a movie she'd watched; a movie in which a clean-up team had cleaned up the bloodied scene of a bloody murder. Fiction. This blood would never leave this carpet. The room already stank of blood, of death. This carpet would only ever be useful as a carpet for an abattoir.

Her task was to confuse the inevitable investigator. Easy; she simply needed to devise a fiction and rearrange things so that the fiction sold itself. Just like a novel, like a movie. So let's see what there is to play with.

Body; one, crumpled in a corner and covered with blood. The body was modest, mostly dressed, no crime of passion this, unless the body became a naked body, and that wasn't possible without too much contact. Charity preferred to avoid contact except when absolutely necessary. Sometimes it proved to be necessary, but this did not feel like one of those times. One room; standard hotel, with big bed (rumbled, bloody), easy chair (overturned, bloody), upright chair (overturned, bloody) . . . and carpets, walls and fixed furniture, all in a state of disarray, most of it bloody. Three bottles, all overturned, all empty, one broken. Charity hummed to herself; a sign of contentment in others.

OK, then. Here comes the plot. Victim is joined by a friend for a drink. They fight. Not much of a friend, then, but enough of a friend to be invited to a private room for a private drink, even though the evening was ageing, the night was young, and the bars were still open. But that was too much detail; all Charity needed was two characters in a room sharing a few bottles. She kicked at the nearest bottle with her toe, read the label. No wine snobs these, plainly. The bottle tried to roll away but gave up, sucked into the congealing carpet.

One of the not-very-good friends whacks the other with a bottle, hard enough to cause death. Hmmm . . . That was not as easy as it sounds. Charity ceased smiling, and practised a look of concern. You need to hit someone awfully hard to kill them. Neither as hard nor as often as is portrayed as being survivable in the movies, but it is difficult to hit someone hard enough to kill them unless you intend to do that final irreversible thing.

In fact, you need to hit them several times to make sure they're dead and not just stunned. Charity's mind drifted back to the days when she had been more actively involved in the killing side of the sisters' business, when . . . but never mind that; time was moving on and she needed to dress the scene.

She needed to believe that her sister was uninjured. She needed to believe that all of the ocean of blood belonged to the victim. She hated to do this, to assume anything, because in every doubt lies the possibility of discovery, of failure, but her sister was unreachable, and Charity was not going to hang around all night.

She picked up the nearest bottle, hefted it for balance and stepped barefoot through the oozing, stinking blood to the body. The victim's right hand was palm down at his side; maybe he had been pushing, attempting to raise himself. Who knows? Who cares?

Charity lifted the hand, pleased that rigour wasn't making her life awkward, and squeezed the fingers around the body of the bottle. She rolled the bottle within the hand, smearing the setting blood so that no prints would ever be found; lifted the arm as high as she could and dropped it back. The bottle fell from the limp fingers, rolled . . . but not much. She walked to the broken bottle, the cause of death. This would be carrying her sister's prints. Inevitably. And the best way to lose these was to apply maximum smearing. The scene needed to look like a simple fight:

8

it must not look like the contract job which it actually was. More confusion.

She scooped blood into the broken body of the bottle and flicked it as high as the ceiling. A little more blood scatter should add to the confusion, as should the final part of her performance. A performance, that is what it was; she smiled and bowed to her audience, her audience of one, her audience of one whose attention would wander no more, whose eyes were fixed on her as she dressed her scene, macabre in her pallid nudity, calm and measured in her actions.

The audience blinked.

Had Charity been a girl given to demonstrating wild emotions, like shock, alarm, she would have done so at that point. Instead, she stared at the body. She stared hard, unblinking, into the eyes across the room. They stared right back, equally unblinking. Unfocused. Unresponsive. The naked, hairless woman stared hard at the broken, bloodied man, wondering whether he was alive, conscious, and if so what he made of the sight he saw. He blinked again, just the right eye, and from that eye there rolled a tear. Just one.

From Charity's eyes rolled tears of her own. She dropped her broken bottle, stood and walked to the body, shaking her head slowly from side to side. She leaned against the spattered wall and slid down it until she was sitting by the body, leaning against him, against his cooling side. She wiped her eyes with the back of her hand and held that hand by his mouth. She could feel no breathing. She pressed her bloodied fingers to his bloodied throat, felt for and found a pulse. Not much of a pulse, but enough of a pulse. What a tale this man could tell. What a tale . . .

Gently, almost fondly, for he was an audience who had paid a fine high price to watch her perform, she clamped a hand over his lips, and squeezed his nostrils tight with the other. Gently. He meant nothing to her. Another tear fell. His left arm lifted, slowly, reaching perhaps for Charity's killing hands, but stopped, dropped to her thigh. Slid the hand to the joint of her legs, pushed against her warmth . . . and so he died.

Charity screamed in silence. She arched her back against the wall and stood, then she stamped across the pain-filled room to the bathroom, climbed into the shower and sluiced the pain from her body, mouth gaping, silent anguish echoing, rubbing at herself until shuddering release found her and she sank to the floor of the shower, eyes closed at last, as the waters washed away the surprise, the unwelcome surprise, and she washed and wiped down the walls and she washed and wiped down her body, and she climbed soaking from the bath, swilled bleach from the maid's bucket around the bath and the drain, dressed herself, still soaking, turned the aircon to full heat and left the scene.

And as she stalked away, her phone called to her . . .

The plan ordained that although it was fine to manage more than a single contract at once, executive actions – terminal actions – were significant standalone events. These things were important, and should always be planned; hence the existence of the plan. Without the plan there was a strong probability of failure, with all the unhappiness for the sisters which would then be inevitable. Communication was crucial. Without communication, confusion would take over; control would be lost. Charity was unamused at being summoned to another action. She was unaware of any other mature contracts. She found no comfort in the unexpected, quite the opposite.

2

ONE MORE CUP OF COFFEE

'Did you see that? Did you just see that!'

Three young men pushed and jostled and shoved their way to the head of a vaguely chaotic queue for coffee. Their leader, the speaker, walked backwards towards the counter, widespread arms underlining his enthusiasm. Collision was inevitable. And collision occurred.

Stoner saw it coming, as was his way. He saw it all in anticipatory slo-mo but waited, fresh, large coffee in his hand, for the outcome. He almost always welcomed an outcome; had not expected to find it in a coffee lounge, but he had no problems with the location. Or with the participants. Arms flailed. Youth and coffee connected. Coffee hit the floor. Stoner stood. Silent. Impassive. Inactive. Waiting.

The young man, the leader, the talker, spun around.

'Guy! Look where you're going! What the fuck! This mess. Everywhere. Shit! Oh shit . . .'

Stoner watched it happening, as was his way. He saw it all in dreamy soft focus but foresaw the inevitable outcome as a hard reality.

'Shit, guy! You've soaked me! You fucking drunk?'

11

The lounge was silencing fast. Families were looking away; sudden interest in anything else, anywhere else. Mothers collected children; fathers pretended tough, hands-off attitudes. The doors only opened to let customers leave; the staff just stared, resigned.

'Aww . . . shit . . . Look at this. Who's going to pay for this?'

The young man was plainly a master of the rhetorical question. By now he was facing Stoner, whose costly coffee was soaking into the offended young man's clothes. Stoner stood, impassive, expressionless. Eye to eye.

'You gonna clean this?'

Another pointless question, another suggestion of intent. Three young men faced Stoner, more anger on their leader's face than there was coffee on his bootleg knock-off football shirt. Stoner stood, impassive, expressionless. Neutral.

Bright-eyed with anger, red-faced with outrage, the young man shoved Stoner hard.

'This shirt's a hundred quid, guy. A hundred!'

He shoved again, harder. Shouting. Stoner stood his ground. Resigned. Afterwards, coffee drinkers agreed that he'd not said a word up to that point. Although he did shake his head, slowly, looking the young man, the much younger man, straight in the eye.

Stoner glanced down, mapped the positions of the participants, then looked up again at the perfect moment to observe the swung punch, the wide-armed brawling bully fist approaching, walked inside it, one single pace, snapped his forehead into full-force contact with the bridge of the youth's nose, slapped his open palms against the young man's shoulders, kicked his leading foot along the carpet and moved forward two more steps, hooked his left foot around the youth's ankles and pulled it back. One long movement, not a series. Fluid.

The young man squealed, an unattractive sound, and fell flat. In the sudden uneasy quiet, the coffee machines hissed their sympathy, their support. Their loyalties were unclear, but their irritation was obvious.

'Don't get up.'

Stoner spoke for the first time.

The young man was going, 'Jesusjesusjesus . . .' in a raising wail as he failed to understand what had just happened.

'Don't get up.'

Stoner spoke softly, but with noticeable clarity and force. The young man ignored this generous advice, and through a rising tide of what could have been misunderstood to be a religious incantation, was wrestling himself to his feet. His companions, sometime friends and potential allies in arms, stood wide apart, staring in shared surprise. Stoner stamped down on the young man's ankle. There was an ominous and obviously painful crunch and the torrent of 'Jesusjesusjesus' soared through tenor to soprano. Blood was running freely from the nose by the carpet.

Stoner looked up at the nearer of the two upright young men.

'His ankle's broken. It will need setting. His nose is broken. It'll be fine, but it will be hard to breathe through it for a while. It would be a kindness to take him to a medic, or call for one.'

Silence. Bewilderment. The invincible superiority of youth facing the demonstrable superiority of a single older man.

'A doctor? A nurse? A hospital? Hello?'

Irritation and impatience were fighting for prominence now. He was bored with this. Amusing while it lasted, the fight was complete.

The pair of friends stared at Stoner. The further started to speak, to strike an aggressive pose. Stoner looked at him. Cold. Quietly.

'Don't even think about it. Not for one moment. Take your friend to a doctor. A&E would be good. You have five good legs between you. Let's keep it that way? You will need to help him. He will be in some pain.'

13

Gently. No raised voices. The nearer of the two upright friends started to move towards Stoner, opening his mouth.

Quite suddenly, Stoner was far too close to him, moving fast, leaving him nowhere to go but in reverse, spluttering.

'Do not,' Stoner repeated himself, 'even think about it. Take him away. Maybe his mother will love him. He surely needs some love.'

The suddenly silent pair, all confidence gone, lifted their fallen hero and negotiated the lounge door, the exit. Gone. Talk restarted. Quiet. Staring.

Stoner turned back to the counter. The teenaged server smiled at him.

'The guy over there . . .' she nodded to a table, '. . . just called the law. Sir.'

She smiled some more. Stoner took out a twenty, handed it to her.

'Sorry for the mess.'

He turned for the door, exit stage centre. Turned back, a plainly and obviously exaggerated hard look wiped across his features; 'I'll be back . . .'

The server clapped, and laughed, and hid the twenty.

'Who's next?'

The lounge manager, previously invisible, hurried by with a brush, collecting the fallen crockery shards. Coffee lounge life continued, and by the time the law arrived there were no witnesses left, just third-party comments on other-third party comments.

All done.

3

SAME OLD STORY

'Let me', said the Hard Man, 'tell you a story.

'Let me', said the Hard Man, 'tell you a tale . . .'

He stood facing Stoner, whose impassive expression matched that of the slight Asian gentleman who was standing to the left of the speaker and a little behind him. Stoner spoke to him, acknowledged him: 'Mr Tran.' And he nodded slightly.

The Hard Man pushed past the door, pushed into the room, pushed on into a place where he was unwelcome. Considerably unwelcome. But he was the Hard Man. That he was unwelcome made no difference to him. If he recognised that he was unwelcome, he ignored that recognition. It may have mattered nothing to him; there was no way of telling. It was unimportant anyway.

'Another fight.'

The Hard Man's statement lay slab-flat between them.

'Another fight, JJ.'

Not a question. No room for doubt, just a simple statement of fact. So there was no need for a reply. A reply could only have been an agreement, and there was no room for one of those. No need, either, The Hard Man stood. Stoner stood too, impassive, although all the space in that hallway was his own, the Hard Man

15

an intruder, an uninvited visitor, no kind of guest at all. There were times when it was right to make a point of property, of possession, but this was not one of them.

'Some thug,' the Hard Man's tone was neutral, no edge nor inflection; 'smacked around a young boy in a coffee shop.'

The Hard Man looked around the hallway, not like he was looking at anything, for anything, more that he was exercising his eyes, flexing their muscles, lubricating their spheres, performing maintenance and keeping them rolling, ready for a call to arms.

'The boy needed attention.' Not help. Help might have been useful at the time of the action, but it had not been forthcoming, and after that it had been too late.

'Stitches.' The Hard Man's tone of voice fell with the second syllable, disapproval, possibly, although why he would have cared either way would have made for another minor mystery. 'Stitches carry questions with them, and questions carry further questions, and questions we would always prefer to avoid.'

The Hard Man raised his gaze, Stoner returned it. But he offered no words in reply.

'Hospitals, JJ. You know this. You know that hospitals cause attention and you neither need nor want that. Something we share is that neither of us wants attention. But still, still you put the boy into hospital. There's no sense to that. None.'

Neither man blinked. Neither man was tense. This was not a confrontation. This was a negotiation. Or at least the introduction to a negotiation. Neither the Hard Man nor Stoner cared about a careless youth in a hospital. Football followers did it to each other all the time. He was just another. A negotiation; rules of engagement.

Stoner dropped his fighter's gaze to signal his unwillingness to engage, then raised it again to reboot the conversation.

'Come in, then. Tea? Coffee? Glass of beer? Are you having a

16

nice day? Is life being kind to you? How's the wife? Kids doing well?'

The Hard Man gazed, smiled. A thin smile and only with his lips, but a smile all the same.

'Keeping it bottled and with a lid on it, JJ? That's good.'

Stoner stood his ground.

'No, really, how is your wife? Kids? Car? Cat? And how is the kid in stitches? Really. Has he learned a lesson? Will he share it with all of his friends? These things are important. Understanding and knowledge are always important, and I feel I have simply helped a misguided youth to tread the pain-filled path of understanding. And what do you care? You moving into social work? Scourge of the crims turns into saviour of the stupid? Lawdy-lawd, it's a miracle.'

The Hard Man eased a little. His smile softened.

He walked towards Stoner. 'Water. Just water. Have you noticed how dying is plainly unpleasant? People seem to do it only once.'

Stoner eased a slow smile of his own.

'Is that some kind of threat? Have we reached that point? Again? Already? Dying? Who's dying? Why are they doing it . . .'

The Hard Man stopped dead. Looked up. Caught the return stare and fielded it cleanly.

'No threat, JJ. No threat at all. Other people are dying. Not you. Not me. No one we know nor even care about. But they are dying. They're being killed. By persons unknown for reasons unknown . . . although the reason is almost certainly financial reward rather than personal passion. Although that is not entirely the view of our friends in the high places.'

Stoner stood aside. Let the Hard Man pass. Custom and caution kept his hands from his pockets, open, in plain sight. The Hard Man appeared to notice nothing, glancing around the cluttered, clean, comfortable room as he entered.

'Did you mention water?'

17

There was warmth . . . almost warmth . . . in the request.

Stoner backed towards a kitchen. Hands still in plain sight. The Hard Man shrugged free from his coat; dropped it over the arm of an easy chair, sat down. Stared at the ceiling. Stoner stood. Watchful. Reserved.

'Pax, JJ. Take it easy. Be . . . calm.' The Hard Man rolled the vowel in that last word. Folded both of his hands behind his head. No threat. Eyes still on the ceiling. 'We have no problem here, you and me.'

Stoner passed over a clean coffee mug half-filled with clean cold bottled water. The Hard Man glanced into the mug. At the bottom was the image of an open hand, palm towards the drinker, fingers straight.

'We may have . . . concerns. Unresolved business.'

He looked again at the open hand at the bottom of the mug, and smiled a sort-of smile.

'But not here, not now, and not serious. Not yet. Although it would help us both if you were to control your hitting boys impulse a little. It's all a bit adolescent. All a bit teenage testosterone. Nice mug. Familiar. The Red Hand of Ulster? That was a while ago. Got any more water? Water with bubbles? Or is that restricted to more welcome guests?'

Stoner fetched two mugs; one coffee, one water. Placed them on a tidy polished table. Leaned back against the wall opposite his visitor. The Hard Man took his water, sipped, smiled.

'And sit down. You own the place, man.'

Stoner sat on the table, rocking himself slowly, steadily, on his hands.

The Hard Man sighed theatrically. Drank more water.

Stoner waited in coffee-sipping silence. There would be a reason for the visit. There would be a request for service, and there would be an offer of recompense. A negotiation would take place. The outcome would be a task, and politeness would insist that the instruction would be presented as a request. British is as British does, and even in the killing business politeness was somehow important.

The Hard Man was a long, long-term preferred employer. From military days, through paramilitary days, through mercenary days to civilian contracting days, he and Stoner had partnered each other. The Hard Man was an invisible arm of government, a deniable limb; Stoner was one of his entirely detached hands. While the Hard Man stalked with deniable transparency through the shadows of the corridors of power, he did nothing he couldn't deny, should that need arise. Stoner and others like him performed the dirty but necessary manual labour; manual, as a good hand should be.

And as hot conflicts had cooled and as wet work dried up, so the Hard Man had appeared less frequently in Stoner's life. The jobs he requested changed from the purely physical and final to the mainly operational; Stoner was also ageing, and while younger, fitter, less scrupulous characters dug the holes for most of the bodies, he found the lost, retrieved the hidden and protected those who the Hard Man decided were worthy of the expense of an off-book contractor.

It was plain that the Hard Man's star shone in a high remote place, and that he moved in stellar clusters which were wholly alien to Stoner – who had only twice attempted to trace him back to a family, friends, hearth and home. Both attempts had failed, both failures resulted in warnings of imminent terminal ill health, and Stoner had heeded those warning. His research had uncovered only well-established and impenetrable false-hoods, lies and deceits. It might not suit a macho image, but Stoner rationalised that he would only seek out the Hard Man if he needed support, documentation, resources he could not provide for himself, and he had never felt those needs. Following his last failed attempt at discovering a lot more about him, the

Hard Man had explained that without an effective cut-out between them they were of no use to each other, and in any case it was simply unacceptable that Stoner knew personal details which he could pass on to a mutual enemy or to a new best friend should he change employers. Stoner didn't care enough to argue. It worked well for them both.

'Most recently, then, was last night's dying.'

The Hard Man didn't do much in the way of introductions.

'I think I can connect four, maybe six, killings by the same person or team unknown. I also think that there are more, maybe a lot more. I think that there's a hit man out there, someone unknown to me, and that hit man may be a hit team. I think that if it's a single man, then he's getting sloppy and inconsistent, and his security will fail sooner rather than later, but if it's a team working together, then they will not fail. Not soon, anyway. A team will need detecting. Tracing. Finding. And then they will need a conversation with us, they will need convincing of the error of their ways, and maybe they will need an instruction to desist.

'The killings are messy. The killings are messy because the killer wants them kept private, away from the media. You know what I'm talking about. You . . .' the Hard Man paused for a flicker of eye contact, a shared moment . . . 'we, have used this technique before. It's effective. As you know. Provide so much evidence that the only conclusion is confusion.'

Stoner met his gaze, without comment. Collected both mugs; refilled them. Returned them, and sat down. All in a curiously companionable silence.

'The only features which link the kills are the targets – they're all men – and the locations – they're all hotels – and the fact that the scenes have been messed up. Very deliberately messed up.'

Stoner rose, stretched, moved to another chair further away, repositioned it so he could stretch out his legs, sat down. He closed his eyes, relaxed a little further.

'The boys in blue cannot make any connections, and in any case they're being restrained by higher powers. As are the all-knowing hounds of the press. Our mutual friends however, our unattributable mutual friends, can indeed see that there is a pattern, and are interested, curious. Which is why I'm here.'

Stoner opened a single eye and aimed his gaze at the Hard Man.

'Not entirely a visit brought about by your passionate interest in the wellbeing of youthful shitheads with loud mouths, bad breath and a misunderstanding of how café society really works, then? So why the opening salvo? Why pretend that somehow and entirely mysteriously you have developed some kind of social conscience? I could easily have misunderstood your motives, and that would have been an unfortunate thing.'

The Hard Man reached once more for his water. 'Playing, JJ; seeing whether you were awake. Just games. The games we boys play when we're alone and there is no fucking booze and no fucking women to buy it for us.'

He laughed, shockingly loudly, and clapped his hands, closing the opening of their negotiation.

'And you're wondering what I want? You're wondering why I'm enduring the grim reality of your less than heartfelt welcome and sipping flat tap water from a mug? Do you not have a single glass in this pit? And why are you here anyway? You have at least three other perfectly good houses, none of them over-filled with tenants so far as I know, but you're subsisting in some miserable squat in a dismal suburb in a crap provincial town. Who was the Chinaman who opened the door for me? The Chinaman with the female family and the pungent kitchen. Are you opening a restaurant? Are you on a job? A job I don't know about? It seems unlikely, but everything's possible. Hell, JJ, even for a no-hope like you this place is intolerably grim.'

'It's comfortable. It's clean. It's safe. You tracked me, not the location, which I prefer. I was aware of your trace. I was waiting for you.'

The Hard Man tensed almost imperceptibly. 'How come? You know something about these killings?'

'It's not me.' Stoner's words relaxed his visitor. 'You were always going to show up. I figured that the time was about right. You see a debt you can collect, and collection is your addiction. Your talent. One of your talents. You can pretend that the blue boys are after me and that your mighty powerful personality has deflected them. I'm being kind, and polite, as you can see.

'And you wanted to check that I'm under control. That there's no danger of unwanted attention, as you said, and I knew that you would need to check, so I arranged an excuse, giving that youth a gentle tap, and I chose a suitably protected venue. Welcome to the world of the mad control freak. It should feel familiar. The youth deserved it, and in any case I was simply looking for a suitable opportunity. Was the family guy on his cell phone in the coffee shop one of yours?'

The Hard Man laughed. An almost welcome sound, and if it was a genuine laugh then it was also a thing of interest; a curiosity. He waved the empty mug about. Maybe he was making a point. It was hard to tell. Stoner stood, collected the mug and refilled it with cold, bottled, aerated and expensive water. Water which cost more than his own instant coffee. Returned it. The Hard Man sank another cup, waved it again and watched its next refill with satisfaction.

'You're too suspicious, JJ. I know your work. I'm a fan. An admirer. This is far too messy for you. If you wanted to confuse the scene then you'd confuse it. Doubt that you'd spray blood onto the ceiling, though. That's excessive, and you're never excessive.

'We're supposed to think that this last effort was a crime of passion. Businessman in hotel. Business girl. Negotiation. Man tries something unwelcome – hard to imagine, knowing the girls

22

who work those places, but there y'go – and she stabs him. Hits him with a bottle, perhaps. But that's where it would end. Stabbed. Bottled. A couple of times, maybe, if things were a bit desperate, but I have never heard of a whore ripping some mark to shreds over a bit of too-rough stuff. Did you?'

He appeared almost interested in Stoner's reply. Just for a moment, but he wasn't, because he had more to say.

'What would fire up some whore enough to make her kill her john, anyway? You know whores better than most men, dealing with them in your own unique way, JJ; share with me?'

Stoner glared at him. The Hard Man ignored it and continued.

'I've asked our blue-suited friends to let me see the autopsies of unsolved single-man killings which match this one. Hotels. Places whores go. Also apparent natural causes without a cause. Healthy guys who've keeled over like the Monty Python parrot with no previous massive attacks. There won't be many. Hopefully. An epidemic of coronaries would be a surprising thing. And in any case, I would have heard of it.'

Stoner supplied more water.

'And you want me to do what?'

'You're going to be my faithful Indian scout, JJ, you're going to invisibly go where I cannot. I have been invited to dig deeper than the blue boys and to dig wider. The blue boys have been told to stay away, so there won't be press leaks. I am visible. I need to be visible. You're unknown at this point, and I'll try to keep it that way. You can do invisible. You can do silent. I will tell you of individuals I find suspicious and you will invisibly befriend them. You will live their lives in parallel, and invisibly, and you will find out whether there is a killing team in place. I think there is. I have no problems with that, but I want to know all about it.

'The blue boys want to catch a killer. I just want to find out who it is. When we find him, then we can decide what we do.

23

No point in planning to spill milk unnecessarily. I can always use fresh talent.'

'Clues? Hints? Tips? Leads? Suspects?' Stoner decided upon the constructive approach. 'And what was all that crap about the kid in the coffee shop about? Really?'

'Him? He'll live. He might come looking for you. Don't know. Don't suppose you need worry about that. But he might. His dad's a copper, so he might be able to find you. That was the point. You bothered?'

'No.'

'No leads. Too many clues. None of them make sense. The guy – the most recent guy, the guy topped last night – he was truly worked over. Not a good job. Horrible. Pointless.'

'You saw the scene?'

'Only photos of the body. The scene had been cleared before I got there. That won't happen again; you'll be free to enter the scene as soon as I hear about another crime in the pattern. I'm claiming national security, only specialists allowed. Mucho secrecy, skulduggery, cloaks and daggers; nothing the blue boys want or need. You going to do this for me?'

Stoner nodded.

'OK. Take a walk around the scene. Let yourself in. Can't have you visible. Knight's Inn; know it?'

Stoner nodded again. 'Is the scene guarded?'

'Only by tape. The big clean will start after SOCO have cried enough, and that will be a day or so, I guess. Walk around the place. Feel it. Smell it. Tell me what I've missed. You'll want the body shots?'

'After I've seen the scene. I'll see how accurate I can get with that reconstructive talent you keep telling me I have.'

'Be invisible, JJ. Just be invisible . . .'

And then the Hard Man was gone.

*

The door to the room didn't close behind him; it didn't get a chance to close. There was a foot in the door. The foot belonged to the listener at the door, the eavesdropper. The eavesdropper who had tried to hide when the Hard Man left suddenly; his leavings tending to be as sudden and unannounced as his arrivals, but who had been unable to get away and had been forced to accept the departing greeting . . .

4

FIRST PERSON PLURAL

'That man is a twat.'

The dirty blonde has a gentle way with words. There's no point in arguing with her, either. Once she's made up her mind about something, someone, chances are that only some radical new information will change her view. It's a charming characteristic . . . possibly . . . but not a particularly helpful one.

'I mean . . . every time you see him, you get nervous. And when you get nervous, you're just tiresome company. A pain in the arse. Why do you bother with him?'

Not a question. A statement in disguise. How could I answer that? For a start, it is so obviously a true statement. So I say a sweet nothing. These things help at moments like this.

'Beer? Fancy a beer?'

I know how to impress a girl. Years and years of practice. Nowhere near a town named Perfection, but possibly I'm on the way there. Equally possibly . . . I'm not, or I may be on the road to nowhere, but let us not seek out defeat and disappointment; those bitter twins can always find you all too easily on their own.

Beer always cheers the dirty blonde. She grins at me in

approval. She may be quick to anger, but she's quick to forgive, too, and despite suffering from an excellent memory, she rarely remembers that she has forgiven. Which is a good thing, not least because she's had a lot to forgive – too much for most folk to forgive – in the time we've been together.

'What did the twat want, anyway?' She warms to her theme. 'He never drops by for a simple chat, does he, that twat? There'll be an angle, like always, and he'll be richer, you'll be poorer, then it'll be time for him to vanish again.'

Which is the truth, although not exactly the whole truth. Because if the Hard Man has one redeeming virtue, it is that he pays his way. Financially, that is. Which is his only currency. Spiritual well-being – his own or anyone else's – is rarely high on his list of concerns. It's one of the nebulous notions, like morality, although he does possess loyalty and a refined and occasional sense of integrity, too, if the circumstances demand it.

I've known him – worked with him – for a long time now. Longer than you would think, given that I look so youthful. That's an attempt at humour, as you would know if you knew me. No one has ever told me that I look youthful. Even when I actually was youthful, somehow I managed not to look it. It's a talent. Possibly. A singularly pointless talent. I remember a description given to a bystander after a moment of fractious collision with some fool. They described the assailant – which was me – as looking like a man of about forty. I was twenty-eight. But this is of use; the plods searched for a man who looked about forty. Which I did. Like I said, it's not a useful talent. Maybe I should disguise myself. Sport a wig, dye my hair, grow a beard. Maybe I truly do not care enough to bother.

Working with the Hard Man almost always involves bodies. In fact, I think there's no need for a qualification there; there are always bodies. He is either responsible for causing those bodies to be dead ones rather than the lively kind, or he is responsible for finding out who's responsible for their deadness. On one particularly wry occasion he was hired by an interested party to find himself, for it was he himself who was responsible for the bodies in question. He failed to find himself, except possibly in a Zen sense. Although that would be unlikely, given his personal chosen path. But he did find someone else, someone who was indeed responsible in a direct way but who had pulled no trigger, twisted no garrotte. And he also shopped that person, sold him to his inquisitive customer and then offed him to prevent unhappy personal embarrassment. Life is packed with humour. It is often a challenge to find and accurately identify it, however.

Today's visit had found the Hard Man being unusually non-specific. He claimed to be checking on my availability, although he could have used the phone to do that. There's no need to perform the actual face-to-face talk-talk business these days. It's possible, if unlikely, that he was concerned that someone as-yet unspecified could be listening in to a phone call. On the other hand, it is equally unlikely but equally possible that the same as-yet unspecified someone could be listening to us passing away the day via some high-tech eavesdropping kit fitted somehow, somewhere, in this apparently unlovely apartment. Paranoia is a terrible thing. Round and around it goes, and where it stops . . . everyone knows. Everyone who's been down the paranoia highway, that is. And that includes everyone in this fine line of work. Indeed it does. It is impossible to survive otherwise. Trust me on this.

In a light moment, I once suggested to the Hard Man that we should name our little joint venture something witty and pithy and relevant. The Kompany of Killers, or maybe The Kuddly Killer Kompany; something subtle, something fashionably alliterative like that. I even suggested that this was so stunningly simple that no one would see through such a subtle double bluff; folk

28

might even believe that we were a charity dedicated to something noble. Like saving whales. Those handsome piebald black and white ones . . . orcas. But we're not. Unless the pursuits of wealth and leisure are noble in themselves. And you can debate that in your own time.

The dirty blonde pretends patience. A sure sign that a little temper is imminent. I know the signs. Sometimes I ignore them, because she can be a whole load of fun when she gets worked up. And even more fun when she recognises that I have been winding her up, and then . . .

But let us not go there. You might be shocked. And we wouldn't want that. Not here. Not now. And not yet.

'And while you're not telling me why the twat was here, parking his filthy feet on my sparkling clean carpet, you can also tell me that he's going to make you rich and immortal. Rich or immortal, should I say.'

Rhetoric, as always, is a fun thing; a good clean game between friends, and like the best of games played between the best of friends, it's best played in private.

Being possessed of a surprisingly strong desire to enjoy the rest of my time in this life, I refrained from reminding her that not only was the carpet neither particularly clean nor particularly hers, but also that the Hard Man had never to my knowledge done her wrong, as the song might have it. I also crave neither riches nor immortality, although a careful balancing of these two might be nice.

It would also have been inappropriate to mention that the Hard Man was one of the very few men of my acquaintance who would have been entirely delighted to remove his footwear in the noble cause of domestic bliss. He would have no concerns about that. He tends to be concerned about things more deadly than the state of the soles of his shoes or their potential for carpet contamination.

29

'There'll be a body,' I tell her. 'There's always a body. That's what we do. Bods R Us. Someone will be dead. He'll expect me to go look at it, and then have a go at understanding it, so we can work out whodunit and he can thus become even more famous in his own secret circle. This is what we do. You know this. Nothing strange, nothing sinister, just a pair of amiable eccentrics going about their daily duties, making the world a better and a safer place.

'Beer? Or curry?' I truly do understand the pathway to my best girl's innermost self.

'Fuck off, JJ.'

She could be a poet if she'd only work on it a little harder.

'Curry. And then you can tell me what the twat is lumbering you with this time.'

I have been close to the dirty blonde for a decently long time now. In a long life packed with irony, she is possibly the greatest irony of them all. For a start, she's not exactly what the pedantic among us would describe as being naturally blonde. I know this to be true, and now so do you. We should perhaps keep that quiet intelligence to ourselves. She might not thank me for revealing her little stubbly secret, but in truth she most likely wouldn't care, either.

Self-presentation is not her greatest concern. Although she does claim to value honesty. This in itself is an amusing notion, bearing in mind that she presents herself as being a blonde, when she is in fact otherwise.

Likewise, she isn't dirty; she is demonically hygienically obsessively clean. I also know this, and in the great spirit of sharing which is currently afflicting me I will let you into this other little secret. I know the reasons for these charming disguises, too, of course I do, I investigate things, I crave understandings, but they're not relevant at the moment. If it is unclear to you why anyone might present themselves as being something which in fact they are not . . . play with your own imagination for the time being. I may reveal more later. Or I may not, of course.

'JJ!'

She smacks me on the arm. This is a signal that I am not paying attention. And indeed I'm plainly not, because she has dragged on her so-cool but so-battered designer combat jacket and big boots and has plainly reached a decision about where we're heading, she and I. Along with tact and diplomacy, democracy is also an alien notion to the dirty blonde.

'You said something about curry. And beer. Have you changed your mind? Forgotten? Are you asleep? Dreaming of some other more pleasant company?'

Questions, questions. Life can be a puzzle.

She wanders around behind me and rubs me hard between the shoulders.

'Come along; I'm hungry.'

She's almost always hungry. She also hardly ever eats, despite spending half of her life in cafés and restaurants, pubs too. She may not be entirely blonde, and she may not be dirty, but she is certainly trim. I'd blame the cigarettes if she smoked, which she does not, so I can't. Life can be a puzzle.

'Unless . . .' Her hands run down my sides, skate around the waistband of my pants. She grates a fingernail down the zip, grasps. I stiffen. Hold my breath.

'Nah. Let's go eat.' Like I said. Dirtiness can be an elusive virtue. Which may make it more valuable. Who can tell?

'There's been a clump of killings.'

The dirty blonde may not be entirely certain what alliteration actually is, but she appears to enjoy flowery speech. It may be why she stays with me, of course. One night, in the sleepless oceans of shared awaking, I might ask her. But I'm unsure that I would in fact want to know the answer.

She grunts. An underrated means of communication, the grunt. She swirls the beer in her glass. Looks up, expectantly.

'He's not sure how many, but several. Messy stuff.'

She swirls her beer more actively than before. This may aid her concentration. I observe that I feel unaffected by this. We are all of us different.

'He thinks that there are connections between maybe a half-dozen bodies in the last month or two.'

That's a lot of bodies. Few folk, so we're told, get killed in the UK, and those who do manage it are usually offed by their friends or family. For example, were I to get myself killed, it would be the dirty blonde who did it. This would not be exactly describable as enemy action, but she can get awesome cross, especially when I tease her by failing to reveal all in a succinct and direct way. She'll swear at me in a minute ...

'Stop twatting about, JJ. Get to the point. How can I play Gloriana the Queen of Sleuths if you keep being mysterious?'

Pointing out that I am currently more hungry than mysterious would be a poor move at the moment.

'Bodies in hotels. All blokes. At the last one there was blood everywhere. So much blood that the killer could paddle in it.' I raise hands in surrender faster than she can raise her doubting eyebrows. 'Literally paddle. Splash about in it.

'No; really. Not a fingerprint at any scene, but plenty of footprints. If there was a national footprint database ... the plods would have caught whoever-it-is by now. But there isn't. And they haven't. Most likely they won't.

'He thinks that the blood is a red ... ah ... herring. He thinks that the killer is a pro. He thinks that the amateur dramatic gorefest is there to distract, and it certainly does that for our boys in blue; they are duly distracted.'

The dirty blonde is interested now. Talk of killings, murder, mischief and marvellous mayhem does this for her. I have theories about why it is that she finds this kind of thing so fascinating, but this is not the time to share them. Later, maybe. Or not, of course. It depends.

She looks up from an emptied glass.

'Blood? The perp paddles in blood?'

Perp. Sigh. A hideous contraction of the word 'perpetrator'. So . . . so very American. She plainly watches too much American television. Slime Scene Investigations, or the like. Improbable romantic comedy with superbly impossible plots. I boast a constabulary acquaintance who watches every episode several times. She watches them because they crack her up with every viewing. Comedy cops pursue comedy killers in comedy lo-cations. Reality is a lot more . . . grimy. Killers are a lot more . . . grim. Murder is not the most cheerful of professions; it would be an odd world if it were that.

'Yes. Apparently the last of the locations looks like something from the really dark side of Japanese noir cinema. Joke blood everywhere. Lakes of the stuff.'

'But it's not joke blood?'

'Not a drop of it. It's the real deal. A body contains lots, and it can make quite a mess. And at these locations it's everywhere; on the walls, furniture, ceilings even.'

'Are there spatter patterns, then?'

She really is getting into the TV jargon. Any moment now she'll start humming whodunit theme tunes. Refilling her glass and changing the subject is a far, far better option. I don't mind talking about work with the dirty blonde, but messy killings rarely involve a cast of characters from the light-hearted, easy-going side of life, and her life contains enough darkness already.

'Splatter? Is it called spatter or splatter?'

A man could so easily despair, so easily lose track of what is a serious business. Murdering men is not fun. Well. I never found it that way when it was my main way of turning an honest shilling. That's got you wondering, hasn't it?

'It's blood, just blood. Patterns can only tell you nice convenient stories if they've been designed by someone who is trying to tell you a story.' I try really hard to sound reasonable. Not least because folk at adjacent tables can become distracted if they overhear their neighbours shouting in heated tones about blood on the carpet. On the walls. And if the Hard Man was to be believed, on the ceiling. That did sound excessive.

'Whatever.' She's looking grumpy now. Maybe food would be a distraction? She flags down an innocent bystander and asks him if he'll just pop up to the bar and get her a pint. He agrees. I have no idea why they do this. But they always do. She often asks total strangers to fetch her beer and they always just do her bidding. The beer is inevitably free too. It's a remarkable talent. I must look unremarkably inoffensive. Maybe they think I'm her dear old dad. Sometimes I could get very angry very quickly.

'Grin, JJ! Grin!'

The dirty blonde is beaming sunshine at me. It is impossible to resist her. A complete stranger is battling his way through the evening bar crush to buy her a beer. She wants to talk death, not romance. Strange lady.

'The new one . . .'

'How many? How many? Is it lots?' She can be a worry sometimes. 'And when was this new one topped?'

Her barslave appears at her elbow, blushing and presenting her with a fresh glass of some faintly fizzing beery beverage. She looks up and smiles. He stammers something inaudible but probably cute and endearing. She smiles more sweetly, reaches for his hand. He looks startled. She pulls his hand towards her and puts his forefinger into her mouth. Pulls it out, slowly, past her scraping teeth. 'You dripped a drop.' He looks more stunned than ever. My

34

turn for panto. We have played this scene many times. There are several possible lines for me to choose at this point, but he looks like a pleasant lad so I select something simple and painless.

'That's as near as you want to get, my friend. Believe me.' He looks faintly affronted. The dirty blonde looks really dirty now. Eyes slitted and languid; the real dark Bacall. The lad is blushing; she is flushing, a deep red rising from her shirt neck and up. She leans back in her chair, reaching for her shirt buttons.

'You want a prize?' She undoes a button. 'A reward?'

'You should leave now.' I smile. 'Really. Thank you.'

You could smell his confusion. He walks away. I have so far not hit anyone and no one has hit me. This makes it a good start to the evening.

'I've already told you. Probably more than a half-dozen, less than a dozen.' The dirty blonde's flush is fading fast. I have that effect on her. It must be a special skill. 'That they know of. There may be more. Probably are. If murder was an iceberg, there could be lots below the surface, invisible but threatening . . .'

'Don't go all whimsical, JJ. I don't want your whimsy yet; poetry comes late at night, not over beer and supper. "If murder was an iceberg?" Get you, Mr Poet Lubricant!' Whatever the drink was, it plainly did contain something intoxicating. Probably a vodka shot or two added to her beer at the bar; she has that effect on folk. Taps into unsuspected reserves of secret generosity. Marvellous.

'Yes. The last one looks like this. Looks like a body in a big puddle of blood. Stinks. In a hotel room. Stinks, a lot. The killer left the heating on full chat. Hideous, he says.' He being the Hard Man. She knows that.

'Time of death?' she asks. 'Tod. As in Sweeney Todd. Call in the Sweeney and they'll tell you her time of departure.'

Sometimes I worry about her grip on reality. It cannot be easy being blonde. Even if she is a fake one. And stubbly.

'Not a her,' I tell her; 'a him.' She beams, looks even more happy. If we were on the TV I'd send her drink dregs to the lab for analysis. We're not, so I tip half my own beer into her glass.

'Cod!' she cries loudly, playing to the surrounding silent tables. Our conversation has been observed. It's time to leave. The dirty blonde swills down the last of my glass. Her own beer has evaporated. She has many rare and unusual talents. Making drinks vanish is one of them.

'Cod!' She's all-but shouting now. The bar is all-but silent. 'Cause of death! How did he die? Was he exsanguinated? Isn't that a great word? Was every last drop of his bright precious blood drained away? Was this like some fantastic vampire attack gone wrong?'

All eyes in the bar are bulging in our direction. I want to point out that had the poor bloke been the victim of a massed attack of the killer undead, then there'd be no mess, no blood, because they would have drunk it all, vampires being conveniently tidy like that, but this was not the time.

'Cod,' I spoke gently, calmly, 'with chips, and mushy peas. And maybe a slice of freshly buttered bread. Possibly curry sauce, as you suggested a while back.'

The dirty blonde snaps to her feet, balancing well on her big black boots. The audience springs away in a massed scuffle.

'Sounds cool,' she announces. And leaves the building unopposed.

'So . . .'

The dirty blonde and I are sharing a large cardboard carton of what claimed to be Kansas fried chicken. I would not argue with the 'fried' bit, but the rest of the description was open to debate. Her mood is pensive, her fingers greasy. Talking about murder plainly gives her an appetite. It has the opposite effect on me. As usual in this situation, I wished that I smoked cigarettes, because this would have been the time for one.

'So that twat has found a body and he wants you to go and . . . do what, exactly? The last job you did for him was something to do with insurance, no?'

She knows exactly what my last job was. She knows because I told her all about it while it was shutting down and afterwards, while I was laying low and feeling a lot lower. It was an insurance job, true, but only in the sense that the man who'd murdered his wife had only been investigated by the Hard Man when the life insurers' own man had been beaten insensible by the supposedly grieving husband. This had been as unexpected as it was unwelcome, as the man from the Pru had only been returning personal effects, which does not normally reduce grieving relatives to moments of mindless violence, and the Hard Man had only become involved because the police had declined, as the dead wife's death was entirely unsuspicious and the police do not work on commission.

This is the thing with the Hard Man; despite being some sort of shadowy government high-honcho he never turns down paying work. You pay him; he works. In a sense. In this case he sent me to ask the grieving husband why he'd knocked out the lights of the harmless man from the Pru, because insurance companies are socially responsible organisations and wish to understand the inner feelings of the grieving. They also prefer never to pay out if they can avoid it, and any straw is worth a clutch when the sums are as handsome as they were in this case. Anyway, I had asked politely enough, only to be attacked myself.

An unwise move on his part. I always attack back. Grieving husband revealed himself to be a callous murderer within an hour. The men from the Pru were suitably delighted, and gave the Hard Man a bonus for his zealous and efficient work. I did the work. He got the bonus. And as the grieving husband would soon discover, lacking most of the teeth on one side of your mouth is not necessarily a disadvantage in the prison showers. Life is always instructive. Popularity needs to be earned.

I strike an imaginary match, light an imaginary cigarette (probably a Marlboro; I always liked tight jeans, Cuban heels, Stetson hats), and lean back. The imaginary nicotine routine provides a genuine real-life excuse to forgo the greasy chicken.

'I need to read about the others, because the bods are all bagged and burned long since, but the scene of this one's fresh, so I'll go look at it later when the man calls. Body's gone to a morgue, though, which is a shame.'

Imaginary smoke curls like the dark blues in motion.

'Some guy, professional guy, aren't they all, in a hotel room. Blood everywhere, like I said. It's impossible to make that much mess without meaning to make a mess.'

The dirty blonde's all ears. A strange expression, especially given that she's staring hard and unblinking too. This is plainly not exactly the right moment to discuss the adventurous application of English idiom. She nods, rapt. Waggles greasy fingers encouragingly.

'What did he die of? No one seems sure. He'd maybe been knifed, bottled certainly, hence the gore-fest, and had been knocked about a lot. The man says there's something not right, though, so he's doing the open mind thing until the coroner's done with it and comes up with a verdict. The room is a wreck. Everything that can be smashed has been smashed. That is such a crap way to carry on. No pro would behave like that, so it's probably a crime of passion. Family, then. Or girlfriend gone loco, like they do.'

I look up, hoping for a smile.

No smile.

'If it's not a hit, your man won't be interested, will he? No hit, the plods will handle everything, and there'll be no cash for the twat, and without cash he'll be gone from there. Am I right? Yes, I am right. Do girlfriends really knife their guys? Really? In real life? Isn't it outraged wives who do the knifing thing after getting ditched for some sloppy tart? I mean, it can't be that common, the killing, or guys would never stray and wives would never stab them.'

The dirty blonde's grip on everyday life is awesome as ever.

And of course she has a professional interest in these things. I decide against mentioning this. It would do me no good at all.

'Killing is rare. Killing is unusual. Killing is not the everyday inevitable result of a little bit of excess bad temper.' I could almost get grumpy about this. She has this effect on me. Sometimes I think she deliberately winds me up just for her own amusement. 'Despite what the television suggests, the streets are *un*packed with deranged killers. Most deaths are natural causes or accidents. You know this. Despite the fact that you watch TV and are a noted armchair expert, you are also not entirely dim.'

She smiles at me, in an encouragingly almost-friendly way. I am encouraged. So I carry on.

'Most killers are accidental killers. Almost no killer does it twice. Most killers are not murderers. Most killers don't do it because they want to. Almost no one wants to kill people. Almost no one knows how. It's a rare skill. I don't think there's a Boy Scout badge for killing. Not yet.

'But this is a murder. You can't easily get accidentally stabbed to death. You can do accidental death to yourself in lots and lots of ways, but this is a difficult one. In any case, there's no knife at the scene. It's particularly difficult to slice yourself brutally to death and then dispose of the knife.'

She sits up, lit from within by her bright and very white grin. 'It's the ice knife!' Erudition is a marvellous thing. 'Solved it! No need for you to waste hours of valuable quality time with that twat. Call him up, tell him you've solved it and ask for the fee.

We'll spend it together.' Grip on reality tenuous here, as you can see.

'Ice knives don't slice. Ice daggers stab. There's apparently slicing as well as stabbing. I'll know better when I've seen it.'

'Gotcha!' She laughs. I am smitten. I surrender limply and eat some of the congealed chicken.

'I won't know all of it until I've seen the scene.'

'Which is when?'

'Later tonight, I think. The phone is quiet at the moment, though.'

'OK. Why don't you call him? I don't know how you can stand the suspense. Give him a call. Do it now?'

'There's no rush,' I hear myself say, telling the truth as a chap should always try to do. 'He'll call when he's ready. I'm in no rush to gaze upon the remains of the departed. In any case ...' I smile in an encouraging way, 'it's good to spend a little time together while we're neither of us in a hurry, no?'

She looks a little shifty. Glances down. Smiles unhappily.

'I do need to work. I do have an appointment for later.'

I try very hard. Like all chaps of a certain disposition I try hard to be uncritical and I try hard to be supportive. It may well be something to do with that long-ago religious upbringing, who can tell? But trying is not the same as succeeding, and every time the subject of the dirty blonde's occupation leaps between us, restraint is called for. My restraint, that is.

The dirty blonde, possibly the most exceptional woman in town, if not in the whole world, is a professional escort. I tell myself that this is unimportant, that I should love her as she is and that what she does to earn her money should have no bearing on my feelings. I tell myself that I should care for her regardless of her occupation. Why I tell myself this is a mystery. Of course I care for her, even though she's an escort. Why it should be the case that I should tell myself that it's no issue is an entire gristly issue in itself. But it is an issue. I do care for her. I do care what she does.

And no, before you ask, sniggering at the back, I did not meet her professionally. Not in that sense. Even though I am of a generation and of an upbringing which insists that a thing is worth what it costs and if a thing costs nothing then that is likely to be its worth, I do also believe that love should not be paid for. I led a confused childhood.

That said, of course I met her professionally, but through my profession, not hers. My profession. I can see your eyebrows soar to the north as you wonder how a chap could meet a lady while investigating a death, timely or otherwise. But killing and seeking killers is only the half of it. What I also do is play loud music. What I also do is rent out places where folk can lay their heads when they are either weary of the world or simply weary, and that is how I met the dirty blonde. She was a good friend of a good tenant and she needed somewhere to live. She still is a friend of that tenant, and she is also a friend of her landlord. That would be me, then.

Aha! you cry, displaying a predictably dull lack of imagination. You have worked out, all on your clever own, that I provide a roof and the dirty blonde supplies certain services in return. If you suggested that while you were in my company or even near it then you would suddenly rapidly and completely enter a violently dark and unpleasant phase of your life. I am sensitive like that. Maybe too sensitive. There are those who have suggested that my sensitivity will get me into trouble one day. They're right, except in that it already has, and many times, but we have no need to go there just at the moment. It would not improve your understanding, although why your understanding should be important to me at the moment I am unsure. My unconventional sensitivity is how I met the Hard Man, and that sensitivity is the single feature among my many, many virtues which generates the balance and calm which are essential to a quiet and fulfilled existence.

It also pays well. Sometimes very well indeed. I have no need for money, not really, not any more, but the more you get then the more you want. No smutty comments please. They can hurt. Hurt you, that is.

The dirty blonde always pays her rent. She is unusual in that she always pays it well in advance. This is particularly unusual given her profession, her calling, as many in similar paths of employ are less than entirely reliable. The dirty blonde boasts several professional friends whom no one could describe as being reliable in any sense. So . . . she pays her way. Got that? Good.

I detest what she does. Think about this, if you can so do without sniggering. Think about meeting the most amazing woman in the world. Think more. Think really hard. Good. You meet this astonishing woman and she's standing there all neat, clean and friendly asking about an apartment you have for rent.

Which apartment, you wonder? You have a couple, also a house or two. Show me, she says. So you do.

You show her around the apartment her friend, my tenant, has told her about. She is interested. It is a nice apartment. Pleasant. Roomy. Airy. She asks you about the rent, the deal, the contract, grown-up important stuff like that. What you want to say is something like it's yours for free if you want it and my sweet lord but you are amazing and what on earth can I say which you'll find interesting and things like that. But you don't say any of that. Instead you name a price and she asks whether it includes local taxes and you agree that it does but really you don't care about anything to do with rental properties. You want to ask her every question anyone ever asked anyone else and then several more.

Then you wonder whether she wouldn't perhaps prefer something a little more striking? Something which she might find more amusing? More involving for someone who is plainly more creative than Leonardo, more beautiful and more deadly than Lucretia and more interesting than the most interesting thing ever invented. She smiles. Your heart pounds. She agrees that something a little unusual would be good. You smile back, in a casual and calm kind of way and remark that one of your properties has a turret.

The upshot of all this merriment and delight is that she rents the half-house which you had lined up for yourself and for a rental rate which is only just enough for her to avoid feeling either subsidised or patronised. You could of course get a lot more money for it, had you wanted to rent it, which you didn't, but you do not meet ladies like this one more than once a lifetime. Meeting this lady was a unique experience in my life, and my life, as you will have understood by now, has been both long and intense, interesting and varied. Fulfilling too at times, less so at others. I hope that yours has been the same.

You subtly suggest nailing the deal over dinner. She agrees.

The evening is as astounding as you could have hoped for. You get on impossibly well. Soulmates drawn together through the wilds of the world and destined to be together inseparably for evermore. At the coffee point, she apologises to you and begs your indulgence while she picks up her cell phone, which has been buzzing in her pocket from time to time unanswered. It might, she says, be unavoidable work.

And so it proves. Work. Unavoidable. She texts ferociously and with impressive dexterity and then looks up ruefully and announces that her departure will be imminent, unavoidable and unwelcome but unavoidable. You try so hard to look unsurprised, staying cool, and enquire with only slight bemusement what can be so crucial as it is not exactly early in the evening? In fact, it is approaching ten o'clock, and . . .

She needs to meet a client, she announces, and she needs to

43

dress and prepare for it, and she needs to do that now because she needs to meet her client at his hotel and she needs to escort him to a club, where they will spend the rest of the night doing whatever it is paying clients and their escorts do in all-night and very expensive clubs. The sort of clubs where the pearls really should be genuine, my dear. You try your very best to appear unastonished. You offer to pay and you offer to drive her home, wherever home is, prior to her moving into your wonderful half-house with a turret.

She points with her smile towards the door of the restaurant. At the large, well-built and neatly suited chap who is just entering. You hate him at once of course. She laughs, gently and quietly and deeply, staring at your eyes, eyes which may just display a little more emotion and wonder than you would like them to. She laughs, as I said, and tells you that, no, silly, that's not the client, that's her midnight wheels. So that's all right then.

And then she is gone and you are sitting wondering who you can kill. Who you can pick a fight with and beat senseless. Who owes you money because now would be a grand time to go kick the debt out of them, maybe breaking a few inessential bones and generally relieving those innermost tensions which can be so damaging and destructive if left bottled up. Or whether you should instead visit a welcoming and familiar friend and fuck the night into light, and then you immediately wonder why suddenly and unexpectedly that option – always such a sublime way of easing tension in the past – is so abruptly unappealing.

You collect your thoughts, gather your wits, call for the bill, discover that she has paid it on her way out and wonder what on God's fuzzy green planet is happening to you.

Right now, here in what we pretend is real-time, the dirty blonde apologises, no, laughs at the moment, and checks her cell phone. Sighs, rolls her eyes and says; 'Difficult, this. Got to go, got to go and party. Don't want to, JJ, but need to. I had no idea you would have a fresh corpse available for the evening's entertainment. Can you put off taking a scan at it until tomorrow? Thought not.'

She is too familiar with my attempts at nonchalance whenever she needs to interrupt our shared time with work. Her work.

My cell calls. Buzzes in a fussy irritated manner in my shirt pocket. I ignore it. The dirty blonde glares a little. She rarely answers her own cell but thinks that I am being rude and awkward when I decline to answer mine.

'It's that twat, isn't it? Go on; answer the thing. Tell him that you're on your way.'

She manages to make it sound as though it's my fault that she has a need to go to work, to accompany some rich sack to some rich sacks' club where she will no doubt party the night away and pick up a handsome shilling at the end of it. Whatever 'it' is. A question I most carefully never ask. Usually never ask.

I pull out the phone. Flip it open. It is the Hard Man indeed. Who else? I share the intelligence. She beams again, unpredictably.

'Give him one for me!'

Then she's up, on her toes and gone. Just like that. I get the bill. We take it in turns . . .

5

LIE IN THE DARK

The stars themselves spat at Stoner. On good nights, they sparkled and they smiled. On sad nights, they gently wept and hid themselves away in silent safety behind the hazy gauze of heaven. But not tonight. Tonight, the stars spat at Stoner.

At least, that's how it felt. Darkness should always be an old friend, to lover, loser and the taker of life. The skies provide mood music for all. How that music is understood, how it is heard, how it is interpreted . . . that's where the mood can deepen with the darkness, lighten with the light. Or none of those things. Because the darkness is deepest when in shadow, and the darkest, deepest shadow comes hand-in-hand with the brightest light.

Stoner felt that he was safe from sudden unwelcome lightness at the Blue Cube. When times are tough and the darkness is falling, the only answer is to make deep, dark music.

Actually, that is arrant nonsense, he decided, but it would have to do, because he was entirely out of uplifting philosophical japes. He wanted a little escape from his understanding of the most probable current whereabouts, most probable current activities, of the dirty blonde. Enough dwelling upon an unacceptable reality, then; time for something absorbing. The Blue Cube.

The quiet door. The familiar muffled rumble. The sense of home for a man with no home. And my, aren't we feeling sorry for ourselves? Stoner keyed himself into the back door, entered by the fire door, a life-saving exit in reverse. Life is like that. The man Stretch was active on the ivories, but apart from the general clubsound background, that was it for the evening in a musical sense. Late evening; night yet to come. Plenty of empty tables, plenty of dark corners, although more of those corners were occupied than he'd expected.

Stretch and the piano played together over at stage right, so Stoner chose a table facing them. Dropped the weighty coat, gazed across the small stage, poured the first of a few from the new bottle and raised the glass to the player. An eyebrow in acknowledgement. No need for more. The first glass is just the first glass; no mystery, no pretence that it will be the only glass or the best glass. The first note is just the first note; no pretence that it will be the only note. Unless a chap is a more adventurous player than any before him. The one-note solo? Stoner almost smiled. Only sax players could do that. And he couldn't work the saxophone; neither point nor need, as so many can already boast this fine skill. Maybe the world awaits the one-note solo? Is this why the triangle is a rarely-heard instrument in the world of club jazz?

The Chimp, occasional and always competent barkeep, eased into the next seat, carefully leaving open Stoner's view of the entrance. Habit. No one talked too much about the ways Stoner might or might not make a living, but over time it had become clear that he always liked to keep an eye on the doorway. Many things are best left unsaid; this is one of them.

Stoner leaned over, looking into his companion's eyes while pouring two more glasses. A neat trick, and scary for an unfamiliar, but easy for any chess player or careful observer.

'It's time.'

The Chimp looked back, leaned back, said nothing. He was entirely familiar with Stoner's self-indulgent word games. And there was always a time to talk back.

'Time, my simian friend, for the triangle. It can't make a comeback, because it's never been away nor indeed come into its time in the first place, but it is time for a new prominence. Mark my words. The future of music is the triangle, an instrument of unplumbed excellence.

'Imagine it. Purity. The single note. Timing, pitch and perfect placement replacing all that hysterical jangling.'

Stoner was warming to his thoughts. Across the stage from them, Stretch ran a neat chromatic scale into an otherwise unremarkable – if entirely competent – rendition of something familiar but too easily forgotten. The small audience looked up, nodded knowingly, stored applause for the end, for no reason any musician could appreciate. A scale, after all, is simply that; a scale. There are lots of scales. School kids learn scales.

'Do you enjoy it when pals talk through your best efforts?'

Chimp spoke softly, no facial posturing to distract the amused pianist.

Stoner smiled at Stretch, replied to Chimp; 'You've not heard my best efforts, and neither have I. And if this is the best Stretch can manage, then maybe he should consider a switch to the triangle.'

Both men relaxed. The piano played on, as pianos do. The bottle drained away, as bottles do. The evening promised to distract, as evenings always should.

Stoner glanced through his glass. Glanced around the club. Bili was there, sitting like a silent stack of golden curls in her favoured corner by the stairway. In front of her, facing her from her table's top, stood her trademark two-litre bottle of gassy water. When life was without sparkle, she would say, from the depth of melancholy known only to bassists and public executioners, then it is a soul's duty to replenish, to revive, to add a little fizz. Her bottle may have been half full; it was hard to tell.

Bili sat alone, which suggested that she was yet to perform. By the time she had left the stage, by the time she had once again beaten black and blue music from her bright red bass, she would sit surrounded by the inevitable acolytes. They would slip secret shillings to the bar to learn of her favourite drink, and send bottles of slosh most expensive to her table. They would line up, the bottles, phalanxes of attention-seeking trophy drinks, and at the evening's end they would return undrunk to their station behind and above the bar. Bili was of the firm opinion that she had owned some of those bottles more than just a few times. It was certainly possible. The bottle which the Chimp at the bar would reluctantly reveal to be her top tipple? Whichever he considered to be the most lonesome. If the bar was down to its last bottle of Stolichnaya, then Bili drank nothing else. If there had been a mysterious run on Cockburns Special Reserve, then her life was incomplete without a bottle by her side. Prices rise with rarity. It is a law of nature. Profit is the name of the only game that matters.

Bili would claim that she rarely drank. That is a demonstrable untruth. Her music was intoxicant enough, she would claim. And that was certainly true, but despite her denials, the brilliance of her playing could not suppress her appetite for alcohol's clouding confusions. She was an almost unique mistress of her instrument, the only sadness being that her chosen vice was the bass guitar, and although studiedly poor six-string guitarists could always stand up and volunteer to crucify another singer's song for the edification of the punting masses, it was rarely considered appropriate for an impromptu half-hour burst of jazz extemporisation on a four-string theme. If a bluesman's lot is to cheer the dank lives of others by sharing their own pain with strangers, the lot of the bassist is to forever stand in the background or to sit at a table awaiting the call to perform. But it bothered her not at all.

Stretch ended his solo set to much applause and with a fine bow. Left the stage by stepping straight over the edge and dropping the full four feet without breaking stride, and stood before Stoner, lips smiling, eyes guarded. 'You're looking bad, my man? Care to share?'

Stoner pushed the bottle slowly, slowly over to Stretch. Who rose to his full, impressive, height, grinned a wild wide grin, raised the bottle to his ear, clanked it against the hugely heavy ring of gold hanging there, swung bottle to mouth and drank it down. All of it. Every drop. A neat trick. Applause from the floor was as loud for that as for his keyboard set. Maybe louder. Stretch turned to the room, and performed a strange mix of bow and pirouette, holding the quite suddenly empty vessel upside down and wondering whether anyone would care to replace it? Inevitably . . . they would.

The house band, a trio, sometimes a quartet of well hidden potential, stood to their instruments and attempted a selection of occasionally familiar jazz instrumentals, mingling their own interpretations of popular tunes in an apparently random way. As is so often the case, interpretation of inspired original tunes was restricted more by the players' ability than by their imagination. Imagination is always a strong suit of house bands. It needs to be. They need, for example, to imagine their own musical excellence, and they need to buttress that with the belief that the audience is their own audience and that it is packed into the club's uncomfortable seats to listen to *them* perform. It cannot be easy to maintain this belief, and this was the subject of the Chimp's favourite regular monologue. It was a familiar theme, and as ever the shock of the familiar raised Stoner's spirits. As was also traditional, Stretch remarked in a less than subtle, quiet tone that less folk were listening to Chimp, who had an audience of . . . well . . . himself, so would he please give it a rest and give the three-piece a chance.

Polite applause welcomed the house set's conclusion. And in the traditional ironic manner, their pianist reminded the audience that there were other players present; maybe they could be persuaded to play?

And indeed they could. They almost always could.

The evening progressed, as the best evenings do, with gentle instrumentals from inconsistent combinations of players. Always a piano, sometimes a sax, sometimes a guitar, sometimes a fiddle; once there was a flute. No one understood exactly why someone who could perform with a degree of excellence with a saxophone would feel the need to experiment with the flute. Maybe a clarinet, which – all agreed – boasted a decent level of soul, but a flute? Whatever, the audience loved it. maybe they believed they were hearing something seriously original . . . and maybe they were.

As the bar clock slipped past midnight, Bili sat herself down alongside Stoner. Swung her cascade of curls away from her eyes and smiled, cautiously. Caution is a kindness when dealing with a friend, particularly an unpredictable friend. A friend who was these days but not always and maybe not for ever a friend only in the club context. A musical friend. She smiled. Stoner smiled back.

'Flying tonight, old man?' As ever, the traditional gentle joke raised the traditional part-smile.

'Not sure. You, young girl?'

Bili shook more curls. They may have been natural; how do you tell?

'I do have my four strings if you have your six.'

They centred the stage. The audience, a packed crowd by now, shouted approval for what they hoped would follow. It was what they were there for.

She sang too. Deeply in G.

'One summer's day, he went away . . .' the first vocal burst of the evening. Songs can be rare events in jazz clubs. The audience went silent, leaned forward, elbows on tables, glasses lowered, conversation stilled. Bili sang as she played; beautifully and with the desperate wide smile the lyric demanded. A sad song of lost love and longing, superficially at least. Stoner stroked the strings of his Stratocaster, Stretch chorded sevenths in time with Bili's wandering bass as she strolled towards the chorus.

'He's gone, but I don't worry. I'm just sitting on top of the world.'

Stoner switched from bass to middle pick-up, pulled the volume control around two points and built a slow, pensive verse around the bass and piano duo, then shook his head to Bili, who sang seamlessly into the next verse.

Stoner's personal internal blues lasted three numbers. Just three. And then, as is sometimes the way, he stood up from his high stool, shuffled his shoulders and glanced at Bili, who flicked a smile to Stretch, who kicked the piano's loud pedal and shifted from minor to major for one single bar as Stoner flicked the pick-up selector away from him, all the way to full treble, reeled the volume control until his little finger could twist the pot no further, pulled his hand back till pick hit string right by the bridge and cranked everything he had into a complex part-chording, moving into ever-louder, sustained single notes. Guitar sang like a sax as he worked his rage, his frustration and his blues away. Feedback and talent battled for control of the instrument in a conflicted riot of exuberance for several verses more than any album producer would permit. Such is one delight of live music.

Dream over, game played, he made eye contact with Bili and Stretch and the latter hammered the keys so that they rattled against the harsh staccato of the brittle Stratocaster, while Bili fretted her bass high on the board, fingers picking the heavy strings and dropping them back against the fretboard to provide a percussive beat to anchor the song. Piano took over from guitar, Stoner sat down mid-verse, switched back to the bass pick-up, halved the volume, killed the conflicts, the audience drew breath and applauded while Stretch on the piano pulled the whole train into the station of silence and the power trio took their bow.

'Share a glass, Bili?'

The unlucky house band returned to the stage, clapping their hands over their heads and nodding with fake respect.

They sat at a table for two, as far into the shade as they could. Stretch sat in with the house band, providing encouragement and occasional ironic accuracy.

'Should we be talking guitars for a while?' She looked for a drink. Music is always a safe playground for musicians, even if they play for rivalry as much as for mutual respect. 'Rumour told me that you were considering maybe, almost, contemplating, perhaps wondering, whether you might replace that old Strat?'

Stoner's elderly Fender was nothing less than notorious for its capricious moods. Ninety-nine plays out of a hundred it would function as Leo Fender had intended, and would sound rather better than a guitar of its age should, due to a little extra in the switching department, but on its off day it could be a bad boy indeed. A bad buzzy boy. Ancient wiring was the problem; the breakdown of the earthing the cause of the buzz. And the ancient nineteen-sixties soldering could possibly be the cause of the occasional inappropriate silence. Buzzing silence. Stoner had been known to threaten it with conversion into firewood. Or worse; conversion into an unplayed ornament, hanging on some collector's trophy wall.

'She's at work again tonight, Bili. It just doesn't get better. You know that. The thing is what it is and there's nothing to be done about it. I hate it. I hate myself for hating it. I try to forget it and when we're together I can pretend that it's going to get right but I always know it won't happen. She's good at what she does. She enjoys what she does. She gets paid well for what she does. Everyone's happy. Why change it?

'And how is life in your world, hey?'

Bili tipped back in her chair, tilted her head forward so that her face was mostly obscured by clouds of curls. She drummed her fingernails along the table's edge; all eight of them, perfect pausing, no gaps between hands. She played keys as well as frets, and it showed.

'I thought you'd deny it. Had a guitar all that time, all those years, all those shared solos, snatches of achievement, bursts of brilliance? Hard to ditch that for a modern impostor. An incomer. Something new which maybe just looks better and has a bit more flash, a bit less abrasion, a little more sparkle and a little less grit. If you did get yourself a new playing mate, a newer younger more flexible friend, then it could just turn into a passing thing. Fun while it lasts, brings an illusion of youth, impresses your buddies, but with no depth. No staying power.'

Bili was, some suggested, older than she looked. She could certainly play as though she'd spent a hundred years practising.

'But then again. You don't necessarily need to get rid of the old Strat to play a different instrument, JJ. You could polish it up, pack it in silica gel and preserve it in your attic . . . You do have an attic?'

Stoner smiled at her. With Bili conversation could be many things.

'There's only one way to find out, and anyway, what if I did try out a different guitar, lined it up side by side with the old familiar, played whichever I thought suited the song better? Just like the pros, with a half dozen guitars lined up waiting their turn. Isn't that all a little organised? A little constraining? No room for manoeuvre, for improv, for a little jamming? How does that work? In any case, just how long have you been slapping that tired Ricky; there are better basses, too, lady.'

'A day will come, JJ, when disaster will strike. It will be like your baby burst of brilliance just now, except in reverse. You will twist the loud knob, launch into the best blasting stomp of your life, and the only guy who'll know it will be you, and even you won't hear it, just feel it through your fingers. One day you'll crank it all up and burst into the loudest silence of them all. Won't that be good? Won't that be a fine thing?

'I'll still applaud, though, because I will know that you have fretted your best, that musical history was made before my eyes, if not my ears, and that those notes will never sing your way again. And then you'll go all Pete Townsend and smash the thing up out of rage. Just like that. How much did you say it's worth, that most weary of Stratocasters?'

'Too much. Far too much to play. You're right, though. Come that bad day when the bloody soldering on the jack socket finally lets go, melted by the burning rays of the bright light of my truthful mastery, a bolt from above will strike down that crappy Rickenbacker, frizz those awesome curls of yours permanently straight, and Stretch will take all the credit, all the applause, all the booze for playing solo blues with no cues at all.'

'Hell, JJ, you are a poet. Let us drink to that. Have you considered a flash young thing, maybe an Ibanez, good enough for Joe Satriani, they say, and he's no slouch . . .'

This is the thing about the Blue Cube. This is the thing about a good club, and about playing good music with good friends. It's a world of its own. It's not the real world. That mad place can be suspended, ignored for a while, for a time when the realities can be different, when we can try to be what we are not, to be less than we are. We can be just Stoner the guitar player, Bili the bass. An all-absorbing, ever-challenging world where playing the blues blows away the irritations of reality, where one single dimension can take over and you can ignore the rest of it. Just for a while.

Stoner was walking home. A walk along familiar streets after a few hours at the Blue Cube to balance his internal books. A walk provides time to think, to consider whether he really should return to his own private, semi-secret half-hidden home rather than to the dirty blonde's. They might be similar, his homes, but only one of them would ever be likely to contain that blonde, even if the timing could rarely be guaranteed.

His head was clear, his senses up and running well, thanks to the emotional purge of the night's playing, the rivalries and the shared music of it all.

Two men stepped into his path. One shorter than the other and chewing gum so emphatically that it must be an act. The other was larger, a little bit massive and using that mass to block his way. Not the action of an innocent friendly stranger who has lost his bearings in the big bad dark. He was sporting a decently expensive and tool-worked leather jacket which showed at least a tiny amount of dress sense, unlike the complete absence of politeness indicated by his blocking Stoner's path.

'Stoner.'

A statement, not a question, and as such undeserving of a response. The lesser of the two had spoken. Stoner watched the bigger. If there was to be action as well as words, that was where it would originate. He said nothing. Took his bearings, took stock. No causes for concern, no reasons for alarm. So no need to produce any response at all, not vocal, not facial; no action required.

'Stoner.'

This could go on all night. Which was fine, Stoner was in no real hurry to find that the dirty blonde had yet to arrive home. So his mood could stay good for the time being at least.

'For fuck's sake!' Gumchew appeared to be a man of little patience. 'For fuck's sake; you're Stoner, yes?'

Stoner continued to ignore him, continued to watch Leatherjacket. The latter appeared mainly to be confused. Maybe silence was less than golden where he came from.

'Jesus.'

Where obscenity fails, the good thug can always fall back on profanity. Stoner held no views on these grammatical subtleties, preferring at this point to observe that Leatherjacket's big hands matched his big frame, and that those hands were flexing, as a boxer's hands are wont to do before a fight. If this was some subtle attempt at making Stoner nervous, to impress him, it would need to ramp up a little.

Finally, Stoner flicked his gaze to Gumchew. He raised a querying eyebrow. Said nothing. Then looked back at Leatherjacket, who looked right back, flexing his fingers. Stoner wondered for a moment whether he was in fact that rumoured triangle soloist and was seeking an invite to display his art at the Blue Cube. Which delightful thought must have registered in a small smile because Gumchew changed his song a little.

'Look. I know who you are. Who I am is unimportant. What is important is that I'm looking for Handy Mandy and you know where I can find her.'

The evening was plainly a variety performance. First there was a little light romance over a soothing drop with the dirty blonde, followed by a few hours of good sweet music at the Blue Cube, and finally came the comedy. It was good, too. Stoner laughed. A real, honest laugh. A laugh from the heart.

'You're looking for a hand job?'

Very few things could penetrate Stoner's customary cool, but his mood was atypically elevated after the night's blues, and this ... well ... it was a new experience for him. Over a long life – long by the standards of those who followed his alleged profession, at least – Stoner had been asked to locate many things, but never a hand job. He grinned. The dirty blonde would have been reaching for the Valium at this point, her hysteria a health hazard.

Gumchew's eyes bulged a little.

Stoner beamed at him. 'You've stopped a complete stranger in the street late in the dark of the night to ask him whether he is who you think he is and if so can he sort you out . . . a hand job?'

His smile slipped.

'Who suggested that I might be the right guy to procure such a service? Do you think I'm a pimp, you silly little boy? If we have a friend in common, unlikely as it seems, then he or she is someone with a considerable sense of humour. I don't know many folk like that. Tell me this is all a joke, and we'll get along much better.'

Stoner leaned back, relaxed.

'A hand job. That's really, really good.'

Gumchew appeared to have chewed a chilli. A hot one. Even under the poor lighting he was starting to puff up purple. Laughter was miles away from him. Stoner saw this and he chuckled more.

'Handy Mandy!' Gumchew yelled.

Stoner beamed.

'I heard OK the first time. And I am an unashamed man, but do you really intend to be broadcasting your secret needs so loudly? And in so public a place?'

'Handy Mandy. Mandy Hanwell. You know her; she hangs around the club you play guitar in. She's always there. She was there tonight. She owes something to the man we work for, her and me; you know where she is, and you will share that knowledge so that I can reclaim what she owes. You tell me how to find the stupid bitch, or you can give me what she owes and I will try to forget this. I will try to let you walk away. I will try

58

to forgive your stupid insinuation, your stupid attempt at humour.'

Leatherjacket was bouncing on his toes and flexing his fingers again.

Stoner was smiling no more.

'I know a lot of people. A lot more people know me. I know no Mandy Hanwell, and I most certainly know no . . . for fuck's sake . . . Handy Mandy. Let me be, let me by and we can both move on. We have no argument. I've told you a simple fact. I have no reason to lie to you, comic though you are.'

Leatherjacket was a deceptively fit and a deceptively fast man. He leaned his weight onto his left leg and swung his right foot in a well-balanced and well-executed attacking kick. The key to defence is anticipation. As soon as Leatherjacket stopped flexing his fingers, as soon as he stopped bouncing on his toes, as soon as he looked at the guitar case Stoner carried in his right hand, Stoner had understood perfectly what would happen next.

What happened next was that Stoner strode forward past the upswinging foot and caught the knee behind it. A well-delivered kick is an excellent attack; the excellent defence is to prevent it landing.

Stoner's weight was on his left foot; his right foot swung a little outward so that the inside edge of his Caterpillar boot sole met Leatherjacket's right shin about halfway between knee and ankle. Stoner shifted his weight to the right foot; all fluid motion; all he was doing was walking briskly forward, and the boot sole ground relentlessly down the shin and onward to the foot beneath.

Fighters who like to fight with their feet face dilemmas when considering their choice of footwear. Heavy shoes are usually loud and usually clumsy; a tricky kicker will often prefer something lighter. As here. Unhappily.

Stoner's hefty Caterpillar boot – not a shoe he would have chosen for kick-boxing, to be honest, but a great shoe for walking in comfort – has a well-defined, heavily cleated sole. Great for grip. One of the ways that tread patterns like these provide better grip than a smooth sole made of the same hard-wearing compound is by concentrating the wearer's body mass through a small area; the area of the studs. These studs can cut through mud and water to find grip on more solid substrates beneath. They can also exert vast point pressure, for appropriate example, on an instep, should they land hard on an instep and should that instep be unprotected by anything more resistant than a shoelace and a thin layer of soft leather.

Leatherjacket, completely off balance and in considerable pain, struggled to stay standing. Stoner carried on walking, still carrying the guitar case containing his heroically valuable Fender, and swung it under Leatherjacket's elevated right knee, catching the case with his left hand and raising both hands and the case as rapidly and as hard as he could. His assailant had nowhere to go but down. And down is where he went. Hard. His skull announced its arrival on planet earth with a sharp and surprisingly loud crack.

Stoner carried on walking. He was unhappy to entrust his balance to Leatherjacket's left instep, so he let go the guitar case handle with his right hand, letting it fall while keeping his grip with his left hand, and swung right, dropping his left foot and its excellent Caterpillar boot onto Leatherjacket's right knee, and bouncing all his weight through both of his feet. This left him unbalanced, and had Leatherjacket and Gumchew been working as a fighting team he could have been in some trouble, but they were not, so he was not.

The new imbalance snapped many of the several small and slow-to-repair bones in Leatherjacket's right foot. He stifled a scream, which cannot have been easy, but he could not retain this admirable quiet when Stoner pivoted again, this time on his left foot – the one on the recumbent unfortunate's knee, and lifted his right foot from the crackling ankle, stamping down as hard as he could on the big man's groin. Leatherjacket was flat on his back with his left ankle smashed and with his right leg in the air. There was nothing he could do to deflect Stoner's punishing foot, with its excellent Caterpillar boot landing with all Stoner's weight upon his genitals. No man on the planet could remain silent through this. A scream, a curious mixture of wail, sob and screech, split the quiet night.

Stoner stepped from his loud human footstool and accelerated towards Gumchew, swinging the guitar case back up and catching its handle with his right hand. Maybe a minute had passed since Leatherjacket had made the cardinal, life-changing decision to attack Stoner. Maybe it was less. These things are important when one man is facing more than one attacker. It is too common for the second assailant to prepare and deliver a crushing attack while the solo fighter is unbalanced and while his attention is elsewhere. Stoner knew this. He knew it very well.

But Gumchew appeared to be ignorant. In fact he appeared to be in shock. He was also and quite suddenly short of breath when Stoner swung up the guitar case and used it as a ram, driving it into his abdomen just below the ribs, and slamming him up against the wall.

All stopped. Gumchew had lost his chewing gum. He had probably swallowed it. This is a better alternative than trying to inhale it, although Stoner judged that the time was not right to discuss this.

Gumchew was also looking likely to throw up, which is a common consequence of having the narrower end of a guitar case rammed hard into your abdomen by a very strong man who cares little for your future wellbeing.

'Handy fucking Mandy? Are you out of your head, you senseless little shit? Do you believe me now when I tell you that I don't know anyone called Handy fucking Mandy?'

Stoner was not angry. Stoner wasn't even short of breath. Stoner enjoyed the physical release of an act of violence. Stoner appreciated his own ability to plan a fight and to execute that plan swiftly and effectively. Stoner was, if anything, in a good mood. He stepped away from the unchewing Gumchew, and looked back at Leatherjacket, who was rather optimistically, but with full marks for grit and determination, attempting to rise. Unhappily, the result was more screaming and a further collapse.

Stoner turned back to Gumchew.

'I can't stand this racket. All manner of idiots are going to be here in a moment, and they'll be here quicker if he carries on bleating and wailing. Nothing personal ...' And he kicked Leatherjacket hard in the side of his head, landing a clean and accurate shot with his excellent Caterpillar boot and cutting the unfortunate recumbent off in mid-sob.

Gumchew was still and silent. A neat example of role-reversal. His role was as half of a double act; take away the fallen guy and he was confused. A less sensible soul would have run; to give him some credit, he had worked out all for himself that running from an irritated Stoner was unlikely to bring escape from grief. He gained more credit by spreading his arms wide and presenting Stoner with his open hands, palms first.

Stoner stepped a little further back.

'Speak. Speak sensibly, explain to me how I am the man you're looking for but how I somehow have no notion of who you are or what you want. Speak rapidly and clearly, because your pal there needs fairly urgent medical help, and if he wakes up and starts that yelling crap again I will shut him up again and there is a limit to the number of times a guy can take being kicked in the head before he either turns into a plant or dies. If he was to do the latter, I would have killed him and you know who I am. This would reduce my options for the immediate future to just the one, and that would be bad news for you.

'I am certain that you see what I mean. If not, speak now or . . .'

'Handy Mandy is a posh tart – some sort of escort, some sort of girl Friday for my boss . . . the guy who pays my wages. She's been talking non-stop about this guy Stoner who plays in this club and she borrowed a decent chunk of money – maybe for this guy Stoner who plays in this club – and now she's defaulted and she's gone. We tracked her to this club, the Blue Cube, then lost her. And you are Stoner, yes? You can't be anyone else, not after what you just did to James, and you can't help me. So I should call an ambulance and get help for James and I never saw you and James was mugged by some guy after his . . . ah . . . after his wallet. I reckon that it would be bad news getting stuck between my boss and . . . you. No mileage there. None.'

'We're doing well. You do have a good grip on things. You've learned how hazardous talking to strangers can be and like a good boy you will not do it again. Good stuff. Yes to all of those things. But before I leave you and return to the gentle arms of the evening, I need to know two things, so that my internal alarms can be quiet and so that I can sleep soundly. I need to know that you are unencumbered with projectile weapons, and I need to know your identity. This would be a bad time to become brave or to obfuscate. Believe me. So open your coat and give me your wallet.'

Gumchew obliged with no hesitation at all. Education should be like this; simple and effective.

Stoner returned the wallet, less the driving licence.

'Tell me that the weight in your inside pocket is your cell phone?'

Gumchew nodded.

'Then extract it carefully, and call for an ambulance.'

Leatherjacket had started to moan softly, and the sky was becoming light in the east.

'And if we meet again, please remember that politeness is a virtue and that virtue is its own reward.'

'Stoner?'

A question, asked quietly in a quiet voice by a quiet man holding a cell phone. Stoner looked appropriately quizzical.

'The case? Hoods carry tommy guns in violin cases, yeah? What have you got in there? A rifle? A howitzer?'

'It's an axe, sunshine. It's my favourite axe, but it's done enough work for one evening. Make your call . . .'

Stoner grinned, rolled his eyes like an amdram maniac and walked away. Nothing called him back.

Walking is therapy. A good brisk walk into the early twitches of dawn can raise the soul. His spirits elevated, Stoner decided that rather than head home, he'd leave his wheels where they were, near to the dirty blonde's house, and would stay with her. Maybe sharing breakfast would make them both happy, and maybe he could grab a little sleep in convivial company.

And maybe not. Standing outside, looking up at a silent window in a silent house from the silent street, Stoner reviewed things, as is only right in dawn's early light. The dirty blonde might not be back home yet. She may be back but asleep. She might be less than completely happy to be woken by him. She might be . . . conjecture is the enemy of calm, and Stoner needed to sleep. He needed to think.

He walked back to his car, searching his pockets for the keys.

6

MONEY

'This is how it works,' said the Hard Man. 'I give you money. You make me happy. Sometimes, rarely, it works the other way around. You make me happy and then I give you the money. This is life as we know it. As we share it.'

He frowned. He showed no signs of happiness. His tone of voice was flat, monotonous. The delivery of his small speech was disconnected, uncaring, almost uninterested, as though he was thinking of something else, his mind preoccupied.

He loosened, and then unclipped, and then removed the belt from his trousers. His trousers fell around his ankles. It should have been a comic sight. It was not. The Hard Man was far too grave a character and in far too hard a mood for that.

He stepped free of his lower clothes, wrapped the belt around his right hand, squeezed the buckle as he closed his fingers, forming a bulky, misshapen fist.

'It is,' he remarked, almost to himself, 'the purest way of life. It is my way of life. The simple life. An uncomplicated life. Complication always has a tendency to shorten the lives involved in it. In complication there always lies unhappiness. We must strive for simplicity in all that we do. In all that we wish for, too.

'Complication is an indication of youth. Only youth believes that it has the time, the energy for complication. Complication only distracts from purpose. Purity of purpose is rarely accompanied by complication of execution. Distraction is always a diversion. See past the distraction, and you'll see the pure purpose.'

The tall black woman was naked below the waist, as was the Hard Man. She gazed at him in silence. He gazed back. She cleared her throat, less than silently.

'Yes?'

'Yes fucking what?'

The Hard Man's tone was shifting from lecturing, dominant, demanding, to irritated.

'You just keep right on talking, if that's what you're here to do, that's fine by me. It saves on the cleaning up afterwards. But I have to tell you that most folk don't pay me so that they can talk to me. More's the pity. Talking is good. You carry right along with the talking. If all you want to do is talk, then you can have a drink for free to help you along with that. Would you like that?'

The Hard Man's eyes half-closed, his face was dark. His right fist gripped the leather of his belt. He closed the distance between himself and the woman in two long rapid strides and slammed his belted fist into her stomach.

Hard.

Breath fled from her and her eyes closed, then flashed open again.

'You're better at talking.'

The Hard Man's face was set. He swung again, hitting the tall black woman above the bones of her left hip. Her eyes closed briefly as she staggered away from him. She regained her balance and her eyes stared once more into his.

'Do you feel like that drink yet? You need some inner refreshment, some extra vigour?'

Her tone was flat. No distress, no pain in her voice. The next blow lifted her sideways off her feet; she regained her balance, sprang lithe as a cat across the distance between them, raised both her fisted hands into two attacks and as his eyes followed them, trying to watch them both. As they moved back ready for a strike she sank her teeth into the muscle above his right shoulder, and as he pulled away her right fist flew in fast, catching him below his left ear.

His arousal was obvious, unavoidable, urgent. She seized him with her left hand and pushed him back against the wall, standing on just her left leg as she raised her long, black right leg, opening herself and sliding herself onto him, dropping her raised leg, clamping him inside her, pushing both his shoulders hard back against the wall with her two hands and working him inside her; fast, fluid, controlled movement raising his arousal suddenly and uncontrollably to its pitch. No time, no subtlety, no nothing and as he climaxed she held his shoulders hard, pushing them against the wall as he punched her with both hands into her sides as he came, and he came in silence, and as the final drilling climax shuddered between them she raised her hands from his shoulders and slapped his face, not gently, once on each side. He slipped down the wall, fell from inside her and sat at her feet, her hands resting on his shoulders.

She took the belt from him. Ran its wide side between her legs, wiping herself, and dropped it in front of him.

'A memento for you.'

There was no warmth in her voice. She hung a dressing gown around her shoulders and left the room, returning within moments carrying a pair of matching glasses, one red wine, one white, and placed them on a small table. She dropped smoothly into one of the two chairs and looked at the Hard Man, whose satisfied expression told a story she was no part of.

'Time to talk now, if you wish. Although you never do, do you?'

He was dressed, decent. Completely in control once more. Walked over and took the other chair, chose the red wine and raised it in a silent toast to her.

'They're both for you.'

'You hurting?'

His tone was as neutral as ever.

'Of course I'm hurting. You?'

His expression was ambiguous, fleeting. Maybe a glimpse of an emotion, and maybe not.

'No. I'm not hurting. You don't hurt me at all. No one does. Nothing does. But ... I feel good. I feel ... easier. As always.'

He paused, emptied the first glass and raised the second to her.

'Thank you. As always. Your fee's been paid. You offer excellent value. If I hurt you, why do you agree to see me?'

'For the money. You always ask that question, and my answer's always the same, and will always be the same. I do it for the money. If I did it for love, then I'd be a strange woman indeed. And just to ease you from any need you may feel to provide small talk, I don't care about small talk, I just want to lie in a hot bath for a half hour so I can feel soothed and relaxed before I meet the next job. That's it. There is no more.

'If you want to construct some fantasy in which I enjoy being hit, then go ahead. At some point you'll move on, or I will. Or maybe one day you'll hurt me too much and then this will simply end.'

The Hard Man stood, preparing to leave.

'Or maybe one day we'll decide to formalise the arrangement, make it permanent, and settle down together to enjoy a peaceful old age.' He smiled.

'And maybe I'll become an astronaut, or possibly king of England. They all seem equally likely.'

She did not look at him as he left, and neither did she bid him goodbye. She simply drew a deep bath, and lay in it for some time, thinking.

7

NO STRINGS

'Forget yesterday's crime scene. It's cold. Try a new one. There's been another.'

The Hard Man's voice was soft on the cell phone's speaker, easy on the ear.

'And it's a mess. A real mess. You need to be there. Now would be a good time. While everyone's asleep. Bar us.'

Stoner checked the time on the message, hesitated. Returned the call. Asked the Hard Man's own answering robot for directions. Hung up. Walked to the furthest wall, rested his head against it and kicked the skirting, grimly and repeatedly. Kicking a wall, he mused aimlessly, is as useful as banging the head against it, and about as productive, but it is less painful. Even with application, high energy and dedication, any damage is likely to be temporary.

The wall banged a fresh rhythm of its own back at him. Stoner stopped. Stood still. Recalled with worrying slowness that there were neighbours here. That neighbours were likely to object to a madman kicking his stress into their shared wall, even if that madman was the landlord. Although they could be forgiven for being unaware of his identity, given that there was indeed a wall between them.

He focused a little, drew his thoughts back from an imminent encounter with the recently and messily deceased, and surfaced into the world which was real to more conventional citizens than himself. A pair of nice ladies had rented the next door apartment. Quiet ladies, if typically nocturnal in their business habits, which would be why at least one of them was awake and kicking in the pale predawn light. Or maybe he had disturbed one of her customers . . . clients.

The phone buzzed twice. A message. Stoner flicked it open, read the address, ignored the criticism, collected coat, keys, gloves and commitment, and headed out.

04.28. Even the clock on his cell phone had a sense of humour.

Scenes of crime are always protected. They are protected against the long noses and longer lenses of the curious. The professionally curious and the pruriently curious. Both can render a scene useless for an investigative kind of chap. They render scenes useless, typically, by tramping about, by weeping, by sneezing, by vomiting and by cleaning the place up. Stoner had once watched in wonder as a uniform sergeant had righted the downed ornaments, picked bits of broken glassware from the carpets and straightened tumbled books on their shelves. He had occasionally wondered whether a spot of therapeutic carpet chemical cleansing would have come next if the sergeant hadn't vomited with violence and then sobbed through the aftermath. Shock can be a peculiar companion.

Stoner was prepared for a night watchman. Stoner was in fact prepared for the SOC team to be busily bagging, dusting, observing and generally investigating. But no. This scene was protected only by bright yellow tape. Exactly why anyone should believe that a tape bearing wording suggesting that visitors were unwelcome and should depart hence would have an effect on any but the most accommodating and innocent of casual spectators . . .

71

well, one of life's little mysteries. Of which there are so many, so very, very many.

Behind the tape, the door may well have been left unlocked. Stranger things had happened. It was however unlikely. And sadly, the door was indeed locked, secured by more than the No Entry tape. But Stoner was a man of resource. He could pick a lock. He could open a door using a bent hatpin to defeat a lock's mechanism. This always works in the movies. It rarely worked when the door's locking mechanism unsportingly included a magnetic code held in a temporary kind of way on a plastic card issued to the room's renter when he or she rented the room.

In a similar way, sliding a piece of plastic, whether it contained the correct secret magnetic code or not, between the door and its frame in such a way that it pushed the lock's levers aside, so enabling entry, always popular in the same movies, also rarely works on hotel doors. They are designed to be proof against this kind of thing. And indeed they are. The march of technology is remorseless and unthinking. It is also often effective. Professional breakers and enterers no doubt have subtle skills beyond the imagination of mortal men, and using these would enable them to enter the most securely locked of portals. Stoner was not one of those men. He could break heads with the ease of long experience, but he could not pick a magnetically locked lock. He could not work magic.

'La Forge.'

The scared receptionist stared at him. Stoner applied studied patience, switched on an approximate smile and repeated himself.

'Mr La Forge. Do you have an envelope for me?'

The envelope contained the key card. Of course it did. And of course the room was a mess. Of course Stoner arrived much later than the Hard Man had intended and of course the corpse had been removed. Most of the corpse had been removed. But of tidying, vomiting or sobbing sergeants there was no sign.

Stoner closed the door gently behind him and gazed around him with eyes mostly closed. The room stank. Ageing, drying, sweating blood does not smell well. The room was warm and the blood was generously applied to an impressively large area of it. This makes for a considerably bad smell. It is the smell which turns the stomach. Visually, blood is fairly unimpressive, particularly if it's been left lying for a while. It just looks messy. Like spilled cold gravy, congealing with added strawberry jam, perhaps. It is not particularly frightening. If the room is a warm room, as this one was, then the volatiles in the spread blood evaporate, providing an olfactory assault while at the same time allowing the blood itself to congeal to a texture all its unpleasant own. It is, perhaps surprisingly, not entirely unlike black pudding.

There were other odours. There always are. Stoner breathed normally, eyes closed, allowing the room to breathe through his nostrils. There was hotel-room odour; not-very expensive cleaning agents, not-very harsh bleach. The carpets breathed the familiar scent of wet hotel carpet; walked-in road rubbish and weary cheap polymers. There was sweat in the air also. It was a warm room, the SOC team would have gently broiled in their disposable suits while they laboured, and they would have left the heating controls as they had been set by the deceased because they all knew better than to interfere with things like that. The SOC team would also have been innocent of the strong smell of marijuana and the weaker but equally acrid scent of sex. SOC teams wear masks to prevent contamination and to protect themselves from it, and masks do little to enhance olfactory detection. Stoner was a firm believer in using all available senses as he attempted to understand what lay before him.

Eyes open; lights on. The expected mess. Carefully placed cardboard provided an officially sanctioned walkway. Stoner slipped off his boots. Rested them heels-up against the closed door. Slipped on slippers; he wanted no further destruction of the scene. Walked slowly into the centre of the room, stood still at the foot of the bed. The body had been on this bed. Its shape, the depression of the dead, revealed its previous presence. Five pillows. One of them in the bed's centre, soaked and black with blood. The body had been arched over this, face up or face down. Interesting. Mostly hidden under one of the other pillows was an eye, an eyeball. Stoner stared hard, focusing intently upon the trailing nerve and connective tissue. The victim's pale eye looked away, in a shy, passive way . . .

Above the headboard was a painting. Faintly abstract but rendered more so by the bloody splashing. Stoner stared for a moment. Three pale purple balls on stalks against a purple background. A fourth purple ball hung below the very artificial purple horizon. If that headboard painting, in that room, in this weary hotel . . . if they were the last sights for eyes soon to be forever blind, then it would be a bleak moment indeed, that moment of passing. Another reason for fighting a killer. Die on a beach; die in the sun, die . . . old.

The dead man had fought. This was evident in the scattering of everything. But he had not fought hard enough or well enough. Stoner pondered. He didn't know anything about the dead man, other than the two facts that he was dead and that he was a man, but subduing a man was not an easy task. Sex in hotel rooms generally involves at least one girl. Girls are usually less muscled than men. Girls often have trouble overpowering men. This is one reason why women get raped. Holding off a fit man is not easy for a slight woman. A fit man who is in a state of arousal should be even more vigorous than might be usual – the experience of illicit sex, hotel sex, tends to produce extra excitement. This is one reason why the few hit men who are really hit women tend to favour the more subtle or remote approaches to that final departure. Poisons, guns, garrottes; that kind of thing. Stoner pondered some more.

For the Hard Man to be interested in this, he must have reasonable suspicion that the deaths were more than simply random attacks. They were unlikely to be a result of the joy of sex gone a little further than expected; that particular cause of death was a real rarity. Stoner's pondering brought him to the notion of the accomplice. Could he picture this conversation: 'Excuse me one moment, Mr Customer, while I open the door to my big bloke buddies?' Not easily, he couldn't.

So then; drugs in the drink. Stoner, still unmoving in the centre of the room, looked at the array of smashed glass. A couple of bottles. Cheap wine. Cheapskate. No wonder he got killed. Could the motive be meanness? Some cheap, white, trashy German wine, not even *mit Pradikat.* Not an easy motive, that one. And in any case, the plods had a fine toxicology team in their various pathology departments; if there were soporific chemicals involved – apart from the marijuana, of course – then they would find trace in a trice. If they looked for it.

He could see no indication that a bottle had been smashed over a head, which is an unsubtle and not always effective way of subduing someone. But the edge of the built-in desktop, as well as being smeared with the ubiquitous blood, also wore what appeared to be a tuft or two of short dark hair. That would have hurt, but by the time the hair left the head, that head was already on its way to make unexpected and close acquaintance with the carpet, so damage had already been done.

So then; an errant eyeball and a stray tuft of hair. They both pointed one way; they pointed towards a degree of ferocity which was unusual – most unusual – in a contractor. Professionals kept their place in their business by being dispassionate. Efficient. Ferocity has its place, but if the only way a killer can kill is by becoming outraged, ferocious, then the moment would inevitably arrive when the ferocity was not forthcoming and at that point the professional might falter, might fail. At that point, only retirement beckoned. Or worse.

Stoner looked around him for more signs of far-flung flesh. And of course he found them. Things turn up once you start looking for them. The same thing happens in reverse, too. It is not usually difficult to hide in plain view of folk, especially if they aren't aware that they're looking for you. And it is the same with objects. Sometimes things hide themselves from the most professional of searchers. Stoner had never yet been unable to uncover material evidence from a scene after it had been declared clean by a SOC team. And the converse was often also the case: after Stoner had passed his gaze over a scene, a new gaze almost always found evidence *he'd* missed. The more intense the search, the greater the tendency to miss the obvious. Sometimes.

Among the glass splinters and shards, two recognisable finger-nails. Make that three; the smaller of them possibly painted ... and possibly not. There was so much muck, so much bloody mess that without picking it up it was hard to tell.

Much has been written, and more has been said, about the information available to the practiced observer from a crime scene. Stoner's view was that although all information had a value, the real value lay in the wider view. He was personally acquainted with several practitioners of the SOC expert's art. He had worked both for and against them in the course of his inter-esting life. If he had cause to criticise them, which he rarely did, it would be because they tended to look too closely, in too much detail. He felt that as much was often to be gained by the standing back and taking a broader view. His own favoured method involved both, but in most police work involving genuine policemen, resources were an issue. Cost and value had to be balanced. In Stoner's contracting spook world, these things were less important, funding being politically invisible and always deni-able.

He was calm now. The shock of the mess had eased, his own organism had ceased feeling threatened by the circumstances of the demise of another similar organism. Carpet was just carpet; blood was just mess and an indication of an event, not an emotional decoration ... or desecration, even. Thoughts of the rights and wrongs of violent death had appeared, said their piece, and then left again. Leaving room for thinking, considering, analysing and concluding, although the latter usually came later. The later the better, Stoner preferred, because conclusions are so often incorrect and so often cloud the case.

On the functional faux timber desk stood a portable computer. A small one. A netbook. It was inevitably spattered a little with drops and fragments of the dead departed, and its screen stood open, if not completely. It was positioned precisely where it should have been, were it to be operated from the chair which usually accompanied the desk, but which in this case was lying on its side on the far side of the blood-soaked bed.

Stoner took a tool from an inside pocket. It was one of three he habitually carried when examining a scene, or when working on a motorcycle. This one was an extendable rod with a decently strong magnet at its end; like many mechanics he used it most often in the workshop, where it was a great way to retrieve small, dropped metallic components. In this case, though, all he wanted was to prod the buttons on the netbook to prompt it back to life.

He was curious to see what a mark who had brought a recreational lady to his hotel would have wanted to see on his computer while he and his guest were exercising in the customary hotel way. It is indeed possible to take one's work too seriously.

Nothing doing. Tapping the space bar with the tool produced nothing; the machine was shut down. He thought about this.

'Excuse me, m'lady, I'll just shut down my computer before we do that sex thing.'

It didn't ring true. Nor did an alternative vision in which ferocious murderer, having just ripped at least one eye and a few desperate fingernails from his victim, paused before his emergency exit to power down a nearby computer. Computers turn themselves into a sleep mode; prodding a key, any key, wakes them up. It's universal. A mystery. He could reach the On switch without wading through the bloody carpet, but only just, and there was always a risk of an embarrassing slip. The carded track through the swampy carpet was not the most stable pathway in the world, and placing lateral loads on the card itself could produce an unwanted surfing effect, which easily resulted in brave investigator on bloody knees and a future explanation to his masters which would be more than a little embarrassing.

But it felt important. If the netbook's screen was open, it suggested that its operator had been using it while his guest was in the room. If he'd finished whatever task had been in hand he would not only have switched it off but would also have closed the lid. So it seemed to Stoner, who risked collapse and embarrassment by reaching to his limit and pressing the On button. The power light lit . . . but only briefly. One very flat battery was the likely reason, then. OK. The netbook would have been inventoried by the SOC team so needed to stay where it was. Time, then, for a mental note.

For no reason he could explain, Stoner stared through the room's window. He may have felt a need to let his eyes rest on something further away, relaxing focus often reveals otherwise lost details. Details like the whole-palm print dead centre on the main pane.

Stoner pulled his cell phone from the leg pocket of his cargoes, flipped it open, took three pics of the print at maximum zoom, such as it was, and sent the least poor of them to the Hard Man along with 'Anyone we know?' which might stimulate a response at some point. There was no sign of fingerprint powder on the glass, so far as he could see . . . not that this meant much. Forensic science moves and improves rapidly.

He also sent an image of the netbook and, entirely to be

irritating, of the lonely drying eye. And then he left the room, a man with thinking to do, and maybe a long walk over which to do it. He dropped the keycard back at the reception, eliciting a 'Thank you, Mr La Forge . . .' said without a trace of humour. Star Trek was a seemingly endless source of worknames.

'Thank Mr Riker for me, please.'

The Hard Man always liked to be Number One.

8

PAST TIMES

'Do you remember .'

The Hard Man was drifting into whimsy, it seemed.

'Do you remember the pornographer?'

'Yes. Of course. How on earth could I forget?'

'It would not be easy. She was an unforgettable person. So few persons you meet in this life are like that.' He stopped. Looked a little lost. Stoner had seen this expression before. It was never genuine, never an honest representation of the way the Hard Man was feeling. And in any case, he remembered the pornographer very well, too well for good sense, probably. 'Do you think there's a connection?' A polite question. Stoner could see one way in which the current case could be connected to that earlier episode, but only in that both cases involved violent death. Which in itself and given their line of work was not particularly remarkable.

'I always felt that she was an unusual woman. It was unfortunate that she ended what should have been a fine career in the way she did.' The Hard Man was still looking faintly sorrowful. Hang-dog expressions were strangers to his generally and falsely genial features. 'And I don't know about any serious connection.

You know how I never place any value at all in hunches, even when they're my own hunches and therefore probably worth no more than anyone else's. Well, I just have a hunch.'

The lady both gentlemen referred to as 'the pornographer' had been exactly that. But with the unusual twist that the co-stars in her take on the very old and very human game of let's make babies were usually unaware of their starring status. It had been an earlier, possibly a more innocent internet age, a time when much of the interconnectedness of the ethers was new and when squalid exploitation of the information hyper-highway was in its youth. Unlike most of the pornographer's willing participants, who were rarely particularly youthful but often shared a tendency towards wealth.

'I can't see a connection here, not a real one . . . a valid one.' Stoner decided to push the Hard Man into continuing. The business with the pornographer was one of the few occasions on which the Hard Man had visibly struggled; Stoner had enjoyed the case, not least because of the Hard Man's evident discomfort. So he continued. 'Mean to say. The pornoperson shot her victims only with a camera. She didn't slice them up and scatter bits of their bodies all about the place. Don't think anyone actually died, did they? They might have been in pain, distress, but she didn't in fact actually stop anyone's heart beating. Put up a few pulse rates, but stopped before actual coronary failure. Put up your own rate, didn't she? At least a little?'

'You're an idiot,' said the Hard Man without animosity, said without heat; said without any indication of intelligent thought behind the mouthwork; on autopilot. 'You mostly are.'

'And thank you for those few kind words.' Stoner's attempt at reactivating the Hard Man had been less than one hundred per cent effective, then.

'She was clever. She misled. She dissembled with symbols everywhere.' The Hard Man was really drifting now. It was an unusual sight; a sight to be relished, enjoyed, appreciated. 'Like this one. This is clever. I don't believe any of it. Apart from the poor sod who's been clipped I don't see any of the truth before me. You?'

Stoner pulled himself away from his gentle amusement at the Hard Man's unusual distraction and dragged his thoughts back to the crime scene. Even in its state of bodylessness it was as close as he had been to the killer.

'I just saw a murder scene. Really messy. Damage done by someone stronger than average. Someone with rage, too.' Stoner remembered. Went silent.

'Come along, JJ. This isn't the first scene you've looked at, and I doubt it'll be the last. You're not a kiddie. Give me something.' The Hard Man was plainly feeling benign, his manner almost gentle.

Stoner looked up. 'Next time, leave the rest of the body at the scene for a while? Give me more to look at than bits. That might be useful.'

The Hard Man ignored him, drifting back to his hunch.

'It's not the body, JJ. It's not that. Not exactly. Bodies is bodies; dead is just that . . . dead. It's the filming. I'm unsure why that seems so important, but it does. Something inside says that the filming is more important than the killing. Hence my thoughts on the pornographer.'

He paused. Stoner prompted him, quietly.

'Heather, wasn't it? Heather' . . . he paused . . . 'someone.'

The Hard Man nodded. Caught Stoner's wandering glance before it escaped.

'You know full well it was. Don't play games. Not about her and not about the thing she did and not,' he paused for power, 'not now. That is unamusing. And I would not like that lack of amusement to cloud my thinking or my respect for your competence and your suitability for this . . . this job to become in any way infirm. Do not fuck about with me on this, JJ. Do not play any games. We would have a fight. You would lose the fight and I would retire you from my very short list of professional friends. Retirement in this case would be permanent. In the same way as the pornographer's retirement was permanent. She cannot recover from it, and neither would you.'

Stoner smiled at his companion.

'Bloody hell, I'd no idea it hurt that much.'

'It did. You should accept that fact and move on. An ability to learn from understanding and from experience is what distinguishes us superior humans from a sack of shit on the sidewalk, JJ, and I for one remember that.'

The pornographer had been a lady of considerable appetite. She had two major attributes which assisted her relentless aim to fulfil that appetite; she was both wealthy and she was stunningly attractive. She did what she did with men – and occasionally with women – entirely for amusement. For personal power. Because she enjoyed it.

She fucked wealthy men and she filmed them enjoying themselves. Not for her the single static lens. These are digital days, the age of the cheap camera and the cheap operator. She set up an ever-increasing number of recording devices around her bedrooms and bathrooms, kitchens, gym and living rooms, and she filmed lots of physical exercises in them all. When she was exercising with a particularly interesting person or two, she would employ the services of a camera operator, who could zoom and pull focus while the players zoomed and pulled things of their own. And afterwards she would sit down and edit her movies into something less like a home video and more like a blue movie. She became the pornographer when she sent the first of these to one of its more affluent participant co-stars and suggested that he keep it as a memento. She said no more than that, and she needed to say no more.

83

At that point she asked for nothing in return. Free home movies, shared with consenting participants.

Her client base grew steadily. She was expert at what she could do with a man, particularly with an older man, where skill and its application are particularly useful in extracting maximum performance from flesh which had already seen it all, and done it all too many times for just another bed-buddy to be arousing in itself. Many of her men friends recommended her to their own friends. Stoner had found it particularly interesting that even when her men had been the surprised recipients of her feature films many of them still suggested that their friends and colleagues paid her a visit. Unity in numbers, perhaps.

Inevitably, she asked for a favour or two. Eventually she asked for a favour too far from a man who was less of a friend than he pretended, and the Hard Man was asked to take an interest. Possibly predictably, the Hard Man was already in possession of a couple of movies in which he was the star, and one in which he played an atypical supporting role to more stellar performances. A subordinate position which he felt did not reflect well on his hard man image, and which he felt would be embarrassing if made more public.

More embarrassing yet was that the Hard Man plainly suffered from feelings for the pornographer herself. He knew what she was and he knew what she did, although the scale and variety he discovered when he sent operators – Stoner among them – to retrieve ever more of the movies was at least a small surprise.

In the end, as pressure on him mounted, as more of his governmental colleagues and commanders suggested ever more firmly that their problems be resolved, he took Stoner into his confidence, and asked that Stoner fix the situation in a permanent way. Which he did.

No one had asked him how, where or even when, but the pornographer's sudden silence talked louder than any obituary. Her impressive movie collection was somewhere in the Hard Man's private archive, mostly. Stoner's relationship with the Hard Man had improved from his own perspective after this case, not least because of the suggestion that he might have retained copies of some of the more adventurous movies, such is the ease of duplication in the digital age. Untraceable duplication. It was a non-subject from the moment of the pornographer's sudden and complete silence and disappearance.

But a connection with the hotel murders? That had been provided by the revelation that the last task of the computers left at the most recent scenes had been recording the bodies they shared the room with. Large movie files, not that there was actually any movement, because the only visible actor was a dead actor. And the movie – the still death movie – had been streamed live to a website; one site among the many sicko sites frequented by those strange souls who were fans of crime, crime real and crime imagined.

The Hard Man had connected the two. The pornographer who filmed her bedmates and a killer who filmed his victims. Stoner was unconvinced, and a little surprised at the alleged connection.

'I'm unconvinced,' he remarked to the Hard Man. 'I can't see any connection at all here. The pornographer is long gone, and she never was a killer. She might have broken a few hearts and damaged a few wallets' – the Hard Man glowered at him – 'but she was no killer.'

'Fool. I'm not suggesting she was the killer. My thought is that if someone's filming the crimes then there's a reason for that, and I doubt it's to keep some sick fansite happy. You make a movie for a reason. Only for a reason. They make good levers. I can't see what it is. Open your mind, JJ. Look at more than the method. We need to find this guy, and soon.'

'You want to offer him a job?'

No humour in Stoner's question.

'Who knows, my friend? Who knows . . .'

9

WHERE SHADOWS RUN
FROM THEMSELVES

'Why do men get murdered in hotels?'

The dirty blonde was plainly getting well into this.

'It's like, y'know, if I wanted to kill someone, not that I would, much, but like you always say, given the right, thing ... incentive, um, need ... then I might. If I did, I'd do it long away, long distance, long range. What's that you called it?'

'Long gun. You'd use a long gun.'

Sometimes I do believe that I am the only person who knows what she's talking about. Including herself.

'Right. The long gun. Why are they always long guns? Do you get short guns also? I've never heard of a short gun. I read a story about a lazy gun once, and there was something ... oh I dunno ... something about a smart gun which could speak and aim itself. That would be superb, wouldn't it though?'

Reality, like food, wasn't always a necessary requirement for the dirty blonde.

'But. Hotels? Why in a hotel? Why not be like that Russian? Kick the guy with a poison shoe in a crowded street, make with the apologies and then clear off quick before he falls over. No one could ever catch you then. Why a hotel? Jesus. It wasn't even a nice hotel. I go to loads better hotels than that one. Didn't even have a minibar. Jesus. I can't see that anywhere would be a great place to die, exactly, but some are less worse than others. Was he pissed up? How could he be? No minibar. Jesus. That is cheap. If I die in an hotel, it needs to have a bar. A big bar. I want a wake before I die. No point afterwards. Why would anyone choose to die in a cheap pit? Why would anyone choose to, y'know, off someone in a cheap pit?'

There are moments when it is OK to take time for a little explanation. This was one. Maybe.

'Hotels are convenient. Hotels are convenient for lots and lots of things. And it's not too difficult to get guys to go to hotels. They do it all the time. Some guys just about live in hotels. Setting up a hit is only an inexact science if you're an amateur, if you're just doing it the once. I think this guy, our guy here, is a pro. So, if you arrange to meet a guy in a hotel, it's not too hard to get into his room. Particularly if you're a girl. OK? You know this better than me.'

I can feel myself wince inside at this, but it's true. The dirty blonde never flinches about what she does. It's just a job. Like decorating or fixing cars. Her wallpaper would peel, her paint would flake and her cars would always break down. And some clown would always be there to fix them for her. In her world there is always some handy guy to fix everything, pay for everything. That's what guys do in the dirty blonde's world. It must be the same for everyone. That's what she thinks. And what she thinks is true . . . for her.

'Yeah, yeah. What you're saying then, JJ, is that the john, the mark, yes, gets invited to his own room by a lady he's just met, or by a lady he knows and is meeting, and then just as he thinks Christmas is about to come early and he's going to do a little of the premature rubber stocking filling thing, zap. Lady pops out for a moment to . . . to do what? . . . and in pops the hitter. Bang-o bingo, and goodnight gay Lothario? Is that how he's doing it? It would be easier, less unreliable, if the lady was a hitter. Is she? Could I do that? Is it murderous, murder? It always seems easy enough on the TV, in the movies. Although it would be crap if you knew the mark.

'Hey look. I've been to hotels . . . yeah yeah, I know you're uncomfy, but . . . I've been to lots of hotels with lots of guys and afterwards, when they've done what they pay to do, well I could off them. Some of them. Some of them are ass. Really ass. Next time . . . next time I get sweaty with some really hideous ass I'll work my thoughts around the idea of killing him. I have to think of something unless the john's actually useful in the sheets anyway. Most of them have no clue. Not a simple clue. Some take bloody ages. You wouldn't believe this, but . . .'

I interrupt. I need to interrupt.

'I'd doubt that, really. There are very few female hitters. I've only ever met the one, in fact. And she was retiring at the time. And shy . . .'

The dirty blonde switched from reminiscing to considering. I carried on before she started with more of the sweaty sheet stories.

'But hotels? They're good. You can arrange for the room to be booked for a few days and hang a Do Not Disturb notice outside so that you are really long gone before the victim gets discovered by an eager public. Not very nice if you're the employee doing the discovering, but you can fix that by calling after you've left and telling the constables that there's a body awaiting their immediate attention. That works well.

'There's almost no danger of being disturbed by soon-to-be-grieving relatives, either. Not in a hotel. Can't imagine that it's very great, having the front door open just after you've offed some fine chap, and his wife, mother, daughter, lover come wandering in, expecting . . . well . . . whatever folk expect when they go see their dad, boyfriend. Whatever. It's . . .'

'Has that happened to you? Has some relative, y'know, strolled in while you were banging away? It's happened to me more than once. Oh yes. First time you think you're going to die of shock, but your shock is nothing like their shock, and . . .'

'What?' Sometimes the dirty blonde's concentration lapses can be amazing; truly they can. 'You've what, been interrupted while offing some clown? You have actually killed someone?' Amazing. Amazing if true. I had no idea. But it was possible. I know very little of her younger days. Surprisingly little.

'Soft lad. Banging for me and banging for you are different beasts. Not that I bang animals. Much. Ho ho. Laugh with me. Hold my hand. But no no; I meant that being caught on the job is a hazard which transcends occupations, at a guess. Although when some third party wanders in it's usually been planned in my world. Some smart ass wants to invite a friend. Takes all sorts. Happens a lot. But usually, usually I know about it before-hand. Y'know?'

I'm not comfortable with this. I say so. Not for the first time. She smiles at me. The dirty blonde winds me up. She enjoys winding me up. She tells me that she only winds up folk she cares about. Why would she wind up someone if she didn't care about them? There's no answer to that. She manages serious sex, sucks and fucks all manner of folk she cares nothing at all about. Why would she be bothered about a little humour at their expense? Quite serious expense, from what I know of her. I try to picture caring so little about someone that you'd sleep with them but not provide humour to stroll alongside the sex. I fail to picture this.

I am no prude. Believe me on this. I know many many girls of the game. It is impossible not to if you are a creature whose paid professions drag you through the long nights, whose preferred occupation finds you sitting in the dark smoky clubs waiting for inspiration and release to descend into your lap. Boredom produces many strange bedfellows, in every sense. Random bedfellows; every shade and preferred delight. It's inevitable

'And if it's a woman hitter . . .' I stop to think about this a little. There is a connection. A chap should never ignore connections. Coincidences are always there for a reason. Few events are truly random. 'If it's a woman doing the hitting, she would have trouble ditching the corpse. Bodies are big lumps. They are inconvenient. These hits get left. Hmmm. A woman. Worth thinking about.'

The dirty blonde glows a little. So little flattery. So little effort is required to make her feel better. A tiny appreciation of more than just her physical attributes. It is so easy to see, so simple to understand why I am so attracted. And of course why so many other men are likewise.

'What do you do with your bodies, then, JJ?'

'I have no bodies. There are no bodies. Once upon a time there may have been bodies for which I was in some way responsible, but no more. Not for a while.'

'Yeah yeah, and if you say it, then it must be true. But what if there were? What if there were bodies. What if you'd offed them? What then? What do you do with them?'

'It depends.'

'Depends on what? Oh come on, JJ, this is fun, tell me lots and lots! I mean. It's always great when you talk about your playing. When you talk about the guys down at the Blue Cube. Some of them are OK. Not all of them are my customers, y'know? OK! OK! That was a joke. I know nothing. I know nothing of them . . . professionally.'

She rolls out the word 'professionally' like it's a long, wet, red carpet.

'But you don't talk about your work. What your work is. Your real work. Killing works for you. That twat comes and asks you to take a job with him. You go away. You disappear. You come back a bit and then you go away again. You go away more often than it is possible for anyone to go away unless they're the queen or a rock star on tour. Then you're back and then you're in the heavy money for a bit.

'You say you solve things for that twat. But what? What do you solve? Why do you solve things? The police do solving. I reckon you kill folk for the twat. I reckon you kill them and he pays you to kill them.'

She draws breath.

I feel sad. Very low-down internal sadness. We talk and we talk and we talk, and OK if she likes the music. And OK if she gets a cheap place to live and to hide away when she wants to forget the life for a while. And she likes the bikes and she likes spending the money. But when she decides that I swan about killing things, then she gets almost excited. She's always comfortable if I'm forced to sort someone out. Always likes that. It turns her on. Sexually, I mean. Real wetleg stuff. She's straight about that. Not much gets through to her sexually – and there is little surprise at all in that. But downing someone? She likes that. She does.

I tell her about the previous evening's undynamic duo. She rolls from the bed, floats over to my Caterpillar boots and lifts one. Gazes at its sole. Really intent stare. 'Is this blood?' She wipes her fingers along the sole. Looks at them closely.

'More likely to be street shit,' I say, suddenly keen on cleaning my boots. I resolve to get myself some stout brushes. She drops the Caterpillar boot. Walks into the bathroom. A tap rushes water. There are the sounds of hands being washed. She saunters back through the door. Her gaze is straight ahead; straight at me. She leans on the door frame, staring at me. Reaches over with her right hand and hefts her left breast. It is impossible to remain unmoved by this. Her left hand's middle finger pushes slowly but a surprisingly long way into her navel. Her right hand squeezes the breast it clasps.

'Weapons,' she breathes. 'What weapons?'

Speechlessness is unbecoming. I feel ominous, piling, climbing, darkening rage. I know what is likely to happen. I need to walk. I need to walk far and I need to walk fast. I will need to hit someone. I will find a fight to finish or I will start a fight if I must. I sit up, back against the bed's headboard. I aim to think. Aim to think of something to say. I don't want to leave. I don't want to spoil the party.

The dirty blonde lifts from the door frame. Her left hand's middle finger is down to its second knuckle in her own navel, her own soft stomach. I can see the luminous sweat on her skin. It shines. Her right hand presses her left breast flat against her ribs, then releases it. Then lifts and squeezes, squeezes so the nipple leaps proudly, hard darkness against a lesser darkness. She rolls spit from her tongue and drips it onto her nipple. Again. Then again. Eyes smiling and lips snarling back into her cheeks, she walks towards me. It is hard not to rise, harder yet not to reach for her. She aims her nipple at my lips. I close my eyes but the nipple never lands. Instead I feel it rest against my sex, I feel the drops transferred from her to me. I wait shaking shuddering for what comes next.

The dirty blonde bounces on the mattress next to me.

'Weapons!'

She laughs. The air is ripped from me.

'What does this guy use for weapons? Guns? Knives? There was bloody crap everywhere, so was the vic carved up? You can't do that with a gun, so knives?'

I stand and walk towards the door, towards the way out. My level of arousal is painful as it is embarrassing. I drag on pants, jeans, shoes. The dirty blonde is talking, calling out. I hear sounds. No words. Drop keys into pocket, snag jacket, leave.

Walking is the answer to everything. If I got paid a penny a mile I would be a rich man. But I don't. Walking needs to be its own reward. Walking is not like playing music. Walking is not like fighting. Walking is not like fucking. Walking is pure and simple walking. It frees the mind and it wears me out. Walking lets me sleep. If I could walk far enough I doubt that I would need to fight. Probably I wouldn't need to play. Maybe I could just play because I wanted to play, not because someone I don't know who lives with me, inside me, drives me to do it and will not rest until the legs ache and the breath comes harsh, when the toes start to blister and all of the sweat has dried. When the pounding twelve-bar beat of the feet and the endlessly repeating verses of the walker drive the screaming, scratching, itching, fighting demon back into its dark little cave.

And of course cities are great places to walk. Cities provide pavements. They provide a million lonely pointless people to hide behind. They provide invisibility and anonymity. City pavements go up, they go down, they pass through canyons and caverns, they lead everywhere and nowhere, they have an endless purpose and no purpose at all. There are tunnels to dive into, stairs to climb. There are alleys and boulevards, wide parades and narrow passages. Not all pavements lead to the Blue Cube, although a surprising number of them do. I always walk the same walk, although start and end points are infinitely different. All of my life is one long interrupted walk. There are always pauses, there are always interludes, always stops along the way, but the walk will always start over. I doubt that it will end until I end, and some days I would welcome that day. Some nights would never end without the walking.

Tonight is not a night for the Blue Cube. Not even for the opportunity to be agreeably unpleasant to the folk who know me there. This is not a night for relaxation. I relaxed once tonight already and it was one relaxation too many. This is a night for tension, which would make the strings sing, but if I picked up the guitar now I would maim someone with it. Maybe myself. A man needs to understand the limits of his self-control. Mine are infinite. A man of my mind can do anything. Of this I must endlessly and always remind myself.

I pull the keys from my jeans pocket and flip the remote. The heavy Transporter's orange lights blink and welcome me. Hazard lights. I am my own hazard. My dark Transporter. I open the door and clamber within. The air is stale, too many times heated and too many times cooled. Tastes of diesel, smells of plastics. And the darkness. It smells of the darkness it transports. Our shared darkness; Transporter and I share things. Many of my walks lead me to the Transporter; the Transporter carries me to places where I can walk further. It introduces order into the randomness of the night. It lets me breathe in peace. It demands only fuel. It is easy to me.

I sit and I wait. I know what happens now. It happens now; the cell phone shudders once again. It shudders with an electronic urgency it does not feel for the message which it delivers but cannot read. I read the message, and wish I was walking again. There is a beat, a tempo, a pace to the incoming messages, and that beat is increasing. I need to be elsewhere. I need to be there now or earlier. And I need to wait outside for further instructions. They will be urgent instructions. Further instructions are always going to be urgent instructions when there are corpses involved. And it feels like a night for corpses. It does not feel like a night for driving. It did . . . and now it does not.

I leave the heavy Transporter where it is and walk to the latest hotel. Another hotel. Another date with the dead. The urgency will wait, as no doubt will I.

10

NO RETREAT FROM
TIME THAT'S DIED

Charity stared at the figure standing by the hotel's entrance. Familiarity knuckled at her. The man had appeared before her before. Not recently, not recently enough for him to register as a known quantity, as a significant item at any rate, but certainly some time. He was waiting for someone, something. His body's posture spoke loudly and clearly to her. Gentlemen in waiting. They have an air, an attitude. They transmit, they vibrate with an aura of . . . impatience? Concern? Nervousness?

She'd been observing him for some time now. He'd arrived on foot with the air of a man in a hurry. The air of someone late for an appointment. He appeared hurried but unworried, expecting to be met. By whom? And why? Charity needed access to the hotel. She was also in something of a hurry. After the last mess, and the mess before that mess, there was certainly a need, a serious and pressing need for a long talk. Several long talks with her sisters in arms. The sinister sorority. But talking followed the action at the moment. Which was exactly the wrong way. Exactly the wrong way to run a business like the killing business. Her business. Their business. The business of her partnership. Their partnership.

To become and to remain an effective elimination service it is important that the partnership operates as a team. Operating as a team involves planning. Planning involves discussion, involves transparent and effective communication. It is important that communication results in decisions, mutually acceptable decisions, a detailed understanding of what was to be achieved, which goals to be met, by whom, how, when and where. It is important that all those involved in the plan understand their roles, their function, their place in the great reality which is a murder, an elimination, a contracted killing. It is important that the team accept and comprehend completely that they are a team, and that they all have positions, places to be, rules to agree and roles to follow. And that they are responsible to each other, individually and collectively, for the successful accomplishment of their shared task. That path leads to a successful conclusion, the results of which include satisfactory remuneration and a degree of job satisfaction.

And indeed Charity had always found her job to be a satisfaction. She took a certain pride in a job well done. Not just her own job, but the job of her team as an entity. She could accept that hers was an unusual calling, her preferred profession was not for the mainstream. How could it be otherwise?

The last job had not run according to the plan, and she had no business being summoned to this hotel because there was no plan which involved action of any kind, at any time, in this place. There was no plan which involved her being here; none at all.

Troubling.

And here she was, watching a man. An almost stranger. Charity had a decent memory for figures, faces and postures, and she would place him, recall their earlier encounters at some point, in some previous context which might or might not be relevant to her current task. Why was she watching him? Why had she not simply passed him by, entered the hotel, walked the stairway to the fourth floor, to the room where her task – her unplanned task – awaited her? Because the man in her view represented a threat. If she had been asked to justify her almost unconscious analysis of the man and her almost immediate identification of him as a threat, she would have ascribed it to experience. To a deep and subtle understanding of the language spoken by breathing bodies. Even in stasis, bodies shouted out a language of their own. Experienced observers could often read it well. It is how snipers survive, how cats kill.

The man radiated energy. To the casual eye he was simply standing near the entrance. Not leaning against a wall smoking, talking a fake talk on a cell phone or casting about him for his missing accomplice. He was simply standing. Quiet. That very quiet shouted for Charity's attention. Almost anyone else would have been blinded by the quiet and would have walked past him and into the hotel. Which would have reversed their roles, she was certain, and the watched man would have become the watcher, she the oblivious watched. Inside the hotel there was a body, a recently dead body, and both she and the static man were waiting to meet it. There could be no other reason for him to be there. He could be here to catch an illicit couple doing the dirty in the deep dark dead of night, but she knew, simply knew, that this was not the case.

No one is invisible. If the man was actually the threatening presence Charity suspected, then sooner rather than later he would become aware of her. He would already feel observed. Time was passing, as time cannot fail to do, piling up between them. It would be a familiar and an uncomfortable sensation to him. At the moment, in the first several minutes of the long view, he would dismiss his subtle sense as paranoia; the result of over-sensitive perception. But this does not last for long. Too soon, he would start to scan his surroundings for the cause of his concern. And he would find her. No one is invisible. Hunters can always find their quarry. And he was a hunter; she believed that. His very stillness, his silence shouted out his status as a hunter. There needed to be some activity, a little street life, to distract him.

In his situation, Charity knew, she would be watching windows for reflections, doorways for shifting shadows, patterns of light and dark which were wrong for the angular environment of the building. And once he started to search for the watcher, he would find her. It would not be immediate, but it would be inevitable. She needed to move. But she could not move.

Stoner was restless. He was waiting for the call, waiting for a signal advising him that he could break whatever door seals were present and break into the crime scene. Because that is what he was doing. Breaking and entering. He could be prosecuted for it. In another life that would have been an amusing thought; at the moment, in this place, it was merely an irritation. He needed to focus. He needed to concentrate on the scene before him. He needed a little access. He needed his cell phone to shake; to tell him that all was clear and that he could move forward. Wasn't that how the suits referred to it? Were they not always in a state of going forward? Wouldn't that be a nice place to share . . .

He felt so conspicuous. There is a limit to the length of time that anyone can stand outside a hotel in the dead of the night, apparently aimlessly, before he starts to feel like a beacon. A fool with a fool's golden light flashing, saying, 'Here I am, look at me; I am up to no good . . .' The only virtue of the current situation was that there was no one else awake. And although there was supposedly a murdered man inside the hotel, no one here appeared to be bothered about that unusual fact. Remarkable. But true.

The mind plays tricks at times like these. Stoner should have arrived by car. It is so much easier to wait unobserved and observing from within a vehicle, despite the loss of sensory input when surrounded by steel walls, windows and a roof. His need to walk, his need for the exercise and the clarity offered by the walk had overridden his need for efficiency. His call could be an hour away, his wait a long one. There was no reason for him to suspect that the scene was clear of other, more lawful, interested parties, and it was impossible for him to enter it invisibly. The desk was manned. He knew of no envelope awaiting him here; no key. And it would be a bad night for burglary.

He gazed around. Dark places, almost by definition, are interesting places. This was plainly a quiet hotel. It was a couple of hours after midnight and there was no obvious traffic, no obvious activity, no obvious guests. This was in itself interesting, although not in a major way, and Stoner couldn't see how it affected his view of a crime scene he was yet to visit. But it was of interest. Why was there nobody home? If he was to avoid going mad with the boredom of a pointless wait, Stoner needed to identify a problem and to solve it.

Why had it been important for him to drop everything and get to the scene? Why had the Hard Man been so insistent upon this? Was he actually alone in the street? Had the officers of the law even been here? They should have been. The crime surely had been called in? Agents of the law would have arrived, sirens wailing, beacons flashing, big boots trampling. It was almost impossible for him to be here first. So, then, how was he alone? Was he in fact alone? Was there an unexpected and unusual operation taking place here? Why was the Hard Man silent?

He gazed around. Reached into the night, looking hard and listening hard. In the dark, as vision fades, other senses take over. Older, more primitive senses. Not quite sight, not quite sound; something ancient involving fear and survival. Was he alone? All nights have eyes, but those eyes are very often nonhuman. Cities are filled with feral creatures; foxes, cats on the hunt, dogs lost and lonely. And humans, too, filling all classes of character. Lost in spaces they could never fill. But the night was watching him; of that he was certain. He looked into the shadows. Glanced along the dim-lit roadway. Opened his eyes deliberately too wide to let every available photon bounce off retinas familiar with the unfamiliar moment of movement in the still quiet. The unnatural quiet. He did not feel alone. Stoner felt . . . observed. He yawned, stretched and raised himself on his toes; the actions of the bored man awaiting someone. His own movement should, could, trap an observer into a shift of their own position. As Stoner reached his hands, clasped them behind his neck, and while he rolled his head in those hands, his eyes watched steadily.

There.

His cell phone shook. Twice. A text. He opened the phone, the bright screen blinding his night vision. A simple message.

'Enter. One hour. Confirm.'

Which he did.

Into the lobby. Straight to the desk. The night clerk was putting down the handset.

'Mr La Forge.'

Stoner grunted. The clerk slid a key blank into the read/writer, tapped things, handed the keycard across the desk.

'You the police? I thought there'd be a lot more. And the press.'

'If there are press, my friend, it will be down to your indiscretion, and that would be bad for you. This is a little bit sensitive, and noise would be bad. Best to keep quiet until someone important tells you otherwise. Which will not be long. At a guess.'

The clerk nodded. Stoner did not give off an air of jovial bonhomie. In fact, if asked, the clerk would have claimed that he looked more likely to commit a crime than to solve one. But night clerks see many things, and they know how to be quiet.

'Where?'

101

'OK. Sorry. 410. Fourth floor.'

Stoner was heading for the stairway. He looked back over his shoulder.

'Shut off the lift.'

No police. No scene of crime tape. Nothing. How was this possible?

Charity sank to her heels. Squatted upon them. The not-quite-stranger was inside the hotel. The flare of his cell phone had both blinded him and called him inside. She watched for fresh lights, fresh fourth-floor lights. None lit.

Blind eyes greeted him as he entered room 410. Blind eyes staring from a severed head. Hard to read, though they stared with focus, weeping for his attention. Stoner ignored them. A sight like this was a trap set to mislead, to confuse, to shock. He was not shocked. Not by a severed head. Not by eyes staring for his attention. The deliberate is rarely shocking. Provocative; not shocking. Casual violence is shocking; a set scene is a performance. An act.

The criminal stink of a criminal death. Stoner disliked it. After all these years and all these deaths, Stoner still loathed the stench. A body. Lights on. A scene undisturbed. He set the alarm on his cell phone. Fifty minutes. A lifetime.

How was the scene undisturbed? A puzzle for later.

There was more. He knew there would be more. No killer leaves a single deliberate signal. Not unless they were playing a game, and why would a killer do that? Killing is not a game. It has never been a game. Killing is the most serious decision there is. It is a bigger decision than mating, breeding or eating. There are no frivolous killers. No successful frivolous killers. Frivolous folk commit murders, of course they do, but they never become killers. Frivolous folk mate, breed and eat; they also kill . . . but they never become killers. The killer here had left a message.

102

Stoner was unsure who was the intended recipient. How could he know? The only way to discover who the message was aimed at would be to catch the killer and ask him.

Or to catch the message's intended recipient visiting the scene. Stoner stood entirely still and considered.

Forty-five minutes. He should spend them wisely. He should become familiar with the scene. He should understand it, hopefully learn from it. Instead he stood entirely still and considered.

Outside. He had waited. For a while. Longer than he'd expected. Than the Hard Man would have expected. But Stoner had in fact been much nearer to the scene than that. And so he'd arrived earlier. And as he'd waited outside, waiting for instruction, for permission to enter, Stoner had not felt alone. There was none of the familiar stillness of an observer alone. He had instead felt like an observer observed. Someone had arrived before him.

There is a school of thought which suggests that when a situation is inexplicable, the best course of action is to file those puzzles into the mental retrieval system for later analysis. That time flies while waiting for no man, that there is no time like the present and that every moment is precious. All schools of thought have their moments. Every dog has its day.

There is another school of thought. This alternative suggests that when a situation is inexplicable, then the wise man waits for understanding before proceeding further. It is too easy to create a situation where the wise man becomes instead the fool rushing in. No angels necessary in the bible of big mistakes.

There is nothing at all pleasant about the smell of death. Stoner intended to spend as little time at the scene as he could, even less time than allowed by the Hard Man's deadline, because of the smell if for no other reason. The unlit lamps of the dead man's eyes continued to stare. No illumination there. Stoner walked slowly into the room.

There are many kinds of hotels, and there are many reasons

for staying in them. And as hotels go, this one was pleasant enough. It was clean. It was spacious. It was well furnished, had a big bed and a big bathroom with a big bath. Big enough for two friends to share. It had two chairs and a table between them. You can infer many things about a hotel user by the items he brought with him and what he did with them.

Some folk carry a suitcase at all times, and it is often the same suitcase. The contents vary depending upon the length of stay. Other folk carry a small bag containing almost nothing, relying upon their hotel to provide for them. Some folk live from their luggage, leaving it open from their moment of arrival until they close it again and depart. Other folk establish a home-from-home, hanging up their changes of clothes, positioning familiar items in a familiar arrangement; taking their known world with them wherever they go. There are as many types of hotel and hotel guest as there are hotels and hotel guests. Stoner had no views on hotels nor on those who stay in them. Unless those guests got killed, and only then if grim misfortune or the Hard Man involved him in their deaths somehow.

Luckless victim had carried a suitcase and a computer with him on his last journey. He had unpacked the suitcase; a travel clock sat on the bedside table along with a novel, the reader's up-to point marked, the spine undamaged. No book-bender, then; a tidy person. In the bathroom would be the victim's preferred soaps, toothpaste and maybe medications in case of headache or hangover. No patent guaranteed cure for death though. The body would be in the bathroom. This was Stoner's theory, based around simple observation revealing that there was no other room and that the dead head was the only visible body part.

At first gaze, there was no sign of any other person's presence in the room. However, it would have been difficult for the victim to arrange his death in such a plainly non-suicidal manner

104

without that other party, so Stoner, on a quest for knowledge tinged with only mild distaste for the fact of the death and a suitable depression at the plainly statemental approach to murder displayed by the killer, cast about him for more clues.

The computer, a laptop of unfashionably generous dimensions, sat open, switched on but blank-screened next to its case. The severed head sat between it and the edge of the desk, leaking a little and looking exactly as surprised and as accusing as it had ten minutes earlier. Stoner headed for the bathroom, body-hunting.

No body in the bathroom. The bathroom was a paragon of hotel efficiency and cleanliness. Branded cosmetics had been arranged neatly, and the victim's washbag stood watch over them. No body. Not even the smell of a body in here.

The bath stood clean and empty, ready for the next soak. The shower curtains hung neatly from their rail and even the towels were stacked tidily, with only one of them moved and hung over the side of the bath itself. Either the murderer or the victim had washed their hands before or after the murder, depending on who was doing the washing. There were no obvious bloodstains in the bath or the sink, so Stoner left all that complicated forensic stuff to complicated forensic types and returned to the bedroom. A little bemusement was permissible, but not too much, because time was pressing.

Thirty minutes.

Stoner walked around the bed and back to the severed head. Its silence told him nothing new, and either the smell of death was fading by courtesy of the air conditioning or he was becoming accustomed to it.

The laptop ticked a soft and gentle tick, the way computers do when they're performing some subtle duty in that smug and impenetrable way that computers favour. Stoner stared at it. The power light was lit and the hard drive's light flicked at him.

Presumably it had been performing some self-inflicted task; hence the tick. Stoner tapped the space-bar, using the forefinger-nail of his right hand; guitarists tend to have longer nails on their right hands and fingernails leave no forensic distress.

The screen lit, obligingly, revealing a full-screen image of the severed head. A rear three-quarter view, in fact. Unusual. There was no doubt that this was the actual head. Stoner smiled at the screen. Picked up an instruction sheet advertising and offering the hotel's internet services and dropped it between the head and the computer. The sheet fell unconcerned to the desk, its short flight watched by the computer's webcam and displayed in only slightly twitchy colour on the screen. Stoner smiled again and felt a tiny delight that he had avoided being filmed. He wondered who was on the receiving end of the webcam's static movie. If indeed anyone was. And if they were, then why?

Was it the same fansite to which the last scene's laptop had streamed video footage? Seemed likely.

The computer's case was unzipped. Stoner retrieved the hotel's internet instruction card, holding it by its edges, and used it to open the case. Inside which lay a single word, laid out in an usually attention-grabbing way. The word was simple; the word was 'SIN'. The 'S' was formed from two detached fingers. The 'N' was formed by three more. The 'I' was a severed dick. An unattached cock. A penis.

Stoner's attention was indeed grabbed. He studied the presentation with all of the attention it deserved, which was a lot of attention.

The sinful word was resting on another hotel internet instruction card. But not a card from this hotel. There was very little blood. Presumably the letter 'I' had been unaroused, uninspired at the point of its detachment and display. Stoner could see how that might be. Few experiences in the life of any dick would be

106

more shrivelling than amputation. He wondered whether an aroused member would retain its engorged dimensions after severance. Or not. But he didn't wonder for very long.

He stepped back gently, keeping away from the webcam's limited gaze and texted the Hard Man.

'Nobody here', he sent. 'No body at all. Only bits.'

'Leave now.'

An instant and unequivocal instruction. So he did.

The clerk looked up as Stoner passed him.

'See anyone? Did you catch him?'

He looked as baffled as Stoner felt.

'The thief? The guy who broke in?'

There were headlights in the street outside, approaching in no particular hurry. Stoner didn't pause in his passage to the revolving door.

'No sign,' he said, 'Mostly. Don't let anyone in, OK? The police techs will need to do tests. Y'know. Prints, things like that.'

'They on their way or what?' The clerk attempted impatience. 'It's been ages since I called. We're busy. I may need that floor. I can't turn customers away. This is a business.'

Stoner looked at the clerk, The empty silent lobby.

'Keep calm,' he said. 'And carry on . . .'

Charity sat on a bench under a streetlight reading a magazine. A pose which would have been nicely inconspicuous were it adopted in broad daylight in a busy street in a crowded city. Hiding in plain view is a common technique. Well-proven. Popular.

From her position of considerable conspicuity she watched the not-quite stranger appear through the hotel's revolving door, turn away from her and walk away. No hurry in his stride, no tension in his posture. A man unconcerned. Which was unexpected. As he departed so a police car arrived from the oppo-

107

site direction, from behind her. It passed her and parked. No flashing lights, no sirens, bells nor whistles. All was calm enough.

A single uniform clambered from the car, straightened his attire, placed hat upon head and headed through the revolving doors. Charity wondered how the door felt about all this nocturnal coming and going. Doors could always tell tales, she reckoned. If doors could talk. Sadly, doors are dumb. This door was not only dumb, but sightless as well. No security cameras framed its frame. It was a discreet door, then. Charity mused upon this while wondering why she was there.

The faintly familiar man had visited the hotel. He was a man of the dark; she had identified that and had no problems with it. He had visited and left, conspicuously unconcerned. This was not often the case when an investigating person visited a site soon after her sister had left it. More usually in that particular circumstance there was running, and shouting, and bright lights and considerable action. Here, tonight, at this unremarkable if decent hotel, there was only quiet. It was as uncanny as it was baffling. Maybe the almost-stranger had been there on another matter entirely? Maybe she had received erroneous instruction? Maybe she should collect her unused cleaning kit and head for home, services unnecessary, not needed until another day. Today had been a day of firsts for her, a very unplanned day, a very worrying day. She decided to wait until the police officer left the building and then she would go home. Plainly there was nothing for her here.

Off away in the city the bright night sky flashed in blues and in reds. Off away in the city a siren shrieked. It was late. There was little obstructing traffic. Sirens and strobe lights travel faster at night. Sirens and strobes arrived in a wave. Men ran for the hotel. The revolving doors revolved, as revolving doors do. Every light in the hotel was lit. More lights lit in more buildings. There was calm no more.

Charity stood, and sighed. Her sister had been here, then. There was no mistake. All the signs said so. She picked up her case and walked away. There was nothing for her here.

11

GO YOUR OWN WAY

'Good game, good game.'

Stoner eased himself into the seat opposite the Hard Man. 'It would be a much better game if you'd give me some idea of what's going on. Of what you want. Of what I'm supposed to be doing.'

The Hard Man gazed at the menu. 'I have no idea what any of this means.' He sounded vaguely baffled. He appeared to be concentrating completely upon the mysteries of the menu.

'You hungry?'

'You buying?'

There is always comfort in a familiar routine. Stoner could play the game as well as any and better than most.

'What does this mean?'

The Hard Man was staring sadly at the menu before him. Stoner was pretending interest. He had wasted a day. Most of a day. Part of a day. After escaping The Baffling Business Of The Severed Head he had walked, walked for miles with determination and frustration, pursuing the possibility of sleep through the wasted dim end of the night, but finding no relief. Then a daylight day without purpose. If he was working a job, then working a job

110

was what he preferred to be doing, nothing else. He was a man of focus. Not a man who found interest in the fine print of a menu.

But he was also a man of method, and if the Hard Man was sufficiently distracted to discover interest in the menu, then Stoner could dip into his reserves of patience and indulge him. For a while.

'Corn-fed chicken grand-mère.'

The accent was hopelessly bad. An act of course. The Hard Man was fluent in French. Occasional in other languages, like Russian, German maybe.

'Grand mer?'

He raised an eye to Stoner, who returned a deliberately bland gaze. A familiar game, this one. And like all games it served its purpose well.

The Hard Man warmed to his theme. 'Grand mer? Deep big sea? The fabled long-lost well-fed chicken of the deep? There's a movie in that alone. James Cameron should make it. Aged adventurers diving on the wreck of the sunken ship *Moronic* take a bite from the fat chicken of the deep and are transported to an alien world. Can't fail.'

Despite himself, Stoner smiled.

'Grandmother. It means Grandmother's chicken recipe. You know that.'

The Hard Man raised his other eye to level with the first, a disconcerting trick even if it was familiar, which it was. If rarely observed. Like the deep-sea chicken.

'Is that supposed to be a selling point? All your grandmother could cook was tripe. She always burned it, too.'

Stoner knew the routine. There was comfort in a routine, although why the Hard Man should find himself in need of any form of solace he had no idea. Unless his day had been as wasted, as frustrating, as Stoner's own.

111

'You'd remember that from when you were lovers, you and my gran? Is that it?'

'Cheeky. Your sisters told me about her while your gran was stewing tea for me and your mum.'

'Makes no sense. It's roast chicken. Why not call it roast chicken? Why film a dead head and send a streaming video of it to a fansite for those strange sad fuckers who enjoy detective stories?'

Stoner looked up as the Hard Man's discourse drew to its close. The impassive waiter maintained his professional air of interest only in their eventual order. He pretended to hear nothing else, as waiters should.

'Chicken and chips twice.'

At least one conclusion had appeared, puffing into existence after a long long flight of fantasy stairs.

'Add anything you like, any sauces, salads and strange breads. Choose a bottle of some decent drink to wash it all down and bring two powerfully pricey whiskies; my young friend has had a trying day. This is the only way to make him happy.

'The hotel called in a break-in. The fire escape door had been opened and left banging. Alarms sounded.'

Down to business at last. 'Alarms do that. They sound. Your wives all told me that.' Stoner was pleased that a moment of shared intelligence, understanding was approaching. They were rare enough, and if they needed a touch of nurturing and if time was not tight, then he was easy with that.

The Hard Man continued with his tale of mystery. 'The local officers advised the clerk, who refers to himself as the manager for no reason I can see, that they would be there as soon as they could, which could have been before some distant year when the clerk will retire to a life of culinary bliss with his grand-mother, although I doubt it, and told him that as he had no guests booked into any rooms at all on that floor to keep it that way, empty, while they got there. They suggested that there could be some risk to his person. They lied a little.

'I do believe that one day an officer may well have dropped by and made a note in a notebook, but I doubt that it would have been any time soon. The officer gave the clerk an incident number, which I imagine runs to a line or two by now, and added it to the great and glorious piece of technical wonder which is the national criminal database, where it would have sat ignored until the hotel was redeveloped into a theme park inviting cruise ship passengers to relive the great heritage of sleazy fleapits or the approach of the next ice age, whichever was the sooner. But it didn't. And we are unbothered by burglaries, you and I.'

The Hard Man looked up at the wine waiter, who stood at his elbow with every appearance of reluctant fascination and with a tray of glasses and a bottle in his hands. Two glasses filled with whisky; two waiting for their wine. A frozen moment. The Hard Man spread his hands, not entirely in supplication. The waiter poured. Twice. And departed, discouraged. Life as a wine waiter must be one endless stream of potential moments of entertainment, ruined by thoughtless customers who want them only to serve drinks.

'So. The next thing is that a nerdy geek deep within the even greater technical wonder which is something to do with but not quite GCHQ presses a big bright red button of great alert. It might have been a bell, and it may have featured a whistle. Whatever, it was a decently loud button and its call reached my esteemed ministerial colleague's ears PFQ. Because the text message which accompanied the head movie was a long-running repeat of its postal code. Which was identical to that of the busted hotel.

'Technology is always better than humans when it comes to making sense of things and even before you could recite the whole of the *Iliad* in its native Greek our distant but worried guardians of the national interest added twenty-two and twenty-two, came up with an answer greater than zero and called me. And no, I shall not reveal what they called me, nor what I called them, for the hour it was late and I was about the serious business of recreation. Or procreation, if you prefer descriptive accuracy to good taste.

'Of course I instructed that they do nothing, a task they find easy, and that they slap a silence upon the whole thing until I had been round to take a look. By "I" I meant "you", as you will have worked out. I had more important things to waste my time on than some batty hoax from an online fansite for sad souls who believe that they understand murder. As you would hope.'

The whisky was a good one; easy on the palate and an aid to concentration. Stoner always enjoyed a good whisky, although he preferred a vodka, given the option. During the Hard Man's near-monologue a whole bottle of whisky had somehow vanished between them. He observed this, being a noted detective, and flagged down the wine waiter. Stoner asked for a jug of tap water to accompany the next and subsequent bottles. It looked likely to be a lengthy evening, and he wanted to take more from it than a hangover. The waiter stared pointedly at the untouched bottle of wine.

Stoner ignored him.

'Where's the rest of the dead guy?'

'It is a curious thing. And that is a good question. The constables have a body. They do now, at any rate. The rest of a body was sitting on the fire escape at the end of the corridor where you found the head. Cool as you like, almost completely intact and living a life of sociable health and purity apart from being dead and missing a few bits. You did well in getting out of there as fast as you did. This is likely to be a long haul.'

'Any moment now, you're going to tell me that there's more to this than meets the eye.' Stoner smiled a smile which he trusted was more encouraging and companionable than simply grim.

'I was going to leave this until later, but as you've seen right through me and brought up the eyes, I shall choose this moment to reveal that your head had none. Or rather it did have eyes but they were glass. Fakes. Artificial. Prosthetics. Certainly sightless. Even among the blind this head would not have been king.'

'Aha! Moriarty!' Stoner beamed. The decreasing level of whisky in the second bottle assisted his apparent, if largely assumed, levity. 'This fiendish eyelessness prevented the ace detective in me from reading therein the image of the victim's last vision, so identifying the killer. Case solved. It was the Black Queen who done it. Or maybe a wicked witch. Always hard to tell at times like these. Can we eat something soon? This tale of yours is so unlikely that it plainly is a work of fiction.'

The Hard Man unleashed an expression which may have majored on delighted sympathy and charitable kindness. Or it may not. Either way, he poured yet more scotch and waved for a third bottle. The untouched wine continued to breathe, or whatever it is that wine does when left to its own devices.

'Have you done? Then I'll continue. There are some bad folk out there, JJ.'

Stoner stared at him.

'Descending into melodrama so soon in the evening? You'll burst into song before the soup.'

'Burst into flame more like. Shut up, drink up and listen. Any day now they will catch their chicken. It better be a big one if it's going to soak up all this scotch. Thought you didn't like scotch?

'I know pretty well all the proper hitters in this fair land of ours. That is indeed the sound of the obvious being stated. I've employed most of them, trained some of them, and buried and shed sad tears over the less successful. So it's always a delight when my masters decide that there's a new topper come striding among us. Some new murderous bastard out there murdering, bastardly. Should that be dastardly?'

'This is to do with the guy in bits a couple of days ago, then?'

Stoner sought some sense from his companion's increasing obliquity. One of the Hard Man's many peculiarities was his tendency to address a problem only when he needed to. He was not a great planner unless he needed to be. He was also not a great communicator unless he needed to be. He tended to work things out in his head as he talked them out loud. If left to drink and think he could simply lapse into silence. He would then become convinced that his audience was stupid for forgetting the wisdom he had imparted, when in fact he had imparted said wisdom only by telepathy and said nothing while lost in his own arcane reasoning processes. This fooled many people.

'Yes. You get a prize. The guy in bits was not the first guy similarly in bits. Nor was he the first guy who my ministerial masters had told me about, but I'd ignored the others.'

Stoner wondered why.

'Swallows, spring, that kind of thing. They watch far too much television, read far too many books. I don't know where they find the time. They see a serial killer every time some sod dies in the same way as some other sad sod. You have no idea. They should all give up the service and become crime writers. They have far more imagination than most of those. And they pick up expressions like "MO" to make their reports read more interestingly. They're a hazard. And overpaid.'

Stoner tried hard to ask something likely to extract a fact. At this rate they'd both be comatose and thrown into a taxi before the Hard Man got around to selling the job, to making his pitch. Not that Stoner needed persuasion; he did what he did, but it made things smoother somehow. Transactions are always transactions. Always and forever.

'MO?'

The Hard Man drifted back to the point.

'Someday my bird will come. I am truly starving, my friend.

116

Has the waiter died? Hideous revenge of the deep-sea chicken? Have we been stood up? Have you worked your usual attraction upon the staff?

'Messy. Obscured. Manic Murder Most 'Orrible. Mainly Obliterated. Not neat crimes, JJ. Not neat at all. Not a jape. Not nice. I can't think of a pleasant way to depart this teary vale, but I would prefer that it was quick rather than protracted.

'About five years back, then. That's when I think this started. Our lords and masters think it's all new, but I beg to differ. I have not advised them of this. An approximation is all you're getting, because it's all I've got to offer. And you're now sitting there picturing where was where, what was what, five years ago, right? Can't see it was a crossover with either of us, although I would indeed be amused to be proved wrong. Crimes of passion, perhaps, certainly crimes of anger; increasingly grimy crimes. Always in hotels, always involving cutting. Couple of bludgeon-ings, batterings, bullets, but always sliced as well. Scenes messed with post mortem.' The Hard Man paused. Stoner pointed an interrupting eyebrow at the approaching laden waiter.

'It is amazing how criminal some people can become if they're compelled to sit around for hours waiting to be given the bird. I hear there's a theory of etiquette which suggests that valued customers should expect to sit drinking complimentary liquor for the same length of time they waited for their food, thus making the waiter wait a similar length of time for the reckoning-up. Sounds like a good idea. Although simply refusing to pay is always a smart trick. By hell, JJ, I'd almost forgotten that time you waited outside for that tardy lardy waiter and bounced him about a bit. You were a cruel man back then.'

The waiter did appear concerned about this. His body language suggested that it wished it were elsewhere.

'He was, y'know. Cruel. Mean, too. Unpredictable.'

The Hard Man beamed at the waiter.

117

'Do you carry a gun? A big one? In case of irritable customer syndrome? I think I would.'

The waiter chose to grin at the Hard Man. A bold tactic. He served the meal with a flourish and risked a question. With only slight nervousness.

'Crime writers, huh? Enjoy your meal, gentlemen. And try not to scare our other guests too much. We don't need them losing their appetites. Bon appetit!'

Stoner observed that although the restaurant was filling nicely, there was an area of calm and empty tables surrounding their own. He forced a smile, hopefully an encouraging one.

'You got toothache, JJ?' The Hard Man was all friendly concern. 'It saps the concentration. Long life . . .'

The food was excellent. Worth the wait. In other circumstances.

'Bullets and butchery too? Interesting. How so? Torture? An inquisition? Connects between the victims?' Stoner set the talk stone rolling, the better to eat more while speaking less.

'Hard to say. Analysts didn't connect the bullets with the carvings. You know what analysts are like. They know all about killers despite never having killed anything bigger than a bug on a windshield. And they only get to meet killers who've been caught. Which should tell them a thing or two, but never actually seems to. You'd think they'd spend time with successful professionals rather than with the inadequate amateur. But then where would we be, you'n'me? I connected those shootings, me.'

Stoner raised a ruminatory and yet quizzical eyebrow.

'The knife was used mainly to retrieve the bullets. Not to do the deadly deed. Maybe there was a time problem. The blades used are always the same type, but I bet they're not the same knives. I'd guess that the killer ditches those. Smart killer, clever killer. Which is why he's not been caught.

'The MO was in the pattern of the attack. There is always a

pattern. The most recent events have seen a lot more mess. So much mess by now that our colleagues in uniform have come over all distressed. Which is why we're here, enjoying this fine chicken, this fine whisky and this fine establishment, rather than sitting in a bar playing the lotto like a regular guy.'

'Do regular guys play the lotto? That's a genuine query. I don't know many regular guys and those I do don't play the lotto. Am I missing something? Do you play the lotto? I can't see it, quite.'

Stoner was intent upon that clean plate moment. He wondered whether the wait accurately represented the time it actually took to cook a fine piece of bird rather than nuking a pre-meal in a microwave. He hoped so. Betrayal is always a worry.

The Hard Man finished his own chicken, pushed the plants to the side. Made a lake of the jus, an archipelago of broccoli.

'The lotto? Every waking hour of every working day I think only of those little numbered balls and the inevitable lucky sequence which will ensure my transport from this vale of troubles to an endless and eternal life of fulfilment and delight. I can think of no more rewarding pastime than buying those numbers and watching those bouncing balls. What is money for, JJ? You have no soul. No wonder everyone hates you and you are forced to work for me, the enlightened one. Are you still learning to play the plastic ukulele? Is that your own escape fantasy? Some day you will strike a lucky note, great wealth will envelope you and you will ease into a relaxed life bulging with fine wine, fine women, endless sunshine and free booze. And how is the missus? Your own private I'd-a-whore?'

He ignored his own rhetorical insult and moved on. 'Taped wrists. Always, in the early jobs. Taped to chair arms, beds, bathroom fittings. Whatever's handy. Then a little slice'n'dice. Which suggests an enquiry or revenge. I'd go for the former; no one can need revenge on so many similar stalwart captains of finance. For that is who they are. Mostly. And mostly unre-markable. Money men; number crunchers. No connections that anyone can see, not even the geeks, analysts and computers. So it must be true.

'If what we're seeing is a whole new approach to information-gathering then I fear that the future is bleak for those who do actually possess information. I know I'm an old-fashioned kind of guy, but I've never yet met anyone who would refuse to hand over info, be it ever so vital and valuable, if threatened with having his nuts stabbed a few times. Once is usually enough, no? No secret on the planet is more sensitive than your nuts. Lots of blood from the initial assaults. Pointless. If there really is a sequence here, then we're looking at a professional. Professionals don't do messy. Idiot amateurs, haters, nutters, psychos do messy. Not professionals. Which is a tiny cause for thought here. But, really, the last couple have involved a huge lot of blood. Unnecessary.'

'But not the head?' Stoner was struggling for a connection. 'I'm struggling for a connection,' he said, 'in case you'd not worked that out for yourself.'

'Fret not, fret not, there is a connection. A serious connection. An unavoidable connection. And I will get there. In my own time and in my own way. Like your van. Do you still drive that thing?'

Stoner refused to reply.

The Hard Man was undaunted.

'The last one. The last one with the complete corpse was one seriously gory place. You know this to be true, because you saw it. Loads of blood. Did anything strike you about it?'

'Too much blood for a quick death. It would take a hell of a time to drain that amount of blood from a victim, and the heart would need to be pumping away to manage it. That was my thought, at least. I expect I was just surprised by it all. Like an abattoir.'

'Bravo, maestro, then.'

The Hard Man gave every impression of being a man impressed trying to appear unimpressed while exclaiming how impressed he was. Bluff, counter-bluff and counter-counter bluff. All entirely pointless, but it played to the invisible audience hiding inside that gently nodding head. Any moment now, Stoner knew, it would be time for dessert.

'Dessert, JJ? Could you fancy something tasty to cover the taste-lessness of the topic? Jam roly-poly? With perhaps a tangy straw-berry coulis?'

'Bravo? Bravo maestro? Order what you want; I'll have the same.'

'Before I summon the penguin with the menu, though; yes. The key word is abattoir. Not all that blood was human. Pig. Looks the same, smells the same. No doubt tastes the same and it all makes great gravy, sausages and black pudding, I'm sure.'

He snapped his fingers and placed a further food order.

'The body outside the hotel had no hands. It was not the body which was originally attached to the head you found.' The Hard Man was finding his pace. Stoner joined in with the spirit of the thing.

'There's a plain message here. But it is so plain, so entirely fucking obvious, that I can't understand it at all. Who the fuck is sending a message? Who the fuck is it to? And what the great screaming fuck is it about? Why the fuck would you lug a head-less body about the countryside just to leave it lying on a fire escape? A fire escape outside an hotel where you've left a severed head?'

All good questions, plainly, if a touch rhetorical.

Hapless waiter reappeared at their side. Gazed at the two men, haplessly. Stoner shrugged, nodding with tilt of the head and a single raised eyebrow towards the Hard Man, who looked up, flushed and irritable. 'The special!' He was almost barking in his irritation at being interrupted. Waiter looked increasingly hapless.

'There is no special, not as such, not this evening; just what's on the menu.'

Conversation in the room had faded again, almost to nothing. The other diners appeared to be hurrying, maybe sensing an approaching storm. But the Hard Man summoned a deep reserve of well-hidden patience and assumed the smile of the killer whale, complete with teeth. 'Do you have a suggestion? Does it involve rhubarb?'

'The chef makes . . .'

'Excellent. Two of those. Now . . . please . . . go away.'

A long drink from the short glass.

'There's killing, JJ, and there's killing. This is just plain mad. Leaving a head as some kind of message? OK. I can't believe that you or me were the intended recipients, but I can quite easily imagine a situation in which I might leave such a message. But a body from another head? What? That is stupid. Meaningless. Except . . .'

'It can't be meaningless.' Stoner finished the thought. 'It means something to the guy who did the topping. And he wouldn't have left that message himself . . . OK, OK!'

He held up both hands in a universal surrender symbol. 'You're having me in on this because you want what I've got. And all I've got is thinking. That's all. It is a message. A strong message. Not a message left lightly. Our problem is that it's obscure for us. Find someone who doesn't find it obscure and you've found a reason for the job. Find a reason and you've narrowed all the possibilities to a more sensible level.'

'Thanks for the egg-sucking lessons, JJ. I was almost taking it all seriously for a moment. I forget quite what the master of understanding you are. That – and your Zen-like calm – is why I try so hard to make you rich. Of course there's a message. My

122

real fret is that it's a message from the topper to *himself.* If that's the case, then we do have a problem, because it shows that the guy doing the offing has several loose screws. Which is good from a catching him perspective, because he'll do it again and again and a-fucking-gain until eventually simple souls like you and me catch him and we can all go home singing hallelujahs and dancing smugly with our loved ones, be they several or be they single. Spot the hitch in this picture of delight; the other deads will still be dead.

'So give me some insight, oh great smart one. You are the pro killer, top topper, not me.'

'Not there. We don't go there. You know more of the past than . . .'

The Hard Man slapped the table. Hapless waiter delivered the desserts. Cleared off again, almost at a run.

'. . .than is good for either of us. Yep. I know that. Put away your reformation, replace it with that cold killer thing. We need it for this.'

Stoner forced his eyes to close. Forced friendliness through teeth.

'Who are you working for on this? How official is it? How off the books? Do you have resource? Facilities? Pudding's nice.'

The Hard Man beamed like a drunkard. Stoner was not fooled at all.

'There's a story. The story goes that there's a budget. So money is pretty much unimportant. It's on-book enough for that. But it's off-book in as much as it would be unwise for you to pick up the phone to your friendly police station and demand of the constables that they provide you with a squad car, goons and ammunition.

'I'll give you enough reading material to prevent your sleeping for a few days. As I say, I do believe there are several more bodies connected to this topper than do Her Majesty's finest. You may

123

disagree. At this stage you're welcome to do so. I would prefer that you are correct that way. The world does not need another nutter on the loose, frankly.

'Deal only with me at this point. Are you going to finish that? Do you need anything more at this point? How much free time do you have at the moment? Questions, questions; endless questions. Here I am, blithely assuming that you're available for all this tedious work nonsense. You are, though? Yes?'

Stoner aimed his gaze at his food, concentrated upon his reply.

'It will fit in. That's all. I'll fit it in. I have no wish to go marching all over the place. If you need someone full-time, then that's not much use. Not for very long, at any rate. You know me; always keen to help, but there are other things.'

The Hard Man nodded.

'OK. Coffee? A club? You on a date? And why would you leave a severed head in a hotel room? I mean that. You. You yourself, not some hypothetical nutjob. I'd rather believe that there is a rational purpose to this, rather than some random headcase who's been watching too many movie mysteries. Go on?'

'Can't see it, I'm afraid. I'm no use. I'm a quiet man. Methodical. You know me. I'd always clear up. Always lose the bod. If the client insisted on it being found, then OK. But that rarely happened to me. Done accidentals, so there's closure, and maybe insurance and a lack of doubt, but I never really enjoyed those. Too easy to screw up, to leave forensic.

'So. A lesson? A warning? It is a message. Can't not be. Can't be anything else. It's a bit . . . tribal. A bit jungle. Are the bod and the head very different? One or the other's not had a treatment? Been left in the sun too long, that kind of thing? Microwaved?'

'Oh yes. No doubt. Two blokes. Should have identities soon. Head pretty much straightaway, bod a little later due to the thoughtless handlessness. But the unofficial officials will most likely find the DNA somewhere. They must have about a third

124

of the population on file by now. But you're correct. It is a sign. A message. If I thought it was a message for me then I would know who'd sent it. I would know whether I should be scared. I would know whether I should be heading for the hills or simply loading for bear. You don't send messages to dead men. You don't need to. If they're dead, chances are that they've already ignored all the messages they're ever going to get. You're sending messages to someone else.'

Stoner sighed, theatrically. A drinker's sigh. 'So all we need to do is find someone who's panicking. Easy. I shall take a long walk home and will watch out for the plainly panicked and will at once connect many many dots, all of which will lead me straight to the killer. What could be simpler? I'll do it for free.' He pushed his chair back and limply flapped a hand at their waiter.

'Coffee! Strong. Loud and dark. Can I say black?'

He looked with mocking query at the Hard Man. Who ignored him.

'While you're out there pounding the ground seeking the legendary panicking man, I shall make a valiant – probably doomed already – attempt to extract from my masters exactly why it is that they're so concerned, who they think is behind it, why they're not simply applying the constabulary to the problem and generally tilting at windmills. But I doubt they'll tell me much in the way of useful truth. How did the head die?'

Stoner almost laughed.

'What?'

Sometimes the Hard Man could be oblique.

'How did it die? Do you think the beheading is the message or simply the cause of death? The body was stabbed. And it was missing bits, as in the other cases. Similar bits. Hands. Feet. Dick. I really don't like that. Chap could get by missing a hand or a foot, but his dick? Fuck.'

'Or not. Under the circumstances.'

'As you say. Where's the coffee when you need it? I must enquire whether the sorry state of dicklessness arrived pre or post mortem. And why "SIN"? What sin is this? The biggest sin of them all is murder, and we must assume that the victim was the sinner. This can't really be a case of wait until you see the other guy?'

The Hard Man was drifting steadily. Stoner felt unmoved by the drink. Sober. Sad, if anything.

'It's been a long and trying day, JJ. Are you up to this? Every murdered fucker is a guilty fucker. There is no innocence. Killing in a hotel room? There is no innocent reason to get killed in a hotel room. What was the dead guy doing there? Apart from dying?'

'You can't say that.' Stoner smiled internally at the unusual sight of the Hard Man drifting on a wave of alcohol. He must have been hitting a bottle before they'd met. There could be no other explanation. The Hard Man was a seasoned drinker and had an enormous talent for it. And an appetite, too. 'Innocent folk get killed all the time. Why do you think these guys are getting theirs?'

'No sequence of stiffs can be innocent, JJ. There must be a connection. And that connection is likely to be their shared guilt. Shared innocence does not wash. Shared innocence is for churches and choirboys, not for middle-aged fuckers in crap hotel rooms. Well-dressed fuckers do not stay in crap hotels. Not unless they're staying with choirboys. Choirboys with no taste. Fuck; even a choirboy would demand a better place to get reamed than some cheap, crap hotel.'

'You think there's a sex angle to this?' Stoner's amusement was drifting away. Weariness and cynicism were more comfortable bedfellows.

'How could there not be a sex angle? Don't look at me like that, either. Do not even think of looking at me like that. Of course there's a sex angle. Why the fuck else would two persons, a man and a woman, most likely, meet in a crap hotel room? On the other hand, JJ, why would two or more blokes meet up in a crap hotel? Unless they want to have sex with each other. Which is unlikely.'

Stoner's face was innocence. 'You speaking in a statistical sense? Or from some deep personal understanding of what two blokes might get up to if left to their own devices in a hotel room? It's more likely that a bunch of blokes would be discussing football.'

'Holy fuck, JJ. You do know how to wound. Football. Jesus. Why did I not think of that? Business executive offed in bizarre football tiff with gay lover in scabby hotel room shock. I can almost hear the headlines. You're a genius. I always said you were, but no one would take me seriously.'

'And apart from that . . . when was the last time you hacked some sucker's head off? Have you ever chopped a head off?'

'It was . . . a while ago. A long while ago. But you're right. It's not an easy thing to do. And it is as messy as all fuck. Seriously so.' Stoner nodded his agreement. The Hard Man warmed to his line of thought. 'How was it done? Could you tell? I'll ask how the body lost its head. You drive that razor-like mind of yours and try to pretend that you can remember what the neck looked like.'

The Hard Man dragged his cell phone from his pocket, thumbed a few buttons. Then he muttered, in a whisper which made their tables of audience strain to hear, 'C17. Yep. U6.' A long pause. Rubbing of the forehead. 'M16. OK. Christ on a pedestal, I feel like the Man from fucking Uncle. Security codes? Even my bloody bank only needs the maiden name of my dead mother to agree that I'm me. Why do you want code of the day, fuck's sake? Yes. Yes. Yes. Don't be silly, chummy, I'm in a restaurant surrounded by passing innocents who will not go away even if I pull a very scary face and no I will not go and stand outside in the fucking street. How did you get this job? M16. Yes. That's right. It's a body. A dead body.'

The Hard Man raised his eyes to Stoner's, rolled them theatrically.

'I know it's not proper to discuss a body while I'm in a public place, and . . .' his voice raised to a point at which it was the only audible source of entertainment in the dining room, 'everyone can hear me because I am fucking shouting. Got that?'

He stood up, staged a badly theatrical bow, and announced to the rapt audience, 'This, laydeez 'n genmum, this is for what we pay our taxes. A round of applause for our public servant to whom I do speak, but with whom I cannot communicate!'

Incredibly, the crowd of diners clapped, and loudly. A small cheer started. Stoner watched in awe. The Hard Man sat down.

'I want to know how the head was removed. No. I want to know now. Not tomorrow. Find out. Call me back. Fuck. Me.'

He ended the call with a flourish. Stood again.

'I am sorry about that. Sorry for interrupting your evening. I shall be quiet now, and my good friend and I will discuss nothing but football until I get my call returned, and at that point we will sneak out, quiet as mice, trying hard to avoid paying, and will leave you to get on with your evening in peace.'

Incredibly, a crowd of smiling faces returned to their tablemates, to their dinners, to their drinks and to their own evening manoeuvres and mating rituals.

'If I live to be one thousand,' Stoner spoke gently, 'I will never underestimate the insanity of the common man. You could have passed a hat around and raised enough to cover dinner. You should be on the stage.'

The Hard Man smiled. A grim and tiny smile. His cell phone hummed, quietly. He flicked it open.

'Yes. C17. OK. OK. You're sure? Thank you.'

He listened in stationary impassive silence for a long time, then clipped the phone closed. Stared at it for a moment.

'That is odd.'

He looked up at Stoner. 'We should walk and talk. No more booze.'

He unrolled a trio of red fifties from an impressive bundle of banknotes, waved them at the waiter, dropped them to the table and rose to his feet. Not a trace of unsteadiness or humour.

'Grab your hat.'

They left. Eyes followed them, but no one called out to interrupt the suddenly serious tone of their departure.

Outside. Dry, dark evening. Night close behind it. Crisp and cooling.

'I don't know how they know this. The head was chopped off some time after the death. The body lost its head while still alive. The head was removed with a saw. Possibly while the body was frozen. How do you chop off a significant body part using a saw? It would take weeks. This is what they think. They also think they'll know for certain tomorrow. Sooner if I need it. There is more muscle behind this than I'd thought, JJ. I like that not at all. Loads of diligent motivated experts contradicting themselves. That is hugely expensive. A single incompetent can get things wildly wrong on their own. Saves a fortune and the result is the same. Confusion.

'Neither of our deceased friends died near the hotel. The hotel room was booked online by a company which doesn't exist. They're chasing the card details ... but that won't get them anywhere, I think. They probably paid through Paypal using a stolen card. You'll like the company name, too.'

He glanced at Stoner. Who in turn glanced impassively back.

'Murder, Mayhem, More Ltd. MMM. Sounds a bit like a law firm. But I do doubt that is what it is. I do doubt that indeed. Because . . .'

Stoner interrupted.

'That's the name of the fansite, isn't it? Murder Mayhem and More. The site where the movie of the head was playing. Crap.'

'Crap indeed, my friend. Crap indeed. There's a game afoot here, and it truly is not football.'

12

DESERTED CITIES, INVISIBLE DISCOS

Stoner walked away. The Hard Man walked to his car. Leaned against it. Watched his employee departing. Watched until he was out of sight. No waves, no fake fond farewells.

The Hard Man pulled his cell phone from its rest, flicked it open, dialled. Lifted the device to his ear. Listened. Listened some more. Dialled another number. Listened again. Said nothing. Tapped out a text message, closed the phone. Climbed into his car. Left the scene.

Stoner walked. Inspiration arises from exercise. A great theory, a fine and laudable sentiment. Stoner walked for many reasons, not all of them involving fitness, and not all of them because he enjoyed walking. The best way to be alone in a city, he felt, was to be on the move. Movement always breeds comfort in the person involved in the moving, and it always breeds concern and doubt in anyone else. Watchers dislike moving targets. Watchers prefer to know the whereabouts of those they're watching. And Stoner did feel watched.

He had been feeling unusually uncomfortable without break since discovering the severed head, the least likely hotel guest of them all. Since before then. Since when? Answers come with exercise and with movement. He crossed the road. No reason to cross it. He could see no other soul taking their exercise in this the late evening, the early night. No followers. Followers are hard to hide in the island silence of the city walker. But he could not shake the feeling that he had company.

Distance will always lose an invisible follower. It is impossible to remain invisible provided the watched puts in the miles. Following a walker is exhausting. Only regular walkers are fit enough to walk hard and long and fast. Stoner was fit and he enjoyed walking. He did not want a confrontation. He wanted solitude. He did not want to trap some know-nothing watching flunky. He wanted to think. Bodies without heads, heads without bodies. Songs without tunes, words without meaning. Connections are inevitable, predictable, but prone to easy misleading.

There was a message here. Stoner and the Hard Man were in complete accord about that. But the message was obscure. No one murders without a reason, and no one gets murdered without a reason. Pointless murders confuse the professionals. If any action in this strange performance was inexplicable but linked, then it was deliberately so. Which reveals the presence of a professional. Amateurs are never any good at killing. They always mess it up.

Professionals are always neat. If a professional is messy, then there's a reason for the mess. The mess will be a neat mess. A structured mess. A mess with a purpose. For a professional, 'mess' is a contraction of 'message'. Always. But messages can be private; they need not be a public statement, an announcement.

There is always a reason. Always. The victim always has a reason to die. The killer always has a reason to kill them. Find the reasons, the connections, and you're well on the way to finding the whole story. And if that's what you want, then fine. Almost nothing is insoluble. Finding courtroom evidence is something else. Finding out the tale behind the killing can too readily involve actions which are illegal and which are beyond the lawful and their custodians. Hence the Hard Man. When the law-abiding forces of the law grind into a wall of legislative obstruction, either the investigation founders or a contractor, an off-book contractor, becomes involved.

Stoner felt watched. This was a familiar feeling. Paranoia is a uniting feature among the clandestine. Those who survive and prosper in the dim-lit world of the off-books operator are always and inevitably cautious, and with caution comes paranoia. He crossed another street. Then he crossed it again. He wasn't hiding. He cared not whether a watcher was aware of his own awareness. He didn't want to catch them. He wanted them to go away. Not because he was in any way concerned that a watcher might be reporting his whereabouts, his actions, to whoever paid them to be a watcher. But because he wanted to think. Thinking is best done without a nagging irritating interference, be it ever-so remote.

He was walking briskly beside a park, a green breathing space long closed for the night. At the end of every day, the custodians of public facilities close them to the law-abiding payers of taxes, leaving them for the exclusive use of the non-legal, the nefarious. This must at some point have appeared logical to someone. Stoner laid his left hand upon the iron railing and vaulted into the park. And he ran. Hard, fast, relaxed and strong. Running hard on a full stomach and a lot of hard drink is not great for thinking, but it covers ground very fast, burns excess energies. And any watcher will need to run to maintain their watch, which renders them conspicuous. If running flushed a watcher then Stoner would explain to them that he felt a need for privacy and would suggest, in few words and with measured violence for emphasis were it necessary, that they respect this and left him to ponder in peace.

He ran to the central feature, a fine Victorian bandstand which appeared deserted. The flesh and drug trades were enjoying a holiday, plainly. He paused, laughed quietly but deliberately audibly, and reversed his run, pounding with no false silence, no attempt at stealth, back to the old iron fence. His watcher was close. He could feel the eyes on him. Back at the fence, he dropped his jacket from his arms and hung it on the iron railings. Leaned on the iron bars and gazed about him, breathing hard. Looking hard. He saw nothing. No one. He waited.

Nothing. Nothing at all. The night was a silent night, not a night of fear. He slung his jacket over his shoulder and walked across the park, alone. Comfortable in this. Able at last to concentrate upon the needs of the moment.

The Hard Man was uncharacteristically concerned about the job. This was possibly the most surprising feature of it. Stoner considered the severed head to be some kind of histrionic gesture, an emphasis in a dialogue to which he was no party. The Hard Man's level of concern suggested that he was more involved than he'd revealed. That although the strangely statemental nature of this killing was a mystery, the reason for the deaths themselves may not be. It is impossible to fully trust anyone involved in the business of commercial killing, and although they had worked together for many years, and although they mostly worked together well, and got on well enough on a personal level, accepting that the Hard Man's private life was completely private so far as Stoner, an employee, was concerned, Stoner trusted the Hard Man only when he felt a reason to do so. The Hard Man hid himself too expertly and too effectively for an operator like Stoner to accept total trust. And his feeling was that, at this point in the job, the Hard Man held an awful lot more facts than he had so far revealed. Which in itself was interesting.

It was also interesting and possibly relevant that the Hard

Man was withholding data. This would no doubt involve some need-to-know justification, but that was usually an excuse, an interpretation, a device. Sometimes legitimate, more usually not. It was, for example, possible that the Hard Man already knew the answers he was asking Stoner to find. Confirmation is valid when black actions are required, particularly when those actions are required by an instrument of government, by an organ of the state. He would certainly hide that knowledge and understanding from Stoner, because if confirmation was what he wanted, what he was paying for, then it needed to be independent. And there is no flaw in that reasoning, unless it stood in the way of Stoner's own task.

Out of the dark park and into the semi-dark of the streets. Stoner was relaxed, confident once more. He was a shadow who hated the shadows he inhabited. He was a spook too easily spooked. That said, he was still alive and practising his arts, both in the dark and in the light, unlike so many others. And mostly he was happy with this. If he felt followed, felt the pull of a shadow, then he was uneasy and ineffective until he had chased it down or chased it away. He believed in himself and in the strong sense of perception which had grown as he had grown into his darker life. Some things are trustworthy, as are some folk. Most folk can be trusted, so long as the limits to that trust are plain and understood. But when push came to fall-over, Stoner primarily trusted himself. The other side to that coin was that he blamed himself when things screwed, as they did. He tried to be honest with himself, mainly because honesty itself is such a flexible, mutable, variable commodity.

The faint worry, the unease he had taken from the evening's meal with the Hard Man had been replaced by a small, smug feeling of pleasure. Had he flushed a shadow? Or had he simply eased his mind a little? In any case, had there been a shadow, it was as likely to be nothing to do with this evening's topic as the

135

other thing. Stoner walked on difficult streets sometimes, and he walked there deliberately. And was rarely alone in this.

But whatever the reason, he felt good, and felt like some good company. He pulled the cell phone from his shirt pocket and thumbed a text to the dirty blonde. The evening may be history, but the night might still have legs. And the blonde's professional callings were rarely of the all-night variety.

No reply. That was unusual, unless she was asleep or working. Stoner walked towards her apartment, a new direction. A sense of purpose, a spring to the step. Still no reply. A half hour of walking to reach hers, then. A half hour's thinking time, with a little added focus in that he'd need to reach some form of conclusion before he settled with the blonde, not least because he felt some regret that he and she had started mingling his work with their pleasure. Rules and boundaries can have purpose; in relationships as in all other areas.

Midnight passed without much celebration. Stoner walked, crossed a street. Stopped. Looked. Listened. No sense at all of anyone following him.

Walkers are a rare species on midnight streets. Citizens tend to drive everywhere. Stoner had never entirely understood the appeal of the inside of some dull family Ford over the airy outdoors. The visual appeal of the plastic dashboard was a minor mystery. He liked his own cars, but he preferred to walk. Unsure whether walking was more rewarding than his motorcycles, though. A familiar diversion, the two-wheeled one. He worked hard to avoid his passions becoming his obsessions.

No reply. He was within a quarter hour of the dirty blonde's apartment. Her home. Her home, which she considered to be hers and treated exactly as though it were hers but which in fact belonged to him. One of the many elephants which inhabited the many rooms of their relationship; the layers of overlap in their lives. The contradictions and conundrums, the chasms of dishonesty with made the shared truths so important, so uniquely, impossibly important.

Stoner was standing outside. Outside his house. Outside the dirty blonde's apartment. His house. The lights were lit. Some of them. Stoner stood and Stoner stared. He could never and probably would never understand how this could be; how it was. It always was. He stared. The night grew deeper. He could stand for hours. It was part of what he did. How he held onto the things he had worked for so long to hold. To the things which held all his value but which had no worth. His delight, his desire and his disappointment. Always that disappointment.

The lights dimmed, one after the other. Once the only light remaining was the welcome home light over the doorway, Stoner shrugged away his anger, his rage, his fury. Sat on them. Squashed them into a hard dark place, the place which grew the music he wracked from his Fender deep into deep nights at the Blue Cube. But that place of focus, that hardest of darknesses, was the place in which he functioned with ferocity, with creative malice. It was the place where mysteries resolved themselves. It was the place which had kept him alive and running when his brothers stumbled and fell. The place where dwelt the darkest of angels, the angel of his frustration and contempt; the angel who thought for him and who found the missing and the lost. Who revealed when he was under threat. His point of focus.

His relationship with the dirty blonde included several understandings, among them the cardinal truth that if he appeared unannounced at her apartment or at her place of work the responsibility for whatever he found would be his – only his. He had his keys, of course he did, and he used them only when he was expected. She was not answering his calls, nor returning his calls.

Stoner reached into the night; seeking with his soul for the answer to the Hard Man's mystery, for a distraction. A killer was out there, another broken soul, and Stoner would be drawn to him. When his world was at its most broken, when he wished only to maim, to rend and to destroy, then he would surely feel the presence of that other torn and weeping soul. He felt nothing yet. The follower from earlier, the evening watcher, was gone. Bitterness and angry bile washed his palate. He turned away from his own house, which was not his home, and walked into the night, seeking someone to take away his irritation. No guitars tonight. He could hope for a mugger, a band of drunken, pill-fuelled fools, but they would not appear. Where are your enemies when you need them?

He turned down into a maze of residential rows and walked on cat feet to his wheels, to his inglorious Transporter. He drove home. His home. His place. His nest. It wasn't far. Less than an hour from the centre of the city, but in another world entirely.

Whoever had named the Parkside Trading Estate had been possessed of a fine sense of irony. It was at the side of no park. Even car parking was at a premium, and was a constant bone of debate between the incumbents. But it was an estate ... or it had been, once. Before it had become an estate, trading or otherwise, Parkside had been a military establishment. A long time ago. Over a half century ago. The historians told anyone sufficiently curious that it had been a military hospital. Which was true in a sense, but only in a sense. Military medicals had been based there, but their function was not exactly the repair and salvation of those damaged by the rigours of war, be they physical or mental damages. Those military medicals had been concerned with the extraction of information from individuals who were suspected of being in possession of such exciting material. Sometimes those enjoying the enforced delights of information extraction were from an opposing power. And some-times they were not.

Before its part in winning the Second World War for the alleged

Allies, Parkside had genuinely been part of a park. Part of the park attached to a minor stately residence, inhabited by a vaguely aristocratic family. The war had not been kind to the family. Not only did all of its sons and heirs fail to return from fatally active service, but their former family home was destroyed by fire shortly after victory was confirmed, hostilities ended, and there was rejoicing throughout the lands. At Parkside, there was no rejoicing. The recently bereaved tend to make for unhappy bed-fellows, company best avoided.

The already bad situation was worsened considerably by the refusal of the family's ancient insurers to compensate the family, their clients for centuries, for the loss of their house, and the military felt in no rush to confirm a connection between the conflagration and their employees. The records of the military medical facility had been lost in the blaze, and it was a blaze whose cause was unclear but whose effect was convenient. Except for the once faintly noble family.

From the unlovely but functional clump of military buildings grew a small, out of the way, almost invisible and largely anonymous clutch of demobbed buildings inhabited by the recently demobbed military types who dealt in allegedly de-mobbed military equipment, of which there was a considerable quantity, much of it impressively lethal and much of it in demand by all sides involved in the worldwide conflicts which had failed to recognise or believe that the war was over and that it was time to give peace a chance.

What had been a notional hospital became a notional scrap-yard for military hardware, heavy and less so, where the operating equipment of several divisions of fighting men was decommis-sioned. There are many ways of killing people, as soldiers and their masters have always known, and many of them passed through Parkside on their way from active service with the Allied forces to ... well, the public view was that the equipment was rendered inoperable and the metals sold for scrap. Firing pins were removed from tens of thousands of rifles, for example. Then the wooden stocks were removed and sold as waste wood, while the various metals, several of them of a high grade and much in demand, were sold off within the metal trade for eventual use in the country's many heavy industries. Not so much swords to ploughshares, but more rifles to rebar, poured concrete for the support of.

As it was with hand weapons, so it was with the heavier armaments. Tanks, armoured cars, Bren gun carriers, motorcycles, Jeeps, bicycles, bridge-building kit and the heavy haulage required to haul them all heavily about appeared at Parkside for disposal. And disposed is what they were. Many of them, most of the killing tackle, perhaps, took to a peaceful post-war world and contributed to its growth and development. But a lot did not. No surprises there.

When Stoner first visited Parkside, he was on the hunt for a supply of untraceable weapons. Nothing in the mass-destructions stakes; he found himself in the market for portable killing machines. Machines intended to be transported easily by a single man and used to forcibly assist in the demise of another single man. Maybe two. Occasionally a few men.

The range available was remarkable. Hand guns, sub-machine guns, light machine guns, heavy machine guns. Hand grenades, gas canisters, flame throwers . . . all suitable for a military museum and entirely risible by the modern weapons standards of the day, but all untraceable, invisible and cheap. And plentiful.

The first handgun Stoner acquired and used just the once for a swift double-tap to honour a decently paying contract had, under the terms of that contract, to be found with the body. Stoner never knew why, and the body was long past caring. The gun was duly discovered, along with the corpse, and while the newspapers failed to reveal the identity of the dead man, they did report that the gun belonged to a subaltern in a defunct regional regiment, who had failed to return to his homeland after being reported missing in action in North Africa, 1943. Much had been made of the remarkable deduction that a long-dead junior officer had returned to wreak vengeance upon some unidentified but presumably unpleasant character almost exactly four decades after his own death. Newspapers can certainly tell tall tales. And, more remarkably, newspaper readers pay to read them.

It would be something of an exaggeration to suggest that Stoner enjoyed a giant revelation of a biblical nature after that contract, but he certainly understood that weapons issued to His Majesty's forces for use in some long-gone conflict in a faraway land were equally effective at ending a life in the old homeland several decades later. These historical death-dealers became his weapons of choice. No need for the fashionable handguns. Sig Sauers, Berettas, Walthers and Glocks were fine for the image-conscious flaunter of fine weaponry; a Webley revolver dispensed death just as well in close quarters, cost little to buy and could be thrown away afterwards without regret.

There was an argument that the elderly ammunition for the elderly guns could be less than reliable, but service revolvers rarely jam and are extremely robust. Stoner had been amused to learn that the national police forces developed a considerable file on the mysterious gang of killers who preferred to use obsolete weapons, and more than one crime journalist sold stories of considerable imagination and no factual base developing a handsome theory that a lost legion of World War II warriors had returned to seek out and destroy those who had somehow and in some mysterious and impenetrable way betrayed them. They even developed a nickname for the deadly band, but he couldn't remember it. And in any case, the gang was a gang of one.

All good things come an end, however careful are the participants, and Stoner was not particularly surprised when his arms dealer decided to sell the truth to a tabloid. The world of the contract killer is a small world, known almost exclusively to its inhabitants, and Stoner got the word before his dealer sold his own revelatory words, and paid an unadvertised, unannounced visit to Parkside.

Reasonably brutal conversation with the dealer resulted in his explaining to Stoner that he had dealt with the reporter entirely via the telephone, that he had arranged to meet that reporter within a few days of Stoner's visit to share the full delight of the newspaper's largesse and the full facts of the story behind the gang of obsolete but deadly gun fans.

Stoner was delighted by the symmetry of the arrangement, removed the dealer from the scene and kept the appointment with the reporter himself. It proved to be a beneficial meeting. The reporter paid Stoner a relatively small sum of money for the information that the dealer was the killer, with the promise that more money would follow with further corroboration.

Stoner was subsequently sad and distressed when he was forced to reveal that unhappily the killer had himself been killed. He supplied photographic evidence of this; the dead dealer lying in a bloody akimbo and with an ancient Webley clutched in his hand. By way of corroboration, the historic weapons murders ceased at the same time as the dealer's demise, remarkably. The newspaper was naturally delighted and somehow Stoner found himself paid for his misinformation, while coincidentally understanding that he had acquired unobtrusive premises at Parkside. He had watched the place for an age or two after offing the loquacious amateur arms dealer and would-be scoop seller, but no one claimed it, so he took it as his own. Life can move in strange ways, if you let it.

And over the years, apparently legitimate ownership of the industrial units on the Parkside firmed up, became legal. The scrapyard dogs were replaced by burglar alarms and Volvo estate cars. Roofs were retiled and brickwork repointed. A curious air of respectability descended. Along with quiet, peace and a peculiarly studied indifference to much of the less than legal trading activity which remained the unsung speciality of the trading estate. All of which suited Stoner perfectly.

He drove the heavy Transporter over the first of several decayed speed humps, pulled over to the side of the disastrously surfaced road and switched off. Engine and lights. Parkside's dark side lay before him. Few lights were visible, no signs of activity. All exactly as it should be. Stoner contemplated the smoking of an imaginary cigarette. He had never actually taken to smoking, failing as he did to understand the purpose, but accepted without question that there were perfect moments for the smoking of a straight cigarette. This was one of them. The length of time demanded by the smoking of a king-sized cigarette would have been the exact length of time required for anyone concerned about being followed to observe whether they actually were being followed or whether a little justifiable paranoia was rearing its wise old head.

Stoner slid from driver's to passenger's seat and opened the door, pretty much silently. He had plenty of practice at being silent. He dropped to the floor, rested the door against its lock while he took a stroll. All was quiet. He knew he was being watched, but he expected that. He did not appear to have grown a tail. He would have been surprised if he had. But relatively few folk died by being excessively cautious, and Stoner had absolutely no wish to lead any of the uninvited to his quiet place.

He walked into the dark, listening for the familiar sounds of night-time Parkside. Strains of music, distantly through the breeze. The hum of electrical power and the murmur of nature. He walked on. Familiar ground. His home from home for many years now. His buildings were silent. A light burned somewhere distantly inside. Telltales shone dimly, suggesting security and cameras. He walked on.

Back to the Transporter. Which was as he had left it. He climbed back in, started the engine, left off the lights and drove towards his units, his own buildings. As he approached he pressed the remote which unlocked the roller doors to the central unit, waited for a count of ten, reversed the VW into its space and switched off, the door rolling quietly closed before him. He took another non-smoking notional cigarette break. Listening. Dropped from the driver's door to the clean concrete of the floor and wondered how many of the estate's band of ferocious feline fighters would be waiting, watching him, as is their enviable and inspirational way. He occasionally considered that if he could watch and wait like a decently feral cat then he would live to see retirement.

As well as being surprisingly clean, the unit was surprisingly spacious. Apart from the Transporter he'd parked, two other VWs, seemingly identical, sat within.

So his house, his own private home, was a garage. As well as the Transporters, the building contained a workshop, complete with tools and ramps, engine hoists and an inspection pit. In short, it looked like the vans' home rather than his. An uninvited casual visitor (there had been none of those in several years) or a slightly less casual but miraculously talented burglar (there had also been none of those) would have observed that the business which described itself as the Transportation Station was indeed a business centred around VW's finest vannery.

And plainly, as was often the way, the proprietor slept above the shop. Or in it, maybe. Stoner was home safe. The heavy Transporter ticked as it cooled and he walked through the workshop, patting a black Harley-Davidson on its black saddle as he passed it, heading through another pair of locked doors – mighty strong locked doors – into a wide and comfortable set of living rooms.

Home.

Safe.

13

THE RED HOUSE

There is a famous saying that things look better in the morning. Like most famous sayings, it's only true when it's true. Which could easily be a famous saying in itself; Stoner was unsure. Although like all practising musicians he carried an endless store of lyrics around in his head and was wont to produce them, either vocally or silently, at unwanted and unappreciated moments, he recognised pretty sayings for what they were ... pretty sayings.

This particular dawn looked no more comfortable than the night which had preceded it. He had slept well enough by his own poor standards; Parkside was quiet by night, and its inhabitants maintained that quiet with as much intensity and ferocity as might be required. And Stoner's premises were secure. In the main, his reasons for occasionally sleeping badly revolved around levels of discomfort. Like most practising motorcyclists he carried his share of accidental batterings, ancient and modern, and they would from time to time intrude sufficiently upon his physical wellbeing to interrupt his sleep, but that was not a common occurrence. Others who shared his means of gainful employment occasionally enquired about his sleeping habits, which was a minor strangeness in itself, given that theirs was an occupation not much given to the sharing of confidences and the revelation of personal details, but those few he had known well had almost always complained of poor sleep.

Stoner slept well. Mostly. But for a decent depth of sleep, the sleep which restores and refreshes as well as merely recharging the cells, Stoner had grown to depend on the dirty blonde. Lying next to her he experienced a peace and a relaxation unique in his world. It was mysterious to him, strangely precious, and he preferred to refuse any sensible analysis of its mystery. The effect itself was sufficient.

His regular and reliable night-time awakenings were brought about by his inability to stop thinking. Unlike most men of his acquaintance, who appeared to think only rarely, and then about matters which he found mostly incomprehensible, Stoner was rarely able to stop or even to sensibly direct the mental churnings which made him so proficient at solving problems. Those problems and puzzles took many forms, and solving them was evidently something of profound importance to some centre, some core, of his being. He had never really figured it out, but knew well enough how to manage it.

The secret was being able to set his mostly unconscious mind a task of sublime unimportance. This distracted it from anything painful or profound, and provided a decently rewarding return of its own. It was quite a buzz to scramble from the twisted sheets and before the eyes of a delighted night-time companion, kick up an amplifier and play a piece of excellent guitar chording which had, only a few hours previously, been impenetrably elusive. At such moments, it was always a fine idea to suggest that the private acts of the night before had provided the inspiration – although that was rarely true – thus ensuring that those delights were repeated.

Had the night been suitably shared but basically unrewarding, it was also always possible to sit entranced playing the same riff over and over until the lady in question recognised her folly in going home with such a self-centred idiot and left. Then of course the day's play could really begin.

Stoner had hoped that after his slightly strange evening with the Hard Man and its subsequent perambulations, he would have understood a little more about the murders in hand. This was not the case. Instead, and this was a minor surprise in itself, he had remembered the identity of a man who had borrowed a tool from his workshop. Not that he needed the tool. In fact he had never used it, which was probably why he agreed to its loaning, but he had noticed its absence when looking for something else, as is so often the way.

Draping a sad-for-itself, huge and ancient pullover over his own warm body, he padded across the sanded and scarred wooden floors and booted up the computer in the unlit corner where it lived. While it loaded and performed its morning rituals, shaking hands with its remote digital brethren, Stoner performed morning rites of his own. Coffee machine loaded with solids and liquids destined to perform their awakening magic, a first indecisive glance into the food cupboards to see whether anything tempted more than morning muesli. He dredged out his cell phones, observed that among the chatter were three text communications from the Hard Man, several others irrelevant but vaguely interesting from the musical crew, two voicemail messages from the Hard Man, and nothing at all from the dirty blonde. But it was early in the day for her. He felt her distance less forcefully in the light of day.

Stoner dropped the last phone into its charging dock without acknowledging any of the messages. They would all wait. And for reasons all its own, the phone – a very smart phone indeed – began playing music for him. Stoner stopped dead in his tracks. He had not programmed the device to perform anything, and was puzzled and a little unnerved by it. Could a distant someone cajole his own phone into playing music unrequested? But then he smiled, recognising Jimi Hendrix's characteristic stretched Stratocaster, playing a long, loud, live take on a short, quiet track from his *Are You Experienced?* album. One of Stoner's favourites, although it was not an album he played much. It was always worth a listen. Genius is always worth recognition. Amusing that his cell phone felt the same way. All on its mysterious own. Maybe.

Sufficient coffee had filtered into the glass jug for the day to officially start, and with a self-amusing air of reverence Stoner carried the first cup over to the workstation, where he sat sipping and flicking through his email accounts. Where once there were letters and a postman, there were now secretive deliveries through the ethers. There was much to be said for this. Where once the peace was endlessly shattered by the shrilling of the telephone, messages now arrived in silence. Without shock. Bad news, good news; they arrived with identical quiet.

Stoner's musical circle was its usual boisterous self; self-indulgent as only performing artists can be, entertaining, tempting as only audiences can be. There was private mail from Bili the Bass and a ring-me note from Stretch McCann, pianist at the Blue Cube. Bili's mail would require more than a single mug of coffee, but Stoner replied at once to Stretch's note with a terse text: 'Now'. He undocked the musical phone and dialled. Stretch answered at once. Some folk never sleep. It was just past six-thirty of that bright morning.

'Someone was after you, JJ.'

Stretch was straight to the point. Silence stretched. Stoner thought.

'Who? Was she nice?'

A gentle joke in case the big man was concerned for his slightly strange friend, the friend who always, but always, needed to know if anyone showed any interest in him.

'She was, brother. Indeed she was.'

Sat sipping on his own, Stoner's eyebrows rose gently and a smile tickled his lips.

'Care to share? Brother?'

He aimed a wide and audible grin through the ethers.

'She missed you by minutes the first time, and Bili handled her with her customary grace and diplomacy.'

The sound-only grin was returned. The morning was starting well enough.

'Did she stay long?'

A chuckle. And a negative reply. A head shaken invisibly but definitely.

'She's a fan, though. Plainly a convert.' Stretch warmed to his theme. 'She was in at the opening last night. Sat by herself. Watching the doors. Just like you do. But you . . . did not come.'

A pause there, in case Stoner wished to share his whereabouts. His silence declined for him.

'Drank expensive water diluted with whisky for an hour. And is brave. She asked Bili whether you were coming in. I do believe that Bili suggested that she fuck right off and ask you herself. No hard response. None at all. Didn't twitch. Asked for your number. Bili gave her a number. Probably a local cats' home. You know what she's like.

'She asked me the same thing when I'd finished the first set. She said that no, you weren't friends, and no, she didn't know how to find you, but a couple of her pals had told her that you were handy with the guitar, and she'd like to hear that. I told her the usual; we never know when your great genius would grace us with your strident string-stretching, so all she could do was keep on coming back and buying our oh-so-affordable water. Maybe something stronger to steady her patience.

'She asked whether you were that good. I lied and told her

that you were. I am your true friend and you are a man who owes me much.'

Stoner grinned again. 'Yep. That is of course true. The big black book of my life, your debt is recorded therein. That kinda thing.'

'She's no muso, JJ. She's plod. Narco maybe. I dunno. You know these people. I don't. I'd be happier if it stayed that way. She was too quiet. One of these spooky types, y'know? Sat there sipping one minute, gone leaving a half glass the next. I didn't see her go. I didn't see her come in. Know what I mean?'

Stoner agreed that he did. Agreed also that he owed Stretch a bottle of something. Suggested that it should be a strong something to soothe the jealousy, as the lady was plainly a talent scout, come to seek him out. And, finding no other talent in the Blue Cube, she'd left. Easy. They laughed and left it at that. Almost.

'When you next here, JJ? Soon?'

'Gotta see the blonde, y'know?' Stoner was a master of the non-committal. 'Maybe she'll be free and fancy a loud night out, huh?'

Then it was the time to dig into the little phone's memories to see what Bili had left.

It was short and to the point. The first message was a text version, abbreviated, of that from Stretch. The second read: 'Need to see you. To talk. When?'

He finished his first coffee of the day. The cell screen lit with an incoming call. It was Bili. It was remarkable how often Stoner found himself thinking of her just before she called him. Spooky. Or maybe he just thought about her a lot. That was less spooky; more strange. He picked up.

'Who's your fan?'

Direct. To the point. Early in the morning, possibly pre-caffeine, maybe even unshowered. Her voice echoed sleeplessness.

'No idea. Sorry.' Sometimes the truth really is the only reply. 'I spoke to Stretch. He thought she was a plod. Drugs, maybe.

Which would not be a problem for me. Did you get a take on her? A feel for her? Maybe she is a fan. Hey, Bili, I do play good enough to have at least one fan.'

Levity attempted, an offer of a humour truce accepted.

'Yeah, yeah. Painted class, JJ. Very striking. She was a model. A model what, though? I dunno. She worried me. More last night than this morning. She looked like . . . y'know . . . a predator. Not a muso. Not a player. Really not a listener. You the morsel, huh? Nothing new there, man.'

She didn't sound as though she were smiling. The words smiled, but not the mouth that spoke them.

'Stretch said you gave her a number. Whose? Not mine, hey?'

'Can't remember. It would have been right for the night. Maybe the AA? Can't remember. Really. You OK, JJ? Not being chased? She did smell like plod. You're not in trouble. Not been fighting again? Slapping guys around too much?'

She really did sound concerned. It was a talent.

'Don't think so. . . but thanks. You around tonight? At the Cube? Just checking up on you, y'know. I do believe you owe me a glass or two.'

Stoner was well into the second coffee. Was considering a second whole brew.

'Love you, that man! Me? Owe you a drink? I been lying for you, man. Hey! Your shout. My drinking. Get used to this, JJ.'

Bili sounded better.

'Hey to you too, Bili. The day is early now. Get some sleep. I've got running to do. People to see. Rents to collect. Strings to fit and a motorcycle to fix.'

Pleasantries and a low tension sign-off.

Stoner's several email inboxes revealed a common theme: incoming from the Hard Man. They would wait. His cell lit again. The Hard Man. Synchronicity in action. It's overrated.

'Yes.'

He was running out of politeness, inspirational guidance also.

'Yes yourself, Mr Stoner. I have a package for you. A physical in your hands, for your eyes only package. Where do you want it? You're not at home, so far as I can see, and I'd not like this to go adrift.'

'The Cube. I'm aiming to be there later. Stretch some strings, ease my worried mind. That kind of thing.'

The Hard Man pretended no interest whatsoever in Stoner's musical meanderings. But they agreed that the package would rendezvous with Stoner that evening. Stoner sensed that there was more to come.

'Have you had another body?'

The subtle, indirect approach sometimes paid off.

'Not exactly. Not exactly. You recall the movie of the dead head on that website?'

Stoner agreed that he did.

'Have you looked at the site again recently?'

Stoner confessed that he had not.

'Then do so. Murdermayhemandmore.com. Go gaze. Then try murdermaybemore.com. This is beginning to feel like an epidemic in waiting. This evening. Love to the missus. Pet the dog.'

And he was gone. Stoner contemplated further caffeine. Considered visiting the websites. Stripped off his ancient pullover, pulled on shorts, socks and a tee, and let himself out into the morning, ready to run. Always ready to run. Whenever there was no time to walk, if he could, Stoner would aim for a run. And Parkside, being the elderly pensioned-off military area that it was, was surrounded by a perimeter. A real perimeter, with the remains of a road. A challenging and interesting running track. All his own, too.

Stoner ran.

In almost instant company

He was running in synch with another runner: all senses so

153

advised him and he listened hard. Feet behind him. Exactly his
pace. Exactly his speed. No one to see unless he stopped and
turned around. A neat technique. He had used it himself oc
casionally, although few criminals could run in any meaningful
way. Heroes of fiction stop and retie shoelaces. Runners'
shoelaces never came undone. Stoner ran on, settling into his
comfortable perimeter stride. He felt good. Followers are fine.
If harm had been the intent then it would have landed by now.
He ran.

A lap. Just over a mile. Steady pace, settling into the stride,
the running rhythm. Common time. Guitar music howled
unbidden and exuberant in his head. Other runners wore head
phones. Stoner's internal system provided more entertainment
than he would ever need. Clyde the Slide's grunting intro to 'Bayou
Teche' scratched and clawed again and again through his inner
ear. His feet hit the beat exactly, as did those of his follower. No
slacking.

A second lap.

The problems of transposing slide guitar music to conven
tionally fretted finger-playing are always a challenge, and chal
lenges are what make things rewarding. So Clyde the Slide slid
the heavy glass bottleneck which wrapped his left-hand little
finger to make the shrill scream, while letting the open strings
play chords behind it. This is less than easy on a conventionally
tuned guitar. The music echoed and howled; patterns formed in
Stoner's innermost ear and his left-hand fingers flexed. He could
feel and hear how the chords and solo notes played out on the
fretboard of his own Stratocaster.

A third lap.

Well into the third mile. The feet pounding in synch to Stoner's
own grew no louder, no softer. He was unworried; unhurried.
The finger positioning of the song's structure became clearer in
his mind; the fingers of his left hand sketched the notes into the

air. A joy rose in his heart. Cajun rhythms could do that. But so indeed could many others.

Parkside was deserted at first glance. It was early. The regular residents would still be deep in their pits, either in the strange land of domestic suburbia or, as in Stoner's case, tucked away in a private hideaway, invisibly close to where they earned an equally private dollar or two. It was a land for night-owls, not for early risers. Which suited Stoner just fine. An unpopulated world was a world without problems, without strains. Over the four-footed pounding, the rasp of chill air whistling through his lungs, the solid double rhythm of his heart and the internal soaring of his incessant guitar soloing, he could hear the singing of the birds. An island of industry surrounded by waves of birdsong should always be unthreatening. He had based heavyweight decisions upon such lightweight thinking before. And running is a great leveller of men. The more he ran, the more tired his muscles became, so it would be worse for his invisible companion. Unless that hidden runner was in fact as much a runner as Stoner himself, in which case ... well, they would both be enjoying a shared pleasure. Where's the harm?

A fourth lap.

Curtains, shutters, blinds, windows and some doors were opening. Life was returning to the strange wasteland that was Parkside. Coffee was calling. Stoner ran on, heading for base. He stretched his stride, raising his pace without altering his rhythm. The gentle interference pattern of the following feet remained steady. His companion was as fit, as tireless as he. He passed his own units and ran on. A door slammed. The second set of footfalls was gone, suddenly. Stoner ran on. At the half-lap he slowed, stopped, stretched and gazed around him. Smell of bacon on the crisp air. He turned and walked through the park's buildings, approaching his own from the rear.

'Shard.'

Stoner nodded and grunted his greeting to the big man sitting still and silent on the wall which flanked the rear of the old buildings. That individual continued to watch, to observe, as he had been doing for some time. Since Stoner had started his morning's running. He appeared no more distressed by the encounter, or by the activity, than did Stoner himself. He waved an arm.

'Head filled with flowers and birdsong, JJ? You are one slow and unrewarding fucker to run with.'

Stoner smiled. One of those quiet mornings.

'Coffee? Bacon? Muesli? Sacrificial goat?'

He let them into the unit, reset some alarms, locked some locks. Revitalised the coffee maker, waved at the fridge and sat down in front of his email. More, ever more of the same thing. Nothing significant, nothing too new. The same message: go look at this murderous website. In time. In time.

'Always a pleasure.'

Stoner was cautious. Shard was a master of his old profession, and although he had once claimed to be as inactive professionally as Stoner claimed to be, the latter had doubts in his mind. But that was nothing new. And Shard did not live locally.

'You moved? Are we neighbours now?'

A friendly enough query, but answers were called for.

Shard pulled his shirt over his head and draped it over a chairback. He was military-standard man, just like Stoner himself. Bigger at the shoulder, narrower at the waist, but not by much. And he was a decorated man. Not only in the military sense, although his time in the military had developed the decorations. His pants followed the shirt onto the furniture and he strode into the shower, ignoring social norms and domestic permissions in the barrack-room way. Water rushed. A cleaner man emerged.

No concealing modesty here. Shard flexed his tattoos, jumped for a rafter and offered a minor display of gymnastics to heat his muscles and dry his skin. Stoner, who'd seen it all before, prepared breakfast, accepting that his guest was unarmed. Unwired. A cell phone buzzed. He ignored it. Set out two plates of bacon, a rough loaf and a bowl of fruit. Two settings. Facing each other. Opposing.

Shard opened the negotiation. 'On headlessness.'

An unusual gambit to start a conversation, but the occasionally taciturn Shard did possess a noted sense of the oblique. And a sense of humour, black as coffee, black as befitted his calling.

'I take it that you're not referring to the Douglas Traherne Harding poetry?' Stoner could do oblique right back. He'd been OK with cryptic crosswords as a youth. '"When I was born, I had no head. My eye was single . . ." that kind of thing?'

Shard smiled over his food, shook his cropped and decorated head.

'Nope. Nice try, though. Your master's voice, more like. You've got a body with no head. And a head with no body.' It was not a question. 'And so have I. It could be that they match. Do you have hands?'

Stoner's cell was once more flashing and buzzing in a mindlessly encouraging way.

Stoner smiled. 'No hands.'

Shard smiled back. There was no humour, shared or otherwise. There may have been mutual respect. A respect tinted with caution.

Shard was a serious killer. He had killed for contractual reasons for a long time. Originally he had worn a uniform and killed out there in the open, as and when his military masters demanded it. No argument, no conscience, no hesitation. He killed whoever, whenever, wherever, with speed and efficiency and with no discernible trauma or emotion. Occasionally . . . very occasionally . . . Stoner had been on the same team. When Stoner had been a military man, Shard had too. When Stoner became once more a civilian, Shard remained military, although he stopped wearing a uniform and a uniform haircut at the same moment that this sartorial transformation also gripped Stoner. The difference was that Stoner left the military's sheltering machine, preferring to ply his trade in his own way, his own selection, his own man, so far as he could. Shard had never cared about the niceties, the subtleties; he was ordered to kill, so he did. He was the perfect military machine, a predictable and reliable asset. He was always happy to serve his country and to take his country's shilling.

The last time their paths had crossed had been an odd event. It was Stoner's last, but probably not his final, kill. While he was setting up the hit, which was contracted to appear as an accident, at least for the media-viewing public, Stoner became convinced that he was being followed. Shadowed. At no point could he achieve the sense of solitude he preferred when undertaking the considerably serious business of removing someone's life.

But although he set traps and baited them, waiting for his follower to make mistakes and to reveal himself, no one was there. Until, quite suddenly, there he was. Shard. Again, Shard.

Stoner had returned from a day of sighting and observation, cementing the fictitious accident which would take the life from his victim. The day had passed well. Plans were laid, tripwires set. Stoner had returned to an anonymous lodge to sleep, to prepare for the victim's last day. He habitually employed anonymous lodges, anonymous locations far enough away from the termination to make his identification improbable at best. He travelled between them, setting up a pattern of movement which would appear unsuspicious to any subsequent investigating officers of the law. He rarely stayed at the same motel twice while setting up a job, and never more than that. Modern hotel moni-

CA LAST ACT OF CHARITY

toring systems are efficient, but relatively risk-free for anyone aware of their procedures.

He had checked in at the desk, been allocated a room. Had been promised a good, sound night's sleep and invited to dine at the character-free restaurant next door. He had declined. Politely. Shard had been sitting waiting for him in his room. Shard's gun had been resting in his lap. As Stoner had turned from closing the door he had been aware of the gun first. Aware that a gun was being raised to point at him. Aware that he was unarmed. This is how it will end. This is how it will end for just about all contract killers.

'Sloppy, JJ.'

Stoner recognised the voice, immediately accepted the futility of resistance, the pointlessness of heroism, and raised his gaze from the gun to the eyes of his better. Because better he was; Shard had demonstrated this simply by being there.

'Sloppy. Bang. Bang. Double tap. You're gone. Hey there, dead man, welcome back. I've booked us a table at eight.'

'That is just so subtle. You want to kill me with kindness? Or poisoning by grease?'

Stoner's voice did not tremble. He was as unafraid as he appeared to be. His imagination was dormant. He swung his luggage, a pair of motorcycle pannier bags, onto the bed. Sat down next to them, heavily. If Shard had wished him dead, dead is what he would already be. The understanding acquired in that moment had remained with Stoner ever since. He occasionally decided that if he was destined to die a violent death, the hands delivering it should be Shard's hands. It would be quick, because that was Shard's way, and Stoner could allow himself to feel grateful for that.

He had been impressed by the ease with which Shard had located him. Stoner had booked the room online that same morning, using an email account created less than a month before.

Shard plainly enjoyed some serious access if he could trace and identify such a short booking. In turn, Stoner thought he knew the access route, not least because he used it himself to extract information from the digital highways.

Dinner had been a peculiarly pleasant affair. Shard was witty, intelligent and interested in many things. But they were there because of a killing. An as-yet unfulfilled contract killing. That subject raised itself finally. Shard had quite suddenly lost all of his animation, his amusement. His eyes had fixed themselves upon Stoner's. A gaze intended to intimidate.

'We're looking at the same mark.' A flat, straightforward statement. 'When do you intend to complete?'

Stoner drank, untroubled. 'Tomorrow. Before noon. Is there a problem? Do we have a conflict? Are you his protector?'

Shard had maintained his flat stare.

'No,' he said. Paused for thought. 'And no again. Go ahead. Let's do coffee.'

Which they did. Then Shard had excused himself, heading for the rest room, from which he did not return. He'd settled the bill, too, as Stoner discovered a little later. An unsettling experience. Stoner finished the job, made the hit, fulfilled the contract and was duly paid for it. Of Shard there had been no further sign. Until now.

Stoner's cell phone buzzed and flashed its idiot message. He continued to ignore it. Drank coffee. Offered more coffee to his guest, who sat, still naked, gleaming across the table from him.

The nakedness was a display, as it so often is. A demonstration of total confidence. Of unconcern. A reminder of shared times in a barracks. In the field. In faraway lands. Over distant oceans and under strange skies. As well as the disingenuous, disarming, unarmed innocence, nakedness was a distraction. Stoner was undistracted. He had seen it all before. And he understood that Shard was his match in close combat, if not more than a match.

Asking questions revealed more about the knowledge of the person doing the asking than it was likely to uncover, so Stoner poured more, sat back and smiled. There were no threats.

'Do we do small talk now, you and me?' Shard smiled right back at him, amused innocence on prominent display. 'Here I am, wearing just Brut and charisma, and you're going crazy with the wonder of it all. Penis envy is a marvellous thing. You're still stuck on that handsome tart of yours.'

It was not a question. It was a provocation, a gentle one. Stoner was unprovoked. Men's bodies were no mystery and held little interest. Shard was very fit, very strong, very deadly. Phones sang out. Several of them. For the briefest of moments, Shard's attention wandered. Stoner was encouraged. He could have taken Shard at that point. He smiled.

'Hidden your cell in a private space? Should I look away?'

Shard smiled right back.

'That will be everyone trying to catch both of us. Your friend will be warning you that I'm on the loose and my friend will be telling me that you're nowhere near that club. Or we've both won the lotto. Wouldn't that be fine?'

Stoner sat. Shard sat. Cell phones sang a conflicting chorus, as harmonising as their owners. The phones went quiet. Then another called, a different signature tune this time.

'JJ, delightful though it is to drop by and share your hyperactivity brew, we do need to talk about our bodies.'

'Yours is exquisite. You should be proud of it. I would be. So would your mother, bless her and all who came in her. It is a tribute to the power of mindless exercise.' Stoner smiled a crocodile smile. An air of assumed weariness settled like a predictable cloud over Shard's features, but relax he did not.

'Thank you. Thank you. Peer approval is always welcome. We

both have a body. Well, to be less imprecise, I have a body and your pet plods have another. Cheerless Charlie – your best mate at the moment, I believe – wants you to find out who's offed yours. We may have a problem. We may have a conflict of interests. Or we may not. Either way, these things deserve a resolution. I am, JJ, offering a co-operative approach to this.'

Stoner gazed at his uninvited guest, his expression as blank as years of studious development could make it. Shard waited for a response, saw none approaching, carried on.

'I think I'm being set up for this. I can't tell you the reason at this point, but when you start digging – and you are an excellent digger, credit where it's due – you will find a road leading to my door. That's a false trail, a red heading or a dead herring, something like that. Make your own joke. There is an intention to bring us into conflict. I can think of several reasons for this and I can think of several folk in whose interests it would be.'

'Care to share this?' Stoner's interest was steady.

'Not if I can avoid it. Can we do the trust thing, you and me?'

A pause. Stoner stretched the silence and then snapped it.

'That is so tempting. It would be so easy to believe we share a motive. Sharing resources can only be good for us both. But it's not a trade, my friend. I have nothing to offer you. You are no kindly benefactor; you give nothing away. Nor would I. I'd like to believe that your offer is sincere, but if I made it I doubt that it would be. We're not that different, you and I. What would you hear if I made the offer to you?'

Stoner, stood, stretched to tiptoe, walked to the coffee and poured more for them both. Set about making a fresh pot. Familiar, relaxed movement of the hands disguising the tension of his thinking.

'Listen some more, JJ. Your big chief is presenting this to you as just another enquiry. Find him a hitter and he'll give you a fat fee and be nice to the wife and family. That sort of thing. You

162

will find the hitter is me. Well . . . you're likely to uncover enough clues to convince you to suggest to himself that I am doing the deeds. Which – and this is true – I'm not.

'My suspicion is that you'll get your fat cheque at that point and that very bad man will arrange a hit of his own; me as the target. That would be more than inconvenient. I don't know how many events you're looking at so far, but you will eventually – OK, quite quickly – find out that I can be placed near the scene of several hits. All uncredited and increasingly messy. "No no!" you'll cry, "Shard doesn't do messy", which is true, but your boss will take it to his masters anyway and they will reach out to me. Not convenient at all. It would be unwelcome, unusually unwelcome. It would interfere with a long job, and I don't want that. You following this?'

Stoner was. Following conspiracies is usually easy enough for paranoids.

'You're telling me that I will find your trail, start following your scent. You will observe that this is happening, take exception to it, and arrange an incident for me. A debilitating incident?'

'Yep. Despite your decent approximation of a good cup of coffee, I would have to act, because the disproving would interfere with a more important venture. Fatally interfere with it, I think. You don't have to believe me, JJ, but I would not be enthusiastic about debilitating you. I have no reason to lie. Unless I killed you, you would in any case come back after me, and life is far too sweet for that.'

'A heads-up, then? Should I believe you? Trust you?' A moment of tension. Stoner had placed the empty mug by the coffee maker, leaned against the counter, his back to his companion. Small silence. The silence pressured slowly, as did the tension. The coffee maker hissed, joining in. Stoner straightened, reached for the pot and poured. 'More? Another cup?'

163

The sound of an empty mug sliding along a table top, reaching exactly to the edge but no further.

'It is good coffee. Believe who you like and trust who you like. Trust your instinct and believe your interest. It makes no odds. I'm only telling you what's in my interests for you to know. My instinct tells me that you will catch a scent soon enough, and you will mistake that scent for my very own spicy odour. And inconsistencies, subtle side-aromas, you will consider to be my own efforts to put you off my own scent . . . and so on. Down that long road lies madness and conflict. A conflict between the two of us is no use. Tell it straight, Stoner; I don't know who would walk away from that. Neither do you. Correct me if I'm wrong in this. It's a long time since we did the dick-waving angry thing, but memory – not perfect I know, but generally reliable – reminds me that it was not fun and it was not profitable.'

Stoner poured. Returned the cup. Stripped off his tee and leapt for the rafter, the same rafter from which Shard had hung himself to dry an hour earlier. Shard watched with a half smile. Stoner strung together a half-dozen brisk pull-ups, repeated them using his right arm alone, then his left arm. Swung himself down, stripped off shorts and showered. Shard applauded, slowly.

'A one-hand clap for a one-arm bandit. That was very good. Good strong legs.'

Stoner towelled down, pulled on fresh clothes, loose black cargo pants, loose black Transportation Station T-shirt, tight knee-high socks. Looked across at Shard and threw him another tee, same logo. 'Have a dry shirt on me. Wear it to confuse our enemies. Who are who, as you're in a sharing mood?'

'Did I tell you how much I like your fortress of solitude, hey, Mister Stoner, sir?' Shard was pacing around the unit. Touching nothing, observing everything on display. Padding barefoot, carrying coffee. 'Always thought it was a good idea. Everyone should have one. More than one, really. And your bike in the

164

living room, too. Very stylish. This the batbike, huh? Press button B and the booster blasters boot you into orbit; that sort of thing?' He was standing by the black Harley-Davidson, slipping his feet into running shoes, shrugging on the free T-shirt.

'It would need a battery. But yes of course. We're all comic book heroes today, no? Comic book villains tomorrow. Great things to fiddle with. Fiddling aids the thinking, as my old mum might have said.'

'Like running. Like sitting all night out in the rain on your big black bike, watching the water slide down the paint, spitting and boiling on the engine. Christ, JJ; how much thinking time do you need?'

'Forgot to ask my old mum that. Sorry. Where are your elders and betters when you need them?'

Shard smiled, grimly. 'Someone is stitching me up. But it's dafter than that. Someone – probably the same someone – stitched *you* up. Set you up for me to find as the operator in a hit about a month back. Nasty job. The mark died slowly and badly. Guts on the floor and him watching them twitch and dry. That sort of thing. Not a pleasant way to end things. Couldn't see you doing that.

'So it's a double game. You fit the geography and the time frames, but not the MO, not the character of the killing. You know how it works. We sit and we sift our way through who's where and who's when and whether they're contracting to any of the usual buyers and – guess what? – you're in more or less that place at more or less that time, and the hit is someone your usual buyers would want their usual hitter to delete for them. But the MO is not you. Be a bad day for us all when you turn sadist. Cause a lot of head-scratching and soul-searching in our tiny little introverted world.

'Meanwhile, your boss hauls you in to investigate a series. Increasingly messy, decreasingly sane hits. Have a look at these, he tells you, and you do. Then you go and consult the mighty timetables of our lives and discover, lordy-lord-lord, I'm in town every time. If I'm a lucky man, you then step back and ask the big Why question. Not why have I done the jobs, because the answer to that is always the same for all of us because we're all the same; for the money. But why the mess? And if I'm especially lucky, you'll come seek me out and you'll sit me down and allow me to poison you slowly with some excitingly dreadful alleged instant coffee and we'll talk it though.

'But if I'm not lucky. Or if you've had another near-fatal fight with your girlfriend, the sweetly professional sex goddess, and if you're feeling very sore at the world you might just notify your boss and take me out. Or seek me out and arrange a forced confrontation, which is much the same, hardly survivable for us both, being who we are and what we do.

'And I didn't want that. Because there's something going on. If you took me on or if I took you on . . . there are only so many of us doing this, Stoner. Only a few. We know everyone between us, pretty much at least, so we know who's playing the piper in this song and dance.'

'It's paying the piper, not playing him. Don't you know your Shakespeare? But I do hear you. I hear what you're saying, and it might make some sense. But not a lot of sense. Seems unreal to ask you this, matey, but why are you spooked? I wouldn't force anything. If I thought you were doing the hitting I'd tell the boss and he'd do whatever he does. I don't take on hits any more, anyway. I do music, me; sweet blues music. And I find things when I'm asked.'

Stoner pumped the pedal of the hydraulic lift his motorcycle was sitting on and raised it so the engine was at eye level. Slid open a drawer of the tool chest and removed a socket. Hooked it onto the engine's drain plug, removed it and watched the oil flow into a pan.

'Shouldn't the oil be hot before you drain it?' Shard sounded interested and vaguely knowledgeable. 'You mechanics are all the same; never do unto yourselves what you preach unto others.'

Stoner looked distracted. 'The engine's never run on this oil.'

'So you're draining it? Why?'

Amusement sped across both faces at the same time: 'To give you thinking time!'

'Exactly.' Stoner stood back, replaced the tool in the drawer and closed the chest.

'The oil in the Transporter needs changing, but you would have considered it impolite if I'd suddenly dived underneath that. Added to which, the Harley is better looking than the VW. How many more hits do you think there've been from this ... competitor?'

Stoner looked around for an answer, but Shard was striding towards the back door, cell phone against his ear, listening intently. He turned at the door. 'OK for me to leave this way, JJ?'

He didn't wait for a reply, simply silently unlocked the door and was gone. The door closed again, also silently. The odour of engine oil provided an all-male accent to the pervasive cloud of coffee.

Stoner's cell phone called him again. He picked it up, flicked it open, observed how popular he was. Voicemail, the screen advised him, he had a-waiting. A-plenty, too. Press 121, it suggested, and he would become privy to its secrets. He did that. The Hard Man was brief at first. 'Call me now,' he had instructed some hours ago. The next two messages were the same. Then there was a string of no-message messages. Finally: 'Harding is looking for you. You need to know that Harding is looking for you. He is looking for you with a view to terminating the relationship between you. Arm up.' Which was strong stuff indeed for the Hard Man.

There was no message from the dirty blonde. Not a one.

Stoner poured the last of the coffee down a sink and set about preparing some weak, fragrant and mostly unappetising floral tea. The ritual gave him yet more time to think. Futures are long and varied. There are many more of them than anyone can ever understand. Shard had no reason to lie; few reasons even to admit an interest other than those he'd supplied.

Hauling the same wrench he'd used to drain the oil from the motorcycle, Stoner re-fitted and re-tightened its drain plug. He poured the clean, unused oil back into the tank. Motorcycles are like guns; the more you strip them, the more you service them, the more you clean them, the more you learn about them, the more they reward your care with reliability, dependability of their own. Lives are like guns; reliability is never underrated, never overvalued. And everyone has but one life, even mystics and musicians. You can share your soul with the devil, but that bad man will always let you down.

14

THE WHITE ROOM

'You do look interesting.'

Dave Reve looked up at the suddenly twin reflections in the mirror behind the bar. The female reflection spoke again.

'I'm Chas. Who're you?'

Chas beamed at Dave in reflection. He gazed back, natural caution disguising itself as shyness; a well-worn technique. Flicked a hand at the browsing barman, two spaced fingers, more stylised horns than obscene instruction, and fixed the gaze into a smile. Too early for beaming. Too early in several senses.

'Dave. Marry me and we become Chas and Dave. We could perform appalling English pub songs on a detuned piano. It would be the making of us. Generations of the drunk would sober instantly and leave their bars as we entered the room. Closet millionaires would share their millions for a promise that we would never again sing in their company. Questions of state would be asked whenever we performed, the UN would sit in emergency jam sessions and nations would go to war to avoid listening to us. The space race would be re-started as there would quite suddenly be a reason to put interstellar distance between humanity and ourselves. It would be an amazing thing, and I would ask you to consider it very seriously.

'There are of course a couple of insects in the smooth liquid of this potential future. Firstly I'm a policeman, not one of the generically laughing kind, and secondly I am a married policeman. Whether that blissful domestic situation has any connection to the lack of professional laughter in my life I could not say. Should not say. Will not say until we're better acquainted. Which I fear to be inevitable.'

Chas slid down from the bar-chair and walked in a wide circle around the bar and its drinking inhabitants. She returned to her seat and sat again. She picked up the bottle of Bud which had landed before her and sliced the soaked label in an exact half with her thumbnail.

'You do look interesting,' she said. 'I'm Chas. How do you do, Dave?'

She extended her left hand; her right held the dewy bottle. Dave Reve gripped that left hand with his own. Slapped it and shared a mocking high five.

'Beer,' he said, 'is one great leveller.'

'They were worse.' Chas sank half the bottle, placed it on its mat, and looked seriously at the mirror. 'The Levellers. Far worse than Chas and Dave. For a start they were serious. They took themselves seriously. It must have been hard for them to face such apathy and derision from the music-loving public.'

'Never heard of them. Life's too short to listen to music you know you won't enjoy, so why do it? Chas and Dave, now, that . . . that was like purgatory for lapsed Roman Catholics; an opportunity to bear the weight of penance without actually dying first. Suffering is always popular with that Church. They encourage their millions to do the suffering while they're alive; dead sufferers rarely contribute much to the earthly coffers, when all's said and done. You can see their point. A clever bunch. Well sorted. Their toast always falls butter-up.'

'So you're that lapsed Catholic, married and joyless policeman, Dave!' Chas was grinning at the unsmiling reflection of the slim man seated next to her, in life as well as in reflection. 'Are you here for the cure?'

'I'm drinking the cure, miss. Ms. Muzz? Missus? I was numbing my sorrows with overpriced and very dilute if entirely palatable alcoholic solution until a delightful apparition appeared both beside me and opposite me. I could write an entire *Star Trek* script about the temporal and spatial anomalies of characters reflected in bars, a sort of metaphor for the duplicities of life, if you like.'

'You could. Brannon Braga would direct or produce it, or whatever people like him actually do to television, and the next generations of trekkies would pointlessly debate your creative genius well into the next century. You do have the strangest bar-side manner I've ever come across. As well as a good line in drollery and wit. Is it the marriage or the policing which produces this? Maybe I should get out to meet married policemen more? Maybe there's a whole world of entertainment awaiting, and I was unaware of it.'

Both beers were empty. Chas flagged for more. Dave raised a single eyebrow at her reflection. 'It's on me. These things always are, it's a tradition.'

'Traditions are just rules, and rules are made to break. My shout. Make me smile and I'll stand for another. Make me laugh . . . and I'll stand you a peanut.'

'Oho!' Dave smiled, meeting gazes through the glass.

'Here it comes.' Chas leaned towards her reflection. 'I'm an unmarried woman. No one misunderstands me. I crave misunderstanding. I am bored to death with men who understand me. Legions of boring, middle-aged and married men understand me completely and know how to make me happy while at the same time caring not at all for themselves or just wanting to get laid. I crave meeting a man who misunderstands me and just wants to get laid 'cos his wife is off with their family jewels being witty and smart and beautiful and intelligent, and who loves his mother and his cat and shares a fascination with his rare collection of genuine 1950s Coca-Cola bottle tops and who awaits his every evening arrival with his favourite tea and who dotes on his every word.'

'What exactly does dote mean, anyway? I've often wondered. That's what my life is like, Chas; I waste it pondering subtle things, like the true meaning of . . . dote. It cannot be easy, but it isn't really hard. Drink up. You must need to find better company by now!'

Dave turned ninety degrees to his left, facing his companion head-on for the first time.

She beamed at him. 'What sort of policeman? You must be a top one. A detective? All rugged and . . . ah . . . misunderstood? I can try to do misunderstanding if you like. It's plainly big in your life. Does your wife misunderstand you? Where is she, by the way? At home with the two-point-four kids and the Ford Focus? Mondeo? Volkswagen? Hold on, hold on . . . she takes the children to school in a Shogun? One of the really really huge ones which can hurdle mountains in a single leap. Am I right or am I right?'

Dave signalled for a further round.

'I'll skip the next beer; get me some expensive water, there's more profit for the bar in that. I think only of others. You? What do you drive? You're a cop so you're forced to drive super-safe Volvos all day, projecting an image of calm power and protection to keep Mr and Mrs Joseph Citizen reassured and sleeping through their lives in a peaceable way. You probably don't drive a car at all. You probably go everywhere on foot and ride a huge motorcycle with no silencing at all at the weekends. You spend all your days chasing felonious drunks and your evenings pretending to be the fond family man. At the weekend you don mirror shades and a lot of dirty leather, then head out on the highway like some fearsome dude. Brother. How'm I doing?'

'No! I suddenly had that walking-over-my-own-grave thing. You don't do that at all, do you? At weekends you dress up in a frilly flowery frock and take ballet lessons. So sorry for the stereotyping. You can tell your Aunty Chas. You're safe with your Aunty Chas.'

Dave Reve rolled his eyes, help up his hands in surrender. 'If that's what drinking water does, then I'll stick to beer. Speaking of which . . .' There was no need to call the barman; two bottles of beer and a bottle of water appeared together.

'I'm a detective. A sort-of accountant detective. I detect fraudsters. I do big sums and catch clever chaps who prefer not to pay their social dues. Or who move money which does not belong either to them or to the guys who claim to own it. It's called laundering. I chase laundry. A tough life, but amusing enough. It's more legal than nicking knickers off clothes lines and possibly even more entertaining.'

'Arnold Layne.' Chas tipped bubbly water from bottle to throat. Sank the bottle in one and belched like a stevedore. Covered her mouth. 'Sorry. Arnold Layne. The knicker nicker. Sorry. I should stick to beer; water is too strong for me.'

'Pink Floyd? You're older than you look, then. Hang on, hang on. That was not at all gallant. Your grandkids play Pink Floyd and force you to listen to it under threat of death?'

'No kids, Mister Policeman. No kids. Never had time. Never had inclination. Too selfish.'

'Yeah.' Dave Reve paused. 'My wife drives a Jaguar. An estate. It's very nice. It has a diesel engine and a wooden steering wheel and its seats are made of leather. It's got a CD player. She chose it because she wanted something to carry around the dogs she'd decided to have instead of children.'

'And then? Nature ran its throbbing course?'

'Yep. Kids. No dog. Car's old now, has no value. No one wants cheap thirsty cars with leather seats and permanent puke stains. She's not great on cleaning it. Why are you interested in the wife? Is this a new ploy? Chat to distressed-looking bloke in bar and offer him only stratospherically expensive marriage guidance services?'

'And you?'

'What?'

'You. What do you drive? You can tell a lot about a man from the car he drives. With women it's the clothes they wear. Possibly perfume. I could kill a Scotch. Or possibly a Scotsman.'

'I . . . um . . . I don't have a car of my own. I just borrow one if I need one. I'm a policeman. Policemen can always borrow cars. I don't really care about cars. Or about football. Does that tell you a lot about me?'

'More than you could ever imagine.' Chas pulled a large watch from a pocket. 'It's getting late.'

'Am I supposed to offer you an escort to your room? That would be normal at this point, I think. I could invite you to mine, although that might be a mite challenging on the domestic front.'

'Do you swim?' Chas peeled money onto the bar, waved away the change. 'This place has an excellent pool. And, do you know what? No one swims in it. It also has an excellent gym. No one uses it. The place claims to be a health spa. Because it's a spa it can charge a small fortune to stay here because it offers guests and their guests free use of the excellent fitness facilities. Guests of course prefer to ignore the free facilities which they've already paid for and sit drinking in the bar, where the prices are unusually elevated because they need to pay for the gym equipment which would be free to anyone using it if they did which they don't. Fancy a swim? Fancy taking the plunge, Mister Policeman?'

As she said, the pool was huge and glowed a pale blue in the night. And it was empty. She kicked off her shoes and dipped a toe into the water, pronounced it perfect. Started to unbutton her shirt.

'Isn't it dangerous to swim when drunk?' Dave was standing by the pool steps, fully dressed, attempting to look much more calm than he was feeling. 'Doesn't it give you cramp or something?'

'Not yet.'

Chas had piled her clothes neatly, revealing a subtle taste in the underwear she still wore. She stood looking steadily down the length of the pool, touched the tips of her fingers to the tips of her toes and dived smoothly into the water. Surfaced a surprising distance away and settled into a lazy crawl to the far end. Reve peeled to his shorts and followed. By the time he'd reached the turn, Chas was back-stroking her way to the shallow end. They were both good, strong swimmers. They swam in silence. Never together. When Reve reached a turn, she was halfway down the pool. He swam faster. Failed to catch her. Swam slower. She failed to catch him. Pleasure for both. Companionable.

She was sitting on the edge in a corner at the shallow end. Dripping in her underwear, smiling at him. He pulled himself out. Sat facing her across the corner, separated by tiles. Both of them breathing harder than their exertions demanded.

'You do look good, Ms Chas. You do swim good, too. You swim a lot, then.'

Not a question.

'You too, Mister Policeman. Mister married Policeman. I'm going to swim a little more before turning in. Think carefully before answering this. You have a lady wife who drives a Jaguar. I love to swim naked. If you're going to share in that with me then you will need to be naked as well. In nudity lies honesty, even in the water. Are you undressing me or are you leaving now?' She rose from the pool and stood before him. 'It really is your call.'

No hesitation. No hesitation at all. Reve pulled himself up and out, walked to her, hooked his thumbs into her unfrilly sports briefs and pulled them down, kneeling so he could take them all the way to her feet. She stepped from them and stood before him, legs slightly apart. At ease. She was hairless. Entirely hairless below the neck. Not even the shadow of stubble. Armpits nor belly. He leaned a little forward and kissed her on the bud of her sex. First contact.

He rose. She hooked her fingers into the elastic of his shorts and dropped with them to her knees. His reaction to her was more obvious, less deniable, than hers to him. She kissed him on the tip of his sex. Second contact. He stared at her, transfixed. She looked up, rose to her feet, turned her back to him. Reve unhooked her bra, held her shoulders and turned her to face him. The straps hung at her side, her breasts holding the clothing in position; an interesting reversal of roles. Interesting at another time, perhaps. Reve pulled the garment away, kissed the nipples of both breasts, already standing as proud in their own way as he was in his.

She stepped away from him and smiled at his urgency. Reve was past smiling, fresh out of smart conversation, clever comment.

'Race!' And she dived cleanly and was gone.

He stood and watched as she crawled a length, turned and backcrawled towards him again. He dived. They passed in the middle, their eyes met, their strokes steady.

Another turn, another length. This time, as if by a signal, they both stopped in the centre of the pool, paddled together. She reached for his head and pulled his lips to hers; he drank in her chlorine, beer, whisky, and she his. His hands found her breasts, floating between them, his right hand traced a steady line past her navel towards her sex. Before his hand met its target, Chas sank, took him in her mouth and trod water, arms out from her sides, feet controlling her depth. He could breathe; she could hold her breath for a longer time than he would have imagined. Her mouth worked on his cock for an impossible time and then was gone.

She surfaced yards away, heading for the deep end at speed. He followed, confusion and lust and longing clouding all of his thoughts. When he reached the edge she was already sitting out of the water, just her feet submerged, her legs spread, her own desire obvious. He planted his lips upon her more private lips, lips set in their quizzical vertical smile, and dived into the heart of her, all else lost to him. She leaned back, bracing herself on her arms and spread her legs as wide as wide can be, the easier for him to submerge, to soak himself in her. And when her climax held her, she gripped his head between her thighs, and he worked his face into her more, her pleasure the only thought active in his head.

Her climaxes grew in both frequency and intensity. He attempted to pull back, but her legs, strong swimmer's legs, held him in place. Not that he was unhappy there. Far from unhappy. Her shuddering and her cries were more compelling than any whisky. She came over and again, until with a long loud sob she slid from the poolside into the water, his head clamped between her legs, his mouth open only to her sex, and sank into twelve feet of bright blue, gently heated water.

He struggled, but he could not break free.

15

THE PURPLE RAIN

'I feel so happy that I almost died, And then he hit me . . .' The Hard Man's singing was as tuneless as it was unwanted and inappropriate. Stoner stopped walking, sharply. Stood statue-still, eyes half-staring, fists half-clenched. He had not expected to walk straight into the Hard Man, leaning casually against the wall of the hallway in his own house. 'Who've you been beating up now, JJ? Did the other guys get away, or do they look worse than you do at the moment? Why are you ignoring me? You returned none of my calls. None.' He was all seriousness, now, the pretence of levity discarded as painfully as it had been employed. 'That is not the way it is.'

'I ran . . . into Shard. Harding. He had things on his mind. We discussed them. After our long, friendly and constructive debate, I needed to think, so I switched off my phones.' Stoner unclenched his fists. Talking with the Hard Man could feel like a fistfight sometimes. 'I still need to think. He and I will need to talk again. In any case, what do you want? I have a business to run and something like a life to lead. This is my house. You're not supposed to break into my houses. It's against the law. It's called breaking and entering.'

'I shall forgive your unkindness, JJ. Any in-depth conversation with Harding could prove fatal for a lesser man. Let's simply say that I was worried for you. You never switch off your phones. You may ignore them but you are way too paranoid to switch them off. It's possibly burglary but not actually breaking and entering. I broke nothing and I entered no one. I only entered the house as far as the hallway, and only then because I wished to be clear of the rain.'

'It's not raining.'

'Yet. But it may. I am, as you know, a cautious man, as well as considerate to my friends and implacably, relentlessly unforgiving to my enemies.'

'Then pretend to be my friend. Let me earn my living and let me think. There was much to learn from the conversation with Harding, and chats like that always repay a replay. Unless you've more gems of intelligence to share with me? You do? Oh for fuck's sake. Not another body? Let's go somewhere quiet.'

The big old house was divided into four apartments, all of which were let, one of them to the dirty blonde. Stoner was a gentle and undemanding landlord, but rents needed collection and buildings always required repair. In any case . . .

'She's not in. So we might as well go eat.'

The Hard Man plainly could read minds.

'Or at any rate, she's not answering her door. To me. Does she have a spy hole? CCTV? I do sometimes get the subtle ghost of an impression that I am not entirely top of her must-invite-to-tea list.'

'She's not answering her phone, either. Would it hurt you if I asked you to wait here while I check she's OK? See how I do consider your feelings, even in delicate matters like this. She hates and detests you, of course. I cannot deny that. She is a lady of taste. Discrimination also.'

The Hard Man raised the edges of his mouth in an expression more like that of a man licking a drain than one sharing a great time with a friend, but he nodded and leaned against the door-frame. Nonchalantly.

'You do nonchalance very badly. Back in a moment. I'll call your cell if I'm going to be unavoidably delayed.'

'She's not talking to you either, JJ. Bet?'

'If she's at home, she's talking to me.'

Stoner pretended a levity and a confidence he did not feel. The dirty blonde was not answering, door or phone. Stoner considered letting himself into her apartment to check that she wasn't lying bleeding or incapacitated somewhere inside, but decided that his respect for her privacy was more pressing than his concern for her wellbeing. Their relationship was an unusual one, but part of the agreement which had resulted in her renting an apartment from Stoner involved his recognition of her profession and of her need for privacy.

'Not home, then? She's left you, maybe?' The Hard Man was as deliberately tactless as he felt the situation demanded. 'Can't you just stick your neck around the door? Reassure yourself that all is well within? Or are you a true bloodsucker of a landlord and in the best vampiric tradition require an invitation before you cross a threshold? I saw a TV programme once, and . . .'

'Just shut it. OK? She's either out or she wants quiet. Both are fine. If anyone had hurt her in there the others would have told me.' Stoner tapped a two-handed pattern on the door to the apartment opposite the blonde's. A roundly expressionless Asiatic face appeared around the door.

'Mr Stoner. Rent is paid.'

'Mr Tran. I am concerned for our friend over there. Is she OK?'

The Asian man practised his inscrutable arts, maintaining a completely expressionless expression. 'I know of no problems. I have heard and seen no problems. Missy is away, I think. For some days. You have the keys, Mr Stoner. You can check up on her.' Still no expression. 'I shall tell her of your enquiry.'

'OK. Thank you.'

Mr Tran appeared to be transfixed by the sight of the Hard Man, despite the latter's studied air of nonchalance. 'Hello,' he said. The Hard Man declined a response. He and Mr Tran ran a brief, silent inscrutability competition. There was no obvious victor. Then The Hard Man levered himself away from the wall, removed his gaze from Mr Tran and spoke softly to Stoner.

'I'll be off then. Leave you two to . . . to whatever it is that you two do. Good to see you're in one piece. Survived Harding. A rare talent. Leave a phone on, JJ. Just in case, huh? Domesticity calls.' He sketched an approximate smile, glanced once at the silent Mr Tran, and left. Quietly.

Mr Tran was an interesting man. All of Stoner's tenants were interesting in one way or another. Mr Tran was particularly interesting in that he appeared to have no identity at all. Stoner knew him only as a most reliable friend, and a sometimes mysteriously invisible ally. He had already been a resident tenant when Stoner inherited the house, the only tenant there, in fact, despite the building containing another three spacious apartments.

Mr Tran had a large and fluid family. Maybe it was less of a family and more an active, shifting circle of friends. Stoner never invited an explanation. Had he done so, both men knew that the reply would have been a lie. A kind, considerate and unverifiable lie, but a lie nonetheless, and some twitch of trust would have been lost, both in the asking and the telling. They came and they went, this family and friends. They were implacably polite and spoke English excellently, although with a consistent and notable southern American drawl. Which sounded odd from the mouths of a collection of diminutive Asiatics, boys and girls, ladies and gentlemen. Mr Tran was also an excellent cook; he sometimes invited Stoner and the dirty blonde to eat with him and whoever was sharing his apartment at the time. And now, with a typically subtle shift in demeanour which Stoner always found vaguely disquieting, a suddenly beaming Mr Tran accosted him with an invitation to eat. Right now. Immediately. A family celebration, he said.

Stoner attempted polite refusal, explaining that he and the dirty blonde had been aiming for a night out together, maybe some music, maybe a meal for two, had she been ... well ... where she should have been. Mr Tran frowned, an expression as theatrically insincere as his sudden enthusiastic welcome.

'Missy has been compelled to be out.' Mr Tran's use of English, while always most comprehensible, could at times be mysterious. 'She has been extracted by an insistent client, perhaps. A gentleman greatly affluential who wished to celebrate a family matter with her.'

Stoner worked hard to keep his surprise from his features; inscrutability was a much-prized art among Mr Tran's kind. Among Stoner's kind, too.

'Influential, Mr Tran. A man of great influence.'

Mr Tran beamed wider still.

'Mr Stoner. I am attempting to share with you that he is a gentleman of considerable wealth.' He looked closely at Stoner. 'A really rich geezer, OK? It is unkind that you are unable to pass your evening with Missy, as was your plan, and so I would like you to share a family celebration. You are a kind landlord and I wish to repay that kindness.'

The smile left Mr Tran's face, replaced by a suddenly stony gaze which would have been alarming under other circumstances. Stoner was unalarmed, but recognised that beating on the dirty blonde's door to check the veracity of Mr Tran's statement would have been as insensitive as it was unnecessary. And in any case, he did enjoy Mr Tran's exquisite cuisine. And he would at least be in the building when the dirty blonde returned from her evening's entertainment. He accepted, with good grace and bowing.

Mr Tran offered him a low bow, and a wide smile.

The evening presented a pair of immediate surprises. Firstly there was no sign whatsoever of Mr Tran's transient family. It was dinner for two, and it was ready to serve. Stoner's presence at the Tran table plainly was no surprise at all to his host. The second surprise was that the food was entirely southern American states; gumbo, dirty rice, Cajun spices, po'boy sandwiches and onion threads, chowder and beignets, hot dogs and hamburger. It was all perfect and it was all delicious. The coffee too. After a long conversation-free time in shared appreciation of Mr Tran's mastery of Mississippi cuisine, Stoner expressed both his delight and indeed his surprise. All the food he had previously shared with Mr Tran had, as he remarked, been Chinese.

Mr Tran swilled noisily from a bottle of Coors and contemplated his guest. 'Not Chinese, Mr Stoner. Never Chinese. Vietnamese. I am a man from Vietnam; Tran the man from Vietnam.' He seemed pleased with his own joke. Constructing a joke in an alien language is never easy. An intentional joke, at any rate. 'And now, Mr Stoner, you have a call waiting.'

Stoner looked up, alarmed. Mr Tran rose easily and smoothly to his feet and lifted some of the evening's debris from the table. Stoner's cell phone immediately shook itself in his pocket; he looked at Mr Tran's departing shoulders with some surprise.

'I would answer that, Mr Stoner. It may be important.'

He flicked the phone open, raised it to an ear, still watching Mr Tran's retreating shoulders. The Hard Man, again.

'Sorry to disturb your evening, again, so soon. But you should know that my own intended time of conjugal delight has been interrupted, postponed, spoiled even, by the loathed pressure from above. Those magnificent men in the ministerial machine appear unable to understand why it is that I am still unable to

183

offer them answers about these damned bodies. My usual entreaties and laments concerning the dire quality of the troops at my disposal had no effect. Well. No positive effect. Their view, vigorously expressed, is that if I cannot provide answers they will employ another agency. Maybe a foreign agency in case there is a cover-up going on. No comment? Then I shall continue.

'I neither want nor need the giant, flat and sweaty feet of some continental cousins stamping across my turf. That would be too unpleasant for words. I need some answers, JJ. I need those answers fast. The time for genial conversation is over. Get out and break some heads. Get out and get me some answers. Do it now. I'll put it another way: please do it now. Or. . .' his voice fell away.

'Or what?' Stoner asked, carefully. 'Or you'll threaten me?'

'The opposite. Or tell me that you can't do the job. Do that before we hang up and I'll root among the sewers to dig out another operator. They won't be as good as you, JJ, but maybe I'd feel easier about threatening terrible things to them when they fail to live up to even my painfully low expectations. Say now if you want out. Now. This instant. Or shift a gear and step up and sort this thing out.'

No hesitation: 'I'm on it. I'll start pushing.'

The Hard Man hung up. Stoner closed his own phone.

Which immediately rewarded him with an irritated tone announcing that two messages were waiting. He listened to them both. The dirty blonde, at last. She wondered, twice and with audibly escalating disappointment, whether he was ever going to answer her calls? Whether he was going to accept her sudden and exciting invitation?

Mr Tran stood smiling at him from the doorway. Stoner's phone rang again. He decided that after answering this last time he would break it into its component parts and flush it down the toilet.

But he answered the incoming call . . .

16

GOLDEN BROWN

'I'm a wife for a week!' The dirty blonde screamed into Stoner's ear. He held the cell phone at bay, bemused more than amused.

'Well, a little more, but a week as a wife sounds better than a bit more than a week as a wife.'

Stoner was silent, unable to think of a reply which was better than unpleasant. Why hadn't she mentioned her revised status? Her holiday? Whatever it actually was.

The dirty blonde, however, was plainly having a better time than he was. 'A bit less than a week to go and I can maybe get back to being single. Being human. Maybe. How're you, lover boy? How's big bad life in the big bad city? You caught loadsa crims, done loadsa fighting? Bloody strange here, baby.'

Stoner wondered at her lung capacity. There was no pause in the flow; she breathed only out, and all the time she was breathing out, she was speaking. Loudly. Maybe too loudly. Stoner felt the hackles of suspicion rising. He pretended to ignore them. To concentrate only on her words.

'But I need you. I want you. Can you drag yourself away from your passionate performance of that twat's every bidding and provide an honest girl with a good day's fucking? Living like a nun, I am. All I need's the black dress and insane hat and I'd be bloody Mother bloody Superior.'

She finally drew breath . . . paused, at least.

Stoner plunged in: 'Steady. Steady. Where are you? I've been calling, I was worried . . .'

'I'm fine. Don't worry about me. You're not my mother. You're not even my father. You can still qualify as my lover if you get your tricky dicky up here sharpish.' There was a certain direct-ness of approach here.

'Here is where, say? Just a clue?'

'Oh. Yeah. It's the old vicarage, somewhere . . . hang on . . . near Woodstock.' A pause. 'Can't you locate me from my phone? You FBI chaps can do that. I saw it on the telly. Can't you just zoom in on my signal and zoomily zoom here with Percy the pink pointer and give a girl something substantial to think about apart from housewifely duties? Which are, really, really, really, dull-oh.' She was re-warming to her theme.

Stoner plunged in once more; 'I'm not an FBI man. I'm nowhere near the kit I would need to find your phone. You must know where you are. Bloody hell, woman! Talk sense, huh?'

'Calm, calm, JJ. Mustn't get your blood pressure elevated. Not just yet anyway. There's a pile of letters in the hallway. I'll read you an address.' The sound of running feet echoing in a large space, and then the address. 'Told you it was an old vicarage. It's a parsonage. What's the difference between a vicar and a parson? Do they get transmissions from the same god, or do they all have different ones? Thought a parson was part of a chicken? Who knows? Who bloody cares?'

'You're staying with a parson?' Stoner struggled to keep incredulity from his voice.

'Don't be a tit, JJ. Just get up here now, give me what I really and truly do need, and I shall reveal all. Then I'll tell you every-thing. Look! I made a joke! Tell you what, though, this be-gloomy old pile is not a place for jokes. There's no bugger here most of the time. Bloody bizarre. Like a railway station at midnight after the last bloody train.

'Then, just as you're getting used to the notion that you have a bit of peace and quiet, and a moment of aloneness to enjoy, it's like a railway station at midday, packed solid with transients you don't know, don't want to know, all of them getting in the way. Only it's worse. It's like they're the biggest rugby club in the world. They all know each other and they couldn't give a shit about you. They just do their stuff, talking, walking about, eating like the pigs they are, swilling booze – not beer though; these inhumans don't drink proper drink – and it's like I'm not there at all? Even though I'm taller than most of them? And I do kinda stand out, yeah?' Her every phrase was now a question. Her voice raised at the end of every thought. She was in fact distressed. Remarkable, that.

'Why are you there, babe?' Stoner tried to be kind. 'It doesn't sound like fun, to be honest.'

'Fun? Oh. It will be fun. Fun the minute you arrive. Promise. Fun from the minute you get here till the minute you fall asleep. Then you'll wake up – come to – and there will be more fun and then you will go away and I'll stay here and then it will be desperate shit again until I get back to town and we can all have a very good laugh about it. Tell you all when you get here. Do that fast. No waiting for glass slippers at midnight, Cinders.'

She was gone. Sudden silence from the earpiece.

Stoner walked to his heavy Transporter. Walked past it and on down the dark street. The dirty blonde sounded ropey but he doubted that her life was threatened by anything more than the traditional hazards of her occupation. He blipped the van's alarm from a hundred feet away. The Transporter grunted as its passenger's door unlocked, the diesel's glow plugs lit; the engine was ready to fire by the time he was sitting before the wheel, sliding the keycard into its slot, tapping in the code to override the alarms and the no-go status. Lights lit, engine running: Woodstock. Maybe an hour. No need for any speed. Plenty of time for precaution. She'd been there for more than a week, he doubted that an extra hour would damage her more than she was already damaged.

He couldn't pretend that he enjoyed being used, but she was only being herself. She was who she was and that was what he wanted her to be. At times like these Stoner needed to remind himself that this was the case. Had been the case for a long time now, although he still failed to understand the why of it.

Gravel crunched. The Transporter ground its heavy unsubtle way around a circular drive to the door of the parsonage. Passed the door and reversed across the drive. Parked facing the exit. Habit. Stoner climbed from the passenger door and slipped it shut behind him. The building was well lit; it looked like a Church of England parsonage should look, like it was a set on an American movie, a set dressed by someone who had watched too many English domestic detective programmes. It looked like a caricature of respectability; one seriously desirable residence.

The front door looked older than Henry VIII would have looked had he still been capable of looking like anything alive. Or which once had been alive. There was without a doubt a doorbell somewhere, but Stoner couldn't see it in the carefully posed Sherlock Holmes gloom under the misted Victorian overhead light. He was illuminated; none of the door furniture was. He could have designed that himself. Any CCTV would have him framed like the performer he felt like.

He hammered hard on the door. It was unmoved, and his hammering produced no response at all. He tried the handle before hammering again. He respected his hands. He could do better things with them than beat them against planks so heavy that they made hardly a sound. He wondered fleetingly whether beating his head against the door would have the same effect.

The handle turned, the door opened. Of course it did. This was rural England; no need at all for security. For visible security. The house's electronic brain would have good images of him. He would need to find that brain and . . . no point. If it was as sophisticated as it would be had he specified it himself, his image would already have been transmitted to his own equivalent in a security company and even now his identity would be whistling through the ethers. Within a few minutes – were he interested, which he might be – the Hard Man could know where he was. Which might or might not be important. But which was certainly a concern for another moment.

He walked inside. Into another film set. Another set-dresser's dream of the rooms English landed gentry liked to inhabit. It all looked genuine, so was most likely either genuine or very expensive fake. Stoner cared neither way. He cared about the dirty blonde, who called him through the doorway of the second room on his left as he penetrated the silent oaky hallway.

'Fuck first or story first?' As ever, subtlety was her strong suit.

Stoner faced her without smiling. 'Where am I? Who owns this place, and why are you all alone in it? Tell me that on the way to somewhere comfortable and a coffee. A hot coffee. Strong coffee. It's been a long day, and it's not getting easier.'

The dirty blonde sprang to her feet. She was less than Stoner's six feet three inches, but not a lot less. And she was a very different shape. She was wrapped in a robe which fell open as she stood. Stoner stared with resolve directly into her eyes. His peripheral vision advised that she was wearing only the robe. He thanked his peripheral vision for this excellent news and instructed it to go away.

'Don't be cross, JJ.' She ran the fingernails of both hands upward from the base of his crotch until those hands found the zipper and pulled it down, unhitching his belt with a sophistication of technique and an utter familiarity with male clothing which would have impressed a first-timer, anyone who didn't already know her well, into a state of wonder. Her left hand slid inside the open zip and squeezed the base of his cock through the cotton underwear.

'Please don't be cross. It's no problem for you. Just me doing what I do and trying to be something I'd like to be. Trouble is, I always do the same things. I always see the same way onward, and I always stay the same. This will be different. I hope.' She had freed him from his pants by now and was cruising the nails of her forefingers along the length of him. He still stared into her eyes.

'Make some sense, please?'

The dirty blonde began to sink before him. She looked him in the eye and parted her lips a little; rolled her tongue into view. He gripped her shoulders, gently but with resolve, and lifted her to her full height again. This was in fact the one hundred per cent opposite of what he most wanted at that point, but times, places; things that go bang in the night, persuaded him otherwise. The dirty blonde lifted her fingers from him, dropped her arms to her sides and gazed hard right back. He returned her hands to their task. 'Carry on. That's as good as ever. Just talk. I can listen and lust at the same time. Not all men can do this.'

She smiled.

'I have a client,' she began. 'Well. I have lots of clients, but this is a special one. You sure you don't need a little something? You do feel a bit urgent. Have you been missing me?'

'Talk. Just for the love of fucking, talk to me.'

Stoner sounded emotional. He was emotional. Vanishingly few folk could produce emotions in him. The blonde had always been able to do this. She had trouble not doing it. Which did have its moments. She held him in both of her long-fingered hands and massaged the underside of his glans with both thumbs. A lesser man might have died on the spot.

'My . . . client . . .' she began again.

'Your john. You needn't tell me who he is. If he's the guy who owns this place then I'll soon know who he is anyway. I didn't know you knew government people. It might be better for us all if I don't know who he is.'

Stoner's grip on his serious expression was hard to maintain. She squeezed and rubbed more; stood a little closer to him. He could smell nothing but her; feel nothing but her; hear nothing but her. His world was centred only on her. Which is a dangerous place to be.

'My john . . . thanks for that . . . I think you're right . . . asked me to come and stay. It's not the first time. I've known him for a while. He came to me from a recommend . . . or was it an agency?'

Stoner remarked with some tension that he didn't need history, he could get history on the History Channel; he simply wanted to know what she was doing here and why he was here too.

'He said he had important news for me. Good news. News I would like to hear. He is a . . . generous man. He pays very well, he is almost always polite and he is almost always clean. He brings me gifts . . .'

Once again Stoner suggested that brevity would be a bonus. Not least because things were becoming urgently messy in a personal way and he didn't want her to stop what she was doing but would need to stop her soon if he was to retain any pretence at focus. Losing focus in situations like this is usually the point at which the bad men wearing bad hair and bad suits and with bad intentions were most likely to appear and ruin his already tiring day. She stood closer to him; pressing her bare abdomen against the thumbs which were inflicting the damage. A lesser man might have wept at this point. Stoner struggled with his focus.

'He told me it was a family matter, and I could share his delight. I thought his son had won a Nobel Prize or his daughter had married a horse and produced prize-winning marrows or something. But no. No. He's thrown his wife out of this house and decided to divorce her. It's funny, but I'd never thought he had a wife. Seemed too . . . tough for that. I think she's keeping at least one of his other houses. He has several houses, you know, and . . .'

Stoner's strained suggestion was that she stick closer to the matter in hand. She smiled. She could appreciate wit.

'He wants me to live here. Forever. If I live here, then he'll give me this house for as long as I want it. He'll pay for it and he'll maintain it. There is a very large garden. I think I could like gardening. All his houses . . . I think . . . I've only seen three of them . . . Have large gardens. Which is a bit strange, because he's not very interested in . . .'

Stoner's demand that she get back to the plot was made through misting eyes and straining senses; she was moving briskly against him.

'He would like me to be his wife. But without the actual marriage thing. I don't believe he really wants a divorce. I think he just said that to sound good. So I'd take him seriously. I don't care about that bit. I knew you'd be really pleased. I know you don't enjoy what I do, but I do need to live. And I thought that I would give it a try for a bit and then surprise you. I could give up on the game and you could stop being angry about it, and we would get lots more time together and I can come with you and we can solve crimes together. That would be brilliant.

'Come on, come on, come on . . . that's better. You'll feel easier now. You were too tense. You are always too tense. There is no need to be tense with me.'

Stoner rocked on his feet. His sight steadied, as did his balance. A lesser woman would have reached for the tissues. The dirty blonde emptied him between them and rubbed herself against him, took her hands from him and ran them around his waist.

'Can you forgive me? Can you kiss me now? Can we go to bed now?'

'Where is he?' Stoner's equilibrium was returning. The moment for bad men in bad suits had passed and he felt more like kitchen for coffee than bedroom for a fuck.

'He's had to return . . .' she switched voices to a thickened BBC radio announcer's; '. . . m'lord has returned to the House. There is a committee or a conclave – what exactly is a conclave? – and he has to be there to make great big important decisions.' She smiled at Stoner. 'He's been whipped, he says. He always enjoys talking about whips but never uses one. Not with me, anyway. Back the day after tomorrow. Sorry; tomorrow now. He won't be early. He's never early. Have you noticed that people who think they're important expect everyone else to be early but never are themselves? Coffee?'

Stoner's cell phone shook in his pocket. He lifted it out, read the message, flicked it shut again and sighed.

She read him clearly; 'Wam bam, thank you mam. Off so soon, JJ?'

He rocked his head. 'Not yet. Not yet. Did you say something about coffee?'

She led him deeper into the house, into a world changing from fake ancient charm to modern honesty; a bright shining kitchen flickered fluorescently into view.

'Fresh or jug?'

Stoner went through phases where he took his coffee seriously. The dirty blonde had never understood why, but respected any oddity. It had often proved to be a professional strength. Stoner merely grunted. 'Hot. Wet. Black.' Nothing too complicated.

'You cross with me, JJ?'

For a moment, the dirty blonde looked serious. She could do this. Stoner wondered whether it was an act; how far from being another john was he, really? How far from the manipulations? Her serious look stabilised, steadied, still appeared sincere.

'Not cross, babe. Not angry. Just . . . concerned. You know how it is. I know how you are. You can control men, but not all men and not all the time.'

A familiar chorus. Familiarity eases tensions. Which is not always a great idea. He looked up at her. 'What do you want? You have a house, a home. You can stay there. Live there as you want. Call it your own. Do with it what you want. Decorate. I don't know. Anything. Isn't it . . . grand enough for you? Do you really want something . . . like this?' He spread his arms wide, taking in the whole gleaming brightness. 'Do you . . . I mean . . . do you even cook?'

She looked down. Looked at the immaculately expensive floor tiles. 'The house is nothing, JJ. The place I live is your house. It belongs to you. You can come and you can go. All the others living in the house pay you rent. Proper rent. You visit me in your house and your . . . friends come and go and I am furniture. Fucking furniture. Furniture you fuck. The fucking pays the real rent. I know how it is. I do this, don't I? I do this for money.' She was shouting, almost.

He looked as lost as he felt. And he felt anger rising, dully. 'You want to pay me more rent? Why?'

'Because then I'd be more than just your whore. I'm everybody's whore. Take the money out of it, JJ, and what's left? What is left?'

Stoner sank onto a stool. This was a familiar conversation. He was weary of it, and knew she was too. 'He'll be listening, y'know. Your lordly nightshade. Your would-be master. He'll have the place wired. Cameras too, most likely. Is he really a lord? A real lord?'

'Not sure. How would I know for sure? If you know who he

is, would that be a problem? Problem for us?' For a moment, the dirty blonde looked almost concerned. Sad, almost. Cautious.

Stoner pondered. 'I don't think so. Depends. I've certainly not been here before. I'd have remembered that. But I'll know the type of guys who do his security, and they'll all be good guys, efficient guys, and he'll want to know what goes on in his house and they'll know how to let him know. That's the way it is. Men in your lord's league always work like that. If he lets you alone in his house then he'll want to know you're not trashing it, not inviting in strange men, doing parties and stuff. He'll have watchers. It's no big deal. I don't think it's a big deal. Does he bring his work home? Does he talk work here? If he does, then he'll most likely record it. He's a minister, is he? Some serious high-up? The Hard Man might know him.'

'Yeah, yeah. That twat? Why is he always numero uno in your thoughts, JJ?' She was suddenly distracted. Off-track. 'Already you're talking about him. Again. He is one pig. One pig swilling with the other pigs like him. Dirty snouts fighting for the trough.' She sounded confused. Oddly worried. Nervous.

Stoner sighed. 'Oh, fuck this, babe. I didn't come here to fight. Why would you living here get us closer? That's all I want to know. I give you all the room you want.'

His cell phone called for him again. He ignored it. As soon as his phone ceased its urgency another phone began to blast out bad music; a phone on one of the shining cutting blocks in the gleaming kitchen. They both looked up, both said 'You get it' in unison, both smiled. Stoner picked it up and thumbed the green icon. Listened. Sat down again, heavily. Said nothing. Flicked the device silent.

'Hope you enjoy being a film star,' he said, raising eyebrows high enough to peer through them at her. She smiled back, dropped her robe to the floor, rubbed her breasts and performed a stately twirl for the unseen eyes.

'Oh, I've done porn. Everybody films themselves fucking these days. Everybody. They got audio here as well?' Her gaze drifted to Stoner, who nodded.

'You know him? The security man?'

Stoner nodded again.

'So m'lord doesn't have to hear why I'd be doing this with you? I can negotiate with security. If you want me to?' She simpered in a professional way.

'Not worth the bother. If he's inviting you to stay here ... to live here, then he'll make conditions, I expect. But you'd have to agree to them first. Probably. I don't know. Not my top subject, this. I just don't see how it's an improvement for you over what you've got. But you don't need to explain it. Just make up your mind, do what you want to do. It's best. You want to pretend to be lady someone, then do it. Just do it. Sort out what you want, tell me and we'll work it out. But you knew that, yes? And ...' he sighed, 'it would probably be best if I keep away from him.'

She nodded.

'There's a price.' Stoner sounded suddenly serious.

'There always is, JJ, but ... not with you, not with me. What is it?'

'If you get serious with him, just tell me. I don't want to know anything else from this point on. You live here and act like his ... consort or whatever. I can handle that. You start having ... feelings, tell me and I'll step outside for a while. Promise?'

She walked to his side and reached for his hand. Held it. Squeezed it. Pulled him with her through the house.

And in the lonely midnight ...

'JJ?'

'Mmmm'

'Can they hear me, us, too?'

'What? Who?'

'M'lord Posh; can he hear us now? In the dark?'

'Dunno. Depends. On what he wants to hear.'
'If you'd done his set-up, would you set it to hear us now?'
'Yep.'
'JJ?'
'Mmmm?'
'Thanks.'

Stoner sleeps like the dead man he will one day become. Unconcerned. Untroubled. Uncomplicated. Pretty much the only time he sleeps like this is when the dirty blonde sleeps beside him. He tries not to recognise this, to be unaware of it. He just accepts that given the chance he would sleep like this, like the dead man he will one day become, every night.

His cell phone flashes its summons into the warmth and the dark of the piled clothes, discarded along with them. It silently cries into the night many times, with decreasing frequency. No one hears it, no one sees its urgency.

In the darkness, her skin is almost invisibly dark, just a dull gleam; a small gloss moment in a dark mass. Her hair is a golden cap reflecting the tiny light. Like a halo. Like a crown of pale thorns in the darkness.

17

GREEN LIGHT

Driving. Driving again. This time into the big city itself. Endless demands from the Hard Man that they meet, that they resume their several interrupted conversations. Stoner could see little purpose to this. Both he and the Hard Man subscribed to the manwatcher's theory that the full content of any serious conversation was available only when all the parties to that conversation were in direct line of sight, sound and sensation of each other, but there was nothing new nor meaningful to discuss since their last conversation. Telephone conversations, text messages, email and loudhailers all had their limitations, but any one of those simple, two-dimensional media would have been fine for two folk to agree that nothing had happened. Nothing relevant. Nothing important.

An agreement to say something only when there was something to say was their normally preferred way of working. Less babble, less background, less clutter. More focus, more opportunity to talk about, something worthwhile.

Today his physical presence was in demand. It could be an irritation, but the invitation would be hard to decline.

The heavy Transporter ploughed its way through light traffic and shrugged off anything bigger with disdain. It was a comfortable way to travel. Quiet, the big engine insulated behind walls of sound-absorbency and performing its motive function in a typically efficient Teutonic way. A lesser advantage of fitting an engine with around three times the original unit's performance was that the engine was never working hard at any even faintly legal road speed. It idled along major roads in a high gear, no stress, less effort, little noise and no vibration at all. The drive train and the engine's mountings were specified to handle that engine at full bellow, and at a gentle canter they transmitted no sign of the engine's presence into the driver's domain.

Peter Green's distinctively thin Gibson soloing leaked from several speakers into the hush of the cabin. His weary, world-stained voice wondered why; why don't you give it up, bring it home to me, write it on a piece of paper, baby, so it can be read to me ... Stoner's thoughts wandered uselessly between the previous night and the approaching meet, between fleshy pleasure and fleshy pain, wondering and wandering with an atypical absence of focus. He had nothing to say to the Hard Man, and the Hard Man could have nothing to say that he wanted to hear.

He swung the Transporter from the main road to a suburban cluster, drifting towards his own part of town, watching mirrors as was his habit. No one following. No menace. Nothing to worry about. Stoner was almost puzzled by this. His presence in the parsonage had certainly been recorded as well as observed, by uncertain friends if not by actual foes. His was a small world, manipulated by the media which described and defined it.

A quiet suburban car park, then. The Transporter was as secure as a vehicle can be. Silently locked, silently alarmed, waiting in silence for its pilot to reappear. If vehicles could boast character, then the Transporter would be stoic, dozing doglike dreams maybe, of oil changes and chases, the sudden sprint and the pounce, the growl and the gripping, hanging on.

Stoner slid from the passenger door, slipped into a fast stride away from his house, crossed the road. Stopped. Sat on a wall, flipped open his cell phone, made a clown's exaggerated performance of reading and sending text messages. Sent not one in fact, but several in fantasy, face pointing hard at the small screen while eyes and ears watched around him.

Nothing. Background noise, the chatter of the living, the mindless random of everyday life. No obviously false patterns and no obvious interruptions to the pointless performance of suburban existence. Folk doing what folk do. As always, Stoner wondered what it was that they did, and why they would choose to do it. But not for long. Life is too short to wonder about the lives of others. Those, the many others, that is. Individuals are more interesting, and stand out from the crowd. There were no obvious individuals nearby. No one of obvious interest.

He walked fast alongside an old wall, mortar and tired brick. A wall of a long-gone building, now a wall containing nothing, hiding nothing apart from Stoner, who strode with the ease and confidence of the long-distance walker toward his own house, a house he claimed to inhabit, but which was not and never had been his home. The dirty blonde lived there, although she was currently waiting for someone to claim her in their own home. Mr Tran lived there, along with a volatile and transient array of companions, fellow travellers and those on the run. And the techno prisoners could often be found nearby, hooked in, as they often were, to Mr Tran's companionable caravanserai. Stoner owned the house. His name was writ loud on papers supporting this view, but it was never home, not for him.

The habitual paranoia of his trade found him approaching his house more than once and from more than one direction. For no reason he could express, he wished his whereabouts to be less than public knowledge for a while. Privacy felt prudent. The old wall was cut by a doorway. Stoner pushed through it, latched it behind him. Ran down a short descent of steps to a cellar door, pushed through that and latched it behind him. Complex gimmick locks are great for the movies; a deadbolt is dead simple and dead reliable. There is no silent way to defeat a deadbolt, no way to break in without attracting attention. Underrated, deadbolts and latches.

Mr Tran was waiting for him. Stoner had no clue how this could be. If he wanted to see Mr Tran, to talk with him, then Mr Tran would be waiting for him with oriental patience; if he had no wish to see Mr Tran, then Mr Tran would be nowhere to be found. Another mystery skill, one of many hidden within the quiet Vietnamese features.

'You have been to see Missy.' It was not a question. 'She is well.' Neither was that. Mr Tran was practising making statements in English, which was neither his first nor his second language. 'You are working a case for that man.' No questions today. This was a day of statements.

'I am.' Stoner agreed.

Mr Tran bowed slightly, recognising the reply as the truth that it was. 'Tea.' He led Stoner through into his own rooms, walking in silence as if it were natural, which it might be among Vietnamese, and leaving the door open behind them. Stoner turned to close it; Mr Tran prevented this with a raised hand and a smile. 'Your telephone.' He held out his left hand. Stoner dropped the phone into that open hand, which opened the phone, flicked the green key. Nothing. No glimmer of electronic life. Stoner dropped the battery into that open hand. Mr Tran smiled and returned both cell phone and power cell to their owner.

'Are you a happy man, Mr Stoner?' A question at last, albeit an unexpected one. 'I am told otherwise. She . . . cares for you. Cares about you. She wishes to pay you rent.'

At this point, a lesser man than Stoner may have stared open-mouthed and incredulous. Stoner was not that man. Nothing, nothing at all was reflected in his face.

'And the people with whom you wish to speak are on their way here.' Another statement. Excellent English. Mr Tran's eyes, the remote eyes which kept watch on others, were less easy to observe than more conventional eyes. Stoner recognised that Mr Tran was not only inscrutable but also invisible, accepted this and accepted the tea. It pays to be polite. 'Menace and Mallis,' confirmed Mr Tran. 'They know you well. And you them also, I believe.' Statements. Always statements.

Stoner supplied a statement of his own. 'Rarely met them. But they are excellent to work with. The techno prisoners. Masters of all things digital.'

'As all should be, Mr Stoner.' Mr Tran poured, gracefully. 'But few are in fact. A common weakness and an unnecessary one. Digital affairs are simple enough for very unintelligent folk to master them. Very many very unintelligent inadequate individuals are indeed masters of many things digital. It is real life which is complex and subtle. Digital binary yes and no endlessly ... mere fools can handle that.'

Stoner accepted both tea and wisdom with an equable smile and a gentle and appropriately slight bow. 'Understanding how to formulate the questions which require and accept the simple yes or no answer ... that is the subtle and the difficult business. I find that Menace and Mallis are excellent at sorting meaningful questions from the meaningless mess of other people's lives.'

Mr Tran bowed gently in return. 'Reducing many of life's variables to the question which will accept only a yes or no answer? Philosophers have passed many ages with that one, I think. The tea cools. It is to your liking?'

'Everything cools in the end, Mr Tran.' Stoner drank slowly and with appropriately obvious appreciation. 'Death cools everything in the end.'

'And cool music provides warmth. Missy is a sympathiser to your own music. She praises it. She plays it when she is alone. She is proud to know you, and to be your friend. As you sometimes appear to misunderstand. Which allows a heated sadness to enter her life, which is unfortunate, because her life, although filled with love-making is not filled with love. Your music is filled with violence ... to my ears. Amplified music has no subtlety, no art. But it drowns pure music, as violence destroys peace. Violence will destroy all of our lives if we allow that, Mr Stoner. If we fail to understand what violence is. That violence is weakness. It is always weakness.'

This was a colossally long speech for the usually almost silent Mr Tran. Stoner carefully, silently and precisely replaced his empty cup upon its saucer, gazed upon Mr Tran's calm features.

Said nothing.

Mr Tran rewarded his acceptance with a smile.

'I lost a war when the USA left my country. I lost my home. I lost most that I held true and dear to me. Violence had destroyed the land and the people who lived upon that land. I was unable to return to my land because the USA lost its war with China. The violence of the Chinese was greater than the violence of the USA.' Mr Tran looked up from his tea and smiled. 'And now I have it back. I am welcome in my land once more. The greater violence has indeed proved to be the weakness. The USA continues to lose its world in its struggle with China, and both of them have forgotten me. And my own country. Their violence has left us. They have moved their battle to another ground.'

'You're going to return, then? To your home?'

'No. My return could cause both of those most violent nations to remember a former fighting ground. There is never a need to resume an old struggle. In any case, I do return. Regularly. It is a land of beauty. But of limited opportunities for me. At this stage in this life of mine.' Mr Tran smiled. 'What was lost to me when the USA left my land is forever lost. To me. That loss is also a gain, to me. Everything balances, as you know, Mr Stoner. Fighting against that balance achieves only a loss of energies, a loss of opportunities and the acquisition of perpetually complicated enemies. Which is a lesson unlearned by your usual, your current employer. He knew it all at one time, but has stripped himself of that learning in his quest for greater understandings of smaller details. He cannot be an easy man to work for. I can see no reason why I would work for him. For example.'

Mr Tran looked across the low table with a chill smile directly into Stoner's gaze. 'Working with you, Mr Stoner, is not a problem for me. Living in your house is an honour for me. I am pleased at the opportunities for balance which accompany our relationship.' He looked down at the drying cups. And looked up suddenly.

'Our guests are here. They await.'

He led the way into the rear of his apartment, into a set of three rooms which Stoner had never visited before, despite having been the property's owner for several years. He had inherited Mr Tran along with other sitting tenants when he'd acquired the properties, and there had never been an incentive to either intrude or to evict.

Siblings. Maybe twins. Maybe almost identical twins. Maybe brother and sister. Maybe they were unrelated, although that seemed like the least appealing option, the least likely. Menace and Mallis, the self-anointed techno prisoners. Digital gurus of the highest calibre. Permanently unemployed and in receipt of state benefits; permanently occupied and high-earning data delvers; digital deliverance almost guaranteed. No find, no fee. Failures always welcomed; the only way to earn is to learn and the only way to learn is to err. Which possibly made them human, although they made few efforts to appear conventionally so.

'Mr Tran.' A pale-skin androgyne spoke softly. No meeting of eyes, no handshakes. Matt black straight hair in a long loose ponytail, dark downcast eyes, black clothes, the speaker was wearing a black long-sleeved T-shirt with a ghostly image of a ghostly well-washed waterfall. Mallis, then. Probably.

'Stoner.' The other seldom spoke. No eye contact, no direct acknowledgement other than a rare vocal interjection. The T-shirt with a pair of washed-out semiquavers dimly visible. Menace. Probably.

Stoner's tension, temporarily defeated by the Vietnamese calm, returned. He could feel a headache arriving, like the clouds of storms on his mental horizons.

'Murders. Bad ones. Several. Can you help?' They either could and would, or could and would not. Conflicts of interest could too easily be fatal in their shared world.

Mallis spoke. 'Yes. Provisionally.' Menace looked up briefly. 'Depends on what you want and who you want it for.'

Stoner ran through the series of deaths. Mr Tran stood by a window, fingered the opaque lace curtains in shadowed silence.

Mallis spoke again. 'When did you last speak with Shard? Are you working this together or in opposition?'

'There is no opposition between Shard and me. No conflict.'

'But there should be. Shard has already entered this investigation, Stoner. Did he talk with you of his own concerns in this . . . this . . . common interest?'

'He did. He thinks he's being set up to take the blame. He says he's not the killer. I believe him in this; he has no reason to lie. Not to me. I want you to link the victims. The way through this mess is through the victims. The fact that there appears to be no link is in itself a linkage. Given the similarities of the attacks and their characteristics it seems impossible that there is no link. Find that link for me and I'll be on my way.'

'There must be a fee.'

'Of course there must be. At this point I've got so little to go on that any assistance you can provide would be of great value, and I'd pay accordingly. You'd not over-charge.' He smiled. 'You never have before.'

Menace was talking inaudibly with their Vietnamese host. Mallis looked up; looked directly at Stoner. 'I know some of this, but only because of my conversations with Shard. Shard and yourself, Stoner, carry equal weight with us. I'll want him to confirm that you are not in conflict. Will he do that for me?'

Stoner nodded. He couldn't imagine where their loyalties lay at the best of times. Their priority was rarely money, which Stoner understood perfectly well, and it didn't seem to be anything personal. The techno prisoners appeared to operate on a private internal code, and were well-known in the shadowy community for their refusal to work against the interests of their friends. Unhappily, only they knew who their friends were, and, more importantly, who were not their friends. They didn't hand out convenient badges or issue press statements.

But they were tools, tools of the trade, the techno prisoners. Tools like a sophisticated and intelligent search engine. It was not easy to become emotionally connected with a search engine. Even if it did have a near-identical partner and wear Goth punk blacks left over from the 1990s.

'OK. How can I help?' Mallis again. The dim conversation between Menace and Mr Tran had concluded.

Stoner had asked himself the same question. Until he'd arrived to his own mild surprise on Mr Tran's doorstep he had been unaware of a need to involve anyone else in what he considered was most likely to be a fairly straightforward investigation. The number of freelance professional killers in any country is small, and although freelance work was hardly uncommon the usual suspects were usually the usual suspects because they usually did the killings. Stoner's intent had been based around the well-worn and well-proven elimination of the innocent. When the innocent have been eliminated, the guilty will always be among the remainder.

The problem of course is that if the guilty party was not included in your list of the usual suspects then the process of elimination could eliminate . . . well . . . everyone on the list.

'There's a connection between the victims.' Stoner sounded almost confident, at least to his own ears.

'You already said that. It may be true. Are you intending to convince me or yourself by repetition? No one is eavesdropping this conversation so you can't be intent upon convincing a third party.' Dealing with Mallis could be an oblique process.

'Just thinking aloud.' Stoner was indeed thinking. Why would anyone eavesdrop, and why would Mallis wish to emphasise that they were not? 'I have stats and stuff on the victims. You'll want them. How do you want them? How much time do we have here, today?'

Mallis surprised him, not for the first time. 'I'd prefer to uncover facts fresh. Keep what you've been told separate from what we tell you. Compare what you know with what we tell you. That way you may discover routes to a more fulfilling reality. A greater understanding. I'm not being deliberately mysterious, Stoner, far from it. If Shard is actually as concerned by this as he appears to be, then it's something bigger than a bunch of butchered bodies. Shard is not a guy to fret about a few stiffs, a mutilation or two. He is not one to be over-concerned about you, either. I want to start from the overlap between you and Shard. I reckon that there is more to that than is plain to me at the moment. But you're right. There is a link between the dead. And if there isn't . . . if they're random somehow, then that is more remarkable than if they turn out to be blood relatives. I hesitate to say this, knowing your loyalties, but I would also consider the motives of your own employer. Does he . . . *is* he, setting you out as a target, for example? That was one of Shard's initial considerations. You know already that you are going to be presented with information suggesting that Shard is in some way involved in these killings. You may already have this data?'

He paused. Stoner shook his head.

'Be ready for it. The form it takes and the source will be interesting in themselves. The data will be false, but a truth will be available in the manner and method of the delivery.' Mallis was plainly happy in his work.

'The murder websites? The sites with the movies?'

'Genuine. Not a concern. I know the provider and the purpose of the sites.'

'Are there several of the things?'

'Yes. But the main one, murdermayhemandmore.com is the central source. It's a fansite for crime fiction freaks.' Hearing Mallis judging other web-dwellers as freaks was a minor entertainment. 'There's been a lot of fan chat and fiction forum stuff on there for a while, judging by the site histories, but only the last couple of entries have displayed actual real-time footage of genuine body parts. It's refreshingly different. It may even catch on. Become something common. Beats endless football as a visual treat for the mindless masses.' Delivered in a deadpan voice.

'Contacts, data? Where do you want it, and how do you want it?' Stoner was always aware of security; his own and others.

Mallis grinned; a faintly unsettling sight. 'The murder website?'

Stoner nodded.

Mallis again. 'The site has a message board. It's unregulated, unmoderated so far as I can see. Packed with fools. You hunter; me seeker. When I have something I'll post a cell number for you to call. You can do the same. Got a collection of sim cards?' Stoner agreed that he did. 'Add the reverse date to the end of the name, so we'll know. Today's the eighth; seeker80. It's not obvious, except to us.'

'Fee?' Stoner repeated himself. Mallis shook his head.

'Later. If it's easy we'll do a reciprocal, if it's not we'll talk further.'

'Shard, then. Does he use the same arrangement on the message board?'

'That,' Mallis was expressionless, 'would be too much knowledge at this stage. Ask him.'

As if by signal, Mr Tran appeared at Stoner's side; Menace turned away, walked rapidly to his partner. They left the room.

'No long goodbyes.' Mr Tran's day of statements was continuing.

18

JUST LOOK AT US . . .

'Just look at them all.' Stoner was talking, tuning, wickedly aware of the open microphone. 'Where do they all come from?'

'It's a lyric, hey?' Bili leaned over her long-suffering long-scale Rickenbacker bass and popped an open-A harmonic, sociably enough, listening as Stoner tuned to it. 'All the lonely people?'

'Why do they all come here?' Stoner was picking harmonics of his own, micro-tuning the elderly Stratocaster in an inevitably doomed attempt at lining all of its six strings up in tune at the same time, all the better to play some vigorous blues. 'Surely their lives would be more complete if they sat at home watching some unreality show on the TV? Or is it nuts' night out at the nuthouse?'

Faces in the audience were smiling. They would be the regulars, the regulars who understood the floor show. Other faces displayed a lot less amusement. They might get the joke. Or they might instead get the hump and leave. Their loss.

'They come for the lessons.' Bili snagged her cascade of curls into a tangle, loosely restrained by a scrunchie. 'They come here for the free education. They come here for the sparkling wit, playful repartee and almost free booze. And most of all, they come here so they can try to answer the greatest riddle known to modern man.'

She was knocking out a steady common time beat against her bass E-string.

'Forget nuclear fusion. Forget the mysteries of the pyramids. They come to learn, man; they come to learn the answer to the lastest greatest mystery; how long can one man take to keep his bloody guitar so perfectly out of tune?'

Applause. Stoner rattled a few glasses with a growl of bass string feedback; the elderly Fender fizzing in his fingers as its strings resonated to Bili's more beefy bass, an octave below his own. She had added a counter-beat to her rhythm pattern, picking a second E an octave above her first and alternating with it; first finger and forefinger alternating and matching on the heavy strings. Stoner switched between the Fender's pick-ups, selecting the middle of the three then winding its tone control back with his right-hand little finger, then lifting the volume to compliment the throb of the big bad bass guitar.

'I've been rollin' and tumblin' . . .' Bili's over-amplified voice startled the audience. She'd sung straight into the microphone; nothing half-heard here, just the full smack of the words. 'Cried the whole night long.'

Stoner's guitar scratched a rhythm; some strings sounding crisply through the muffle of the heel of his right hand, which deadened their resonance. He was picking the strings with his fingernails, the flat pick tucked away behind the guitar's scratch plate, ready for use, should the song head that way.

'And when I woke up this mornin', all I had was gone.' Bili tossed her head and stood up, slinging the big bad bass guitar into a better position and beating its strings with renewed vigour. Stoner remained leaning against his high stool, watching her more than listening. He knew the song; he had little idea of where she would take it tonight. She walked away from the microphone,

211

singing out a high-crying yeah . . . trailing from audible sound as she walked away from the audience, moving her left hand higher up the guitar's long, long neck until she was picking out a harmony to Stoner's battering rhythm, a neat exercise in role-reversal, one which would be recognised by the regulars, who were used to four-string guitar solos and appreciated the burst of creativity which they demonstrated.

Newcomers were welcome to join in the appreciation, although few would. Bass guitar solos are fairly rare, and are viewed by some as an acquired taste.

Bili was playing way up the neck now, pulling and bending the strings as well as slapping them hard against the fretboard and then pulling them away from it, letting them snap back with an explosive percussive punctuation to Stoner's solid, scratching, too-treble accompaniment.

A set of descending triplets and she was quite suddenly back at the microphone, back face-to-face with the audience, who were by now stamping and stomping and even clapping a little as six-string Fender and four-string Rickenbacker snapped their waves of rhythms together.

'If the river was whiskey . . .' Bili beamed at a regular who had threaded his way to the bar, recognising where the song was leading. 'And I was a diving duck . . .' She bobbed her head, walked back a few paces, leaving more room to swing the long bass neck again, completing the verse and hammering halfway into the next one with the instrument talking instead of her voice. Stoner smiled and scouted the edge of the stage, half-wondering whether more instruments would be joining them. Not this time.

Halfway into the verse, then: 'I'd swim right to the bottom, Drink myself back up.' The small woman and the big guitar bounced together through another verse of purely improvised duet with Stoner watching, listening and waiting for his cue for some closing chords. None came.

212

'That's it!' Bili just stopped.

Stoner stared wide-eyed. He'd stopped at exactly the same moment, unbidden and for no reason he could understand. Utterly and unconsciously in tune with his companion. Where there had been a bouncing, rollicking beat of blues there was now the silence. Followed by a pause . . . then the applause. Followed by Bili accepting a bow and a multiple measure of spirits from a hand in the audience.

'Why do they come here?' Stoner was laboriously pretending to re-tune his Fender. 'It's bloody noisy sometimes. Can't hear to tune this bloody thing. Not that anyone would notice . . .'

'It's the cheap beer.' Bili beamed at the audience who'd supplied a long drink. Bili beamed, the audience looked away, flattered but a little sheepish, too. It's as though they had made an offering to a minor deity of some kind, only for the godling to pay attention, look up and say thanks. That never happens in religion, making music a better bet for those of a generous and worshipful disposition.

'I do believe that it is the sheer art of it all.' Stoner leaned back against his stool and watched carefully as Stretch eased himself into the piano player's seat. Stretch was a big man, but delicate and subtle with his hands. He lifted heavy eyes across the piano's scratched lid, and breathed heavily into the open microphone above his keyboard.

'They come, my man, for inspiration. They come from a world of desperation and despair, keen to share with the Cube's bright and optimistic vision of a future powered entirely by the blues and the booze. A world . . . they seek a world where all that matters is that the booze flows and the blues follows it, faithful, like a hound. Faithful, like love following beauty. Faithful . . .'

'Christ!' Bili pointed the long slim neck of her bass at the wide pianist. 'Are you going to peddle philosophy? I bet these guys chose to pay us a visit to learn familiarity and understanding

213

of the piano hammerer's take on the world. Christ, man, they'd get more sense from ...' she paused for effect '... from a drummer.'

'A drummer?' Stretch and Stoner chorused like the well-practised act they were, while the former kicked off into an instrumental version of a tune so often stolen and plagiarised by generations of jazz club musicians that no one could be certain what the words were until someone started singing them. No one sang. Bili and Stoner chugged along following the piano's leadership and the audience forgot whatever it was they were escaping, avoiding and evading by sitting and sharing expensive drinks in a grubby club late into the night.

Stretch shifted key twice and the guitars followed. Shifted time signature twice, unannounced, and they followed that too. The audience shared the stormy passage. Stretch started to sing, in the wrong key for his voice but with considerable force; 'There is ... a house ... in New Orleans'. Got no further than that; the key was perfect for Bili and she picked up at the second line, howling the verses through slitted watering eyes while the piano ground through its chording and Stoner appeared to drift. He picked up a pint glass of tap water from beside his stool and sank it all, raised the empty vessel to his companions and relieved Bili of the lead spot. It's a good tune to jam to, for guitars and pianos and almost anything else, and the jam lasted for a half hour, shifting key once more before it returned home and Bili howled the last verse as though she really meant it, as might have been the case.

The audience added their own appreciation, and applauded Stretch as he took a bow and introduced both himself and his venue and his fellow musicians.

'Now walk', he instructed them. 'Now is the time for a little ivory magic.'

And so he proved it to be.

Bili headed off to the table of the free drinks provider, who shot comically to his feet, bursting with surprise and delight to be so honoured. Stoner laid his Fender into its case, wiped down the strings, and walked to the bar.

'Your boss,' announced the Chimp, the perfect bartender, 'is not your friend. He leaves you messages. They are not sweet little love notes. Increasingly they are not. I have promised him that should you appear, no matter what the hour and no matter your condition, I will demand that you call him. Immediately and at once. If not sooner. Do you have a problem?'

Stoner shook his head. 'No more than the usual. Missing persons, you know how it is.'

Chimp did not, of course, although he may have suspected. 'Even for him, quiet man that he is not, he is being insistent. Not aggressive, but that condition is approaching fast, I think. Call him. Why not?'

'Why not? How long have you got? How many reasons would you like?' Stoner waved a hand towards the bar. 'A drink while I think? Anything will do. Water would be best. Water makes lions strong, y'know. Failing that, whisky runs it a decent second. Has a package landed here for me? Maybe something you needed to sign for? Addressed to me? Looking – y'know – important? Personal? For me?'

The Chimp shrugged his shoulders, shook his head, handed over a padded bag, and reached for an industrially proportioned bottle of sparkling water. '"Water is the strong stuff. It carries whales and ships . . ."'

'"But water is the wrong stuff, don't let it get past your lips."' Stoner knew the same song. As indeed did Bili, who had appeared at his side. '"It rots your boots and wets your suits, puts aches in all your bones; dilute the stuff with whisky, aye, or leave it well alone,"' they chorused, to the bemusement of customers, audience and musicians alike.

215

Glasses clinked. Bili spat out her first mouthful. 'It's bloody water!'

'Of course it is. Stoner has a call to make.'

Stoner tipped a cell phone, a note and some spare batteries from the bag into his hand. He sighed, read the note, sighed once more and dropped phone and batteries into a pocket.

Bili turned to him. 'The blonde? Your blushless paramour? A new romance? Your new fan from last night is here somewhere. At least she was a moment ago. Where, where, where she gone?' Bili pointed at a bottle. It was uncertain exactly which of the many she was pointing at. 'Fill me up, o Chimp. Make my life complete. The muse for my blues comes from a bottle. Like a genie. Rub, rub, rub, pour, pour, pour and kabam! Express solos are us. The blonde, JJ? She running you around as usual? I wish she would stop that. Or that you would stop trailing after like that two-dicked dog.'

'Nah. Not her. The boss. Knickers twisted into more than their usual knot.'

'You know why? If it's urgent maybe you should call.'

Chimp had gone back to keeping bar, Bili was acting as temporary conscience.

Stoner sipped. 'Another missing person. Thing is, I don't know why he's pestering. I've done no real work on this yet – although I did agree that I would. Wheels in motion, vague stuff like that. He knows that but is still pestering. Not like him, truly.'

Stoner maintained a legend; a nebulously vague but consistent story that he was a private investigator who specialised in finding missing folk. He was never specific. Never entirely honest, but never entirely dishonest, either. And he was a fairly private man anyway. So folk tended not to ask. It is a minor oddity of folk in general that they are more usually curious about themselves than about others. Very often, when they quiz nosily into another's affairs it is a competition thing. They want to see where they fit.

216

They want confirmation that they are successful in whichever parts of their lives they value, and a way of confirming their supposed success is to delve into the lives of others and run a comparison. Sometimes out loud, depending upon their levels of self-confidence and intoxication. Stoner almost always deliberately failed in comparisons of this kind. He rarely competed with most other men. Most other men had nothing, did nothing, he would value, so he was unrewarding in competitive conversation.

And he could . . . and would . . . talk for as long as anyone could want on his favourite subjects. Although most men know that a Harley-Davidson is a large American motorcycle, and that a Fender Stratocaster is a guitar, and that the blues is a kind of music, few of them could compete with Stoner's considerable knowledge on those subjects. So they usually retreated to discussing politics, football, beer and women, at which point Stoner could always pretend ignorance.

'So call him. Cut the crap out of the way and we can stretch some strings, hey?' Bili often talked sense, even when her grip on the real world was compromised by alcoholic intake.

Stoner dug the new cell phone from pocket and flicked it to life. Nothing. Not a glimmer. He dug a battery from the pocket and fitted it, causing snorts from his companion.

'Wow, JJ! What kind of super-asshole takes the battery out of their phone! Man! You worried about those black helicopters?'

Stoner rolled his eyes, thumbed the button to call the only number in the phone's address book. It was picked up at once. Stoner walked steadily and with deliberation to the rear exit, his favourite entrance, too, but doors work both ways.

'Where've you been? Never mind. You're where? At the club? OK. No need to leave. Just important to know where you are.' The Hard Man viewed his troops as pieces on a board and moved them impersonally sometimes. 'There's another fucking body. It's getting insane. Can you hear me yet?'

Stoner had left the raucous environs of the club, the door had swung closed and only city background chatter interfered with the one-sided conversation.

'It's a cop this time. Another hotel. You can't go look yet, so enjoy your evening. It's someone we know, I think. Not so messy but more personal.'

'A cop?' Stoner was surprised. Killing police was usually so counterproductive from any criminal's perspective that it was a rare event. 'Who was it? Where?'

'Near Oxford. Nice of you to be in touch. One question: you keeping this phone switched on or do I need to send someone to collect you?'

Stoner agreed to leave his pocketful of electronics in an active condition, and they both hung up. There was no obvious winner in the hang-up race, either.

A click.

A metallic mechanistic click. A mechanism.

Stoner slipped to the wall. Into shadow. No weaponry to hand. No sense of presence. No clue that he was not alone in the yard. Internal flinching as he recognised that he was not watching. Had not been watching. Caught. Unawares. The light click; a safety catch. He tensed in his shadow. The light click; again. This time the lighter lit and it flared and it lit its target cigarette. In the brief bright flare he saw a tall woman. Blonde, very blonde. Then all he could see was the dim glow of the cigarette.

'Nice playing, mister music man.' The blonde voice matched the hair. 'You do your reputation no harm.'

Shadows shifted and pooled, the haze from the doorway and the scattering of starlight did the view no good at all. None at all.

Stoner was not at ease. He could not have missed her leaving the club to enter the yard behind him. He could not have missed her entering the yard from the silent street. He was neither deaf nor blind, simply dangerously distracted, which was as bad as a combination of the other two. Or she had been there through the whole of his phone conversation. He silently eased further into shadow. A woman who could move cat-silent was a concern. He could see an outline behind the leading light of the cigarette. Which did not phase in its brightness. It was not being smoked. It was an announcement, then. A marker. Perhaps.

'Oh. Thanks. OK . . .'

The bar door opened, the dark was damaged and Stoner's retreat into platitude was shattered by Bili's eruption from the door and her flight across the yard to its centre, where she stopped. The door closed. Darkness blinded again.

There was no cigarette glow. None.

'Hey hey, JJ.' Bili was turning slowly on her feet, arms stretched wide as a tightrope walker. Her eyes gleamed a little with reflected starlight. Stoner wondered how that could be when he had been utterly unaware of the other woman, the blonde woman, the smoking woman. He slid to Bili's side, tapping her shoulder from behind. She span, and fell against him. He caught her of course. And there they stood. Silent. Motionless. Daring to breathe. Staring. The light in the sky was the light in her eyes. Stoner found her beauty intolerable. She hung from him, turned her face up to his, eyes reflecting the infinity above. He leaned lower, kissed the top of her head. Slowly. For a while.

'We making more music, babe? You calling me back inside?'

Bili looked silently into him, turned, and with a 'Yeah. Whatever . . .' trailed back to the door. Her silent body slouched, displaying whole unspoken chapters of misunderstandings in its own unmistakeable language. Stoner watched her walking away from him.

The blues come from the heart, straight from the heart – sometimes.

19

HELLO DARKNESS . . .

'The geometry of violence has always been a particular fascination.'

Stoner slipped into the shadows, silent, listening, feeling for the dark.

No outward signs of intrusion. No lights where there should be no lights; no darknesses where darknesses were abnormal; none darker than they should have been. Stoner's tradecraft was endless, relentless, excellent and plainly inadequate. The clue had been olfactory. No sight, no sound out of place. Until the short speech, delivered with humour. No menace. Stoner sank into a squat beneath the vague haze from the blacked-out window which was leaking a little light for exactly this situation. The shadow was deep, deeper against a faint haze of light than on its own. Contrasts could be killers. He sat in a comfortable squat, easy, relaxed. He knew the voice, was unthreatened by the voice. But unsettled by its presence. Here.

'People always study the causes, the effects, the reasons, the results, techniques and consequences. Only easterners recognise the potential beauty in the unique opportunities of violence.'

The trigger had been an aroma, the alarm intended to both reassure and unbalance.

Stoner stood up, slipped silently into the shadow at the side of the dim window. Spoke, then squatted once more.

'You brought your own blend, friend? This is serious stuff. And you even took time to grind it.' He injected a tone of awe into his voice. Delivery otherwise flat and even. Unhurried and unworried.

A single light clicked. A reading light illuminated Stoner's favourite reading chair. Shard sat motionless facing him. One hand held palm-out, the other holding a beaker. He was unsmiling as well as unmoving, and he looked exhausted.

'Pax, JJ. And an apology for the intrusion. The coffee is a gift, and there's a kilo of beans less a single cup. We need more talking. And we need to reach an understanding.'

'What was that crap about geometry?' Stoner stalked grimly into the light. 'Anyone else here I should know about? Your funny friends with garrottes and the Geronimo approach to relation-ships? Shouldn't you have brought a box of almost inedible choco-lates?'

Shard remained seated, in as unthreatening a pose as he could manage. Stoner continued; 'And how did you break in? I'll need to fix that.'

'You will. I didn't break anything, although I am about to. Break something. Break a trust. I entered through the front door, and I used a key.'

'I do have a problem, then.' Stoner stalked in thought to the coffee tackle. Measured beans. Ground beans. Boiled water.

'You do. Do you run to a refill? It is good, and it wasn't cheap.' Shard was holding out the beaker. His expression was too serious to be threatening. Stoner walked to him.

'Care to share? Care to show me something like ... respect for my place? And your presence in it? Without my invite. Old friend?'

'Catch.' Shard threw the empty beaker.

Stoner left it to fall to the carpet.

No splash. No drip. Shard stood, shuffled legs out wide apart, raised arms level with his shoulders; Michelangelo Man made flesh. 'More than that?'

Stoner nodded. Shard stripped, completely, unhurried and not unhappy. Reached for the beam in the centre of the room and commenced slow, rhythmic pull-ups.

'No excitement, JJ. No thrills.'

And that much was clear. The prospect of violence, of harm, of physical action had always been an arouser to Shard, and aroused he was not. His body art mocked Stoner; rippling with no life of its own yet appearing amused, inked eyes following him.

'Do you feel the need for a cavity search, JJ, or can I drop back to earth and sup a little more of my rather splendid coffee?' Shard appeared heroically unflustered by the idea of a cavity search.

Stoner turned away, returned to the coffee. 'You started taking milk yet? Cream? Sugar?' No reply. None needed. He turned back to Shard, now dressed and decent, handed over a fresh beaker of the hot stuff. Both men drank.

'My problem, then. How bad is it?' Stoner welcomed the fizz of the caffeine, and was thinking fast. He leaned into a tall chair, set the beaker down on a table and lifted a guitar from its rack. 'Who? When? And most importantly, why?' He fingered some chords but sounded no strings. Thinking. Watching. Waiting.

'I have no secrets from you in this,' Shard spoke flatly, a monotone intended to conceal nothing, although concealment and revelation were both untruths in hands as expert as his. 'You are being set up.' The emphasis was slight but the active verb had it. Stoner nodded.

Shard continued. 'As am I. We are supposed to be in conflict.

I need to ask this again, JJ. Are we at odds in this? If so, say so, and we'll resolve it. I will walk away if we agree on that, but I'll be replaced before I'm out of sight. And I think we would both be targets from that point.'

Stoner nodded his agreement. 'The key?'

Shard pointed. 'By the bike's.'

'Very good. Where from? More usefully, who from?'

'My employers gave the key to me, but that's not what you're asking. It's plain that they've got others working the case. At least one other. And the finger is aiming at you. They know I know you, maybe suspect that you may trust me and that trust might well be misplaced, displaced in favour of a cash transfer. As is usually the way among thieves, after all. Nothing remarkable in that. But where they acquired the key . . . your key . . . I have no knowledge . . . but we both have ideas. They told me that it was the key to your house near Oxford, that I would know which if I know you as well as he thinks.'

'At which point you remarked that I have no house near Oxford . . .'

'I did not. I accepted the key, pocketed it, said OK and left. It was easy to leave quickly as we were in a safely public place, and in any case I have a habit of leaving quickly. There was no point in lying and no point in being honest either. So I did neither. I left, like I said.'

'And you couldn't call because they know your numbers, my numbers, everyfuckingbody's numbers.'

'Just so. Exactly so. Tangled webs. Spider geometry. Which is where we came in. Actually, we came in less than a half an hour apart, so someone's surveillance is first-rate. Had you been far away?'

Stoner paused. 'No. Not far. And not working. Not on this. I've done nothing on this. I have . . . things . . . things on my mind. There's no rush. Not from here.'

223

Shard walked a little, relaxing a little. 'Your boss, Cheerful Charlie the laugh-a-minute lad, sees an urgency. That said, that said ...' he lapsed into a moment of muse. 'That said, his name is not coming up. No one has commented on his existence recently. Which in itself is remarkable in a small way. My lot know him well.'

'But he,' Stoner looked at Shard; right at him; 'he *has* mentioned you. He's warned me of you and of your interest in me. Your interest in taking a hit. On me.'

Quite suddenly and without warning, Shard was holding a blade. A black non-stick twin-edged killing blade. He raised it slowly in front of his face. Pointed it at Stoner, rolled it through his flexing fingers. Balanced its point on his thumb. Caught the killing edge, the serrated edge between thumb and forefinger. Lofted the blade into the air, gently, heading for the arm of the chair in which Stoner sat, unflinching.

'Catch, JJ. A gift.'

Stoner reached out and caught the falling blade cleanly, turned it and hurled it into the ground between Shard's feet, as exactly halfway between the feet as could be measured without a tape. 'Point taken.'

'No offence, JJ, but you're getting soft. If I had designs ...' the sentence faded.

'We need to do this every time we meet?'

Shard looked up at the question. Raised an eyebrow and almost smiled. 'Maybe. I can almost trust you, JJ, because I have the upper hand. I'm fitter and my sources are providing information more effectively and more efficiently than yours appear to be.'

'It's a good blade. You should keep it. I have several.'

'Me too.' A second knife sprouted next to the first. Both men laughed. A nervous and combative humour.

'How far can you trust Cheery Charlie?' A serious question. 'You're in decently deep with him, JJ; does he feel clean to you, with you? And how many bodies has he told you about? Why would he even care if I was killing them, anyway? Who are they? My own lords and masters tell me that there's nothing special about them, the bodies, but it's kind of hard to believe that. Only nutters hack up other people and play with bits of bodies, and nutters never last long in this line of work. I imagine you still know freaky folk who do freaky things with data? You using them?'

Stoner nodded. 'They're on the case, but as I keep telling you, I'm way behind you in this. Way, way. Tasked the techies only recently. Very recently. No reports yet. In a way that's encouraging. In another way it's the opposite. They did however speak kindly of you. A welcome reassurance.'

Shard looked long and hard at his companion. 'You're detached. It's still not real to you. What's the haps, JJ? A lack of focus is too easily fatal. You starting to listen to dem ol' retirement blues?'

'Don't you hear them?' No banter, just a straight question from Stoner, a momentary whimsy. 'Don't you think that this is a power play, and if it's time to move on ... again ... then it's time to move on? Don't you get tired with all the pretence? The insincerity? The bullshit? The endless repetition of it all? Don't you ever want to walk away from it? Just walk on?' He looked into Shard's dark eyes, eyes which stared back, flat and calm.

'No. No. No, I do not. Nor do I want to have a house on a hill, nor a sweet baby in waiting, nor a groovy crowd of best mates. Nor do I want to hand over the hat to some new, young thing. Nor do I want to be plain and straightforward honest Jack Shit. Nor do I want to be poor. It's not a game we can retire *from*, JJ, just isn't. We ... you've always known that. Fuck it; you told me exactly that when ... whenever it was. And you were correct. There's no getting away with it. There's no relaxation. Retirement is only hiding. Hiding, hiding, hiding until a debt you thought you'd cancelled comes calling and calls collect. You pay and that's it. That. Is. It.

'I'm not ready for the hiding yet. Surprised to even think that you're even thinking of it. Fuck yes. You're not a runner. Not a hider. If I'd thought you were about to cut out, to run out . . . fuck it, JJ. If I'd thought that I wouldn't have come.' Shard was on his feet. Towering. Mighty. Pacing, restless. 'Is this a goodnight call for you, with you as head boy on the last list? Are our lords, ladies and gentlemen setting you up for the long fall? Is their scheme that they build a case against you, I take you out or provide entry and exit for some young disposable hero to take care of the head shot? Is he sat outside now waiting for that shot? And if he doesn't hear that shot will you hear it as I leave, as he blows me away then reloads, re-arms and re-enters to come see you? That would fit.'

Stoner was still. Quiet. The more Shard paced, the more agitated he grew, so Stoner shifted further into silence. He looked up.

'No.'

Shard stopped, looking at the door. Then at the black Harley-Davidson which dominated the room. Then at the coffee pot. He collected mugs and set a fresh brew in motion. Finally he looked at Stoner.

'No?'

'No. There is no one out there. Not unless they followed you, and you would know if they'd tried; not unless they followed me, and no one did that.'

'They know where you are. Where we are. They gave me a key, for fuck's saintly sake.'

'No. They *have* a key. They have no idea which lock it fits. They tried to follow you and you lost them. Did you feel a tail? Did you shake some tail on your way here? Was your route a clean route?'

'Virginal.' Shard was pouring, serious, steady and concentrating. 'No tail. But it always feels like there is a tail, y'know?'

Stoner nodded. 'Keep the brew hot; back in a minute.' And

Stoner was gone. Out into the back of the building, down a flight of steps into a vehicle inspection pit, through a not-obvious door and then gone. Shard waiting. Patience. Stoner knew his homeland, needed no one to clutter his security.

Then he was back. The front door opened silently. Shard was in shadow, blades in each hand, but Stoner stepped alone into the light, arms wide, hands open.

'Nothing. If there's anyone there then they're better than I am, better than you are, and we're dead if that's what they want. But there is no one. How's your phone?'

'Asleep, and as clean as you'd expect.' He lifted a cheap pay-as-you-go cell phone from a pocket. 'No battery; never used by me.'

'Coffee, then, and thinking caps on, my dark friend. Let's do plotting.'

Shard agreed, nodding. 'And scheming. Sorry about the paranoia, too.'

'Paranoia? I heard none. We live by wit, by an instinct for preservation. Ritual. Routine. Recognition of wrongness which most never see, never understand, never even dream of until it's way way, way too late. We are not amateurs. We are the caffeine cowboys, and we never forget it!' Stoner ended on a top note of droll melodrama, took a slight bow, and poured yet more coffee. Always fresh, always the same strength. Habit. One less thing to worry about, in a world where everything was a worry.

'Caffeine cowboys? Shit me, when was that? Back to the old Father Jean, eh, JJ?'

'Let us hope not. It's far too long ago, in a distant place, and that was not a good place to be. Not a good place at all. Though we did learn a lot. How many keys?'

Shard looked up. 'Say again?'

'How many keys. How many keys to my place were you given?'

'Why?'

227

'Work it out. How many?'

'Four.'

'You have them all?'

'Indeed.'

'Handover time.'

Shard reached into clothing, passed over three keys. Stoner looked at them carefully. 'Interesting. How many of them did you try? How many doors did you try them in?'

Shard looked at him, straight. 'Just this door, this place. The only key which fits that posh lock is the posh lock key. Come along, JJ, why do you ask?'

Stoner dropped the keys onto the table, separated the key to the Transportation Station. Then one other. Looked harder, sat back. Reached again for his drink. 'This one is for the club, Blue Cube. No idea what the others are. Interesting, huh?'

Shard looked closely at the remaining keys. Stoner looked at his companion. 'You recognise these?'

A shaken head. A puzzled expression, unguarded.

'They're like . . . I should know what they are. But I don't. Odd. It's like, you tell me that they're the keys to something and I go, "Oh, yeah!" Know what I mean? But I don't know. Seen their like before, though. Seen a lot of keys, JJ. A lot of locks. Lots of locks locking lots of things. Churches to chastity belts. More likely the latter than the former.'

Stoner swung to a shadowed desk, seated himself in an atypically big, comfortable chair and pulled a keyboard from a drawer. Thought for a moment. Reached down to his right and powered up one of several desktop PCs.

'Time to ask the technotwins what they've found, I think. Before we decide where we're going to, we need to decide where we're starting from. And this is a new-to-me PC, acquired from a seriously illegal source, so should be packed with someone else's ID and cookies and handshakes and . . .'

'Oh my!' Shard faked his own exclamation marks. 'You do not mean to imply, to suggest, that this is a stolen computer?'

'Afraid so. I shall surely spend many ages in purgatory, atoning for my sins.'

'If there was any justice, we should expect the heavy tread of the boys in blue as they come to arrest you; assuming that the previous owner of this stolen machine was a well-known purveyor of kiddie porn and that said plods will descend on you as soon as you log in. Or is it log on? I can never remember.'

'No idea. The machine is supposed to be clean of all infections, viruses, that kind of thing. I assume that the PC cleaner would have removed anything particularly unpleasant or incriminating. But it is true that you can never tell, and that postulated higher powers do indeed move mysteriously where complex questions of morality are involved. For example . . . it's certainly taking its own sweet time to boot . . . for example, consider the morality of using a stolen computer to assist in the apprehension of a serially murderous bastard . . .'

'Christ, JJ. Father Jean the Confessor is one thing, Father X the swinging vicar of suburbia I can quite do without. I'll put the kettle on. What are you looking at? Strange time to surf seeking adventure. A bit public for porn?'

Stoner ignored him. He wandered instead around the unfamiliar machine's web browsers, selected the most familiar and used the world's most popular search engine to locate the murder fansite. Entering it via that route felt more secure, although he had no idea whether it actually was. Shard drifted over, faux concern for screen privacy shining like fool's gold.

'Anything you'd prefer I didn't see?'

Stoner shook his head, apologised for the screen's poor resolution and slightly bizarre colours. 'You've seen this, surely?'

Shard shook his head. Silence. Jocularity forgotten. Focus. 'Am I seeing what I think I'm seeing, JJ?'

'New to you?' Stoner was puzzled. Shard confirmed that he'd not seen the site before, that the sight of the dead head was a new one. Not a particularly welcome sight, although he'd seen better sfx body parts at the movies.

'Not sfx, sadly. This is my lost head. The head once attached to the body whose mysterious demise my master wishes me to investigate. As indeed I am doing, in the leisurely way folk find so very frustrating.'

'It's not my head, JJ.' Shard displayed a little puzzlement. 'Wrong race, colour, ethnicity. And size. Age too. Too young. Got any others?'

Stoner looked up. 'You sure?'

'Yup. How many others you got? And while we're at it, where is this? What are we looking at? Murdermayhemandmore? What's that? They've got strange tastes. Is that a real dead head? Colour's not good. Who wants to just look at some sad fuck's dead head anyway? Apart from some other sad fuck?'

'And that, Tonto, is what we're here to find out.'

'Cheerful Charlie gave you this site, did he? Doesn't seem his style, to be honest. Always thought he'd go more for the torture stuff. Wouldn't have thought him a necro at all, except in the righteous satisfaction and gloating senses.'

'He's a very hard man with many strange tastes. He did give me the site. Access and info about it from the techno prisoners. You're using them too, I believe? Saves on effort if we can avoid duplication.'

'Those gothic weirds? No. Not much. Don't really get on with them. Paralleled on a couple of cases, and I know you rate them, but they're too up themselves for me. Too out only for themselves, not altruists like you and me.'

'Irony at such a young age, Shard? Proud of you. Got the impression from Mallis that you were all in signals. Certainly seems to know what you're up to and where you're up to, too.'

'Wheels within wheels within wheels, JJ. I am not faking this innocent expression. Behind the innocent expression lies confusion, plain and simple. What's the website? What's it for? Why are we looking at it? And whose head is that?'

Stoner clicked open a fresh window, another head. 'Come to think of it, why is it there at all and how was it removed so cleanly from the rest of him? Beheading is not as easy as it looks in samurai movies.'

'You'd know that, huh?'

Stoner smiled. 'I try to be more subtle, myself. Chopping off heads is a little . . . statemental, don't you think?'

'More likely just mental. Doesn't make a mark more dead, hacking off bits of him. But if we have different heads, presumably we have different bodies too? Time to compare notes, Kemo Sabe? Are we trusting one another yet?'

'OK.' Stoner left the window open on the last dead head, turned to his companion. 'That's not live any more. When I first saw it, the image was a live video. If that was still running in real time you'd be able to smell it from here. I'm not sure whether that means anything. The site? Techno prisoners are looking at it. It's some sort of route, contact to the killer. Perhaps.'

Shard nodded. Stoner grumbled some more.

'Mallis . . . Menace, I can't tell them apart, gave me some idiot access code using this site's forum, or something. I've not used it. Not even been there. A forum? What is that? Fuck's sake. What's wrong with talking coded nonsense from an anonymous Hotmail account? These geeks are all up themselves. Up each other. Who gives a fuck?' He turned back to the screen. 'I'd been planning on taking a stroll through the whole site, but you sort of interrupted that.'

'Techno prisoners? OK. The geek freaks, right? Mallis and his strange friend. You'd thought they were working for me? OK. OK.' Shard appeared to be a man confused. 'Why everyone and

231

his dog insists on using fake names these days I dunno. Wish they'd not. Techno prisoners? Is that some kind of joke?'

'OK, Mr Harding. As you say, Mr Harding.' Stoner grinned.

'Fuck right off, JJ. You know what I mean.'

'The plan, in so far as there ever was a plan, was that Mallis and her (his? You sure?) mate would research the data they have and communicate using this very site. Which, as you can see,' Stoner opened the appropriate window, 'boasts an unregulated – well, it looks unregulated – forum for death freaks. I've not looked at it yet, so let, us, share . . .' he tailed off, dramatically. 'It's going to take ages. Which clown thought this up? I'd expected a few sad fucks pretending to be killers, acting some childish online fantasy about how they're great killers of our time. There are stacks of the idiots. I'll need to scroll down the entries to see whether Mallis has left something for me. Amuse yourself. It might be an idea to take a run around the estate anyway. We've been here for quite a while. There might have been an invasion of humans.'

Shard walked over to inspect the motorcycle on its high bench in the middle of the workshop Stoner appeared to call home.

'Never thought I'd see you on one of these things. Aren't they bikes for bankers? Harleys? All style, no substance? Great looks, no go?'

'Got three.' Stoner was skimming through the entries, the names of the forum's inhabitants, looking for Mallis's mark. 'They do what they do. That's the only big one. The others are trail bikes; perfect for town and country, sir.'

'Bit bloody obvious, though. "Here I am! Come look at me, Harley-Davidson Man," surely. For one who likes to skulk about they're a bit brazen.'

'That's the whole point. Part of it, anyway. Folk see the Harley, assume the rider's some urban wannabee badass and ignore you. Even other bike riders ignore you. Perfect invisible machine. Like the Transporter, only cooler. You can sit on any city street on that and so many folk see you that you are completely hidden. You can wear body armour, Kevlar kit, hide your face and carry all manner of offensive weaponry and no one, absolutely no one takes a blind bit. Perfect, as someone once sang.'

'Three? Each one more ... ah ... menacing than the last?' Shard was mocking, but not much.

'No. The others are dull ex-army camo trail bikes. I keep one in town and one in the van. Perfect. Same reason as the big hog, but one hundred per cent disposable. Used them all the time before I . . . retired. Great for following, shadowing, surveillance, dodging traffic, riding footpaths through parks, one-ways, ratruns, the lot. Nice NATO specification, too; big carriers, even a box for a light rifle and an invisibility switch which kills the electrics apart from the sparks. Made for me. Love them. Dog-cheap, too. Fuck me.'

'Not while there's a dog on the street, JJ, what's up?'

'There's a message from Mallis. Contact number. Time for a drive. Need to be away from here, then. Time for tea somewhere, plainly. Want to come? Any preferred destination? How'd you get here anyway? Helicopter? Ninja midget submarine? Something even more James Bond?' Stoner shut down the PC, pulled leads from ports and plugs from sockets as he did so, shrugged into shoes and a jacket. Shard was ahead of him, standing by the motorcycle.

'Is there room in that wagon of yours for my bicycle?'

Stoner stared. 'Bloody hell. Fit bastard.'

20

AND I PRACTISE WHAT I PREACH

Stoner closed his cell phone. Sat, silent for a moment, looking at it. Looked up at Shard, who gazed back impassively.

'Well?' he said. 'Well? That all sounded most amicable,' Shard raised a mug of supposed coffee halfway to his lips, changed his mind and set it down again. 'But you are so good at the paranoid security thing that I have no idea at all what you were both talking about.'

'All. All talking. Both prisoners were talking with lucky old me. The marvels of modern science, so forth.' Stoner looked around. They were alone, pretty much, the grim roadside eatery proving unpopular even with hurried men on the move. 'Big, big coincidences. And they're always trouble.'

'How so, my man? Share with Shard, your local confessor.'

Even Stoner looked alarmed at that.

'Identities of the heads are confirmed; details even now wafting to an email address I'd forgotten I had, so it should be decently secure. If I can remember its passwords. If not . . . Mallis no doubt knows them. Little of interest there. The interest's in the coincidences. But I need to think a little. Do you know anywhere which serves actual coffee? Even an entirely addicted caffeine cowboy could not survive on this piss.

'OK. The deadheads are no-marks. Nobodies. Oh the jokes just keep pouring out. It's a laugh a minute here. There is no reason for us to be involved. None. Apart from the fact that our employers wish it. They're messy deaths, but the plods will probably catch their man eventually, and if they don't it's hardly a matter of concern to our masters and lords. What is a concern is that on each day of the dead there's another death. Always close geographically, and always an alleged accident. Or an alleged natural cause. Of someone of interest. Someone too young and too useful to be dead. The latest is a plod, in fact, quite a senior one, offed in some spa hotel. Drowned in their posh pool while taking an early morning swim before power breakfasting, or whatever top cops do in spa hotels.

'What's interesting to the terrible technical prisoners is that so far there isn't a messy death to match up with mister dead policeman. No dead head. If their theory is something like correct, there will be. My theory is that the other guy, the head donor, won't be found until some clueless innocent cleaner goes to clean his hotel room, innocently.'

'Then there'll be shrieking, and running and shouting, and panic and plods all over. Just, exactly what we – that's thee'n'me, JJ – do not want. Can your master hold the scene for you before SOCO whip in and stomp all over the place in their size fifteens?' Shard sipped, with caution.

Stoner was almost amused that Shard was plainly intent upon them working as a team, a partnership. That would be the first time for a very long time, and although he preferred to work alone he was well aware that Shard's skill set was perfectly complementary, and so long as Shard would accept that any partnership between them was not going to be a democracy, then it could work well.

'It's more likely that Mallis will catch breaking news on police channels about the death before my boss does.'

'Have you asked them to keep an ear out?'

'No need. Not with Mallis. He'll call as soon as. If theory is good theory, then the next death will be close by the last death. Drive time. Do you and your bicycle need a lift?'

Shard smiled, nodded. They drove. But not far.

'Here it comes.' Stoner swung the Transporter to the side of the road, flicked on the hazard lights. Answered the shaking cell phone: 'Yes?' Then a long silence while he listened. Followed by a couple of affirmative grunts, and he handed the phone to his companion.

'There'll be a text any moment now with an address. Get that, memorise it, then climb into the back and dig out anything that looks a little like current police ID. There should be something in one of the racks, drawers, y'know. There'll be a blue flashing light, too, somewhere. I always prefer the subtle, silent stealth approach.'

'Messy again?' Shard was all business.

'Hard to say from the panic, but we'll need to press on a little if we're to get there before the blue boys. Pass the phone.'

Blue lights flashing from the windscreen, phone in hand, Stoner dialled the Hard Man, waited less than a single complete ring for the reply.

'OK. So we have a body. We have two bodies. The first is the plod you know about, the second is a civvy stiff you don't. Yet. But you will. As soon as you get notified about the second, the messy one, will you keep the law away from the scene? Thanks. I'll be there in fifteen, need another fifteen in peace and quiet. No, I'll be on my own. Why? There a problem?'

'OK. Can you do the delaying thing? It would help. No, I don't know who he is. Do you have firm ID on the dead plod yet? OK. I'll be arriving in the van with lights flashing. I'll pretend to be legal and lawful and things like that. Really could do without the real plods appearing while I'm there. No, I won't touch anything, I just want to feel the scene before SOCO turn it into their own private playground. Thank you. I'll leave the cell on.'

He closed the call, pocketed the phone. Grinned. 'Here we go.'

'Going alone, JJ? There are two of us. Hello?' Shard looked expectant.

'You're the lone bicyclist, matey. The last scene I saw, I was watched. Know it.'

Shard nodded. Paranoia was a trade technique all its own.

'I need you to watch the watcher. Find the fucker and follow him. No contact, no fighting, no being seen. You do that?' Shard nodded again. 'I'll drop you a couple of blocks away. Use this number. All good, 'cos we're here.'

'Yep. I'll call.'

The Transporter scraped the kerb and stopped to release its passenger. Shard piled around to the back, removed his mountain bike, vanished down an alley with a hiss of tyres and was gone.

Blue lights strobed from the Transporter's screen, and Stoner parked it outside the unremarkable motel.

Flashing lights, an air of hurry and authority. A waved ID and a shouted demand. They all work together to open doors and gain directions to a hotel room. Milling. A tight knot of frightened folk. Stoner pulled them around him, told them to sit down, calm down and drink a few cups of anything they might find soothing. Instructions: stay away from the doors. Wait for the boys in blue. Keep their valued statements fresh by trying not to talk about what they might know, think or have imagined. Talk instead about the weather, the football, the government. Meanwhile, Stoner assured them, they were perfectly safe; the criminal was long gone. Even as he spoke the words, Stoner wondered whether they were true.

He ran up endless flights of endless stairs, found the offended room, slid the keycard and eased the door open with his toe; both hands free, senses switched on. Stripped off jacket and shoes and pulled on the familiar white paper suit and the white paper shoe covers and the white paper hat with the elastic and the light blue surgical gloves. He intended to touch nothing, nothing at all, but he also intended to leave no trace of his presence. No point in causing extra work for the real workers, after all.

Death. A reclining corpse. A man in repose. And in pieces.

21

NO TRAINS TO HEAVEN

'Little Willie in a johnnie?' The Hard Man was plainly entertained by the whole thing. 'You caught a dick in the bog? You went fishing in the toilet? Jesus weeping Christ, JJ, what is all this? And how did you know about the stiff before I did? Professional interest only. I'm not suggesting that you killed him.' That was perhaps an example of his sense of humour. Maybe an attempt at levity. It was difficult to tell.

Stoner shifted in his seat. As was his way, the Hard Man had met him in a restaurant, although eating was a long way down Stoner's list of priorities. A very long way down a rather short list.

'The head was sitting on the desk. Just sitting there. Leaking. It had not been easy to remove it. Most of the mess in the room came from the effort involved in hacking the thing off the neck. It sounds as though it should be easy enough, but it's not. It's not like chopping the head off a dead chicken. At a guess, I'd think the killer used a proper butcher's cleaver or something very like that. Something heavy, sharp, and with enough depth of blade to stop it twisting around and going nowhere every time it encountered bone or sinew. It's too easy to get the blade stuck in gristle. Bugger to pull it out. You get crap flying everywhere.'

'Not a samurai sword, then?' It was never easy to know whether the Hard Man was making a joke.

'Doubt it. The *katana* is supposed to be sharp enough to remove head from neck in a single slice, but you need a lot of skill to do that. And hiding a sword in your back pocket isn't too easy. A butcher's axe would fit into a suitcase. Briefcase. Overnight bag. Why the thought, though? Do you have another serial somewhere which involves some tough nutter flailing about with a sword? Some cretin with a fixation for bad Japanese movies who's watched *Kill Bill* too often?'

The Hard Man shook his head. Said no more. Watched Stoner, silently and steadily. Did not even pretend his usual stoic fascination with the contents of the menu. Not that any waiter seemed over-keen on serving them. Maybe they'd been told to keep away from the debriefing. Which was, Stoner recognised, exactly what the working lunch actually was. Although it was late afternoon, the Hard Man had suggested that they consider their meeting to be lunch. Stoner had no problem with whatever they called it. Time is just time; it ebbs and it flows, labels applied to it generally fall off at inconvenient moments.

'The head was the proud possessor of a shiny new Apple laptop, and that fine machine was connected to your favourite murder fansite, transmitting – guess what – a video of the head to that very site. Or, to be more accurate, it had sent about an hour's worth of video, lost the connection and shut itself down. No idea why. Computers should remain a mystery to everyone except those who understand them, that's the way things should be. No doubt the sad fucks at murder merry mayhem or whatever it's called are even now creaming their collective unwashed and ill-fitting jeans over what they imagine to be a decently realistic dummy dead head. Bully for them, of course. I'll check. Unless you'd rather do that?'

The Hard Man shook his head a little. 'Done that. The site's still running about an hour of utterly pointless and not even faintly pleasant footage of some sad fuck's head. Techs are even as we speak manipulating the early part of the show to see whether they can pull more from it. There's shadow movement at the beginning, which I'd imagine to be the killer moving around the room until he leaves. But I'm not hopeful. This guy is too smart to leave reflections of himself in things. But looking harder never hurt, so looking harder they are. Tell me more, Sherlock?'

'Clothes neatly piled on the single chair. These motel rooms are small. Functional. No wardrobe as such. Coat rack with a jacket and an overcoat. Nothing remarkable. Shoes together beneath the chair. Suitcase against a wall, case for the laptop on the desk. Body on the bed. A lot of blood. Lots. The head had been hacked off with the bod lying on the bed, face-up and alive. Spray of hard blood all over the wall and the nicely meaningless picture above the bed.

'Heart had run for a decent while after the neck arteries had been cut, so you can work out for yourself how much blood was on the bed, the floor as well as the walls. Sodden in places. No, I did not walk through it. It was well set, though, congealed. Room was cold, but the drips had stopped dripping long ago. The plods will give you ToD.

'Bod spread-eagled, so not conscious for the excitement, the entertainment. No one on the planet would lie still while some maniac chopped their head off in front of them. They'd need to be seriously out of it. You'll get toxicology, I expect?'

'Yes. Won't take long. They don't get many murders out here in the shires. They go in for death by a thousand glares rather than hacking folk apart with axes. Backstabbing rather than honest-to-goodness full frontal assault. Each to his own. The dick?'

'Cut off after the ticker had ticked for the last time. Blood oozed rather than pumped. Cut off with a knife or similar. Sharp; a cutting not a chopping blade, so two blades used at least. No hacking, chopping, no particular mess nor gratuitous disfigurement. Circumcised but a long while ago, and not by the killer. Clean cut, balls left where they should be.

'Cock in a condom. Your merry forensic men can tell you whether our man enjoyed a last blast before meeting his maker in the jolly hereafter, unless it had been in the pan for too long.'

'Yes, JJ. I'll get the usual from forensics. If you want and if it helps, I'll pass it on to you. You've been fishing in dangerous water again.' The Hard Man was offering encouragement of a sort. 'And you've answered a question?'

'As you say. The last two bodies you showed me were dickless as well as headless, but we'd assumed that the killer had some bizarre trophy fetish and had kept the dicks for kicks, or something. But I bet they went down the toilet, too. Then there was just that one message, that "sin" thing. In truth, I wondered about that. The scenes were so messed up, deliberately messed up, that I'd felt something was being hidden. Just pointless confusion. Distraction.'

'The pig blood was a bit of a giveaway there, JJ. Do you have any idea what that particular nastiness was all about?'

'No. Apart from some serious attempt at obscuring something bloody. How many human blood types were present, that sort of thing. There was nothing at this scene which didn't come from the bod, so far as I could see. But I did have the feeling that if I'd waited for SOCO and the plods to arrive and do their stumbling about, then someone else might have got to the scene before I did ... maybe before the regular plods, even. I'm not the only guy on the planet who can listen in to emergency calls or pay folk to do that for me.'

'As you say. Why did you go rooting around the plumbing, though? Did you really think that the regulars would have missed it?'

Stoner nodded his reply. The Hard Man sighed, leaned back

in his chair and flicked a hand for a waiter, who materialised instantly, accepted the Hard Man's order for the two of them and vanished again.

He looked up: 'So this is a sex crime? Whore lures john to motel, pimp does . . . does what? Pimp kills, hacks heads; whore chops off their dicks? I can't make much sense of this. I mean . . . I can offer endless suggestions, we can all do that, lord love us, but none makes much sense. Got any thoughts you'd care to share? Be as off the wall as you like. This makes little sense to me.'

'What makes the least sense to me, oh great master, is why your own deities are interested or involved. If you felt an unusual urge to level a little more with me on that score I think I could make more progress, frankly. No offence intended.'

'None, as they say in the movies, taken. It would be disingenuous of me to tell you that I have no idea why my own employers are sufficiently bothered about some string of whack jobs to employ us, rather than letting the more mundane forces of law and order do their relentless jobs, but I can't see how my own theorising could fail to obstruct the clarity of your own thinking. No shit, JJ; I'm being straight. If you can convince me that you need to know more, then I'll think about laying more of this crap on your shoulders, but I don't see how it will help. But I can repeat – in case you've managed to forget – that your pal Harding is apparently fingering you for at least one of these jobs.'

'That's exactly what I mean.' Stoner glared across the table. Food arrived. He ignored it. Both men waved away the over-attentive waiter. 'He, Shard, Harding, is completely certain that my involvement is purely investigative. We've discussed the subject at some considerable length. And in depth. And with near murderous intensity.' Stoner's voice had risen. 'Which we both assume was someone's intention. Any idea who that someone might be? Because I truly do hate being set up, being set up to act the idiot.' He was almost shouting.

The Hard Man chewed slowly, with the air of a man reflecting.

'I do believe that I called you – after many hours failing to make a connection – to warn you that this was more than just a possibility. That Harding may consider you to be responsible in some way and that I was concerned. Both for your wellbeing and for the possibility that he might be wrong and might act precipitously. Although I should also say that I have no doubt that you would be able to look after yourself should there be a conflict. Unless a long gun was involved. Harding is an excellent shot. First class.'

'You would know, I'd imagine? You've employed him?' There may have been a little bitterness in Stoner's question.

'Not directly. Not recently. But I have respect for his abilities. As I'm sure you do too. If it's worth anything, I'm pleased you've sorted it out. Should I assume that you're working together?'

'Assume away. Assume what you want to assume. There's one big fat fuck of a lot more to this. That you're not talking to me is a loud shout in itself. You're not interested in finding a killer. Plods can do that. What's going on? What are you actually after?'

'Eat up.' The Hard Man continued chewing. Stoner looked at his plate, as if noticing it for the first time.

But the Hard Man offered an answer. 'I don't know all of it. And I can't tell you all of what I do know. It's not riddles. Any operative needs direction. You don't need me to tell you that. You've run enough operators in your time. It can too easily be that too much information gets in the way of finding the truth.

'And the truth I want you to find is – you were wrong about this – the identity of the madman who is killing these johns. That has to be enough for you. From that point on, others further up the food chain will make decisions. They may or may not involve me, and I may or may not involve you. You should know that there is a lot of flapping. There's no panic. There is concern at levels which concern me. Political levels, which is always bad news. I don't know who, but I do know why. Or rather, I can guess why.

'It'll be a loss of control. A wobble in the established order of how things work. I'd lay odds on that. Maybe a shift in loyalties somewhere behind doors so closed that they're more solid walls than French windows. Even if I did know more than that – and all I have is suspicion – I'd not willingly tell you more because it could hamper your judgement, impair your sense of direction. Things like that. It might also lay you open to easy identification by parties I'd rather remained unaware of your involvement. If that happened, then you might face rival recruitment, which would be bad, or removal from the field, which could be disabling or fatal. Which would also be bad.

'It feels like the manoeuvring of a private army. I've got no problems with that; many of us have our own private armies. It's usually the easiest way to get things done in these dark days when everyone sits on a committee and everyone sat on that committee reports to another committee, and everyone on those committees reports to another committee. It gets utterly inefficient. Which is what it's for. It's all a huge, expensive and insane control and check on everything, accidentally intended to prevent anything actually happening. Like major wars, cleansings both ethnic and otherwise, genocides, mass destructions, nuclear annihilation and the unpalatable understanding by Joseph Q. Public that none of it actually matters and that the whole world is run by big companies anyway, leaving government by media as a palatable and allegedly accountable fairy-tale front. Which is as it should be.

'Where was I? Is any of this actually any use to you? I doubt it. I tend to believe that information only clouds the thinking. There's a struggle going on somewhere. There always is. There's no need for me to know who's involved and why and where. There never is. Can you ever believe that I might actually be helping you to help me? Does it ever occur to you that it is in my own interest for you to be successful? Why are you always so fucking paranoid?

'Guinea fowl's good, isn't it? Why is some maniac filming these dead heads and posting them on that sicko site? Why is the same maniac murdering people who I can find no sensible connection between and chopping off their dicks? I could almost have understood keeping them as trophies. I can see the appeal in that. There are a few gentlemen whose detached dicks I would happily keep in the freezer so I could laugh at them from time to time when things were feeling just too fucking serious, but ... chopping them off and flushing them down the lav? That's a bit extreme. Why's he doing it?

'These questions are much more interesting and involving than the machinations of self-deluding pensioners desperate to retain their grips on power, office or whatever they think they're doing. Or should we swap jobs? You stand well back, be uninvolved, do nothing but seek patterns in the famous big picture, while I go digging in the dirty detail looking for actual, tangible, provable facts. That would make a refreshing change, as cider drinkers say on telly.'

He resumed chewing with obvious relish and looked across at Stoner, who was prodding at his food with the air of a man who's just realised that he's guest of honour at his own last supper.

Stoner was feeling familiarly resigned to his lack of progress. 'There is no getting a straight answer from you, is there? Can I ask some questions and will you answer them with a simple yes or no?' To his surprise, the Hard Man nodded, waved his cutlery in what appeared to be an encouraging manner.

'Do you have any idea who the killer actually is? If so, that knowledge could save me a lot of dicking around.'

'No. Simple answer.'

'Do you know who's behind it?'

'No.'

'Do you have suspects?'

'Yes.'

'Will you share this with me?'

'No.'

'Why the fuck not?'

'There is no yes/no answer to that, my keen, impetuous but grammatically challenged friend. And that was the deal. Any more questions?'

'Is Harding working for you?'

'No.'

'Do you know who he *is* working for?'

'No. But before you ask again, yes I do *think* I know, but if I'm correct in my thinking, that information could seriously impair your own work, would cloud your vision when it needs to be clear, and might send you off down roads to nowhere. Would certainly waste a lot of time, yours and mine. However, if it helps, I'll guarantee to tell you should I get proof. And if I think it's in our joint best interests. OK?'

'Are you aware that there are two sets of murders running in parallel?' Stoner sat back and watched for any signs of impact. The Hard Man stopped chewing for a moment, then resumed.

'Interesting,' he said. 'Parallel? I'm aware that there may be other bodies in this sequence of which I am as yet unaware. But parallel? What do you mean by that?'

Stoner ignored the question. Asked another instead. 'Do you genuinely know of no connection between the dead heads?'

'No. The very fact that they are so completely unconnected is what worries me the most. I can see no pattern in it. If it was just some nameless nutter extracting a terrible revenge from a society that hates him . . . I could live with that, but our employers would not care about that at all, so we would not be employed. The lack of connection is the key to this. I think so, anyway. Find the connection and we can all retire to Barbados and watch the cricket. If you're not eating that bird, pass it over and I will. It's too good to waste.'

Stoner stared at his plate with distaste, then stood up. 'I've had enough; you eat it. This just goes around in circles. We're getting nowhere sitting here chewing chunks of undernourished, overpriced chicken. I'm off to the club to make some noise. I'll leave the cell connected unless I'm feeling paranoid about it, and if that happens I'll leave a message for you. That OK?'

'It'll have to be. How did you find out about the last killing, by the way?'

Stoner ostentatiously checked for eavesdroppers and whispered; 'Elementary, my dear fellow. Elementary.'

Both men laughed aloud. A surprisingly happy ending to what should have been a more difficult conversation.

'Nice evening for a walk, Mr Stoner,' the Hard Man sounded almost avuncular. 'Enjoy the air, and keep an eye on those dark doorways.'

22

IT HURTS ME TOO

'I'd do anything to play in your band, Mr Stoner.' The chubby young woman had been hovering around the stage like a lost soul for the entire evening. 'Anything. Absolutely anything.' She gazed at him, eyes wide in lonely appeal. Bili rolled her eyes, grinning from behind the supplicant, pointlessly but with pleasure tuning and re-tuning her bass.

'It doesn't really work like that.' Stoner's mental processing was preoccupied more with murder than with music; badness real rather than recalled and turned into song. 'We're not a band, as such. It's certainly not my band. We're just a clump of guys, y'know? We mainly turn up and play, as and when. The house band, Mellow, that's a real band. We're more . . . y'know . . . ad hoc. More of a loose jam kind of thing. Mellow are good, really good. They learn numbers and rehearse and everything you'd want. And they play a lot. Do you want an intro? I can do that. What's your name? What do you play? Hey! You any good?' He beamed encouragement.

Bili beamed right back over the young woman's head. 'It's a fan!' she mouthed, rolling her wide eyes.

'Oh. Mellow? Yeah, they're OK. They're good enough, but they're not . . . ahh . . . special like you guys. You guys really do make it work. It's just . . . it's like it calls out to me. Makes me want to play too. It's like . . . when I hear you guys getting really into it . . . really deep into it, and especially you, Mr Stoner, on the guitar, then I want to play it too. I work the saxophone. Tenor, alto. It would fit right in. Would blow side by side with your guitar, Mr Stoner. When you solo'd on "It Hurts Me Too" in your first set I knew I'd have to ask if I could audition or jam or join in or whatever. Your playing gets right inside me. I think you'd know what I mean when you hear me play. I'd pick up your lines, harmonise. You make your phrasing work in a way that would work on the sax, I think.

'Really. I'm not pushy. I don't mean to be pushy. It's just, I dunno, it's just that I've never met anyone who plays the guitar like it's a sax before. It really digs into me. I really would do anything you want if you'd let me play. Anything. Just say what.' She wound down, eyes wide, hoping for encouragement. Stoner stared at her. Bili had ambled off to conspire with Stretch by the piano.

'OK. Couple of things. Like I said, it's not really a band, in the formal sense that you seem to think it is . . .' He was floundering a little. 'We just . . . know each other really well and we've played together forever, so we don't rehearse like most bands do, so they can get to know each other. We just come together here when it's right. The others do more gigs than me, but I . . . I work a lot of evenings so I don't get a lot of chances to learn many new numbers, so we mainly stick to blues we all know . . .'

'Oh yes! I can see how it works. Couple of guys told me all about how your band plays, and how you stick to a pretty short list of numbers in the set, and that you don't ever play the same thing twice. I'd love to try that. I can play lots of stuff, from formal jazz to bebop, and I think that some trad alto phrases would work just perfectly into the way you play. Your solo in "It Hurts

Me Too" just made my lips and fingers twitch. I could pile a whole extra layer onto that. Couple of run-throughs to sort out the timing, your approach to scales, this that this that, and ... it would be brilliant.'

'I'm sure it would.' Stoner looked up, seeking help. Chimp waved, obligingly, from the bar. Bili pointed her eyebrows at the lights overhead. 'Hey, look. I'm getting the evil eye from the others. Looks like they want to play some more. Could chat about it later if you're around. Before the last act? What's your name, anyway?'

'That would be great. Great. Amanda. I'm Amanda. Do you do requests?'

Stoner paused on his way to his stool, stage left. Looked back. 'I don't usually choose the numbers. Bili on the bass usually decides what she fancies singing. I play it if I know it. You got a request, best ask Bili. She does bite, so look out!'

He grinned, and Amanda duly grinned in reply, headed off to speak to Bili the Bass. Who listened to her, smiled. Looked across the stage to Stoner. Stuck out her tongue at him. Fingered a third-fret G on her bass's bottom string, dropped the string to sound the open E. Hit that note twice, left it ringing. Fretted the G to E sequence twice in slow succession then hit that bottom E twice again. Looked at Stoner.

Who nodded, fell into the tune, adding part-chords to Bili's grumbling, mumbling bass. He switched to the Stratocaster's bass pick-up, his little finger wound the tone control down to dull so the clicking of the bass strings cut staccato through the muted guitar chords as Bili stalked her microphone.

'The night fell a spoonful of diamonds ...'

Stoner's Stratocaster coughed a sliding chord.

'The night fell a spoonful of gold ...'

A cluster of minor harmonics sang from the guitar.

'Just a little spoonful of your precious love ...

'... satisfies my soul.'

And Bili growled out her take on Willie Dixon's most famous ballad, her eyes laughing at Stoner while Amanda swayed on her feet in front of the audience, staring at her very own personal guitar hero. Who delivered a succession of steady workmanlike single-verse solos until after the third sung verse, when Bili stepped back from the microphone and Stoner fingered the Fender into its most abrasive, sax-impersonating throaty roar and improvised on the two-note, two-chord Spoonful theme for maybe a half hour before resting back on his stool, muting the loud red guitar and letting Bili wind up the single-song set.

Before his newest and greatest lifelong fan could reach him, and while the applause was still gathering strength, Stoner hopped from the stage and headed fast for the bar. He snagged the key to the club's upstairs apartment from the fingers of the ever-aware barman. 'My next is a weak beer, Chimp, my last is on its way back to the ocean!' And, almost laughing with the appreciation of the back-slapping audience, he ran the short stairs to the apartment and its private facilities.

As is the case with many basement clubs, the Blue Cube's owner also owned the rest of the building, and the overground levels contained a decently-sized apartment, most often used for visiting musicians or other guests of the club. The apartment also offered a little personal privacy for performers and their guests, should they prefer to pee in peace, away from the stares of the well-meaning.

Stoner unzipped and took aim, humming disconnected guitar jottings as he awaited the flow and the relief.

'Great solo, Mr Stoner.'

The voice was close beside him. He sighed. Gazed ahead and waited for the interrupted flow. Which, inconveniently, declined to arrive. He sighed again, more loudly.

'Let me . . .'

A chubby female hand reached around and took hold of him. He stood still, concentrating on breathing steadily, silently; on the pattern of the wallpaper. The hand squeezed, gently; 'Come along now. There's a good boy,' and stroked while squeezing some more. The inevitable erection overtook Stoner's close inspection of the tiling, fascinating though that was, and the urge to piss retreated. The hand was dextrous, too, reaching inside Stoner's pants to the base of his cock, squeezing firmly then running that squeeze out to the tip, which swelled and purpled obligingly, doubling both his urges while satisfying neither.

A face appeared at waist level, an eye winked at him. Lips moistened and she drooled spittle onto the end of his cock. Licked her lips again and muttered ironic encouragement; 'Come along, you know what to do, little chap.'

Searing genius wit is never easy at times like this, and Stoner was rarely interested in appearing cool anyway, so he felt mixed feelings as the first pale yellow drips hit the bowl. 'Thanks,' he managed as the flow improved.

Amanda pulled herself between Stoner's cock and its target, hoovering his cock into her mouth with impressive speed and drinking fast from it. Almost as fast as he peed, she drank. Impressive stuff. If messy, because capable though she was, his flow was initially uncontrolled and overflow was inevitable. But she swallowed heroically and with apparent relish; he eventually controlled his output, and balance was maintained until his seas were dried up. He looked down and raised both eyebrows, unusually at a loss for words at this point. The world of the gigging musician is always unusual; this was faintly extraordinary even by those standards.

Words came instead from Amanda, who removed cock from mouth long enough to suggest that she recalled that men's personal prongs could perform more than one function, and remarked that his appeared to be up for further exercise at this point, as indeed was unarguably the case. He nodded, words still strangely absent.

'Control of the reed is key to getting a decent sound from a sax,' Amanda observed, running her tongue under Stoner's personal instrument to demonstrate her point. He leaned back against the wall; stared imploringly at the ceiling. There are many points of no return in a man's life, and he could feel another of them fast approaching.

'Umm . . .?' he managed, with a faint hoarseness.

She played her tongue on the fleshy purpling reed with visible amusement, contrived to grin while squeezing him with her lips. Being the perfect gentleman, Stoner of course exaggerated his delight. Being a perfect lady, Amanda removed tongue from cock to suggest that the saxophone analogy could perhaps be replaced with something more flute-like, where the sound is produced by blowing across the hole nearest the end of that other brazen instrument. She once again demonstrated her prowess at this curious musical technique using the increasingly rigid instrument to hand.

'Accurate fingering is crucial, though, particularly while extemporising,' she announced, managing to simultaneously squeeze and rub the shaft in demonstration. Combining her manual skills with the tongue technique and breathy blowing had by now reduced Stoner's world to a tiny place indeed. Maybe a dozen cubic inches contained all of it. He was considering neither music nor metaphor. Sex was all. Pure physical delight. The whole world contained just two folk propped in a bathroom above a club from which the steady bass beat provided an eccentric persistent background sound. She sucked, rubbed, squeezed, blew . . . he leaned, weak-kneed, and groaned a little. Hardly a fair division of duties, but currently acceptable to both.

'Ummm . . .' he managed again, feeling the typical male need to announce the next coming, mindlessly forgetting or ignoring that a player as proficient as Amanda would be well aware of this. As she indeed proved by lifting her hands from his cock, resting the teeth of both jaws lightly upon it and sliding them his entire length, all the way back until her face was buried against his body and her teeth tightened to hold their grip, forcing the action end of his cock against the extreme back of her mouth. Which she opened as she swallowed the end of him, gulping hard as he penetrated her throat.

Surprise and his reflexes pulled him back, but she reached around, grabbed a buttock with each hand and growled, gargled almost and her throat muscles convulsed in their gag reaction at the intrusion. She jammed her face against him. He soared, stretched, cried aloud for salvation or something as he came, pumping pumping pumping, his hands gripping his own head as worlds exploded before him.

She coughed.

And again, overtaken by her gag reflex, and sat suddenly back from him, cock flying from her wide-open mouth accompanied by a shower of fluids as she spewed up most of what she had recently swallowed. Most of it found its way back to its donor, Stoner, hosing his groin and soaking him south of the waist. His cock squeezed out a final contribution to the mess and lost its tumescence rapidly, hanging increasingly limply in a swamp of semen, piss and beer, stirred in with other stomach contents which were probably best left unidentified.

Amanda leaned back against the bath, wiping semen and snot from her face, hair, mouth and eyes.

'Came down my bloody nose!'

She burst out laughing.

'Look at me, Ms Cool, snot and spunk running down my bloody nose! Fuck, Mr Stoner, am I sorry about that.'

The ingloriously yellow lumpy mixture dribbled down over her T-shirt, smearing the words 'Jesus Saves – Devils Drink' with presumably unconscious irony.

'Oh I am so sorry; I wanted something special for you! Something really really special. Something you'd remember and something . . . oh . . . something to persuade you to let me play. Fuck. It doesn't usually make me sick. I don't usually throw up.'

'Usually?' Stoner stared at her in feigned disbelief. 'This is something you do . . . a lot? Only with strangers? Guys you meet on trains? Close friends?'

'No,' she was still beaming desperately. 'No. I wanted . . . wanted to . . . impress you. Oh shit.'

A voice interrupted. Bili, from the doorway.

'Well done. You passed the audition, girlie. Earned your moment of fame. Bring an alto next time. Tongue that as well as you tongued JJ and you'll do good. Won't she, matey?' She stared, expression flat, at Stoner, who nodded, limply.

'And put that thing away; poor little jobbie's trying to hide anyway. Dear Christ, but you have seriously fouled your britches. Gonna look good for the last set. I'd play sat down if I were you.' Bili, practical to the end. Wiser than she was old.

Stoner shook his head, speechless, mopping ineffectually at his groin with the second towel; the first he'd passed to Amanda, who smeared her face some more, mumbled what sounded like a mean mix of expletives and apologies and ran from the room, stopping briefly in front of Bili, looking into her face but saying nothing before fleeing downstairs to the club.

Stoner sagged to the edge of the bath and sat, wiping at himself, tucked tackle and zipped up.

'I'm soaked. Holy shit, Bili. I wasn't expecting that. I came up here to get away.'

'You certainly came. That was a sight to behold, my friend, and will be a source of blackmail for years to come. Wish I'd filmed it. You'd have been an instant overnight internet sensation. Well . . . she would have been. Yours was just a bit part, a supporting role, of course. A little bit part. We gonna close the

256

show, or do you want just Stretch and me to handle it? Sorry.'

She smirked at her own humour.

'Is it dark enough? Oh fuck it, I don't care. I'll just wash my hands. That mess would rot the strings in seconds. I'll come back later and clear the room up. Shame you arrived when you did, Bili. I reckon she'd have got better with a little more practice.' An attempt at levity.

'You old men couldn't perform like that twice in a single week, so don't come it with me, soldier.' Bili was smiling, shaking her head at the nonsense of it. 'Come on ...'

'Do not laugh, Bili. Laugh not.' Stoner was attempting, and failing, to sound stern. 'It's just ... just the way it is. The way it's always been. You know that. You get fans all the time. Far more than I do. You drink a river of their whisky.'

'But I don't fuck them, JJ. Hardly any of them. Hardly any at all. Here I am, trying to remember that last one I fucked. Hmmm ... Nope. Can't.'

They were sitting side by side in the silent, dark club, at the side of the empty, quiet stage, all alone in the night.

'But never mind that. She surely does have an unusually inventive ... creative technique. Was it as good as it looked?' Bili appeared to be genuinely interested. Stoner looked at her suspiciously.

'Yes. Excellent. She needs to practise her last verse closures, work out how to stand an encore or two, but apart from that the performance was outstanding. Not that a gentleman awards marks to a lady. If a gentlemen did that, he would expect that ladies would do likewise, and no gentleman would wish to be compared to another. These things ... performances ... are all relative, in any case. I hope.'

He smiled.

257

'And I stink, Bili, I truly do stink. Like a drunken tramp in a whorehouse.'

'Do you care about that? Care enough to clean up before tackling dawn's early light, so forth?'

The hour was a late hour. Stoner dragged his cell phones from his pocket, glanced at their displays. Messages from here and there; nothing compelling. Nothing from the dirty blonde. Nothing from Shard. Nothing from the Hard Man. Bili looked at him again.

'You going home to anyone tonight? Is she, your lanky friend, is she around tonight? Or is she as professionally engaged as you? No offence intended of course.'

'Of course. None taken. Too tired to take offence. Offence could bite me on the arse and I'd take it without complaint and turn the other cheek.'

'Not seeing your little friend Amanda again tonight? Hasn't she called you, suggesting another rehearsal?'

'Don't be a pig, Bili. Unless you gave it to her, she's not got my number.'

'Oh . . . I'd say she's got it, got your number absolutely spot-on. In a sense.'

Stoner sighed. 'OK, OK. I'm all in. Can't do the fighty banter thing much more. Need some sleep. Gonna take a bath, too tired for a shower. There's a washing machine upstairs too, might even be a change of pants somewhere around. I'd better lock things up first, let you out, so forth.'

'Just lock up, JJ. I'll crash here. I'll even scrub your back in the bath for you. You look too tired to be a threat, and I doubt your elderly shagging tackle's up to another go-around for a while.' She smiled, quietly and without sarcasm, with no angle at all.

'You sure?' Stoner stood, walked behind the bar, punched the combination into the safe and pulled out the club's keys. 'That . . . would be . . . nice. Really nice.'

He locked everything; doors, windows, cellar door and fire

exits. Walked upstairs to the apartment, greeted by the welcome sounds and smells of a filling bath. Sounds of running water from the kitchen, too, followed by the question about it being too late or too early for a pot of morning tea. He shouted a grateful affirmative, locked the doors between apartment and club, stripped off messed clothing and piled himself into the bath, sinking under a layer of fragrant foam. Heaven.

'Heaven,' he sighed as Bili padded into the bathroom, a business-like mug of weak tea in each hand. She smiled down at him. Parked their drinks, picked up his clothes.

'You got a change here?'

He nodded.

'Upstairs. The other flat. Unless someone's walked off with it, flogged it all off down the market.'

Bili loaded up a washing machine. 'Look at me,' she smiled. 'Quite the domestic goddess, huh? Make someone a great housewife one day.'

'You surely will. Surely. Be a lucky guy, that one, huh? That's what the blonde's doing at the moment. You know that?'

Bili's arched eyebrows confirmed her ignorance.

'You and . . . her,' she said, carefully. 'Confuses the fuck out of me. Don't take the hump, JJ, I'm not being mean, but I really just don't see it. I mean, she's a fit critter, no mistaking that, and I'm not qualified to make moral judgements any more than you are, shagger, but . . . I honestly don't understand why you carry the torch like you do. Makes no sense to me. Hey!' She laughed. 'Lean forward and I really honestly will scrub your back for you. Years since I did that.'

She stripped off her shirt, leaned over Stoner to collect soap and cloth. Stoner watched as her breasts sailed in and out of his hazy, tired vision.

'Oh, the Sloggi sports bra; my favourite. Go to it, wonder woman. You do look sweet enough to eat, Bili. No word of a lie.'

259

'And you look like you've already been eaten, cowboy, so lean forward ... but before that, your tackle appears to be bleeding. You OK?'

Stoner lifted himself out of the water on one hand, and with the other swept the suds from his cock.

'Does feel a little tender. She's bitten me. Just a flesh wound, right down by my balls. That was one pretty far-out blow job; you've got to hand it to her; A for effort.'

'That's just a scrape. You're bleeding from the end.'

Stoner peeled back his foreskin, revealing a pair of symmetrical scrapes at the rim of his glans.

'You didn't notice that?' Bili was incredulous as she laughed at him.

'My mind was ... occupied. Really, Bili, at that moment she could have bitten the fucking thing clean through and I'd have asked for more. But it's clean enough. Unless you reckon I should bathe it in disinfectant? Scour it down with a little wire wool? Drain cleaner? Flame thrower? You really pissed with me? Sorry if so, Bili. Love you, you know that. Don't hurt. Not for me. I truly am unworthy of that.'

Bili peeled his foreskin back as far as it would peel, washed the limp pink dick gently and let the skin roll back.

'I was a tiny bit bothered about the vomit; piss and puke are probably not recommended for open wounds. That said, I expect that thing has been in worse places, old man.'

'You know that to be true, Bili, so I'll not embarrass you with a reply. Far worse places. God I'm knackered; the old chap hasn't even twitched. Lovely lady handling him and all. Amazing.'

'Rub him yourself; you can pretend that it's all in the interests of personal hygiene. She'll be back for more tomorrow. You do know that? Know her type? Obsessive? But ... what she said about your playing; she's dead right. Last few sessions you've been seriously smoking that old Strat. Seriously. Real squeal blues from the heart. Your tart, JJ; she breaking your heart? Tell me to fuck off if you want.'

'Nah. She's ... she's the one. The real one. Makes my heart sing, just like the song says. Really. I know it makes no sense at all. None, but that's just how it is. You're going to laugh – feel free – but I have an ambition. It's my only ambition. I want to make it ... right for her. I want her to do well. I want to make her happy, and I want to make her mine. And now she's shacked up in the shires playing housewife for some fucking lord of the land, or some such.'

Bili grinned, opened her eyes as wide as wide could be. 'Really?'

'Really. She reckons ... oh for fuck's sake, you don't care about this, Bili, and it makes no sense to me. I don't understand what she wants. She wants us to be an item, the item, the only item, but ...'

'She's on the game, JJ. She's a whore, a working girl. So she must be an awesome lay? Presumably the best fuck on the planet, right? So why are you sticking it into the faces of chubby wannabe saxophonists? Why do that when you can enjoy sweet expert lurve with your very own not-blonde?'

She reached into the bathwater, squeezed Stoner's cock with a proprietorial air.

'Oh look. It's not broken. That's a relief.'

She let him go again, leaned back against the wall.

'Surely she can fuck you so far and so fast that you just wouldn't want girls like whoever she was tonight?'

'I can't remember the last time Lissa and me actually fucked together, Bili.' Stoner was suddenly serious. Looked angry. 'Sex is ... different for her, sometimes. Somehow. She ... sees my need. Fixes it. Gives monster head; you've seen her do it. Anywhere, any time. I last less than one minute. Or a hand job. Efficient. Fast. Can get tissues out of nowhere faster than it takes me to come so there's never any mess. Any time, any place, just like they say in all the songs. But we don't . . . fuck. Hardly at all. Started off like she didn't want to just do it. I could see that. She does it for a living. It can't be an exciting thing for her. Never new. I understand that. Same for stagehounds like me . . . and maybe you too, hey? Then later she wanted to make love. Take real time over it. All night. All morning. She's brilliant. The only time I'm so relaxed that the voices in my head just shut up and fade away and leave me in peace. But that was then. Now she wants to save us time for when it's love time, not shag time, but she knows I'm a horny old goat so provides instant expert relief any time she thinks I need it. And I can't fault that. Seems like she's more interested in my job than she is in my cock. Can't fault that, either.

'But it works both ways. If all I wanted was a quick jump, a BJ at the club, whatever, well . . . it's always there, isn't it? The poor fan is always with us. You've got yours, I've got mine. Like troubles. I want more than that from Lissa, I've told her but she believes me not. She knows what I really want behind the kind words, which she thinks are just flattery. I'm a bloke; she knows that all blokes want the same. And it's true. But only to a point. It's a huge suffering subject. So, let's be honest, it's all over. It should be all over between us. That's what it sounds like. But it's not true. If anything, I feel more for her than I've ever done. You're not asleep yet, then?'

Bili had moved behind him and was soaping, scrubbing gently at his back. Massaging his shoulders and the sides of his neck.

'Not yet.' She picked up a vast soft towel, offered it to him. 'Dry yourself and come to bed. Pull on some pants too; I don't want himself poking me in the arse every time you roll over.'

She stood, stripped off the brassiere and pulled a clean T-shirt from a drawer, heaved it over her head.

'You really are fucked up, y'know? It'll look brighter in the morning. Honest. Whoever wakes up first gets the milk in.'

'There's milk in the club. Coffee's better here. Thanks for listening, Bili. How long is it since we slept together, huh?' Stoner towelled; Bili threw him a clean set of tracksuit pants; he staggered into them and fell beneath the sheets.

'Just under three weeks. Your memory really is fucked. But so is mine. Remember your other fan? The blonde well-dressed one? The one Chimp thinks is a narc? She was in again tonight. That was actually what I came up here to tell you when I found little miss tingle-tongue trying to explode your dick all over the walls. I quite forgot in all that excitement. She'd gone by the time we came down again. Sorry about that. You need another fan.'

She smiled, but Stoner was sound asleep.

23

ANOTHER LONELY DAY

The morning after found Stoner awake early, mind racing with a sense of urgency which years of experience would not let him ignore. He rolled silently from the shared bed, admiring the rise and fall of Bili beneath the flat linen sheets, and skimmed silently across the rugs to collect his cell phones. They held the morning's news, as he had known they would. A voicemail heads-up from Shard confirming his continued existence, a series of missed calls, a couple with their identities withheld, and a text from Mallis, suggesting blandly that both email and a meeting should be a priority for them both.

Confirmations first. Texts to those who needed reassurance, email to others. Text reply within instants from Shard; someone was awake and living their life, then. A coded message from Mallis containing a place and a time, along with an instruction that he bring a netbook or something similar with net access and a screen bigger than that on a cell phone.

Distant atonal music and the rhythm of a vacuum cleaner revealed the activities downstairs in the club. A glance to the bedroom revealed no signs of activity beyond a steady silent breathing. Stoner showered, dressed, slipped downstairs, leaving a note: 'Hope it was as good for you as it was for me.' Irony is an unappreciated form of wit, and would certainly not be lost on his last night's bedfellow.

Stoner eased the apartment door closed, let the lock click a note of security, and drifted behind the bar, coffee in mind, along with a need for glasses of water and a laptop or similar. His own was nowhere near. The vacuum cleaner droned on, sometimes closer sometimes not, accompanied by a trail of music he could not recognise.

His phone shook.

Shard.

'Where have you been? Never mind. You were right. You had a watcher. Watched you all the time you were nowhere to be seen. You were in the hotel. He and me were outside. I couldn't see you; he couldn't see you. What was he watching? Why also? You leave as plod arrives. Less than a quarter hour. Your miserable mate has less pull with the plods than you think he does. They charge into the lobby, then stop. He does have pull. Maybe the blue boys are afeared of a dead man. Who can tell? You wave at the top plod, a sergeant. How'm I doing so far?'

Stoner smiled, despite himself. 'Doing good, Shard, doing good. And then?'

'Then you're off. On foot. Why on the foot, JJ? Your truck'll be towed by now. Your problem. There's movement. He's in sight. Not a big guy; easy to take down. Big coat, watch cap, gloves, silent shoes. A pro tracker and a good one, I'd guess. Maybe military, but didn't smell like it to me. I kept well back. You took a call, made a call, whatever; waved the bright light of your phone for all to see. Maybe you were surfing the porn, who can tell? You stopped. Your trail stopped. You looked around and, fuck me, he vanished, right in front of me, right before my eyes. Panic rises. Mistake time; I was watching you and not the guy with the soft shoes.

'You move on; he reappears. It's like a switch. If he's that good then he'll know I'm there, so I allow some distance, follow you for a little. But no; he's still there. You change direction, head off somewhere east. He follows for maybe 400 metres and then stops. Looks like he's talking; a headset, earpiece, something. Turns around, scans, scans again. Shows no sign of having spotted me, but I don't know. Walks back to the hotel. I'm in doorways, in bloody front, no shoelaces to tie, no excuses for being there. I ring a doorbell. Avon calling. He passes me on the far side of the street. No glance my way; I can't see a face, not a hair, no clues. Big hat, high collar, cold night.

'Walks straight past the hotel. Not a pause. Meat wagon's present and correct, boys in blue and men in white idling the way they do. He stops and he stares. No hurry, just another rubbernecker. Turns the corner we came in by, lights up a car, climbs in and gone. Number's on the text to yours. I lean on the pedals but there's no traffic and a bicycle is not too clever when the enemy's driving. End of. Went home and shouted at myself a little.

'Good idea about the bike, JJ. Shame it's not got an engine, huh? Bloody shame. What now? Where are you? You were silent all night. Strange time to go to a party.'

24

MOTOR VANS, ELECTRIC SOUNDS

'Sometimes I think I've wasted the last twenty years.' The dirty blonde's lament scraped from the cell phone's struggling speaker. 'You there, JJ? You hearing me?'

Stoner grunted. The heavy Transporter's cabin was technically and expensively quiet, the darkness all outside. The ride and the roads were smooth, the phone sat snug in its dock, no bad connection crackles interrupted the one-way flow.

In the same way that the dirty blonde would sometimes achieve an almost magically manic level of excitement over matters which appeared to Stoner – and probably to the rest of the functional world – to be mundane, so at other times her excitement turned into an equally manic form of misery, mixed with doubt and defeat. Most of the peaks and most of the troughs came and went of their own volition. Stoner was always made forcefully aware of them, but he rarely actually understood the stimuli. Sometimes the mania thrilled him, brought new life to old emotions . . . sometimes he simply switched off from it, refused to let it interfere with the constancy of his own uniquely intense feelings for her. It often paid a dividend to be aware of but undamaged by emotional extremes in others, he felt.

'I've been doing this since I was twelve. You know that. You know that, JJ, because I've told you before.' Her voice sounded flat, empty. It might have been the low quality of the signal or the weedy speaker. And it might not.

'I always tell you, JJ. I only tell you. Only you. Don't know why. Why is that? You there, JJ? You still there? You hung up? You never hang up. Not on me.'

Stoner grunted. Kicked the side of the transmission tunnel. The heavy Transporter was resolutely solid, it made little noise. Its carpet was thick and dense, its steels robust, impervious steels, efficient steels. He kicked it again, harder. With extra conviction. The cell phone shuddered in its dock, the signal crackled in a gratifying way. Stoner felt increasingly calm. He had felt calm enough before this, but greater calmness grew and spread within him.

'You're driving again. OK. I know you don't like talking when you're driving. Just say hi or something.'

Stoner grunted. Kicked the car again. The phone rattled obligingly. 'It's not a good line,' he shouted, face pointing away from the cell phone's microphone.

'Not a good time?' The dirty blonde sounded momentarily concerned.

'It's always a good time, babe.' Stoner aimed to reproduce the sound of a man concerned but harassed, interested but interrupted. He had no idea why this might be important. Or to whom.

'You're always driving. Driving, driving, driving. We don't get enough time together because you're always driving.' Petulance was defeating concern. Her voice sounded exactly as a voice sounds in the morning after a lengthy and chemically fuelled night. 'We should spend more time together,' she sounded, almost angry. She was rarely angry.

Stoner grunted.

'Where are you driving to? You won't tell me. You'll tell me that I don't need to know and I don't need to worry and you'll tell me when you see me. Have you found another body?' The voice sounded suddenly more alert, a glint of optimism lightening the thunderclouds.

'Many more bodies?'

Stoner grunted.

'I know, I know. You'll tell me later. You're not the only one who's busy, either. His eminence, his lordship . . . whatever, got a whole pile of calls last night. I'm shattered. Hardly any fucking sleep. Every time I managed to drift away some twat called him up. He's not like you, JJ. He doesn't turn that bloody phone off. I turned it off when he went for a slash, but do you know what? Some twat called him on another phone. He's got loads of them. Why would anyone have more than one phone, for fuck's sake?'

One of Stoner's other phones lit up and shook in an enticing manner. Shard. He left it. He was finding the dirty blonde's monologue almost relaxing; monologue therapy. Excellent stuff. It eased a tension from which he was not yet suffering. A sort of down-payment investment for future tensions. He enjoyed the idea of that. Maybe there'd be a profit in it? The Hard Man would know. But would certainly steal the notion if so. A conundrum.

'He's rushed off, too. We were supposed to be having some friends around for lunch. His friends of course. Don't think he'd like my friends. Don't think I could invite my friends around for lunch. For anything really. The fucking catering people turned up about an hour after breakfast, said they were setting up for lunch. Lunch for twelve. Thought I was the fucking maid. Fucking housekeeper. I told them they could fuck right off and fuck themselves. Didn't they know who I fucking am? They fucking do now. I told them I was the mistress of the fucking house, their fucking boss, the useless fucks. That fucked them, complete mind fuck. They didn't know where to look. Never mind where to put themselves. Soft fuckers.

269

'The head fucker asked where I wanted to eat. I mean . . . where they should set up luncheon for the luncheon function. Fuck's sake. Luncheon function? Sounds like a dose of the honks. Bad lobster, mixing coke and sardines. I told them that one would luncheon in one's summer house. Didn't know this place had a fucking summer fucking house. Fucking does though. Made me feel completely fucking stupid. How come those sad café fuckers knew that my fucking house has a fucking summer house when I didn't fucking know my fucking self?

'Jesus, JJ. Only sane man I've ever known is you. Why do I miss you so much? Why do I feel so crap? I want to see you . . .'

This might have been the magic moment. This might have been one of those rare moments when it would have been right to speak the truth, to speak all of the truth. She missed him. He missed her. They both shared their beds with other people, the wrong people and for all the wrong reasons. If she would just stop talking for a moment, maybe they could start communicating. Stoner considered speaking. Considered bridging the gulf between them with words. Considered the risk, the exposure.

A text landed on his other cell; yet another summoning, another obligation, another complication.

Stoner remained silent.

The dirty blonde battered on.

'What are you doing now? Where are you? Why don't you come here? No idea when his eminence will drop by but if he dropped by and found you here he would just have to . . . well . . . I don't know. He'd just have to fuck off out again so you didn't murder each other. He did say I could have this place. I could own it. As in, it would be mine. I got a table set for twelve for lunch. There's no one else here. It's insane. Catering dickheads are coming back at eleven-thirty. That's . . . now. They're not fucking here. I'll fucking rat them out for being bastards and not turning up. Oh fuck, the door's ringing. Gotta go, JJ. Kisses, yeah?

Give your little guy a big squeeze and a big rub for me. Fucking doorbell. Do those fuckers think I've got nothing to do but answer the fucking door? Sorry this was so short. I've gotta rush.'

Stoner drove on, bemused.

The matt black van sat in the car park where one of the techno prisoners had said it would sit. Inconspicuous it was not. Apart from being matt black, a non-standard shade for any known vehicle apart from mythical helicopters, it boasted a huge and well drawn universal anarchist emblem in fluorescent pink on each side. If anyone believed in the notion of hiding in plain view, of conspicuous invisibility, this would be a great opportunity. Stoner stared as he rolled the Transporter alongside; driver door to driver door, gazing into the doped, dulled gaze of Mallis him/herself.

'You're not . . . early.' Said in a not unfriendly way. Mallis appeared too dim at the moment for unkindness. More of an observation, something which may be interesting at some other time. 'We have a lot of material for you. You a quick reader? Good listener?'

Stoner nodded.

'Don't get out. Catch this.'

A rubber model of a cartoon Tasmanian Devil flew gently through the gap between the windows. Stoner caught it, reflexively. Nodded thanks.

'Read it,' instructed Mallis, 'and return it. I'll wait.'

Stoner examined the rubber devil. It pulled apart in the middle revealing a USB connector. It was a memory stick. Science is a source of constant advance and wonder. A rubber cartoon animal packed with information. Who could have thought it.

'You can listen to *The Archers*,' smiled Stoner, attempting levity.

'*Desert Island Discs*.' Mallis didn't smile much. 'My favourite. I collect the podcasts and save them up for waiting time like this. Expands the mind. The benign nonsense of it all.'

The matt black van's gloss black window rolled silently closed.

Stoner flicked open a laptop, booted it and pushed the memory stick into place. It opened with a movie. The dead head. Possibly another dead head. They can appear uncannily alike. A second window opened next to the moving image and a text file scrolled down it at talking speed; a voice unfamiliar to Stoner read the script aloud. A description in cripplingly impenetrable and pointlessly technical garble described the source of the movie. Strings of numbers and terms meaningless to Stoner apparently revealed where the signal had been posted and hosted.

None of it meant much to anyone unfamiliar with satellite co-ordinates, but it would be no doubt useful information for a techie as techie as Mallis. Stoner opened a screen window to copy the information to his laptop's drive. Nothing happened.

Mallis popped the black van's horn and wound down his window. 'Don't do that.' The window wound back. Information technology is miraculous. Omniscient.

The rubber cartoon devil resumed its monologue. Seventeen killings could be connected, apparently, to the messy heads-off murders; all but four in the UK. All of them could be linked politically or organisationally, all could be considered to be professional hits, all of them disguised, either as too-obvious accidents, improbable suicides or as unlikely natural causes. Parts of the MO were similar, mainly in the deliberate misdirection of the inevitable investigation. And when Stoner's mind boggled gently at the thought of such a high number of deaths, he reminded himself that if a decent researcher shoved out the parameters of their search far enough ... they could connect anything to anything. The skill always lay in the analysis.

The range of victims was also interesting enough. All men. No pattern of age, particularly, although none was old and none was young. The analysts' view was that there were further cases as yet unlinked, and that there would be more in the future. All of the UK hits had ended the careers of men connected to the

A LAST ACT OF CHARITY

security industry in some way, although only the police official had been so involved officially and openly. The other links were less obvious.

Menus offered themselves. The gloriously misnamed techno prisoners had opened up an entire world into the lives and identities of the victims. Stoner was as amazed as he always was whenever he enlisted their services. And as frustrated as he always was that until payment had been made – and made in full – he would be unable to keep or to copy the information. This was one of the oddities of dealing with them; they knew his word was as good as his money and that he would never betray either them or himself. However, they also believed, as he did not, that he was likely to depart the land of the living suddenly and unexpectedly.

The twins themselves, Menace and Mallis, had of course never actually explained this to him. They pretended sublime disinterest in mundane matters like money, preferring instead to concentrate their self-proclaimed genius in the rarefied world of information, its acquisition, verification and transmission. A colleague of theirs, a seriously muscled man who rejoiced under the nickname of Hazardous and who shared the twins' taste for gothic theatrical excess, had once outlined their only way of working. Stoner had been amused ... mostly amused, by this display of quaint paranoia, and had pointed out gently to Hazardous that if he seriously wanted to extract data from the prisoners then he could do so, being who he was, how he was and being connected as he was. Hazardous had smiled and remarked that no matter how low Stoner may be able to stoop, they could stoop lower still, and, really, it only boiled down to whether he wanted the information the techno prisoners were so expert at supplying. They really had no rivals in their world, not in this country and quite possibly not in the entire Anglophone world.

273

Stoner had wondered how this might be. Hazardous had smiled again in an almost engaging way, but had also declined to comment further.

Their relationship had worked perfectly ever since. Only once had information supplied by Mallis turned out to be substantially incorrect, and to Stoner's surprise the fee had been refunded. Although the opportunity to emphasise their technical expertise had been taken even then, the money transfer had been from an apparently non-existent account into Stoner's most private and most personal hidden account. The unspoken suggestion was that in the same way that they could place funds into a hidden account, the prisoners could also remove it. Stoner had no idea whether this was in fact possible, but he preferred the quiet life.

He drifted past fields of information. Far more than he was ever likely to read, let alone need, but when the inevitable reckoning, the reporting, arrived, it was always helpful to be able to supply acres of data for the Hard Man to present to his own bean-counting masters. At the bottom of the last page were details of the fee and the numbers of the account into which it could be paid. He paid it. Started the Transporter's engine and wondered why the driver's window of the other van wound down at that point.

Mallis aimed his inevitable dark lenses in Stoner's direction and leaned forward, almost far enough to be outside the protection of his vehicle's steel walls. He called out: 'Be careful with this, Mr Stoner. The information you have is incomplete. There will be more, and you should wait for it before moving far. You've paid the whole fee. We'll be in touch.'

A speech. And a worry. Stoner assumed complete stillness and stared hard at the shiny black lenses. Then he nodded. Both windows elevated themselves. Both vehicles departed, stage left and stage right.

25

THE COLOURS OF THE RAINBOW

he shot came from nowhere. He was so surprised that he almost iled to recognise what he'd seen and heard. A gunshot? A quiver the drift of dust in the lights? In broad daylight and while he as occupied with tasks both innocent and mundane? He laid own the oil can he'd been emptying into the black Harley-avidson on its bench in the centre of the room, turned to face e door and sat down.

Slowly.

Silently.

Shifted the breathing from nose to mouth to reduce the inter-rence with the hearing. The tools he'd been using were well ained, they lay in a clean line on a cloth bed; easy to find and lent. Habit is a life-preserver.

No unusual sounds. An unusual lack of sounds, in fact, which ld a silent story of its own. He waited. Background noise levels eadily returned to normal; the customary animal ambience, uman and otherwise, birdsong and trees. A shot interrupts bird-ong, but the apparent silence of the trees was all in his im-gination. He rose, silently. Switched on the spotlights which lit e bike on the workbench with a brilliant, hard clarity, a clarity which eased the strain on the eyes when wrenching on something small. Walked silently to the room's main lighting switches and doused them all. The only light was the light illuminating the Harley. The motorcycle shone, gleamed dully, flat black paint contrasting intensely with the higher gloss on the black exhausts. It added to the atmosphere of watchfulness. The tense quiet. It cast unpredictable and unusual reflections. He reflected. This place was his place of safety. His private place. Not a place where guests were invited, and all uninvited guests were unwelcome until proved otherwise. The burden of proof was theirs. His concern was privacy. Quiet.

Stoner slipped into shadow. Observed through wide-open eyes and listened with stretched care. No shadows moved to interrupt the windows' illumination, and no abnormal sounds disturbed the watch-keeping birds. Until the second report. Closer than before. No doubt this time, a shot, and a heavy shot too. Big calibre, low velocity. Pistol. No rifle's high-speed bullet whipcrack but no silenced sibilance either. Big-bore handgun, fired close by. No sounds of impact. No splitting brickwork, no breaking glass. Someone else's problem, then. It is not easy to miss a building at close range in daylight. Scallies bagging rabbits, perhaps. But scallies rarely use handguns for rabbits. That would require skill, scallies blast away with small-bore shotguns when hunting the scary rabbit. Usually. Scallies save pistols for use on each other.

First one, then two of his cell phones lit up in the half-darkness. He stood still, ignored them, watching and waiting. Took another phone from the leg pocket of his cargoes. It was silent and unlit. No missed calls. No more shots. Nothing from the phones. The motorcycle shone, a darkly shining show of its own. He moved around the room, listening, watching the windows for interruptions to their patterns of light and dark.

Exactly the wrong thing to do at this moment would be to go outside, to investigate. Another wrong thing to do would be to do nothing, nursing concern and providing a home for worry. He fixed his gaze upon the motorcycle, letting his eyes wander over its many familiar mechanisms while his ears ran loose and random, seeking a message from beyond his walls. None came.

The phone in his hand shook silently and its screen lit.

Shard. He lifted it to his ear.

'Did you feel it?'

Stoner grunted. He enjoyed many games, especially those involving wit and wiles, but in their own place at the right time. This was not that time.

'Feel what?'

'The passage of an angel.'

Cryptic, even for Shard, who sounded far from his best. Sounded breathless. Tired. Not running but showing every audible sound of a man who has run very fast and very recently. Stoner said nothing, tapped the mouthpiece rapidly twice to show that his silence had a purpose beyond simple antisocial behaviour. Shard caught that. His breathing was slowing, so no injury insult there.

'You have a guardian angel watching over you. He passed close by and now is gone. Can I come in or are you coming out? It's clear out here. I think.'

An odd admission. It was either clear or it was not. Shard would know. Should know. If Shard was unsure then the safest place could be inside. On the other hand, rats get caught in traps, rarely in the open.

'I'll see you. Blue van. In five.' Stoner hung up. The blue van was a Parkside fixture. It looked derelict, unwelcoming, although its tyres remained miraculously inflated, and its windows miraculously unbroken, its doors impenetrably locked.

'Very good indeed. Very, very good.' Shard looked tired. Sounded stressed. 'Watching you. How did he know who you are? And if he knew who you are, and he could only have known that if he'd been told, how did he know where you are? No one follows you, JJ, you are the most paranoid man on the planet, and if you'd been followed you'd know you'd been followed. If you led them here then you intended to lead them here. Am I missing something? You playing me for a fool? Playing a game you're not sharing? No prob with that; you want me gone, just say it.'

The two men sat in the silent, closed dark of the blue van's interior. It was dull, damp and smelled derelict, a faint odour of long-ago death lingered, providing a vague psychic sense of unease and disquiet.

They sat on silent swivel seats behind the two front seats; rearward-facing seats made for watching, unobserved. Seats from which the occupants could see without much risk of being seen. The blue van was a lookout post. An inconspicuous, almost invisible, tired Transporter van of a certain age and anonymity. Unremarkable. Not worth a first glance, never mind a second, better look. Certainly not worth stealing. Not that such a theft would have been an easy undertaking, given that the blue van's ignition system was a thing of minor wonder and a certain robust complexity. The last person to break into it had died in it. Maybe car thieves could detect the lingering confused spirit of their departed brethren, and maybe they couldn't, but no one had tried since that unhappy day, long ago though it was. The would-be thief had died quickly, as was Stoner's preferred approach to such things, but his remains had shared the blue van's interior for some time. Which may have added to the vague odour of death which lingered. Stoner occasionally wondered whether the odour was noticeable to anyone who was unaware of the thief's passing, but he wasn't wondering that now.

'I have a watcher?' Stoner's query was quiet. He was thinking.

He asked again. 'How? I've not been followed here. Not unless someone is very, very good.'

He adopted a consistent approach to followers. As soon as he became aware of the tail he led them with enthusiasm. He led his followers to watch depressing Scandinavian monochrome movies, desperate domestics a particular preference. He led them for expensive meals in appalling restaurants, and on occasion he led them to galleries packed with art of the most catastrophic kind, the kind which would have made anybody sensitive doubt their sanity. On one particularly favourite day he had led a grimly suited and unsmiling woman to a display of art featuring female sex organs displayed in utterly mysterious but certainly unpleasant ways, and had stood stationary, apparently transfixed by a hideous image of genital mutilation, for over an hour.

The watchers inevitably lost their faith or discovered another, and then Stoner reversed their roles, following them in their turn to discover their own basic secret; who was paying them to follow him and, preferably, the reason for their interest. The creative use of sensitive paranoia can never be over-stressed as a tool of this trade. But he had not been followed, of that he was as sure as he could be.

'They followed you, Shard. No other way.'

But Shard shook his head slowly.

'Nope. Not unless they're psychic. Your guardian angel was here before me. Whoever he warned away arrived after me, sure, but not by my route. I came by bicycle, me, and they came and left by car. I think that's how it went.'

'You sure?'

'Yup. Eggs is eggs. Stuff like that.'

'And it was a warning shot? How come?'

'Warning two shots. Anyone who can find this place, who can watch you without being seen by you, and who wants to watch you not kill you . . . that person is competent in the extreme, and that person does not miss. That person is in the game with us, knows who we are and what we do. What they don't know is what we don't know either and we all need to find that out.

'Nope. The shots cleared away someone else. Your most secret hidey-hole is turning itself into a regular Times Square, endless coming and going. And you're really getting slack, JJ, if you were aware of none of this. Did you know *I* was here? Had I magically landed in your own private hideaway unseen, unheard and . . . unknown? As well as the intruder and the angel? Have you really lost the edge?'

'Negatives on all counts. I'm not so slack. I felt observed . . . but it's getting so that I feel that way all the time. I need a holiday. A quiet life. I need to be loved. Think I'll go on a cruise. Tell me what you saw?'

'Nothing. Patterns in the leaves. Heard it all. Arrived, hung the bike from a tree. Took a scout, like you do. Movement patterns in the leaves around your shed; patterns closing in. One, maybe two. No more than that, and not expert . . . not as expert as us. No way as expert as the shooter, who fired once. Odd echo. Non-directional, no flying foliage. Shot straight up, I'd guess. Patterns all ended. Much listening. Everybody's listening. A world of calm and quiet; you did things with the lights in there.

'Second shot. Same handgun, same non-directionality. One, maybe two, people left. One person followed, but that guy is very good. Proper tracker. No tracks. We'll find the other guy's traces, but not the second. Very good.'

'And now?' Stoner was not enjoying this conversation at all. Not a word of it.

'Now we're being watched again. Betcha. You feel it too, no?'

Stoner nodded. 'Why, though?'

'Who you pissed off? Who're you . . . umm . . . we working for? No jealous husband this, JJ. No breathless groupie. You're being protected, man. You. *You* of all people. Fair boggles the mind, that does. Who would want to protect you right at the this time, and why? You're looking for a hit man, a slicer, a head cutter-offer. It really does look like someone wants you to find him. So your watcher, protector, is a friend. A friend good enough and scary enough to scare off anyone getting near.'

'I'm just working for the man, the same man. Same as ever these days. You know that. You're ... well, you're doing what you're doing and we're supposed to be looking for the same thing. This dickhead headchopper killer. We're doing the seeking thing, not playing at being targets, right? And in truth I'm strug-gling with the whole thing anyway. There are signs, there are signals, all the usual crap, but truth is that if it wasn't for the bodies I'd think this was just some ruse to set me up for the long fall. And that has been a long time coming, to be fair.

'And ask this: this protector of yours – nice theory by the way – this hero lets you pass by? Or is he not as good as you and doesn't spot your subtle camouflage as an elf on a bicycle or a tree sprite or whatever you're meant to be dressed up in Lycra to look like. Tree sprite. I do like that. But it doesn't dodge the question. Why let you all the way to me, but not the mysterious unknowns? Or ... another question for you, Sherlock the cyclist; was the watcher protecting the second lot from you and me? You'd already seen them, I would have spotted them at some point long before they were a threat. That said, I would have wanted a serious conversation, not just a fight.'

Shard was quiet for a while. He took a cell phone from his pocket, lit its screen and read for a moment. Shook his head. Passed the instrument to Stoner, who swore a little. Passed it back.

'Coast clear,' read the text message. 'Number withheld.'

'Your phone?' wondered Stoner.

'Hmmm,' agreed the younger man. 'Indeed. Let's see.'

He eased open the door nearest the building's shielding wall and stepped out. Was gone. Stoner followed, walked briskly and openly to the perimeter road and started to run along it. Eased up his pace and ran steadily as one with no care in the world. The old industrial estate showed as little sign of industry as ever. Stoner nodded to a couple of familiar faces as he passed them. This running man was no stranger here, and fellow inhabitants kept their own counsel, minded their own business, as ever. He ran back to his building, let himself in. Tapped his terminal to life, left secure messages for both techno prisoners, contact points both physical and fallback, stressed urgency. Collected keys and left.

Left as far as reaching the door and reaching for the lights. Stopped. Stood. Listened. Nothing. Nothing out of the ordinary, the predictable. The phone in his leg pocket shook again. He opened it and read it.

Shard: 'On my bike.'

Point made. Or . . . a point avoided. Why was Shard at Parkside anyway? He was supposed to be investigating . . . whatever he was investigating. Or he could have been there to share data face-to-face, which was fine, except he hadn't. Hadn't shared anything.

Shard could have made the whole thing up. Could have fired the shots himself and simply acted a part. That kind of paranoid thinking drives a man to drink. Stoner was too familiar with that; drink was a familiar country, he was no stranger there, nor to its less legal chemical neighbours in intoxication, delirium, denial and destruction.

The Tasmanian Devil memory stick sat by his laptop. Uncopied. Unread in any great detail. He had been avoiding it – spannering tasks on a motorcycle are excellent displacement activities – when interrupted by the shots and the subsequent mild headfuck of his dealings with Shard, which were reassuring at best, ambivalent at least.

Changing the transmission oils on most motorcycles is a task often neglected, Stoner considered. Although modern lubricants are of remarkable performance, especially when compared to earlier varieties, they still suffer from a lack of attention on the part of the motorcycle owner. The oils may appear to be as golden and as smooth as the day they were poured into their new metallic homes, but a combination of short rides and long intervals between those rides meant that the oils rarely reached the temperatures they needed to achieve to cleanse themselves of condensation and other undesirable contaminants. Stoner was of course aware of this, and unlike most of his fellow riders he looked forward to an hour of mindless spannering to provide him with thinking time.

He unbolted the Harley's transmission drains, after positioning a plastic tray beneath them to catch the released lube, and while the cold, thick, golden oil drained down he sat back to think. Watching oil drain slowly is more relaxing than playing an instrument. An instrument demands much of its player, and playing while thinking and dreaming produces solos as exciting as music for the funerals of the deaf, possibly less exciting than that. He sat back on a stool and watched the oil drain away as the daylight did the same. And he pondered.

The victims were employees of organisations unfamiliar to him, with the exception of the policeman. Stoner was familiar with the police. He enjoyed a decent relationship with most of their officers most of the time. OK: some of them, some of the time. Mallis had provided job titles for them all, but again they meant little. 'Chief Operating Officer' could mean anything. It depended on what the business did to turn its shilling. 'General Executive Manager' likewise.

The Tasmanian Devil did however include details of their bank accounts and the sums which flowed into and ebbed out of those accounts. They made interesting reading, as is so often the case.

'*Cherchez les dollars*', as a sage may once have suggested, and you could certainly find many things, although those things were not always obvious. A common feature of all the accounts was that as well as the regular, presumably salary payments, each of the dead men – and they were indeed all men – received a steady and substantial quarterly payment, which accrued through each of the three years the accounts revealed and were then paid to another account. The same account for them all. Mallis was not usually one to offer suggestions unless invited, but in the case of that account he'd appended a note suggesting that it did not exist. At any rate, it plainly did exist but he and his partner could activate it in no way at all. That account even aggressively refused to allow them to deposit funds into it. Stoner wondered what 'aggressive' implied in this context. How can a bank account – a series of numbers controlling other series of numbers – be aggressive about anything? As he watched the last drips of draining oil he decided that he most certainly did need an aggressive bank account. Whatever it was. The Bank Of Aggression. The Mutual Unfriendly Aggression Bank. Great idea. Can't fail. No one would even attempt to rob it, surely?

So the dead men were all conduits of some kind.

Mallis had entrusted the Tasmanian Devil with no suggestions about what kind of organisation was involved, so Stoner sent a message to ask. The reply was swift: the techno prisoners could find out, but it would take a considerable amount of time and involve a considerable level of risk, which is translatable as meaning that the cost of such a seeking would be high . . . higher than usual.

Stoner was sufficiently intrigued to dig further into the soupy mass of stats and facts encoded within the Tasmanian Devil. The mysterious account was certainly not based in the UK. This was no surprise, underhand banking was a global business and the fact that the prisoners considered it to be non-UK based made

Stoner's criminal mind decide at once that it most likely was in fact UK based. Deceptions inside deceptions. Enough to make the brain hurt.

The last of the motorcycle's oil drained into a stationary pool. Stoner dimmed the lights and evening descended, as evenings do.

26

FIRST LIGHT, LAST CALL

No response from the Hard Man. No reply from Shard. Nothing new from the techno prisoners and not a single bleat from the dirty blonde. Stoner sat neglected, frustrated and a little confused. Irritated, also, although he would have denied that.

Times of tension were always opportunities for enjoyment, either to ride down the road on one of the motorcycles, or stretch a set of six bright strings in the company of friends. In both cases, preparation is the key to delight. He had already and unnecessarily changed some inoffensive oils on the motorcycle he currently favoured for road use, so he turned his attention to his small collection of guitars. The Fender whose strings he preferred to bend was at the Blue Cube, so there was no opportunity for displacement behaviour with that fine instrument. Undaunted, Stoner fetched a guitar case from a steel cupboard. He paused.

He kept his guitars in flight cases to protect them from the hard knocks of long-term storage. Damage sustained while in use, while actually being played, that was OK in his musician's world; damage caused by clumsiness while the guitar was resting between stages was unacceptable. The patina of regular and hard work was valued by electric guitar players to such an extent that the mighty Fender guitar company produced brand new guitars which were factory scratched, scraped and sanded to make them appear worn and played out. This was a mystery to Stoner. His preferred Fender guitar was actually worn and played out. It had been refretted a number of times; three or four, he was unsure. Its once lustrous sunburst finish was scarred on the back by generations of belt buckles. Its tuners were occasionally prone to a little slippage, its control pots to a little electrical leakage, its frets to a little buzzing and its rosewood fingerboard had built up drifts of muck which were a mute to both the strings' accuracy and to any claims he might have made to being a safe pair of hands for such a rare and valuable – or simply old, depending on your viewpoint – instrument.

Stoner loved the cantankerous old machine . . . if loving an assembly of woods, wires and plastics is sane. And if 'love' is indeed the wrong emotion, then he certainly valued the thing, not least because others ascribed such a mysterious value to guitars like this one that they sold for large amounts of money when they appeared on the market. He suspected that those who paid the high figures rarely played the old instruments, but respected the fact that these high prices made the guitars eminently stealable. He considered it unlikely that anyone either could or would break into Parkside looking for elderly American guitars, but stored them in steel cabinets in case they did.

The cabinets were fireproof, too, which had seemed like a good idea until he thought about it during another unwelcome period of inaction. If the tasty combination of motor oils, fuels, wood and plastics which packed the buildings did indeed go up in flames, would it not be good to know that the prized guitars were safely stored in flameproof steel cabinets? Superficially, perhaps, but if the temperatures rose high enough to wipe out the buildings, the guitars would surely suffer. It would most likely be a challenge to extract the most rudimentary of blue notes from large lumps of charcoal.

Procrastination is an undervalued virtue in men whose nature is to react suddenly and often with violence. There are plenty of times when action itself is probably the least sensible course of action. But men of action are notoriously and properly admired for their ability to leap feet-first into risky situations, caring not a damn for the dangers which might be involved. This is how they die. Or, worse, how they become seriously injured and cause the deaths of others, sometimes innocent others. Stoner's experience of life had confirmed this truth to him, hence his tendency, when all about him were losing their heads, to immerse himself in the subtleties of his music or in the delights of maintaining and riding his motorcycles. Others of his acquaintance in similar occupations indulged in recreational pharmacy to calm their nerves, which were then so dulled that they failed at their tasks, often fatally, when the need for action became suddenly imperative.

He removed the guitar from its case. This particular instrument was a Gibson, a model obscure, which he had purchased only because it shared its model name with a motorcycle he had ridden once, hated and returned to its owner with flattering protestations of delight and a silent understanding that he would much rather walk over broken glass than ride another.

The Gibson was much the same. Beautifully made and handsome in its deep lacquer and expensive woods, it impressed everyone who saw it, who remarked upon its rarity. A justifiable rarity in Stoner's view, given that it was much better to look at than to play. It sounded wonderful, though, as indeed did the eponymous motorcycle, but his Fender-familiar fingers found the fretting experience to be more of a challenge than a reward. However, when he had decided to attempt the bottleneck approach to playing his blues, where the fingers fretting individual notes to play tunes or to form chords are replaced by a cylindrical slide worn over a finger to perform that duty, he had retuned the Gibson and discovered that it was perfectly suited to the task.

This conversion came after staring with disbelief and with ears whistling from the power of the world's top slide guitarist. 'I can do that,' Stoner had declared – but only to himself, fortunately – and had launched into a concentrated study of the technique. Bili the Bass had, after hearing his early efforts, suggested that he take up the triangle, coining a shared joke which had now lasted for several years.

Stoner fingered the strings on the Gibson. They were tuned to an open-G chord and familiar finger fencing produced unfamiliar tunes. He gazed again at his phones and at the screen of his laptop. None of them seemed likely to save him from the dreaded practice. He performed the perfected coffee ritual. That dark, almost black brew hissed, bubbled and wheezed into his mug. He picked up a blue glass slide and slid it over the ring finger of his left hand. It felt unfamiliar. He removed it, powered up a Marshall amplifier, connected the Gibson. As it was an efficient Gibson and not an elderly Fender, there were no buzzes and clicks, no pops nor crackles, just an amplified mains hum. He wound up the volume until the air quivered around the speakers and the strings of the guitar attempted to sound themselves, aching for the screaming release of feedback. Rested the glass slide on the strings and rocked it gently; the strings chimed in chorus.

He leaned back on his stool, sharing the weight of the instrument between his left knee and the shoulder strap, and began at the beginning. The scale of G-major; one, two, three. The first scale, the first octave was perfect. He was as pleased as he was surprised. The second octave likewise.

He was encouraged.

Three of his phones lit up.

*

Shard again, all three messages the same.

'Outside. Company. North.'

Interior lights left as they were, Stoner, wrapped in black and with a mood to match, armed himself, unobtrusively exited the Transportation Station and merged with the evening. Stood in the cooling air, breathing it in and listening to the chorus. Footsteps, quiet and confident. A confidence misplaced, hopefully.

One set of clever steps, near-silent steps, heading for him. He wondered whether he could hear a second set following the first, but decided that it was unimportant. What was important was that he intercepted the incoming intruder. The only reason for a stealthy approach like this was malicious intent. He hoped so. He stood still and silent as two sets of steps approached. Two. Definite. A team. Quite suddenly, Stoner felt himself wake up. As if a switch had been thrown, he was spoiling for it. Movement, maybe; contact, maybe; progress, answers . . .

A slight figure, moving in the shadows of the unkempt roadside shrubs. Indistinct in the failing light, excellent tradecraft and casual camouflage; hiking gear rather than military; innocently effective, always deniable.

The figure drifted past Stoner's stationary post. He was no longer aware of the second intruder. All senses focused upon the target. In sight now, but not for long. The edge of evening; a perfect time to intrude . . . and to defend against that intrusion.

No time for genial introductions. Stoner announced his presence with a stunning sideways blow to the back right side of the intruder's head. Glancing success – maybe the slight sound of the air parting before the blow or the movement of that air; maybe the second sense all stealth fighters learn as an essential survival tool – the target was alert and moved to avoid the strike, twisting left and away from the initial blow . . .

290

. . . directly into the path of the main assault, the rapidly closing left fist, the heel of which landed hard against the intruder's left ear, snapping his head sideways and back into Stoner's right fist. Ears seriously boxed, the figure paused; Stoner stamped the deeply cleated sole of the weighty Caterpillar boot of his left foot hard and accurately into the back of the right knee of his opponent.

The effect was exactly as the manuals suggest; the intruder fell, stunned and unbalanced, to Stoner's right. Arms thrown out for balance. The correct reaction would have been to relax and roll, but the dual head strikes had – as intended – delayed the brain's higher functions and instinct attempted to preserve balance.

Stoner caught the rising left arm, twisted it higher, pulled it back, and down, and hard, and followed the figure to the ground as it fell, landing a precise elbow directly and with maximum force into the intruder's left temple at the exact moment the right side of his head made contract with the exhausted, worn concrete of the old roadway. The impact was as loud and as violent as a gunshot. The body fell limp. Stoner stepped back, stood tall, turned to face the second figure as it closed in rapidly.

And stopped, well short, well out of range.

'Wow, JJ. That was neat.' Shard. Inevitably. 'Did you need to kill him? It would have been good to get an answer or two first.'

Stoner paused. Accepted Shard's presence and turned back to the fallen. A calm descended upon him. A familiar calm. Acceptance and a little denial. 'He'll be OK. A bit tender and in need of a little joint repair . . .' His voice tailed away. He reached for a pulse.

'Fuck. Sorry about that. He's gone. To somewhere better, let's hope for that.' Stoner stepped back, while Shard moved in close and rolled the body over, face up.

'Anyone you know?'

'No. You?' Stoner focused on Shard's face in the failing light. Shard re-checked the pulse, rocked back, sitting on his ankles.

'Yes. But a long long time back. 2 Para. Maybe a Hereford squaddie. I'm not sure.'

'Do you have a name for him?' Stoner, practical, calm.

'Nope. But we can print him. That should be simple enough. Why d'you kill him? He would have talked to us. More use alive than dead.'

Shard looked up. Stoner stood silent, darkness settling around them.

Shard tried again. 'Why d'you kill him?'

No reply.

'He could simply have been coming to listen, to watch, to warn, to . . . oh I don't know, just to talk about Transporters and Harleys, fuck's sake.' Shard wrestled with the dead man's clothing. The long, dark, sound-muffling coat fell open to reveal a sawn-off shotgun hanging from a lanyard around the neck.

'No loss. There are plenty more. The world is full of assholes. You'd bring a neat killing thing like that if you wanted a chat? Hmmm?' Stoner scanned the increasing dark.

Shard stood, gazed from motionless body to impassive killer. 'You want someone else to come after us? You can be strange. Damn fast though. For an old man. Impressed. Any thoughts about how to dispose of the evidence?'

'This was a message. Everything's a message of some kind.' Stoner massaged the elbow which had delivered the killing strike. 'Snag is I have no idea who sent it, what it means, who this guy was or who he worked for. I just knew that his job was to deliver a killing shot or to die trying. That was his job . . . his function. I doubt he knew about the dying trying thing, though. If whoever sent him knew he was sending him up against me . . . against *us*, then they also knew he would fail. Which is a message in itself. On the other hand, he could simply have accepted a hit contract without knowing the target. That's usually the best way, no? Saves on the jitters. So, if someone was sending a message, the best message in reply is always a return-to-sender. Except we don't know who the sender is, which is unhelpful.' Stoner paused. He was icy calm, calculating a response. Shard displayed none of the sudden fear he felt.

'So . . .' Stoner thought aloud. 'It'll be another unexplained accident, messy enough to make the media sit up, and public enough for our late compadre's employer to work out what happened. I can do that. See what comes out of the woodwork as a result. If anything. It may of course be unrelated.' His tone made it plain that he felt this to be unlikely. 'Stick him in the van. I'll take him for a drive and drop him off somewhere. Big road or a railway track so he can get a bit messed up, confuse the issue for the plods.'

'Christ, JJ, do you always think this much?' Shard stood over the body, lifted the shotgun and its lanyard from it, trawled the pockets for other weapons, found only a knife. 'You going to help me carry Mister Happy?'

But Stoner was gone.

293

27

EVERYTHING'S WAITING FOR YOU

'You were recommended by a lady.' One seriously smartly presented individual had seated himself at the café table, uninvited, opposite Stoner. Who was unimpressed, unamused and uninterested.

'Recommended for what?' He was in no mood for conversations with strangers, no matter how well dressed, how well mannered.

The intruder sat back, looked around, flashed gleaming teeth in a fine attempt to attract service. None came. Unlike a shared silence. Both men appeared comfortable with that. Stoner removed a phone from his pocket, opened it, confirmed that there were no outstanding instructions warning him to beware tall, handsome strangers, and replaced it in its pocket. He gazed at the man opposite, neutrally. This could perhaps be a welcome encounter. It was unlikely, in the light of his past experience of these things, but it could be. His guest smiled. Again.

'Is service likely? Possible?'

Stoner nodded, encouragingly. The stranger mistook the nod for a thawing, and showed further wider whiter teeth in a truly winning and welcoming smile.

'She told me you always stop at this place when you're passing. So I waited.'

'For very long?' The notion of parking up outside an anonymous roadside café and then waiting for an unknown, if recommended, apparently, stranger to drop by was a good one. Amusing, perhaps. 'Many weeks, for example?'

'About a half hour. You sure about that service?'

Stoner shifted his gaze over his guest's shoulder and tracked the approaching coffee as it progressed glacially towards the table. The stranger smiled on, aware of the shift but undisturbed, undistracted by it. Professional, then. The plate and cup landed, the waitress turned away in silence. Stoner raised a hand.

'More, please.'

She stopped, turned, looked only at Stoner. Silence.

'Same again, please. And thanks.'

He nodded towards his guest. The waitress left in her maintained silence, with as much vigour and bounce to her step as when she arrived. Immune to displays of dazzling dentistry. A true waitress, an example to her profession.

'You want something.' A statement. 'Other than breakfast?' Stoner sipped his coffee, winced. It was as bracing as ever.

'That good, huh?' The smile was still convincingly in place, no sign of tension or intent. 'Yes. I'm a policeman, Mr Stoner. I know who you are, who you're working for and that you're good at what you do. I have been told to find you and to talk with you. Your employer, public-spirited and helpful though he always is, claimed to be unaware of your immediate surroundings. The very tall black lady in his office suggested that I might find you here at around this time. And here you are. She knows your movements well.'

Stoner sipped steadily. Carefully.

'You do have a name? You know mine, so it seems only reasonable to share these things. Your coffee might be on its way. Be cautious. You do not want to drink it. You should eat the bacon in bread – hard to describe it as a sandwich – and leave the coffee for me. I'm immune to it. Almost enjoy it on a bad headache morning. Try water, maybe a drink from a can. A new and unopened can. They're the least dangerous.'

He took a bite from his breakfast, revealed no visible distress and sipped more of the coffee.

'What you after, anyway? Guitar lessons? Tips on traffic control? A guide to good coffee?'

'According to the information you hold, I should be dead.' The smiling policeman appeared unworried by this.

'OK. I had wondered.' Stoner chewed, with inexplicable relish. 'You're not the wrong policeman. You're the right policeman. And you should be a dead one. You're a man called Dave, right? Tell me all about it?'

And so he did.

Stoner listened while chewing. He signalled for more coffee. More coffee appeared. But only for him. He looked up sharply at the waitress's retreating back. Waitresses do not have eyes in their backs. Or in the backs of their heads. And the strange grunting snorting noise she made when walking away, a noise with a distinctly porcine flavour, was perhaps a clue to her behaviour.

'For. Fuck's. Sake.'

A series of statements. Staccato. Clear. Almost loud. With violence behind them. Stoner smiled no more. His gaze lacerated the calm and the quiet of the café. It lit a path to the waitress, who turned, returned and delivered two big mugs of coffee.

'Food in a moment. Sorry Mr Stoner. Didn't know it was a friend.'

Stoner raised his eyes to hers, bloodless. 'He's not. He's a plod. But he tells a terrific tale. Bring him ketchup for his bacon, and bring me another coffee.'

She glanced at the table.

'Yeah yeah, so I've got two already. I need strength. OK with you?'

She left. No little piggy grunts trailed her.

'I'll get this straight. You met some tart in a bar, in a posh hotel filled to brimming with fellow constables.'

Dave Reve nodded. Sipped. Grimaced only very slightly.

'The wife's upstairs counting sheep, so you decide to quench the hots with the blonde tart in the pool. How do I do so far?'

'You're good.'

'You fuck about in the pool some, and then she half-drowns you by jamming your face into her snatch and taking the deep-end dive? Is this correct, Dave? It sounds truly unlikely to me, but if you're telling me it happened then I should believe you. You have no reason to lie, or at least I can't think of one. How . . .' he drank deeply, shuddered only a little. 'How did you escape? Dear gods. What a way to go. Killed while muff-diving in a hotel pool. Glorious. Would your widow have got your pension? It would surely have given your forensics a bit of a day, taking oral swabs, as they do. "The deceased had eaten a hearty beefburger with relish and a lively cunt for dessert." That would have made their day. Sorry, it's a pleasing thought. Go on, how did you escape? Bite very very hard? I doubt that harsh thoughts would have done it. Interesting geometrically, though . . .'

'I didn't escape. She let me go. Try it. It's not easy to break the grip. My mouth was tight up against her, so I couldn't bite, and she had a grip of the pool's rim, I think. I just flailed about. Got water up the nose, started coughing, swallowed, breathed more water, panicked like a fool . . .'

'Thought about the grieving widow, how she'd explain it to the kids, stuff like that . . .'

'Nope. Punched her in the body as hard as I could, which wasn't very, started to cough, choke, horrible way to go, drowning, despite what some folk write about it. Couldn't see, couldn't breathe, couldn't break her grip. Hell of a grip, she had. Great . . . really great legs. Fit as you like. Then she just let go. And she went. Was gone when I got out of the pool. No sign. No trace. Took her clothes and took my clothes too.'

'Oh! I love that. She took your clothes? Left you strolling about the midnight lobbies in the starks? Excellent. Sense of humour, then. How d'you explain that when you got back to your room? "I say my dear, a funny thing happened on my way back from the bar?" That would be a challenge.'

'Didn't even think about it. Was still coughing up water and crap from my lungs. The chlorine is really bad for the lungs. They're still sore.'

'Sympathy of course. Fuck of a way to go, though. Epic. You report it? What were you doing in the hotel anyway? Some jolly for the plods? Happy taxpayers buying you all a good time?'

'No. A conference. All about money. I'm an accountant. A police accountant. A banker. I'm on the force because they wanted it that way.'

'OK. You investigate financial crimes, is that it?'

'No. I move police money around. Do you have clearance for this? Who are you anyway? I don't know you well enough to care about you, but I've skimmed your short file which tells me that you're some kind of freelance. What kind of freelance, and why?'

'I bet you know what kind, and I bet you know what I do, too. I bet you pay me, or men like me. Are there limits to what you can discuss with me? What have you been told to tell me? More usefully, what have you been told you must not discuss with me? In denial lies the truth. Usually, I reckon.'

'The brief was to tell you what happened. I've done that. Interpretation is more your game than mine.'

'That is true. Most certainly true. I can't . . . interpret without facts and background. The more facts, the better background, the better my . . . interpretation is likely to be. I'm looking for a killer. The fine lady didn't kill you. She killed someone else. Another porker. That very night. Which is all very excellent, she will have done it for a reason. If it was indeed that lady who killed that cop. There are few lady killers. But your masters and mine seem to think that she killed another cop. What do you think?'

'I think lots of things, but I'm not sharing until you tell me what you think. You show me yours, you know how it goes.'

'OK. I think she was a distraction. I think she distracted you while her oppo, the real killer, went and did his dirty deeds. That's how I would have done it. If I did such things, which of course I do not and never did.'

'Nice theory. Distracting who? I was hoping to get laid, not to wander around for an hour in the nude coughing up chlorine water. And distracting me from what?'

'Not you. You were the distraction, not the distracted. Although . . .' Stoner almost smiled. Thought better of it, and hefted one of his coffee mugs as though weighing it to throw. 'OK, then. You've rubbished my idea. Let's hear yours.'

'I think I was the target. I think she liked me. I think she deliberately killed someone else and let me go. I think you know that already and that you're playing a fool or a sophisticate or something out there. I think you're trawling for information which will help whichever investigation you think you're investigating at the moment. I think you're trying to mislead me, too.'

Stoner smiled down at his coffee. Raised his eyes. 'Why would she let you go? Professionals do not do this, otherwise they would either be dead themselves or out of work. Either way, they would no longer still be professionals. And if she could overpower a cop in his prime armed with nothing but her twat and a pair of good legs . . . she was certainly a pro. Most certainly. Did you fuck her? You carefully left that bit out.'

'Is that important?'

'I have no idea. No idea about most of this, to be honest, but it all adds a little spice to the tale and its telling. Maybe if you didn't, hey, maybe she'll come after you for a happy ending. Maybe if you did, you were so ace that she was not only stunned into letting you go but she will come back and insist that you do it again. I am sure stranger things have happened. I still reckon that she wasn't the killer. I reckon that if she'd been the killer then you would be one dead cop. So did you? Fuck?'

'No.'

'Interesting.'

'How so?'

'Christ's sake. Keep up. Her behaviour was bizarre. Utterly bizarre. What was your meeting, your conference, what was it about? Money, you said. You said that you move money about. What sort of money? Why do you move it? From where? To whom? You're a decently senior plod, so it must be important. You're at a posh hotel, so your constabulary pals must be decently senior. Just a moment. Was it all constables? Or was the guest list rammed with crims as well? A giant slush party? Handing over wads of taxpayer largesse to keep the villains under control?'

'You do have a great imagination, Mr Stoner.' Dave Reve appeared to be genuinely amused by this sudden flight of fantasy. 'Mostly cops. Cops of one sort or another. There are several sorts of cops, as you must know, being who you are. In case you've not worked it out, I am the man who pays you. Sometimes. Although in the same way that you wouldn't recognise me – I hope – I don't usually have any contact at all with operators.'

Stoner spat into his empty mug, sourly.

'Operators? Is that what I am? An operator.'

He appeared decreasingly happy.

'You're a transport consultant, if memory works. You supply

advice to surprisingly senior officers in the intelligence community. Advice which, excuse me if my near-death experience has muddied my thinking, generally involves senior officers or their appointees hiring your services and indeed your vehicles to carry out tasks which are somehow logistically vital to the realm but which need not be specified to a mere money-mover like me. And as my figures are checked only by secure accountants I could be viewed by persons of a depressingly suspicious nature to be acting not only as a money-mover but also as a cut-out between official ... ah ... officers and ... ah ... unofficial consultants. Of which you are one. A well-paid one, although my memory could be confused, as I've already suggested.

'It could also be of course that I am not unique in the function I provide to, say, legitimate officials, and that from time to time my colleagues and I get together to ... well, I doubt that the reasons we might get together could be very important at the moment. You specialise in Volkswagen Transporters, I believe? You have a fleet of them. They are wonderfully versatile and can be used in a vast variety of circumstances for all manner of unspecified but nationally essential jobs. Were I a curious man, I might even have observed that the noble and selfless taxpayer would appear to have paid you rather more than the cost of a large selection of Transporters over the last several years? Presumably they wear out fast. Maybe the service they provide proves fatal for them. Maybe they find themselves cut off in their prime?'

'Rather like your own position in that respect?'

'Exactly so. The same thought had occurred to me. It's an unusual notion, to find myself comparing myself to a VW van, but life can be strange.'

'Transporters rarely go swimming in the middle of the night with shapely assassins, though.'

'True. Being human appears to have at least one advantage

over being a VW van. Even though your own VW vans appear to cost a lot more than the life of, say, your average human.' He smiled. 'Any chance of a glass of water?'

'Almost certainly. But I'd only drink it myself if it was boiled first and then probably diluted with alcohol to maim the more resistant bugs. It is a little early for that, though, and I do have some miles to drive.'

Reve looked up, settled back. 'In a VW van, presumably?'

'Yeah. Whatever.' Stoner flagged down the sullen waitress, both of them failed to smile, he placed an experimental order for water.

'Why are we having this meeting? Pleasant though it might be, I confess a little puzzlement at the leading up to it. You were nearly but not quite killed by a tasty lady who seduced you in a swimming pool. You have a fine theory that after failing to kill you, which she was supposed to do for some as-yet unknown reason and for another unknown reason changed her mind and instead went off and killed someone else. It's not easy to believe this. A long series of non-coincidences. I need to ask: why was she supposed to kill you, do you think? You're a money man, nothing useful. No offence unless you want to take some. And if you do . . . well fuck you, hey?'

'You're supposed to know more about this than I do, Mr Stoner.' A tinge of irritation, steel almost, in Reve's tone. 'You are supposed to be asking me relevant questions, getting answers which mean something to you and thus gaining something of an understanding of whatever it is that's going on. You are not supposed to be sitting here like a sulky teenager, being ill-humoured and tricking me into drinking some seriously unpleasant mess in a cup.'

Stoner pulled a cell phone from his pocket.

'Excuse me.'

Texted the Hard Man. Who replied as though he'd been sitting

302

waiting for the call. Stoner replaced the phone in a leg pocket of his cargo pants.

'You're clean, then. Also cleared. I can tell you anything. Impressive in one so young. Information can be fatal. Think carefully. Do you want information? Do you wish to share my thinking on this? You can say no. Wives, families, pensions and the like can get awesome vulnerable, awesome quickly.'

Reve nodded. Stoner shrugged.

'Heads. You know about the heads?'

Reve shook his own, a puzzled look fixed to the front of it. 'Heads?'

'As in severed. Cut off. Sat on hotel desks and filmed. Instant movies instantly uploaded for the instant furtive delight of . . . well, I'm not sure who, really. You don't know about these?'

Reve shook his head again.

'OK. It's guys. Always guys. We have a number . . .'

'We?' Reve interrupted.

'Me and others. You don't know them. If you do know them, it's better that you can't connect them. We have a number of headless bodies. The number varies depending on who you're talking to and where you look. These things are never as definite nor defined as in the movies.'

Interruption again. 'Where? How d'you mean? A body's either a dead headless one or it isn't. Surely?'

'You would think so. But it's not clear. At first there was no obvious pattern to a bunch of increasingly messy killings. Plod was baffled, as you'd hope and expect. No offence, officer. But the bodies were complete. Well . . . all of the bits of the body would be in the killing room. Scattered around a lot . . . increasingly a lot . . . but all there. And there was an escalation pattern. The killings were getting worse. Messier. And someone was messing with the scene. Either the killer or someone else. I can't get my head around a lot of this, not the least because I've only received the bulk of the data in the last twenty-four hours or so. And no, don't even ask. I'm under no obligation to tell you who tells me what or in what order they tell it to me. The data is trustworthy, and I need to assume that it's accurate so I can work with it. It may not be complete. Hence the caution. Hence my reluctance to claim facts.'

Stoner paused, Reve stared at him. Wondered aloud whether something a little more fortifying than coffee – be it ever so strong – might help. Stoner agreed that it might indeed. But what? And where?

'You have a car?' Stoner raised an eyebrow in Reve's direction.

Reve nodded. 'I have a Jaguar.'

'Bully for you. I have a VW van. Let's go take a drive in it to a place I know where they might serve a quiet drink to a constable without scowling a lot. Better yet; I drive, you follow. How's that?'

Reve shrugged. 'I'm a family man. I know plenty of family-friendly places. You spooks like families, right? They make you feel safe.'

'You've been watching too much TV. Children just make a noise, pretty young mums distract the eye. I prefer quiet dirty places where they serve beer from jugs.'

'Whatever.' Reve had the air of someone who truly cared not a lot. 'Drive on, so long as you bring me back to civilisation at some point.'

'That I cannot guarantee. You adept at following? Done the police course in chasing a tail for beginners?'

'Mine's a Jag, yours a van. I should be able to keep up.'

Stoner smiled. 'I wonder. Where're you parked? Outside here on the double yellows which deny convenient parking to us mere humans? No doubt with a big bright badge in the screen to ward off the wardens? That sort of thing?'

'You got it. I'm not a spook. I don't need to hide. And the job needs at least one tax-free perk.' Reve was standing, buttoning into his coat.

'Yes of course, folk just try to murder you in swimming pools. We all love the quiet life.' Stoner moved scarily swiftly to the door, leaving a crumpled banknote on the table. 'When the big black van comes up behind you and flashes those big German headlights, pull out and follow. It's easy enough.'

And he was gone.

To reappear as stated a few minutes later, almost before Reve had fired up, belted up and called up to the office. Stoner pulled up behind the Jaguar, flashed some lights, passed and led away and out of town. To a grand old country house hotel, where the staff were welcoming and discreet and the drinking hours flexible and discreet.

'So why do you think the pattern's changed? Why did the killer – is it one or more than one? – switch from a progression, an escalation, to filming dead heads? You will have a theory, I imagine.' Reve stared at a soft drink. Stoner ordered a bottle of vodka and a litre of chilled water to chase it. And an orange. A healthy lunch. Balanced.

'Drugs.' Stoner busied himself pouring generous measures of the spirit into two glasses. He poured water for himself, pushed one of the spirit measures to Reve, who shook his head gently. 'I think it's a drug thing. Escalations and unpredictabilities often go together with dopers.'

Reve sipped the mysterious fruit drink he'd ordered, twitched a little at its bite and shook his head. 'A drugs thing? You reckon this whole business is about drugs? I don't think I'm payman for any drugs ops. The paperwork I get is all national security, very occasional organised crime, very rarely political. Drugs, though. Don't recall any drugs. Except maybe incidentally.'

'No. The chopping of heads is a drug thing with the cartels of Mexico and parts of the States. It's a way of attracting attention.

Dunno whether they also film them, but they certainly leave heads lying around to make a point. I gather they also deliver them to the person they're making a point to. Sending messages is important. You can see that it would have an impact.'

'Would certainly wake me up!'

Reve reached for the spirit bottle and poured.

'Yes. I could be completely wrong, but . . .' He ground to a slow stop.

Reve prompted, waved his glass a little. 'But? But?'

'I don't think I've heard of a serial, an escalating killer, who suddenly shifts MO.'

'OK.' Reve pulled an encouraging face.

'Can I show you something?' Stoner stood, pulled a wallet from a pocket, pulled banknotes from the wallet. Reve lost his encouraging face, replaced it with a more honestly bewildered expression.

'We're dealing with the same thing, but you don't actually understand, comprehend, recognise that thing.' Stoner spoke with an air of decision; Reve responded only with blank confusion.

'Grab your coat, grab your hat, we're going somewhere quiet.'

Reve's air of wonder coagulated into an almost physical cloud of confusion. 'We're leaving? We just got here. I was just getting used to the idea of getting wrecked at the expense of the noble taxpayer, a worrying notion for public servants, as you know.'

He made no move to leave. Stoner towered over him.

'Come on. I want to show you something. Something which will increase your bean-counter's appreciation of the realities of what's going down.'

'What? Where?' Reve stood, only a little unsteadily.

'What proper policemen call a body of evidence, I think.' Stoner smiled a distantly grim smile. 'It's all in the van. The other van,' he added, attempting to clarify a point which had quite plainly become lost somewhere in translation between them. 'It's not far. And we can share that drink immediately afterwards. C'mon; you might learn something today.'

They piled into the heavy Transporter, leaving Reve's smart car where it was, and headed out. Reve, in an excellent alcohol-fuelled humour, demanded to know what they were going to view. Stoner's companionable silence was companionable enough, but it was also silent.

As they swung through a complex traffic interchange, Stoner pulled into a faster lane to clear a dawdler, impressing an impressionably cheerful Reve with the sheer performance of the heavy Transporter, so Stoner glowered from driver mirror to passenger mirror, to central mirror and back to the driver mirror again.

'For fuck's sake,' he growled, mainly to himself.

'Say what?' Reve stared around, lost in the van's lack of rear windows.

'Some prat on a motorcycle.'

Stoner accelerated the Transporter past the slower car, started to change lanes to allow an overtake, when a large, loud and very fast motorcycle stormed through an invisible gap between the Transporter and the car it had passed. The rider – or the passenger – banged gloved fist and booted foot against the van's side and door as they screamed through a gap which was visible only to them. Stoner gave them no more room, continuing to change lanes, to close the gap between the motorcycle and the Transporter.

Then the bike was clear and accelerating away, rider and passengers both gesticulating their disapproval of Stoner's driving with a series of lurid gestures. The girl perched on the tiny rear seat, Lycra-clad knees held high, and clamped to the rider's sides, demonstrated her view that Stoner's virility may be a feeble thing, if a thing at all. Stoner watched, but did nothing, held to the speed limit as the bike accelerated away.

'Stupid. Why pull that crap?'

The bike had pulled off the carriageway and had parked up with a clump of other machines and their riders. The passenger climbed down and joined the rider and his companions; much vigorous gesticulation as the Transporter reached them. Dave Reve raised two fingers in salute as they passed. Stoner's sigh was long and loud.

'Dear, dear, the posturing policeman; now you'll inflame their egos, prod their manhood, expect noise and bad riding.'

'You can outrun them in this rocket van, surely?' Reve's face reflected sudden concern. Not a combatant, then.

'Nope. Not in this. This maxes at about ton-twenty; they'll get another thirty on top of that. And there's not much traffic, either. Here he comes, riding like the lone deranger himself. They do love to pose, these lads. Makes me feel very old.' Stoner's voice was flat.

The bike was back; the same one from before, along with the original rider, judging by his crash helmet, painted to resemble an alien head. The back seat hero was now another man, open-face helmet, leather cut-offs and a swinging chain replacing the original woman and the Lycra legs. Stoner watched the mirrors as they approached . . . and as they passed, pulling into the path of the Transporter and braking hard ahead of them. Stoner swung out and accelerated past.

'What's this about?' Reve looked more nervous than he sounded.

Stoner sighed again, glanced at the mirrors.

'OK, they want to stop us, to shout and swear at us for driving on their road and somehow in some pathetic way they want us – me – to apologise while they push us around and scare us to death. This is because they are big scary boys and everyone is scared of them. It makes me sad to be a bloke, to be a biker, frankly.'

The bike passed them again, making a lot more noise from its open exhaust, while the passenger swung the chain against the side of the van.

'They have no respect for my paint,' rasped Stoner, watching as the bike pulled past once more. 'Paint is important to some of us. Paint costs money. Some people spend a lot of money achieving the exact paint job that reflects their personalities. It's a personal style statement. You'd know nothing about that, you being a cop. And a married man with kids, so forth.'

'Are you like that?' Reve sounded surprised.

'No. But they don't know that. They're treating me with great disrespect, though.'

'Does that bother you?' Reve sounded concerned.

'No. But they don't know that either. But they've done this before. I'll bet they're the absolute scourge of other low-life tossers who drive their mates around in fucked-over hatchbacks with wrecked engines and great paint jobs. Here we go again.'

The bike had braked hard, slowing in front of them. This time Stoner accelerated hard at the bike and its riders, switching on his headlights and spotlights to suggest his intention. The bike accelerated again, but late, too late to avoid the onslaught of the heavy Transporter, and Stoner swung it out to overtake them again, missing them by only a metre or two. Reve clung to the grab handles, although the Transporter's suspension matched its hefty engine and the van was track-car stable as it shifted lanes . . .

. . . and shifted lanes again, as the barriers and demands of highway maintenance closed the outer lane to traffic, cutting the flow to just a single lane.

Chain clattered and rang along the sides of the heavy Transporter as the bike carved through between the van and the barriers. Once again it slowed, this time to a stop, the rider swinging his motorcycle to block the lane and dismounting, standing behind his machine and folding his arms with unmistakable intent.

'Can you drive over it?' Reve sounded worried now. 'Push it out of the way?'

'Not easily. It would damage the van, and why would I do that?'

Stoner braked at the last minute, rolling the heavy Transporter right up to the motorcycle, and before Reve could say anything, Stoner was out of the van, running with astonishing speed at the passenger, who raised the chain ready to swing it. Before he could Stoner had hit him full in the face and as he tried again to swing the chain Stoner was on him, hooking his feet from under him grabbing and wrapping the chain around his right forearm, pushing past, causing him to fall, then turning.

Suddenly.

And stamping hard on his face inside the open-face crash helmet, cutting off a scream before it was properly born.

With no pause and no hesitation, Stoner vaulted over the leaning motorcycle, straight into the body of its rider, knocking him off-balance while screaming at him, 'Die, die, die, dead man, die, die, die!' He jammed the stiff straight fingers of his right hand with all the force of his upper body directly into the rider's windpipe where it was exposed below the chinguard of the full-face helmet.

Then the chain was suddenly winding around the rider's neck as he stumbled, clutching his throat and emitting a musical gargle all his own, falling to his knees and trying to swallow and to stop the chain. Stoner moved fast, so fast, around to the rider's back, placed his left foot between his shoulder blades and pulled the chain, pulled it tight and pulled the struggling gargling man to the roadside barrier, where he wrapped the remaining length of the chain, holding its prisoner entirely captive.

With no pause, Stoner ran to the struggling fallen passenger, who was rubbing at his face and spitting blood and teeth and

310

trying to stand while enduring not insignificant pain from his broken jaw and broken teeth. Stoner kicked him hard as he could in the side of his head, protected as it was by the open-face helmet, and when he fell he kicked him again, this time in his stomach.

Maybe a single minute had passed. Maybe two. Certainly less than three.

Stoner returned to the motorcycle. Wheeled it to the side of the road, removed its ignition keys and rolled it down the embankment, letting it overbalance and fall on its side.

He returned to the rider in chains, slotted the bike's keys between the fingers of his right hand and smashed them into and through the polycarbonate visor of the full-face. The face of the alien bled red blood and bubbled.

'Never, ever, ever again try that stupid shit with me.' Stoner ran back to the heavy Transporter, its engine idling patiently, its occupant staring in silent disbelief at the display of unarmed combat, climbed aboard and drove off. Another car, just one other, had arrived, but its view of the altercation had been blocked by the black bulk of the heavy Transporter, and as that heavy vehicle pulled away, the following car followed it, driver oblivious to the carnage he was passing through, concentrating on the conversation he was enjoying with his cell phone. It's a question of perspectives.

'It's a question of perspectives,' Stoner remarked to his companion, who sat silent, staring straight ahead as the van accelerated again. 'Consider it a public service. No fee. The only effective form of self-defence is an offensive self, which I believe I've mastered. The moment you recognise an attack is on its way . . . attack first and harder. If the enemy cannot attack you . . . they can't hurt you as much as you can hurt them. The only alternative is running away very fast and very far. Being a target is never an option. Not for me. Not again. Never again.'

'You could have killed them,' Dave Reve finally found his voice. 'I'll call an ambulance.'

'Go ahead,' Stoner was as unconcerned as he sounded. 'They'll have your number from the call, so they'll come to see you, and you can explain what happened. It'll make an entertaining coda to the swimming pool saga, and your status as a guy who gets half-killed by a naked lady but then beats a couple of hard-boiled bikers to bits will reach new heights.'

'I didn't do anything! You beat them up, man!'

'I was nowhere near. I have a dozen witnesses who can place me anywhere else. Anywhere I like. Call your colleagues, an ambulance, a couple of priests, the AA, anyone you like. I'm sure you'll make a great story out of it.'

'This is your world, isn't it?'

'It is. And welcome to it. No fee.'

'I feel sick. I think I'm going to throw up.'

'No you're not. You'll be fine. I'll open the window. And I'll take you back to your excellently prestigious and suburban Jaguar. The body of evidence – where we were going – can wait.'

'Does this happen a lot?' Reve's colour was returning through the pallor of his face. 'And where did you learn to fight like that? Did they even touch you?'

'If one of them had got to me, I would have fallen. Two fast men will always beat one fast man, all things being equal. But they weren't fighters. They were fools. Noisy fools.'

'Who taught you to fight like that, though?'

'The army. The army trains hundreds of us to fight exactly that way. Remember this next time you feel like a scrap with someone you don't know.'

'I never feel like that.'

'Then you'll be safe. Always walk away. Leave fighting for fools like me.'

'Are there lots of guys like you?'

'Oh yes. More every year. Left-over warriors. Depend on it.'

Reve stared ahead through the windscreen. 'You could have killed them.'

'Yes. But I didn't, so you can relax.'

'And it just doesn't bother you. At all. Really?'

'It's just how I am. Always have been, maybe, certainly since the army and Ireland, Iraq.'

'Can't believe that the . . . the violence doesn't affect you. That's . . . inhuman.'

'Of course it affects me. Don't be stupid. If I wasn't affected I'd be dead. Long since.'

'So you just control it? You . . . what . . . zone out?'

'Not really. You can't zone out in a fight. You'd lose focus and lose the fight. Folk do that, fighting folk. They're all dead or out of the business.'

'Doesn't it build up, though?'

'Aren't we the profiler, now?' Stoner's amusement might have been genuine, though the dead gaze suggested otherwise. 'But yes it does build up. We all have ways of dealing with it, of handling it. Nearly there now.' He was swinging the heavy Transporter into the car park containing Reve's parked car, pulled around it, pulled up, already facing the exit. Unlocked the passenger door.

'Go on, tell me. How do you control it, how do you work it out?'

Stoner's smile gazed ahead, through the screen. 'Sex. Also rock 'n' roll.'

'Drugs?'

'They have their place.'

28

LIE IN WAIT

'It's the demons, isn't it?' The woman who styled herself Amanda intercepted Stoner as he headed towards the bar. He stopped. Walked away from the bar towards an empty table and beckoned her to follow him. It was loud by the bar. People enjoying themselves. Good for business.

'What's that? Demons who force you to attack strange men in strange ways in strange places?' He was smiling. It felt to him that this was his first smile of the day, which it may well have been. He looked over her head towards the bar and flapped a hand for service.

'No.' She returned his smile. 'No, the demons in your head who make up the tunes you play. The demons who force you to play the way you do. Demons who drive everything. You certainly do know them. You'd be unable to play like you do without them. You even try to drown them, don't you?' She looked around, back towards the bar. No approaching refreshment rewarded her attention. 'Don't laugh at me. I'm not joking.'

'I'm not laughing. It would take something really funny to make me laugh tonight, and that's not faintly funny. I don't think I do demons, though. I think . . . I think there are too many demons.

I think my own music exorcises them. I think if I didn't play the blues then the blues would drag me down. Drown me. The blues is the demon in me. I think that players are so much more lucky than everyone else. I think we're a different breed. I think you can't play unless you're driven to it, and that everyone else wraps themselves in blankets of stupidity, dishonesty and distraction to keep their attention away from the demons. I think they succeed, too. I think that almost no one knows about the demons . . . recognises them. I think they waste the entirety of their lives avoiding the demons of their own realities; they just rattle around for the whole of their lives. No point, no purpose. They do nothing I can understand. They squander their one and only chance, because although Buddhism is a great and comfortable thing to believe in, none of us is coming back. The darkness is every-where and the darkness is filled with the demons. It's where they live. Inside the dark inside us all. I'm not laughing, Amanda. The opposite. The night is filled with crying tonight. I will break a head or two tonight. I have no wish to do this but I will need to do it.'

Drinks arrived. Water for Stoner, something frothy for Amanda.

'Did you order that?' She looked surprised. Stoner shrugged. Shook his head and glanced at the bar.

'Everything is a message. The message here is that I should stay sober. The message is from Chimp, the guy behind the bar, the guy with the epic tats and the muscles. He is messaging that I look like a fight and he doesn't want a fight and he is suggesting by subliminal secret messaging that I stay sober. That is unlikely, frankly.'

'You saying that there's a message in my drink, too? What the hell kind of message is in . . . this?' She flapped capable strong fingers at the creamy concoction before her. 'I mean, what the hell is it anyway?'

'It's a cocktail. Chimp likes making cocktails.'

315

'I can see that it's a cocktail. Thank you so much, Mr Stoner, sir, for sharing your sense of humour with a mortal. I know it's a cocktail. It smells and it walks and it talks like a piña colada. I don't care about that. It will taste great if he really can mix a drink. What I care about here is the message.' She paused. Shrugged. Smiled in a minuscule way. 'What message is here? For me, that is. Or is it a message to you?'

'Both, at a guess.' Stoner almost smiled again. A faint glow of comfort threatened to derail the deliberate darkness of his mood. 'Could be he sees you for a frothy frilly tart, of course. Could be that he's telling me not to waste time on an inconsequence. If that's what you are. He doesn't know that, and neither do I. I don't actually know what you are. Or who. And don't start telling me now. I have no patience for life stories. Not today.'

The transient experimental glimpse of happiness had retreated again.

Stoner's phone shook in his pocket. He rose and walked to the bar, walked fast; folk cleared from him.

'Has Bili left us any Stoli? Is there a drink left in here?' He tried to smile at Chimp, but it was an obvious struggle. He gave up, banged both elbows onto the wet wood, shook his head and knuckled his forehead. 'Feel crap tonight, mate. Want to drown something. Me, for example.'

An unopened bottle of supposedly genuine Russian vodka slid towards him. Chimp hadn't moved. He did now; rolled his eyes to his left, towards the far end of the bar. A blonde woman raised her glass. Stoner nodded to her.

'What's she drinking? Fill her up when it's her time, OK?'

He picked up the bottle, pointed it to the woman, nodded. She looked at him over the rims of her spectacles, nodded, made a pistol of her right hand and fired him a shot. She might also have said some words, but the ambient was too loud to allow passage to anything less lively than a full shout. Or a real shot.

'Who's your friend?' Stoner was back at the table. Amanda stared with intent towards the blonde at the bar. 'The smart blonde lady? Good hair.'

Stoner drank the entire contents of his glass of water and refilled it from the vodka bottle.

'I'm not sure. She's been here a few times. She asks after me, I'm told, but somehow we manage never to actually meet. But she's good with her hands. It's not easy to slide a bottle along a bar. Not and keep the thing upright. Takes practice. Maybe she's after a job waiting bar. Who knows? Who cares?'

'A fan, then?' Amanda smiled a little. 'Like me?'

'I doubt that she's exactly like you, Amanda. Really. If she was like you then she'd be sat at this table joining in, not sitting on her own at the bar, staring at the optics and the mirror and avoiding all comers. Strange behaviour.'

'But she is a fan?'

'You get used to this when you play. You brought your bellows? The big brass sludgepump? You want to wheeze some noise tonight? Is that the plan?

'I thought you weren't going to play? Going to have a fight tonight?' She smiled some more. 'Yes. The sax is in the car.'

'In the car? It's no use in the car. It'll be lonely in the car. I feel sorry for it. Poor lonely sludgepump, alone in a lonely car. Makes me want to break something, the sadness. That's what it does to me, sadness. Want to stop feeling sad? Break something.'

'My dad always called trombones sludgepumps. Not saxes.'

'Your dad sounds great.' Stoner had drunk a full glass of the vodka and was relaxing. He looked up. Chimp leaned over him, carefully placed a litre bottle of sparkling water in front of him. Walked away. Stoner poured a glass of water, sank it. Poured more spirit. Sank that. Looked at Amanda. Sweat appeared on his forehead. His eyes remained entirely focused.

'Your dad a player? Tell me about your dad.'

'Jesus.' Amanda walked to the bar, carrying the cocktail before her as though there was a danger of an explosion. Placed it in front of the blonde woman, who looked at her, expressionless, said nothing.

Stoner's phone shook, rousing him suddenly from the approaching and welcome dullness. 'Oh fuck off, Shard,' he muttered as he flipped it open to read. But it wasn't Shard. It was Dave Reve. Asking his whereabouts and if he could intrude. Stoner replied in the affirmative. Amanda had retaken her seat. She waved at the open phone.

'More fans?'

'Nope. A gentlemen of the constabulary persuasion, oddly. Not every night I find my company so in demand. The plod will come calling any time now. You OK with that? Where's your drink? Did you throw it away?'

'Gave it to your fan. She looks the sort to enjoy a good cocktail. Great wig she wears, too. I know wigs. That's a posh one. Any chance she's not an actual blonde? Who would have thought it?' She turned to face the bar. The blonde woman raised the cocktail, shared with them an unreadable expression. 'See. My friend.'

Amanda produced a shot glass and poured vodka.

'*Naz drovie!*' she said, and threw it back.

'Steady with that. Too much booze too fast can make you throw up.' Stoner's half smile was showing signs of revival.

'Oh what wit! Very funny. Practice makes perfect.' She sipped. 'Perfection in many things. Something to aim for. Did you know that all men believe that only men can hold their drink? It's true. I mean it's true that they think that. But women can absorb alcohol better than men. It's because of the higher fat content in their bodies. Did you know that? I'm betting another drink that you did not.'

She drank that other drink before he could reply. He didn't

318

reply. Poured himself another spirit and turned his gaze to the stage. The house band had left for their break. Stoner observed that someone had placed his Fender on its stand next to his amplifier, that the amp was switched on, lights were glowing. He admitted temptation. But only to himself.

Amanda studied him. 'Play or fray, Mr Stoner?'

'JJ. I think you know me well enough to call me JJ. Friends do that.'

'I'm a friend? That'll be the booze, then. In the morning I'll be nothing. Just another fan. Or will your morning bring tea and toast with the classy piece in the wig? She never looks away from you, y'know. Never. Do you always have this effect on women?'

Stoner looked back at her. 'No. No, I don't. Do you ever actually shut up?'

Amanda smiled, wider and wider and the smile split into a laugh. A loud laugh which stopped the conversations at tables around them. She wound down to a wide smile and flicked back another shot.

'I'll go get the sax.'

She bowed to the nearby tables, turning more than half a circle while doing so, ending up facing the door.

'Back soon.'

'Who's that?' Dave Reve settled uninvited into the still-warm seat. 'Looks nice. Welcoming. Not blonde, so I can feel safe? No?' He did the quizzical eyebrow thing, settled a soft drink on the table. 'You getting smashed, Stoner? Thought you were going to do some of your musical stuff. Or do you perform better when rocket fuelled? Do you need a fight first?'

'Fuck off, Dave.' Stoner's expression was as welcoming, as amiable as his words. 'Welcome to the club. The Blue Cube welcomes all-comers to an evening of booze, schmooze and bluesy music. What's so urgent that it's dragged you away from a lovely evening of domestic delight at the family hearth? You hoping for

319

another magic blonde? This place is crawling with them tonight. Chap can't move without tripping over some classy tart or other.'

'Who's your brunette, then? Looks nice. Nice shape. Wide mouth, decently upholstered.'

'You make her sound like an easy chair. A sofa. She's a saxophonist.'

'Any good?'

'No idea. Shall maybe find out in a little while, although I am no judge of techniques on things without strings. What d'you want anyway? Tell me now. If I carry on with my Russian friend here, Miss Stolichnaya, and most especially if I remake my fond acquaintance with her sister, the bad lady Pertsovka, I shall soon lose all interest in everything but the girl, the music, the bottle and the night. I'm halfway there, so . . .'

He looked up, quite suddenly becoming aware that Reve was paying him no attention. He was staring at the bar.

'What's up?' Stoner was rushing back to sobriety. 'Who is it? Who've you seen? Is there a threat here? I see none.'

'Back in a minute. You armed?'

Stoner shook his head.

'No. Do I need to be?'

'Maybe.' Reve stood slowly, made a show of draining his glass of its non-alcoholic contents, and made his way to the bar, displaying conspicuous politeness to those he moved gently aside. He leaned, elbows to the counter, attracted attention, and ordered.

'Stoner gets no new bottle till he's played. You tell him that. Please.'

The barman was a big man.

'You tell him. Man wants a drink, he has a drink. You want to be his mummy, you be that thing for him. I'm sure he'll love you for it.' He looked around at the faces around the counter, shrugged, displaying no recognition, and returned to his seat.

'There a problem?' Stoner appeared harshly sober. No trace of a slur. Eyes active, hands out of sight. 'Tell me now.'

'The blonde at the bar. The beautiful one.'

'Yes? I have eyes, I can see. She bought me the bottle here. My friend Stoli. You fancy her? You're acting more like you want to call in an air strike, mind.' He was relaxing, misunderstanding. Reve's tension was hidden, controlled.

'She's the woman from the pool.'

'Say again.' No lightness now. Stoner took his phone from his pocket. Keyed a text message to Shard.

'The blonde woman is the woman who tried to drown me. No doubts. I was very close. I know exactly what she looks like. She's the killer. She nearly killed me.' Reve's voice was rising, in both pitch and volume.

'Look at me. Look directly at me.'

Reve did as he was told.

'Pick up the bottle, Amanda's glass, and pour yourself a drink. Take your time. Look one hundred per cent relaxed. She's looking this way. She's very nice looking, my goodness me, yes. I am unarmed and have no wish for violence in here. Unless it's my own and I'm in charge of it. Look at me. Say something funny.'

'Holy sweet fucking mother of God, that insane bitch is sat at your fucking bar and you ask me to say something funny? You off your fucking head, Stoner?'

Stoner smiled widely, shook his head. 'Oh that was funny. That was so funny. You are such a comedian, Dave! Dead right. I've called for reinforcements. They're on their way. Any moment now the cavalry will arrive.'

'You're talking crap, Stoner. I'm going to arrest her. You might be acting some stupid part as an unarmed superhero, but I have a gun in here, and . . .'

'Oh do shut up!' Stoner was actually laughing. 'Forget all talk of guns. You're not waving some fucking bazooka around in here.

The place is crawling with civilians having a good time and no one, cop or no cop, shoots them. OK? Speak up. Are we OK with this, Dave? Say yes and you live, fail to answer and I'll disarm you and break your head to shut you up. Simple.'

'OK. It's OK. I don't understand a fucking thing. Why are you grinning like some sort of fucking maniac, you fucking maniac?'

'Talk about anything. Tell me again what a great fuck she nearly was. I need to do a thing with the phone.'

Stoner texted. Reve stared, tried to speak. Mumbled. There was a ripple of small applause from near the stage. A distraction.

'Amanda with the saxophone and the wondrous lip technique,' Stoner replaced his cell phone into his pocket.

'What? I'm losing this.' Reve reached for a drink. Stoner poured a clear spirit into a clear glass for him. Water for his own.

'Shard's here. Outside. You know Shard? Harding? Do you pay him?'

'I've seen the name, but I only pay to account numbers. But we're all big buddies tonight, right? You and me, you and Harding? Do you work together, then?'

Stoner nodded; 'We do today, I think. I'm going to invite the blonde bombshell over to our table.' He stood.

'You're what?'

'You heard me. Turn and look at her.'

Reve did as instructed.

'Fuck,' under his breath. 'It really is her. Fucking madness.'

'Then why doesn't she recognise you? Why is she smiling at me like I'm Mr Wonderful and ignoring your handsome, manly features? It can't be easy for a lady who's clamped those same manly features into her innermost self to forget them in just a few days. Really. I think you've got it wrong. I don't think it's her at all. I think it's time to find out who she is, though. Stay there, I'll go get her. Do you know Amanda, by the way?'

That expert player was moving importantly through the audience in their direction.

'You don't pay her, do you?'

'Surname? Real surname? Account numbers?'

'Not a clue.'

'Then I've no idea. Idiot. Who is she?'

'Saxophonist. Strange girl. Saxophonists are often strange, but she's stranger than most. A clue for you. If the blonde bombshell leaves, let her go. Shard will tail her. Have you ever done field-work?'

'Yes and no. What do I talk about?'

'Improvise. It's the stuff of dreams in a jazz club like this one. Just make it up as you go along. Beats learning anything. Follow my lead if you feel the need.' Stoner walked towards the bar, intercepting Amanda as she headed tablewards.

'Hey. I got the sax, the alto.'

'Cool as cool. Go sit down and introduce yourself; he's called Dave. He's a good guy. But nervous. He's never been in a place like this before and it's doing things to his sanity. He needs calm. Can you do calm?'

'Ask nicely.'

'I never met her. I'm asking you, Ms Notnicely.'

'Can we go out afterwards? Can we go and, y'know, talk, take a time? I want to hear how you like the way I play. And to, y'know, talk more.'

'Yeah. Fine. Might be very late. OK?'

'I go do calm, o master. Tranquilo is my middle name.'

'Liar.' Stoner approached the blonde.

'Hey. Care to join us? We keep nearly meeting, but somehow not. You here for the music? You a follower of the blues or something?' Stoner was sounding almost human. He flicked a hand for another bottle.

'This suit you?'

323

The familiar Stolichnaya bottle stood between them.

'And thank you for the other little Russian soldier. Come help sink its brother with us, hey?'

She smiled. She truly was a looker, Stoner mused as he led her towards their table. And she was over-dressed for the club, so carrying, concealed. Life was packed with visual delights. None of them could be what they seemed. Life was also packed with sadnesses.

Stoner did introductions. 'Amanda,' that lady bowed. 'Dave,' that man smiled with strain and looked away. 'I'm Stoner, as you know, and you are?' His voice trailed invitingly.

'Charity,' she smiled. 'Charity. I believe it's a virtue. In some. A burden for others. It's very good to meet you all, but I actually know nothing at all about jazz music and I don't have a lot of free time this evening. I wanted to talk with Mr Stoner here about a personal matter.'

She smiled.

'But it'll keep. No rush. Another day.' She turned to Amanda. 'I saw you carrying a saxophone. Do you, y'know, play it here? Isn't it . . . heavy? Loud?'

Reve interrupted.

'Charity? That's one rare name. But don't I know you? Haven't we met before?'

She returned a gaze and a pause.

'I don't believe so. Where? I don't believe I've seen you here before, but I have seen Amanda and Stoner. Are you another musician?'

'Hardly.' Reve's stare was intense. 'No. But I do know a lot of songs, I suppose. Didn't we meet before? At . . .' he paused. 'A hotel? Near Oxford?'

Charity's smile was steady, unflinching.

'Rings no bells here. Was it a concert, a gig or something? I'm

324

no great fan of popular music. I only came here to catch Mr Stoner.'

She smiled at Amanda. 'You have talent. Think I've heard you play before. Another club, another place. But I thought that was a trumpet, not a saxophone. I'm no real judge of guitars, but understand that Mr Stoner here has something of a reputation.'

Reve persisted. 'The hotel had a great indoor pool.'

Charity looked blank. Shook her blonde head.

'Do you swim?' Reve could not drop it.

She ignored him and turned to Stoner.

'Can we meet soon? Just the two of us? I have a business concern which I'd like to share, but it's a private thing, as they usually are.'

She turned back to Dave Reve. 'I do swim, but mainly in rivers and the sea, almost always outdoors. I've not swum indoors for a long time now, and I don't think I've ever swum in a hotel. Ever. So whoever you think I am, it's not me. I would remember you. I've a great memory for faces.' She looked at Stoner as she rose to her feet. 'I've a great memory for names, too, Mr Stoner. And places. May I call you?'

'You leaving?' Stoner stood. Reve also started to stand, but Stoner's hand lowered him back to his seat. 'I'll walk you out.'

They headed towards the exit.

Stoner spoke close to her ear, fighting the noise of the club. 'I'm sorry. What did you want to talk about?'

'We have a mutual concern. It's quite serious, and it is not, I'm afraid, going to go away on its own.'

'You've lost me now. Something to do with the club?'

'Don't play silly with me, Mr Stoner. My concern is your current problem. We have a conflict of interest, although it can be resolved. Most things can, given a little effort.'

She stopped, turned, looked hard at him. 'We can resolve the problem. And we should.'

Stoner's expression drained of any pretence at humour. He looked levelly back.

'Am I looking for you, then? Should I be knocking you on the head and calling the cavalry?' No twinkle of humour. None was returned.

'That would be a bad thing for us both, Mr Stoner. We have much in common, many shared interests at the moment, but we are not on the same side. It's important that we keep our heads clear and our tempers cool. Can we meet again soon? I keep coming here and I keep missing you. And I don't wish to cause a conflict by calling on you at home or accosting you in the street.'

'Give me a number and I'll call you. Tell me a time and I'll call then.'

'I have your numbers, several of them. What time do you breakfast tomorrow?'

Stoner shrugged. 'Nine? I don't mind, really. I'll clear the day for you. Would that be a wise thing to do?'

They were at the door.

She smiled. Offered her hand, which he took.

'It would be a lot better if we could work together on this. Better for us both, and a whole lot better for those close to us. I'll call.'

'I look forward to that. Text or leave a voice message if I can't pick up. One thing?'

She stood by the door. The door manager stared fixedly away from them.

'One thing?'

'Dave, back at the table. Dave Reve. He really does think he knows you, doesn't he? He's a copper, doesn't really do mistaken identities. You do know him?'

There was no trace of a smile in reply. None. Charity looked through him, eyes far away for a moment. A cold stare towards a cold place unknown to Stoner.

'I've not met him before. I do know the name. You sure that's his real name?'

'What? Of course it is, why?'

'You known him long?' Wherever she'd been to in her mind, she was back now. Returned and focused.

Stoner shook his head. 'No. But I have no doubt who he is. And he does tell quite a tale.'

'I honestly never saw him before, not in the flesh, although I believe I have seen his likeness. And I do know who he thinks he's met. He spells his name Reve, not Reeve. French. Dream, it means.'

Stoner remained silent.

'Dream,' she repeated. 'As in bad dream, wet dream, if you like.'

'Nightmares? That sort of dream?'

'All dreams are nightmares, Mr Stoner. If they're bad, violent and aggressive dreams, then they're bad dreams for the dreamer. If they're dreams of success, fulfilment, winning and accomplishment, they're bad for the losers, the lost. Someone always plays the loser in every dream. His dream is no different. It's not possible to make happy endings for all.'

Stoner reached for her. Failed to make any contact. She was unreachable, untouchable and almost out the door somehow, as though the door had moved to meet her. The door manager looked over. Stoner shook his head. Called across the noise to her.

'Tell me.'

'Later.'

No room for negotiation there, Stoner could see that.

'OK. Later it is. Look forward to it.'

'I bet!' She smiled, bleakly and without any warmth at all. And left. Stoner's cell phone shook a minute later. Just once. No message. Shard.

'What the fuck was that about?' Dave Reve's voice was raised, and not simply because the background sound was loud. He looked confused more than angry. Amanda more bemused than anything. She looked up. 'You're not friends, then. You and Charity?'

Stoner stood by the table, suddenly too tired to sit.

'No. Never spoken to her before. You've never seen her before, either, Dave, but she knows, she says she knows, who you're confusing her with. She knows my cell numbers, too. She should not.'

Amanda appeared increasingly baffled, and bored.

'Why not? Someone must have given them to her. Obviously. Come on.'

Stoner looked at her, no smiles.

'Do you have a number for me?'

Amanda shook her head.

'Neither should she. I hate that.'

'What's so important about a phone number? Christ, JJ, there are bigger things in life than phone numbers.' She tried to smile. 'The guys are on the stage. Are we playing? Is it OK if I play?'

Reve shook his head again, pouring a drink for himself. 'I have so lost the thread of this. We need to talk, Stoner. I came to this madhouse so we could talk.'

'You're correct. This is a madhouse. The time for talking is later.' Stoner leaned across the table until his face was close to the other man's. 'Tomorrow or the next day. Promise. Nothing strange will happen to me in the meantime. I cannot say the same for you. I feel ... concern for you. You should go to a safe place. A hotel or the nearest nick. I think you should go there right now and I don't think you should tell anyone – including me – where you're staying. If your car is nearby, leave it and walk somewhere. Anywhere. If your car is parked a decent distance away, which would be better, then walk to it by a very roundabout route, and check to see if there's a tail. There shouldn't be if you leave quickly. Like right now. Go somewhere secure, park your car as far as you can face walking away from it. Use some police safe house. Any one you have access to. And take the card out of your phone. Battery too. I'll leave messages for you when it's safe. Pick them up at six o'clock tomorrow evening. Make that the first time you put the battery and card back into your phone. After you've read my messages, take the card and battery out again and text back to my number on the brand-new pay as you go phone you'll have bought before then. Do not use that phone before then. Go now. Go quickly to a place you know is safe. If you actually have any tradecraft, now is a great time to remember it and implement it. Truly. Don't talk, just go. Out the fire door.'

'I need to call my wife . . .'

'No you don't. Oh. OK.'

Stoner handed him a phone.

'Call her now on that and explain that you're on a secret mission of national security or something. Be very quick about it. Also convincing.'

'This is a music club. She'll just think I'm in a bloody club. Drinking and chasing women.'

'Then don't call her. You must *not* call her on your own phone and you must *not* tell her where you're staying. What she doesn't know, she can't share. Ignorance is rarely bliss, but it does offer a little safety. It's up to you.'

Reve punched in a number, spoke with some little agitation, passed the phone to Stoner. 'Speak to her.' Stoner shook his head, rolled his eyes, but accepted the phone. Spoke abruptly and without listening to the remote voice, the querulous voice.

'Stoner. Reve will be working with me for the next seventy-two hours. He will be unable to contact you in that time. If anyone should contact you asking his whereabouts, tell them that he's been called away. Which is the truth. This is urgent, and it cannot wait. Apologies.' And he hung up. Reve stared at him, stunned.

'How do you spell your name? Your surname?' Reve spelled
it out, slowly.

'Go! Now, just go, for fuck's sake!' Stoner shouted. Reve left.
Amanda stared, mouth hanging open, a caricature of bafflement.

'Got that alto?' Stoner was standing at her side. She nodded.

'Come along then, little miss nice, let's go play some blues.
Play them loud. Drown some sorrows. Cover our confusion. Cloud
all issues and shed some tears.'

'Oh hello.' Bili greeted Stoner with obviously and deliberately
fake forced enthusiasm and friendliness. 'Good of you to drop
by. And you have little Miss Munch with you too, I observe. How
fine indeed, how very fine.'

She was drunk, stoned maybe, rocking from foot to foot in
time with the burst of boogie she squeezed from the big bass.

'Is tonight the night we take requests?' She mimed a caricature of a bow, swinging the bass guitar's long, long neck in a
wide and dangerous arc. The audience chuckled, companionably.
The mikes were live and the regulars were familiar with the
banter.

Amanda stood uncertain. Embarrassed. She nodded to Bili, to
Stretch on the piano. He beamed back, broad white grin splitting the shining ebony of his features.

Silence suddenly on the stage. Stoner leaned back against his
stool, Bili looked vaguely around her. Stretch looked at Amanda
and smiled even wider. And with a deep breath Amanda blasted
the quiet with the unmistakeable opening bars of a slow blues,
playing it in the key of C, the better to suit her estimate of Bili's
vocal range. Immediately she was transformed from nervous
newcomer into a confident instrumentalist. Bili and Stretch
entered the verse with immaculate timing, playing as though
they'd been playing together for years, which they had, and as
though Amanda was a familiar friend dropping by and sitting in.

Which she was not. The intro verse let itself out with no contribution from a preoccupied Stoner, who watched the doorways
one after the other with no obvious interest in the music around
him or the guitar in his hands.

'Have you heard about my baby?'

Bili wept into the microphone, singing so close to it and so
loud, so penetratingly loud, that the speakers released a feedback background harmony of their own.

'Where's he gone, where's he gone; I just don't know . . .'

And Stoner's sharp strings cut in suddenly beside her, holding
her hands as she sang of her loss. He still stared at the doorways, at the bar, anywhere but at Bili, but his timing was exact,
his pitch perfect, the notes bending from flat to sharp and the
edge of the flat pick scratching across the strings instead of
plucking them. Abrasion not complication, fingernails down the
blackboard, the individual notes crunching crisply one into the
other. He looked up only when Amanda's alto saxophone added
a defiant and questioning trailing harmony to his notes.

The unoccupied stool behind the stage drum kit remained
unfilled, but as the bass guitar's speakers boomed, so the bass
drum added its own resonant echo; unplayed, the cymbals hissed
and the snares on the smallest drum sang a metallic backdrop
of their own. Ghost drums, playing themselves, their own blues
for their own pleasure behind the living band. The audience stood,
rapt. Bili sang. Two verses of loss, longing and a lover's agonies,
and then she stepped back from the microphones' range, looked
straight at Amanda, and bowed with her eyes, smiled with her
mouth. A challenge.

A challenge accepted. No trace of nervousness. Amanda bent
lungs, lips and fingers into the brazen sax. Its response was alive,
alive as only a brass horn in the hands of an instinctive expert
can be. The notes hit their peaks, a complete twelve-bar verse,
carefully constructed to end on a high note, which faded along

with the player's breath, overtaken suddenly and shockingly by the double-speed interruption, interrogation, of Stoner's battered Fender. A barrage of hard full-treble notes. He was bending every note on every string as it sounded to make every note sharp. Out of tune. Deliberately putting every ear in the place on edge, hairs rising on the necks of anyone in earshot. True blues at its intense, insistent best. Stoner played while staring at Bili. Just looking at Bili. Gaze unwavering. Whether there was focus, consciousness behind the eyes, it was impossible to see, and only Stoner and Bili would have known that, their own shared musical chemistry being almost a member of their shared stage world, an exclusive world of their own.

And quite suddenly the moment was broken by the alto again. Interrupting mid-verse this time and intercepting the guitar, joining it in an ascending scale; playing in unison, the same notes doubled, two very different voices. One of them powered by living breath, the other by electricity.

Stoner wound up the volume on his Fender, then dropped it swiftly back to silence, watching the doors, always the doors, while Amanda's brazen alto completed the verse. Playing exactly what Stoner would have played had she not been there, or so it felt to the audience, and to Stretch, judging by his smile. And after the final sung verses, the saxophone completed the number and the audience revelled in their loud appreciation of an unexpectedly fine piece of big, brassy, band music. Amanda took her bow, sat down on the edge of the stage and unscrewed the reed from the sax, shaking the spit from it, nodding at Stoner. 'I'll sit this out, hey!' She looked exhausted. Deflated. After a single number. Less than ten minutes.

Stoner nodded. Shouted '"Hideaway". In E,' and launched into that fine instrumental, the band chugging along into their own rendition of Hound Dog Taylor's classic tune. Played well, too, and as the middle section neared its end, Stoner nodded an invite to Amanda to take a verse for herself, but she appeared to be losing a staring match with a face in the audience which was unwelcome but familiar to Stoner, and plainly to the lady herself.

The expressions striding across Amanda's features marched through unhappiness to anger, via frustration and despair. The band played on, all bar Stoner, oblivious to the tiny drama. The small man wearing the too-large leather jacket leered triumphantly at Amanda, who was fast approaching a perfect impersonation of someone who had passed through annoyance and was moving rapidly towards resignation.

The small man had eyes only for Amanda. The number ended, quite abruptly, with none of the usual and expected self-important percussive flourishes from Stoner. Instead and uniquely, Stoner laid down the guitar halfway through the final verse, dropped it to the floor beside his vacant stool, left it feeding back gently through the loud Marshall amplifier while he paced across the stage and dropped from it, landing with his full weight upon the small man in the too-large jacket, and bringing his gripping fists down together with his full weight upon that unfortunate's head. The dismal crunch of spinal bones compacting together was mostly drowned out by the background sound. Mostly. Leatherjacket fell as though he'd been axed. Lay unmoving at Stoner's feet. His eyes stared without seeing, then closing slowly, one after the other. One eye held out for a few moments, staring in blind accusation at Stoner's innocent foot, then flickered shut. The fingers of one hand twitched in silent applause.

The audience voiced their raucous approval of the number, and although those nearest the altercation appeared confused, it was plain that they had no real idea of what had just happened before them. Amanda stared, silent. Expressionless. Eyes unreadable and silent. Saxophone hanging from her neck like a bright mute bird.

Stoner stood similarly silent, still, unmoving while gazing around him. The man at his feet posed no threat, none at all, any threat would come from a man still standing. None appeared imminent. The Chimp and a door heavy appeared. The audience, with a glorious misunderstanding of the performance they'd missed, shouted for more. Chimp and the door heavy lifted Leatherjacket, looked at Stoner, then at the door, a silent question.

Stoner shook his head.

'Keep him. Somewhere safe. I need to ask him who he is.'

'You enjoy attacking strangers? Fuck, JJ . . .'

The Chimp and the heavy staggered towards the bar, Leatherjacket semi-conscious, feet dragging. Stoner hopped back up to the stage, retrieved the atonal Stratocaster, nodded thanks to Bili for winding down the scream of its feedback, and set about tuning it. He glanced across the stage at Amanda, who stood, still, looking worried. Unhappy. The audience was buzzing, aware of tension and mistaking it for the tension of the music, of the new face, the new brass player, maybe.

Bili punched Stoner in the ribs, made a joke of it for the crowd. They applauded. An involved audience, then, unaware of what it was they were involved with. 'You good, big man?' Bili slurred her words, dropped her face and peered up at Stoner in mock supplication. He nodded.

'Stormy Monday, huh?'

He nodded again, and tried to appear unsurprised as a sudden drummer tapped up the intro count, added a shouted 'Two, three . . .' and Bili, Stretch and Stoner slid seamlessly together into an old familiar friend, and time stood effortlessly still, as time can when fine music, fine blues music, is being played live.

Stoner glanced to the bar. The Chimp was back at his post, cheerfully exchanging drinks for money, a job he did well and always with good humour. Of the evening's latest casualty there was no sign at all. And the band played until the end. And they accepted the reward of applause. And bowing, they left the stage.

Wallpaper music replaced them. The audience headed for the bar. Drinks appeared as if by magic for the musicians. Stoner smiled grimly as Bili vanished into a swamp of appreciation, curls swinging, silent smiles floating along with her as she acted the gracious one. He looked for Amanda, who had packed her sax into its case and was sitting alone in the darkness at the edge of the stage, the corner nearest the fire exit.

'OK. Who he?'

Stoner passed her a bottle of water, something neutral to share. If not a pipe of peace, at least a bottle of it. 'You're plainly not strangers.'

She passed the bottle back. Looked up into the air above them and sighed.

'There'll be another one. They always work together. Big bloke. Big as you. Heavier.'

'We've met. Just tell me who they are, who you are, and why I don't like them.'

'Why *you* don't like them?' She appeared at least a little surprised. 'I doubt they'd give you any grief. They're more into scaring drunks and women than attacking big, fit blokes.'

Stoner shook his head a little.

'I met them both before. The fat guy tried to play the heavy with me. He's in hospital, I would think. He should be, in any case. There's no sign of him here. He certainly won't be up to a fight. So I've met them twice, been in a fight with them both times. The first time they were grilling me, the second . . .' he paused. 'What did happen tonight? You looked really really unhappy to see him. Why? Who is he? Tell me something useful before my patience runs out. The Chimp will have him stashed somewhere, and I'd like to at least know who he is and why I'm kicking some sense out him before I do it. Give me a clue. And tell me who you are and why you're here. No fairy-tales. It's too late and I'm too tired and too pissed off for tales.'

'I work for a man.' Amanda spoke at the edge of audibility.

'We all do, one way or another.' Stoner sounded as unsympa-
thetic as he felt. 'What does your own man do, and what does
he employ you to do? Keep it simple, so I can understand it, and
keep it short. The night is too young to throw out the crowd and
we . . . I need to play a little more. And I'd like to know what I'm
going to be saying to your friend in the leather jacket. Whether
I can say a few short things and trust him to go away, or whether
he and I are about to become great pals and talk all night.'

The Chimp appeared, silent, at the table.

'He's in the cellar. He's fine. Nothing broken. No gun. He's
confused and a touch unhappy.' And he left, leaving another litre
bottle of water on the stage at Stoner's side. The audience, wisely,
stayed away.

Stoner looked again at Amanda.

'You work for a man?'

'Yep.'

This was plainly not going to be easy.

'He runs an establishment. A club. Several clubs. Not like this
one. Big. There are different sorts of clubs. He has a couple of
clubs in other countries. The States. Russia. The Baltics. It's a big
company, really. They sell food and drink and . . .' she hesitated,
'lots of things. I work for him.'

Stoner wore his patience like a weary cross.

'Yes. OK. You work for a man who runs some clubs. Hooray.
What do you do for him? Whore? Musician? Ventriloquist's
dummy? What?'

'You miss the point. Sorry. I'm not doing this well. I work for
him. Just for him.'

'Doing what?'

'Anything. Anything at all.'

'I have no idea what that means.'

'True. You don't. How could you? You're a man. You're a

336

successful man. You have respect. Everyone respects you. You're a great musician. Everyone loves hearing you play. No one tells you what to do. You just come and go and you play whenever you want to play. Whatever you want to play. It's like this club is your very own club. Like everyone just wants to do whatever it is you want to do. You want to play the blues; everybody loves it, every note. You could play – oh, I don't know – reggae rubbish, and everybody would love that just as much. You're just brilliant. No one tells you what to do. It's written in your face, in the way you play, the way you talk.'

'Oh yes. And I crap out diamonds too. Still doesn't tell me what you do for your boss though.'

'Everything. Anything at all. One of the things I do is be confidential. I can't talk about it. Not to you, not to anyone. What I do is for him. Just him.'

'Girl Friday? Lady Friday? Assistant? Private secretary?'

'All that. Anything.'

'Bedpal? Lover?'

'Those too.'

'Carpet? Dishcloth?'

'You're getting the hang of this, JJ. Well done.' Amanda glared at him, defiance and sadness walking hand in hand across her features.

'Just ease my mind a little. I'm a curious man. I think in straight lines, not in ellipses like a woman. Be easy on me. What does he get out of it?'

'Someone he trusts. Someone who is his alone. Someone he can tell anything to. Someone who he knows will do anything he asks.'

'That's rubbish. You're here. If you weren't your own self you'd be at his side, panting like a puppy, waiting for him to toss you a bone or a biscuit. Or something. Imagine he pays you for these nebulous services? A lot?'

337

'There's a lot of money in my account.'

'There you go. Don't complain. Never bite the hand that feeds, so forth.'

'Good gods, he's a philosopher too. Stoner the psychic. He has access to the account. He can take money out as well as put it in.'

'Then open another.'

'He would know and he would tell me to close it.'

'You always do that?'

'I do everything he tells me to do. If I stop doing it, he would unemploy me. I expect he would clear the money from the account and send men after me.'

'Like our leather-jacketed friend in the cellar?'

'Exactly like that.'

'You scared of him? Does he slap you around?'

'Who? The boss or the guy you beat up?'

'Either.'

'The guy downstairs is OK. He's just some operator or something. He does security stuff, runs errands. He's OK. If he beat me up . . .' she looked up at Stoner and smiled gently around eyes like bruises. 'If he beat me up he'd be in deep shit. So he wouldn't do that. He's more likely to stop me getting into trouble than to cause it.'

'But he was looking for you. He was looking for someone he called Handy Mandy. That's you, yes?'

Amanda sighed in a weary way, like someone who'd heard it all before and didn't enjoy it much the first time.

'Yeah yeah yeah. Common view is that I'm the boss's own private playmate. You know how it goes. Handy Mandy. Yep. That's me. Add your own hilarious bloke jokes. I shall of course convulse with laughter at your searing wit. Not forgetting the originality of course. Where did you meet him before? Here? At the club? What are you going to do with him?'

'Is he really harmless?'

'To you? Yes. To me? Don't know. Last time he felt he had an edge with me a hand job kept him quiet.'

'Men are simple, basic creatures, then?' Stoner grinned at her.

'Yep.' She only smiled. Grimly, at that. No grin.

'I'll let him go, then. Tell him you left hours ago. I'll get Chimp to let him out when the club closes. Two-ish.'

'Me?'

'What?'

'What am I supposed to do?'

'Whatever you want. Stay, go, go now, go later, stay all night. Up to you.'

'You don't care. You just don't care.'

'I don't *mind*, Amanda. I don't mind. Caring is something else. There is a world of difference. If you need to be elsewhere, then that's where you need to be. Go there. If not ... stay. It's quiet here. You're safe here. Until your leather-jacketed pal tells your big bad boss where you are ... or at least where he saw you last. Whatever.'

'What are you going to do?' She stared hard at him.

'Another set. Then I need to get hold of some folk.'

Amanda's stare was set in place. She brought its focus closer to Stoner.

'You beat up one of the boss's musclemen, didn't you? I heard them talking about it. It was you.' She grinned, quite suddenly and entirely unexpectedly.

'The fat guy. Yes. I already told you. Keep up.'

'I'm sorry. Lots to think about. I could almost feel safe with you around.'

Stoner ignored the compliment. Signalled the Chimp for refreshment. Bili brought over a bottle. Water.

'You look like you need fluids, big man,' she spoke with a lightness of voice unmatched by the seriousness of her expression.

'Another set? Or do you want to sit it out and draft Miss Twinkle-lips here into a spot of singing for her supper? Playing for it, at any rate. Know any jazz standards, sax goddess?'

'All of them.' Amanda ignored the barbs. Wisely.

Stoner took three cell phones from his pockets. 'Go make noise,' he said. 'Keep the customer satisfied.'

There were messages. Several of them. Shard. The Hard Man. The dirty blonde. Stoner read them all. Including two offers of life insurance and an announcement that he'd won a lottery without even entering it. Nothing could be better than that.

29

DARK HOURS

'I cannot believe that you're still talking about music.' Bili leaned dishevelled along the door frame, a bottle – almost full – of clear Russian spirit in her hand. Amanda rocked slowly back and forth, up and down, in and out, in Stoner's lap. She looked up. Looked towards Bili, smiled.

'Oh. Hi. Hi Bili.'

Stoner's eyes were closed. He and Amanda maintained their slow steady rhythm. Bili slid down the door frame, sat, folded her legs. 'Don't let me interrupt such a fine philosophical discourse, my friends. Carry on. Just ignore me. A soliloquy for two. Is that even possible? Just don't get JJ talking about triangles. He's mean about triangles. Serious, even. Musical triangles, Amanda, not what you're thinking.'

'Shame.' Amanda smiled again, wider this time. The pace of her and Stoner's shared movement was slow, steady. Relaxed. 'You play, Bili. What's your take on this?'

Bili raised her gaze, poured, and raised her glass in a tired salute.

'Take on what? Whether you and JJ make great music together? I imagine that's your only shared subject, or have you really got more than physical music on your collective mind?' She drank a little, poured some more.

Stoner, eyes resolutely closed, stretched out an arm, opened the hand at the end of it. Bili placed a glass in his grasp, poured. 'Half full, JJ, or half empty?'

He smiled in reply, vacantly, lifted the glass with impressive accuracy to Amanda's lips, tipped it as she sipped. Smiled more, sighed a little, said nothing, shifted his hips.

Amanda looked over at Bili. 'We were wondering whether the sax is the pure instrument, because it plays only pure notes. A guitar, a piano, hey Bili, even the bass, can play chords, more than one note at once. The sax is pure, unless you're Rahsan Roland Kirk and play two at once. It just plays the one note at a time.'

'The bass is the centre. It holds things together. Doesn't take great lungs to play it, either. You got good lungs under there, sister.'

Stoner smiled at Bili's humour, but said nothing. She continued. 'The guitar's an accompaniment, that's all. Sax, though. You can't accompany anything useful with that. It's a voice. It's like a woman. A woman is the entire chorus, the full orchestra, men just add an accompaniment when they're needed.'

She laughed gently.

'What you say, JJ?'

'Me? I say carry on ladies, just carry right on.' His eyes were half-open, they appeared to be tracking the gentle movement of Amanda's heavy breasts as they swayed above him, although it wasn't easy to tell. He waved the empty glass in Bili's direction, She took it, refilled it, passed it back. He sipped, his eyes closed.

'Every solo note I play is a true note.' Stoner's voice was quiet. 'Chords are often lies. They cover errors. The more complex the chord, the more room for mistakes.'

Amanda reached down between them and squeezed him.

'Shh . . .' she sighed, 'keep this going.'

'Don't worry about JJ,' Bili sipped from the bottle, but gently, now watching the couple on the floor before her. 'He'll go on like this for ages. Hours if you'll let him, Hey, JJ?'

No reply.

'It's just . . .' Amanda squeezed him again, less gently. Her face and neck and shoulders were flushing a deep red. 'It's just . . .'

Bili stood, crossed behind Amanda and leaned down, taking one of the other woman's breasts in each hand. Stoner's eyes opened, stared into Bili's. He smiled. Amanda was almost silent, her breath puffing. Both of her hands were moving, squeezing and rubbing between her legs. Bili smoothed her nipples, Amanda's bright flush travelled down to include her breasts, her head fell back against Bili's and she breathed harder harder, faster and faster. Then she shook, silent, sweat standing out on her forehead, around her eyes. She took her hands from herself and squeezed Bili's fingers into her flesh until the bass player's hands were all-but invisible. Then she shook again. And again. And again. And then relaxed. Opened her eyes. Sat still.

'No need to stop now,' Stoner's smile was easy and relaxed. 'You cool? Bili?'

The bassist returned to her door frame, resumed her seat, raised her bottle in a mock toast.

'Carry on. It's OK to be an audience. You were saying about the purity of the sax, Amanda?'

'I so like this.' Amanda had recovered a more relaxed shade of skin tone, was rocking slowly in Stoner's lap once more. She smiled again, wider this time, at Bili, who mock-toasted her with another sip of the clear spirit. And rose again to her feet, crossed to a table where four cell phones were ranged in a row. She picked the right-hand of the set up, and flipped its screen to life.

'You have incoming, JJ.'

She returned the phone to its place, picked up the next, then the next, then the last.

'You have a lot of incoming, JJ. You OK to ignore it all? Sorry, Amanda. Didn't mean to spoil the party.'

She walked over and placed the cell phones by Stoner's side. He took the first, lit it up and read its views, closed it down and read the second's call log and messages. Sighed. Swore a little.

'Time for me to go and do a little work. Sorry.' He squeezed Amanda's buttocks, then her hands, pulled her over him and kissed her slowly and gently.

'Needs must. I hate phones. All of them.' He lifted her from him. She stood and reached for him, but he moved away.

'Quick shower, and I'm away for a while. You don't need to leave. Bili has the keys and knows where everything is.'

'You're just ...' Amanda seemed more puzzled than angry, 'leaving? Just leaving? Right now?'

But Stoner was already halfway to the shower. Bili waved her over.

'He'll be back. Some business. Grab a bath, grab some sleep. Or not. I'm not tired. We can finish the bottle. There's a wall of fresh bottles downstairs. More than enough to poison us both.'

Amanda's confusion was obvious.

A cell phone's strident call sliced through the conversation, such as it was. Bili stared around her in unusual confusion. Amanda stared at Bili, who had risen to her feet and was standing rock-steady, seeking the source of the sound. The door to the bathroom flung against the wall and a naked, shower-drenched Stoner was suddenly reaching behind a television screen, a pistol black in his left hand as he retrieved a serenading phone with his right. He stared at the small screen, made no move to answer the call. Pressed the call denial button, ending the alarm, opened a closet and dressed carefully, choosing each garment.

Bili spoke first.

'All black, JJ? Going to a midnight funeral?'

Stoner ignored her. His focus was complete, his calm total and all-denying. He pulled on and tied with care a pair of stout black Caterpillar boots, took a black bag from another closet, replaced the silenced phone behind the television, collected the others from the carpet and dropped them into the bag. The gun was somehow gone. He stood still in the centre of the room for a small count, turned to Bili.

Tilted her face up to his, 'Love you, see you.'

Was quite suddenly by the door and then disappearing through it.

Amanda stared open-mouthed at Bili. Who shrugged.

'You need a shower,' she said. 'A bath. Come on. I'll scrub your back for you.'

30

ANOTHER MAN'S FLOOR

'Broadcasting again. Murdermayhem. Another head.' Whichever of the techno prisoners had answered Stoner's calls was wasting no time on unnecessary pleasantries. 'Another man. Caucasian again. Live feed, blood still leaking. No indication of whereabouts. More as we get it. This number or the panic number?'

'This one.' Stoner closed the phone, dropped it into the black bag. Opened the second phone which sat with its peers, mute on the dash of the Transporter as they drove, quiet through the night. He punched the call-return button.

'On my way. Location the same?'

'Yes.' Shard was as brief, as focused as all the night's players. 'ETA?'

'You'll see me in five or less. Meet at the van.'

It took less than the suggested five minutes, and as Stoner switched off the engine and the lights a sharp rap on the side door announced Shard's arrival. The door opened and closed in almost silence and the two men sat for a while, listening, watching and waiting.

'The follow was simple. I don't think she was even trying to evade or to lose a tail. She was easy to see – bright blonde as she is – and the traffic kept her completely honest at all times. No stunts, no back-doubles, no switches.'

'None you spotted, anyway.' Stoner was not asking a question.

'There were none. She collected her car; it's in the multi-storey, which has only one exit and we can both see that. She drove here on the most direct route, no sudden side streets, no breaking the one-way rules. Nothing. She either didn't know I was there on the bicycle or she didn't care about it.

'As soon as she went in through the front door, she went to the desk and collected a key. There are three other ground floor exits; I put tell-tales on them all. None have been opened.'

Stoner reached for one of his phones. 'Much traffic with the hotel?'

Shard's tone of voice shrugged for him. 'Just the usual for a midweek night in a place like this. If she left, she left with a different walk, a wig, extra weight and a different height. If she left, she left in disguise. Or in a balloon. You sound spooked, Stoner.'

'There's another head. Another body.'

'OK. And?'

Stoner passed him the open phone. Shard read the text message on the screen.

'Ah. And this is who? Do I care about him? Your brief was to watch the blonde lady, which is what I've done. Who's this? Why is he here and why is he telling you that he's here? Is there a meet? Do you want me to sort some backup or have you done that already?'

'The guy was in the club earlier. Long dull story. He's a plod of some sort. I identified the threat to him, connected dots in the shape of the blonde lady, delayed her and told him how to lose himself and to lose himself very rapidly. Told him to locate an anonymous junkyard hotel or a safe house and to go to ground there. He's had some basic tradecraft training from the plods; I told him to use it and to lose himself. I also told him to strip out his phone and to use a new one, pay as you go.'

'Was he a target?' Shard was plainly joining his own dots. 'Is the blondie doing the icing?'

'He fits the profile and has some entanglement with a previous dead head. At least, he has some geographic overlap.' Stoner fell silent.

'And I don't need to know more?'

'At this point no. At this point it's better for us both that you share none of my preconceptions. And it's better for me that I know what you know rather than you knowing what I know.' He smiled, bleakly.

'So much for the trust we discussed, hey?' No smiles from Shard.

'I trust you completely at this point and you can do likewise. There's no advantage in sharing my opinions, frankly. You'd just develop theories and cloud my thinking. That's all.'

'And you're thinking that the head's his?'

'I am. That thought is large in my world at the moment. It is too rapidly forcing me into a confrontation, and into a conclusion which is too easy to be correct. If the blonde lady, for whom I do have a name, is in fact our mad axeman, then she would be always aware of a tail, and she would always be able to shake it, and she would therefore have brought you here deliberately. If you and she truly don't know each other – and yes, I do trust and believe you – then she would have spotted you simply as a tail and harmless. Or, and this is more of a worry, she spotted you and assumed you were a tail I'd set, and she left you in play while remaining in plain sight herself. Which means that she's led you here, and most likely assumed that you in turn have brought me here.'

'Some long reaches there, Stoner. Some big assumptions. Like, we're the only players in this? Your masters and mine could both easily have teams set up.'

'Do you see any? Have you seen any? The place looks decently deserted to me.' Stoner looked around through the wide wind-screen of the Transporter. It was dark, it was late. Few lights burned in fewer windows. He felt entirely unthreatened.

'Where's her car?'

Shard nodded towards an hotel garage entry. 'Through there. She drove in. Left on foot a little later and went into the hotel itself.'

'Did you check the car?'

'For what? Bald tyres? An empty screenwash bottle?' Shard impersonated a patient man, but with less than total conviction.

Stoner pulled the keys from the ignition.

'Watch the place, OK? What's the car?'

Shard passed on make, model, colour and registration details. Then settled back into the Transporter's interior shade. Stoner swung himself into the rear of the van, left it through the silent sliding side door. Walked steadily across the dim street and into the utter dark of the parking garage. As he entered, movement sensors picked him up and lit the harsh bright lights on the first level. The target vehicle was close by the entrance, standing alone but unlit. Stoner walked around it, the first time as far away from it as he could manage without losing sight of it. Nothing stirred. He circled it again, this time much closer than before. The car sat silent, betraying no secrets. He approached it from the driver's side, keeping the entire vehicle in full and steady view.

The driver's window wound down. Charity looked at him. She might have been smiling, and then again she might not.

Stoner stopped. They shared an entire lifetime of silence collapsed into less than a minute.

'Mr Stoner, I believe.' Still no welcoming smile, but no obvious unwelcome, either.

349

'Ms . . . Charity. I believe I've forgotten your other names.'

'If I'd given you another name you'd not have forgotten it, Mr Stoner. Would you care to join me out of the night's chill?'

'I'd prefer to stay where I am. I may need to run away very fast, and that's not easy to do inside a car.'

'Quite right. There are no eavesdroppers nearby.'

'My man observed you going into the hotel. He failed to observe you leaving it. He is a very observant man, very careful, cautious and, as I say, observant.'

'I'm sure he is. And you?' There was the shared shadow of a smile.

'I have trouble trusting what other folk observe. I prefer to check things out for myself.'

'Wise.'

'Are you in fact inside the hotel? Is this a great illusion?'

Charity's returned, reflected smile was a sad smile.

'I've not left this exciting car park since I got here some time ago. Keep your hands where I can see them, please, Mr Stoner. I confess to a slight nervousness.'

'I'm not carrying. My man makes few mistakes, and I'm currently more curious than dangerous. Who is in the hotel?'

'Nice thought about curiosity versus dangerousness, Mr Stoner, if disingenuous. Many kind people are inside the hotel. I am not, and you are not. We are the only important persons in the current situation. Please stay still. Although you may not be armed, I am, and I am under no illusions that although I'm not much of a killer, you most certainly are.'

In case confirmation were required, the sound of a cough came from the car, and a flake of concrete flew simultaneously from the garage flooring a metre from Stoner's position.

'I need to ask this; are you alone?' Stoner's hands rested at his side. He was too far from the car to rush it; they both recognised that.

'Wrong question. Ask one I can answer truthfully and I'll do so.'

'You're not alone, then?'

'That's an assumption, not a question, and it deserves no reply. You've no reputation for being sloppy, Mr Stoner. Ask the questions to which you need answers. From your questions I'll learn what you know already and can then decide whether it helps us both for you to understand more.'

'You sound like a schoolteacher, Charity. Is that actually your name?'

'It is. Next? You may be up for staying here chatting for the rest of the night, what's left of it, but I'm not, and your friend will be wondering where you've gone. He's armed, I'm sure, and unpleasantness would be inevitable.'

'Dave Reve, the guy you met at the club, the guy who was convinced that he already knew you. He's here, isn't he?'

Charity's eyes fell from Stoner's face.

'What can I say? He *was* here, I believe. I doubt that he is any longer. You should go check. That would be the correct thing to do.'

'We can check together.'

'No. No we can't. Dave Reve checked in . . . I think he may also have checked out.' She looked at something on the car's instrument display, and started the engine. 'Third floor. Room 310. Sorry about the mess. Don't try to stop me and don't bother trying to trace the car. Or stop it.'

The window powered its way closed, and the car rolled lightlessly and unhurriedly forward. Stoner ran in front of it. The car accelerated steadily towards him. He stepped back, trailed tough fingernails along its passing roof. He followed the car as it left the garage, and ran to the hotel entrance. Charity's lights lit and the hazard warning lights flashed once as she passed the heavy Transporter, accelerating at a rate which would defeat the most powerful of bicyclists.

351

Stoner pounded on the door of the hotel's reception. Leaned his weight against the night bell. After a short while, Shard joined him.

'There should be a law against this.'

Shard and Stoner stood in the doorway of the hotel room, a room anonymous and exactly like so many others apart from the carnage it contained.

'You knew him, then?' Shard may have been talking to calm his nerves. Then again, he may have wanted answers. In that he would not have been alone. Stoner stood back into the silent early morning hallway.

'Yes. Not well and not for long. Long enough to know that he was called Dave and that he was an accountant. A police accountant. Not the greatest vocation in the world, but hardly deserving of this.'

They spoke quietly. The rest of the hotel, with the unconscious surrealism of similar situations, slept on unawares. Real policemen and their attendant disturbance would follow soon enough. The half-closed eyes of a severed head regarded them accusingly, perhaps, as they stood framed by the door.

'You think the blonde tart did it?' Shard was direct. Stoner shook his head slowly.

'Can't see it. She'd have been blooded from head to foot. Just look at this mess.'

The room was as filthy, as gory, as it was possible to imagine it.

'Can't understand the quiet of it, though. You can't do this to a decently fit guy without him making one fuck of a fuss about it.' Shard's level gaze swept the room for understanding. 'Chopping his head off didn't kill him, then? And if he'd not known the killer, then he knew enough to refuse entry. So . . . no sign of a break-in. He knew the killer? Even if it wasn't the blonde tart, like you say.'

Stoner shrugged. 'Electronic keys. Easy to copy if you know how and if you come equipped. Easy to lift one from behind the reception desk. Easy to make a new one if you know how to drive the machine behind the desk. I don't know these things personally, but I do know those who do.'

'You'd just shoot the door off its hinges, like in the movies.'

'I would.'

'It would make a big bang.'

'Big bangs have their place. Big bangs scare the shit out of the innocent.'

'You say the vic's a cop, though, so not too innocent?'

'He was an accountant. Didn't strike me as the sort to be scared witless by a big bang, but you never can tell. Let's go. There's no more here. No more answers.'

'You don't want to search the place? Do the heroic and always illuminating CSI deal? Always works on the TV.'

'My sides, they are splitting with the wit of it all. No. If you care to keep your manly feet away from the blood, and reckon you can search the place without leaving a Here I Am postcard for the plods, then be quick and see whether you can find his phone. I want to see who he called. There's nothing else for me here.'

'You don't want to look for the phone yourself?' Shard looked at Stoner with curiosity. 'You want to leave no trace at all?'

'In one. I would rather not have been here at all, so far as anyone other than us is aware.'

'And the blonde tart in the car. The one with the great big gun?'

'The blonde tart you watched get out of the car, go into the hotel, and who you think offed our hero here? I don't care if you paddle through this shit, but I want to be unconnectable with the scene. Not sure why. Let's call it a hunch. Let's pretend that I know what I'm doing. I don't think it matters much if you leave trace. It's not you who's being chatted up by beautiful if unhappily deadly blondes. Who should not know that I have any connection to this mess. Which in fact I don't. This is very confusing.'

'You like being confused.'

'I don't mind it.'

'Confusion's a great excuse when you need to hurt someone a lot.'

'You think I want to hurt someone?'

'I think you always want to hurt someone. Do you really want the phone?'

'It would help. Might help. And why do you say that? I never want to hurt anyone.'

'That just isn't true.' Shard trod a fine line to the headless corpse. Looked at it for a time.

'None of the bodies has been booby-trapped,' Stoner suggested, helpfully. 'I'm just being helpful. Supportive. Encouraging. Hurry up. We broke in, remember? Some day the plods will come.'

'Thank you for those kind words.' Shard moved away from the body, reached into the jacket which lay behind it, discarded on the bed. 'No phone.' He returned to the corpse and eased his hand into each of its trouser pockets, with neither noticeable enthusiasm nor success. 'Nothing.'

'OK. That tells us something. We're going now. Soon as you like. Take another look around first. Could he have hung the phone in the bathroom?'

'Tells us what? Nothing in the bathroom bar the bath. He doesn't even have a bag. Tells us what, exactly?'

'The killer took the phone. He probably had two. Why take the phones?'

'Same reason. Killer wants to see who the vic's been calling. Maybe these are crimes of jealous passion and are connected only by strings of telephony. Maybe the answers are all in the phone bills.'

'Do I pay you for your stellar sense of humour? The answer's as likely to be written in the stars. Can we go yet?' Stoner's tone was mild still.

'You don't pay me at all. In fact, as you are presumably being paid a fortune for your ace detective skills, maybe we should sort some kind of deal?'

'Not here, not now, and not with me, I think. We're leaving through the fire escape.'

'It will sound the alarm.'

'Plod is already here, so unless you fancy several hours of tedious questioning, accusations of the most unpleasant kind and then a rescue by someone who I'd imagine will be very pissed off, I'd say that speed was better than subtlety right now.'

A door opened. An alarm sounded. Feet pounded. Stoner and Shard shaded through the darkness back to the Transporter. Where they sat in darkness, observing the arrival of constabulary and medical reinforcements.

'Mate of yours, was he?' Shard broke into Stoner's brooding silence.

'No. But he was a pleasant enough guy.'

'For a cop.'

'For anyone. Hang on.' Stoner pulled out a phone, keyed a message, closed the phone again. Repeated the exercise identically with a second phone. He speed-dialled the third phone. Waited for pick-up and asked, 'All quiet?', then 'OK.' And he closed that phone too.

'You do have a lot of phones. And they don't light up. How do you do that?'

'It's a secret technique. You can find it on the internet, somewhere near the entries about How To Make Big Bombs and Distant Detonations For Beginners. Everything is on the internet. Even tonight's corpse is on the internet. The internet is a wonderful thing. Even the fact that not of all its free facts are either free or

355

factual is a wonderful thing.' He sighed. 'Dave Reve was OK. He survived an earlier killing moment. He was honey-trapped in a much larger and much more pleasant hotel than this one. The killer – the woman I believe to be the killer – let him live. Sucked his brains out through his dick in a swimming pool, grabbed him in the nightmare killer grip of death and then . . . let him go.'

'You're getting poetic, Stoner. Nightmare grip of death? Idiot.'

'Well, he was happily eating her out at the poolside, like you do, when she clamped her thighs around his ears, jammed his face against her snatch and . . . held his head under the water until he started breathing water. I know, it sounds deranged, but next time you find yourself with a loose woman and a spare moment, and you happen to be in a swimming pool, try it. He couldn't get away, and blacked out.'

'But she let him go?'

'Evidently. Killed someone else in the hotel. Usual provisos; someone else in the hotel got snuffed, same MO as this.'

'Why? Why did she let him go? And then why did she change her mind and kill him again?'

'I do have a theory. It works for me so far, but it is just that, a theory.'

'Do tell.'

'Nope. Not yet. The problem with theories is when the guy whose theory it is believes it to be true. Then he fiddles the facts to fit the theory and the truth goes out the window. He tells his oppos his theory and they all fiddle the facts. That is the high-road to fuckedness, and I do not wish to take it. If theory firms up to fact . . . then I'll tell you. Until then . . .'

'Why are we waiting here? Nice to chat, of course, but while the plods rush around doing the flies around a corpse thing, we're not going to make any progress.'

'I'm waiting for the killer to leave.'

'She left an hour ago in her own car. You let her go. Remember?'

'If my theory is anything like correct, then she isn't the killer.'

'OK. A stunner blonde killer was too bad to be true, anyway.'

'Not so. Just not that blonde. Not that particular blonde.'

'Fuck. There's more than one killer blonde? Be still my beating
. . .'

'Dunno. More than one woman involved here. My theory fits the facts. Snag is that there aren't enough facts.'

'Any sign of her leaving? Your mystery killer blonde, that is.'

'I'd lay odds that she's not blonde at the moment, and I'd lay more odds that she looks more like a man than you do . . . at the moment. I'm just watching. Going to sit here and do more of it. I'm in no rush. You've no need to stay.'

Shard pulled a cell phone from his pocket. Stoner reached out a hand, preventing him from opening it.

'I don't need the lights flashing, if that's OK. Hop into the back; it's out of sight back there.'

Which Shard did, returning with the announcement that he would be on his way, and after the usual slightly preoccupied pleasantries, he left.

Stoner sat. Waited and watched. It was a long night. Policemen and medical men came and went. Blue lights and red lights and white lights flashed and flickered. Eventually quiet returned. A lone watchman in a police uniform stood by the door of the hotel.

Dawn came. And turned slowly into day.

31

STEPPING OUT

Stoner ran. He left the Transporter after changing into the pretend athletic clothing which provided a cloak of invisibility on any urban street, left behind him all contact with the real world, and ran.

The streets were shifting from night life to daylight, and other runners and joggers, creatures of the transition, were his companions. A few drunks and no-hopers littered the doorways, very sound sleepers lay wrecked on benches. Stoner's early morning mates varied from the agile and the mobile to the social flotsam which all parks attract and who are either ignored or invisible to the common man. Stoner ran past them all. He answered no greetings from the similarly attired morning athletes and he ran straight into and over and through any drunkard or beggar who blocked his path. They assumed that he'd not seen them, lost in the self-insulated world of the runner, but he saw them all, and he ran at them until they moved ... or until he collided with them, at which point they were bumped out of his path or fell down with the shock of it all. Either way his path was soon always clear. Jungle law is universal, even when unwritten and unacknowledged.

The park had a series of formal tracks. Stoner ran a pattern in a rough figure of eight. Three laps in, maybe a mile, he was into his stride, his rhythm. The park had settled down to run its own event around his own private race for one. Other runners, joggers and walkers cultivated their airs of privacy by donning headsets of several kinds. Stoner occasionally wondered what – if anything – they listened to. He'd never seen the point in applying a layer of artificial sound over the constantly shifting backdrop provided by the city, by the park and by nature. He'd never understood how the achievements of a musician could best be appreciated by listening to them while concentrating on running, nor how the pleasures of a decent run could be improved by adding distraction. He ran steadily and without fuss; his thought processes attuned themselves to the pace of his running and while his organism handled all the physical side, the navigation, the length of stride and the level of effort, his mind powered away into its own semi-conscious world, where it thought, looked and listened, and then thought some more.

Guitar solos, musical moments, came to him as he ran, as did combinations of facts which, rearranged, presented previously unseen scenarios. What he had taken to be minor details re-established themselves as pivotal moments, small errors revealed themselves as disasters in the raw; vague insights cleared themselves up into obvious facts while he ran. While he let his thoughts arrange themselves with as little conscious input as he could manage, his running took on a life of its own. The more tired his muscles, the more agile his thinking.

His senses likewise worked at their best when left alone. They often discerned patterns which he may have missed completely if he'd been looking for them. And they found breaks in the patterns around them, interruptions to the steady development of the waking day's own rhythms. As the dawn light shifted from

FRANK WESTWORTH

glimmer and glow into light and bright, so the sounds of the city and the park within grew into their own maturity.

There was a car parked behind the Transporter. A family four-door saloon of refreshing anonymity. It was out of pattern. Stoner ran on. The Transporter was parked on a no-parking stretch of the road. Stoner was unbothered by parking fines, even by some remote threat of wheel-clamping or a tow-away. He carried enough identification, both legal, genuine and otherwise, to fear no minor minion of the parking police. Laws never applied to him when he was working, and when he was working for the government, as he was now, at least in a tenuous way, then if the government wished to penalise him for parking oddly while working, well, they could reimburse him later.

This was unlikely to be the case with the saloon parked behind the VW. Stoner ran on. He ran another set of three laps. Another mile. He was warmed through and completely comfortable. No one was running with him. No one ran at his pace; when he speeded or slowed, no other runner, jogger or walker shifted their pace to match. And as he completed his ninth lap, his third full mile, the running, jogging and walking population had changed completely; turnover was steady until the 08.30 mi-gration moment, when runners transformed into office-dwellers, and after that came the 10.00 shift, non-workers, workers of unconventional hours. They mostly fit their own predictable patterns, and none of those patterns involved the illegal parking of a family saloon car in a no-parking spot.

After twelve laps, a notional four miles, Stoner looped away from his park centre track and ran the perimeter. The saloon car was empty. The driver sat relaxed and apparently dreaming on a park bench nearby. She sat facing the traffic, not watching Stoner. That amused him. Had he been under observation, he would have sensed it, of that he was certain. He ran to the bench, approaching it from behind, and sat down, pulling off the track-suit's top half as he did so.

'Apologies for the smell,' he remarked. 'It's going to be warm today.'

Charity maintained her level stare into the motorised middle distance for maybe a half minute. 'It could get too hot. But only if we allow it.'

'You'll get a ticket.' Stoner the ever-helpful was playing at being helpful.

'Got one. Get another any minute now.'

'Do you want to relocate? Breakfast?'

'This is taking cool to an impressive extreme, Mr Stoner. A friend of yours died last night, and you're inviting a lady you consider to be involved in that death out for breakfast. Impressive.'

'Running always gives me thinking room. I like running. Do you run?' Stoner paralleled her gaze, they watched the flow of traffic together.

Finally: 'No. I train. In a gym. I don't run. I swim as often as I can for as far as I can.'

'In a pool? In a lake? Rivers? The seas?' Stoner sounded sincere and serious. He and Charity maintained their parallel gazes into and across the endlessly unfolding street scene. Not once did they look at each other. Not yet.

'Anywhere. Anywhere outside. Do you just run? Running always seems so one-dimensional compared to swimming. Sometimes when I swim I dream I can fly.'

'That's a quote. Who said that?'

'Is it? No idea. It's true, though. When you run, and I know you run a lot, Mr Stoner, you just pound your feet down. They always carry your weight. You are always planted on the ground. Panting. Sweating. When I swim I am weightless. I can let go. I can drift. I can dream of flight. I can dream of drowning.'

'Do you? Dream of drowning?'

361

'Of course I do. You of all people do not need to ask me of all people that question, Mr Stoner.'

'You swim to escape, then.' Not really a question.

'You run to hide, Mr Stoner.' Not really an answer.

'No. I run because I like running and because I like the opportunity it gives me to think. I rarely hide. There is rarely anything to gain in hiding.'

'Confrontation is your way, Mr Stoner. I know that. I respect that. It's one reason I am sitting here collecting parking tickets rather than leading you by the nose in a more subtle way. Dealing with your friend Mr Harding is less . . . direct. Also less stressful. Maybe.'

'Why the formality? A chap could get tired of this "Mr Stoner" nonsense pretty quickly. I think you know me well enough to use my given name. And why in any case are you dealing with me directly? Aren't I supposed to be hunting you?'

'You made little effort to hunt me, Jean-Jacques. Very little effort. I was surprised by that. It made me think. Although, truth be told, it's not actually me you're hunting. It's ain't me you're looking for.'

'Babe. That is a quote. I play the damn song sometimes. Dylan. I prefer JJ. And as I said, one reason I enjoy running is that when I run I can think. I find that I think my best when I run. And while I was running I understood that although I consider you to be my opponent in this mucky, filthy business, you don't see me in the same light. Which is why I've sat here like a civilised chap and why you're sat here like a civilised lady, and neither of us is attempting to kill the other.'

'You have a sister.' A statement, not a question.

'I have two sisters. You've met one of them, although I don't think you would recognise her – we're not much alike – and you're looking for the other. When you find her I think you'll kill her. If you don't, then I think your Mr Harding will do it. He may not have told you this, of course.'

'If your sister is the person behind all this utter shit with the chopped-off heads and the insane online movies, then she has no reason to be left alive. But she wants stopping, not killing. My instructions are to find her, not to kill her.'

'Are you sure about that? My understanding is that your job is to find her and kill her.'

'No. Just the former. Are you really called Charity?'

'Yes. My sister is Chastity. She was well named.'

'Really? She would have been better named Psycho, surely? Maybe Chopper, if you crave the alliteration.'

'She struggles with herself sometimes. But we all do that, don't we, JJ?'

'Why is she killing all these guys? I mean . . . accountants? And why are you talking to me? Don't you worry that I'll lock you up and use you as a bargaining tool to collect your sister? That would appear to be a sensible course of action.'

'I'm not worried about that at all, Mr Stoner. You have nothing to gain from that. Trailing me as bait won't have any effect on Chastity. Other than more killing. And if she felt that you were attacking me, she'd attack you.'

'Of course she would. That's the whole point of a hostage. To provoke a response, an attack. Or something like that.'

'She's not stupid, Mr Stoner. She may be increasingly insane, but she has never been stupid. And she is killing because she has . . . we have . . . a contract to fulfil.'

'It's a joint effort? Both of you are involved?'

'All three of us, in fact.'

'Oh for fuck's sake.' Stoner stood. 'This is a pig of a thing. Can we at least have some breakfast if it's going to go on for much longer?'

He walked towards her car, collected two parking tickets from its screen, along with a couple of his own.

'I'll deal with these.'

Charity smiled sadly at him.

'No need. The car doesn't exist. Follow me. Let's do brunch. Or something.' She climbed in and fired up the saloon, pulled into the mid-morning traffic. Stoner sprinted to the Transporter, fired up and followed.

'The contract is simple. It's open-ended. We have a target list. Exactly like you followed when you were operating yourself.'

'Operating. A great word.' Stoner leaned back in the coffee shop's least comfy chair and reached for his cup. 'Does the contract specify the butchery? The stupid fucking video? And why are you talking to me anyway?'

'The original target was an accountant. We didn't know that; I've only learned it by following your investigation.'

Stoner's cup halted halfway to his lips.

'You're following the investigation?'

'Which should tell you something. Something more than I'd be prepared to confirm, so don't ask about it. The original contract was simple, and specified that the method should be distinctive. It left finer details up to the operator. She ... and I'm unsure how and why she decided this ... made the job so messy and so ... apparently unprofessional and psychotic that it was bound to attract attention from more specialist agencies than the regular police. That worked, and although the police have been involved all along in parallel to other investigations, your own included, their role has been restricted.'

Stoner attempted to speak.

'This would be easier if you let me say what I can say, JJ. This needs to be resolved. I can't take questions and you do need to understand that Chas knows I'm talking to you. She is very good.

Her tradecraft, her streetcraft . . . when she works she's pretty much unstoppable. But she needs to be stopped.'

'One hundred per cent agreement on that. Tell me the where and the when and I'll take her down. Or send others to take her alive. If she's as good as you say I might be unable to do that myself. Seriously.'

'There are two more jobs.'

'Fucking heavens, there'll be no accountants left! Forgive my levity. This is the twenty-first century; we have a billion spare accountants. Who cares about a few more or a few less?'

'I don't think the contract is actually about accountants.' Charity paused. 'The longer you do this job, the harder it gets to keep your interest to a minimum. You start to wonder why you're being contracted to kill people. You shouldn't. By becoming involved it's inevitable that you're going to learn too much about the business of those who you've been contracted to kill. And by association you learn the business of those you've been employed by. That sort of knowledge is never a good thing to carry around. It is in fact a burden.'

Stoner nodded. Moved the crockery around on their table, no recognisable pattern emerged. No tea-leaves revealed themselves. No enlightenment resulted.

'It's why operators like you move into investigation, Mr Stoner. JJ. Otherwise you get too knowledgeable and unless you also understand that knowledge is not power – knowledge is a liability in many circumstances – that knowledge, the stuff you accumulate when you start working out why you're sanctioning who you're sanctioning, that knowledge is usually fatal. And in case you're wondering, I'm telling you this because I want you to help me.'

'Very kind. Why would I do that?'

'I think you'll die if you don't.'

'Is that intended as an incentive? A negotiating position? It's a little clumsy. Threats usually don't work. I am a man who is convinced of the merits of direct action whenever I feel threatened. I have been known to become almost violent at times. So they say.' Stoner stared from the window. The café's car park contained cars. The number and variety changed. He saw no pattern. He stared from the window at the cars simply because that was something to do with his eyes which was other than staring at his companion.

Who shrugged and spoke, gently enough. 'No threat. Not really an incentive. I have, I think, learned too much of the reasons behind this series of contracts. The snag is that there is no way to confirm it other than by watching and observing what happens as the pieces fall. The pattern behind the contract isn't just a series of deceased accountants. It appears to be more a removal of funding. The final targets, the end-users, appear to be those being paid, not those doing the paying. One recipient in particular seems to be especially unpopular with the customer.'

'Does this curiosity bring benefits?' Stoner sounded genuinely interested. 'I just got . . . tired of it all. It is very wearying.'

'No. No benefits. Knowledge is like cancer. Once it takes a hold it's impossible to stop it growing without surgery. And the surgery looks like murder to me. More murder. What we're doing now feels like surgery . . . butchery. We're contracted to remove someone else's problem. Our problem is that we understand it too much. When I say "we" I mean I understand it, Chas doesn't care. She cares less and less about less and less. That's the escalation you're seeing. She's way beyond the brief now.'

'Can't you cool that yourselves? Involving someone else seems damned risky to me.'

'Not while the contract is ongoing. Not easily.'

'And you're not going to tell me who the target actually is?'

'No. Mostly because I might be wrong. You're going to follow me away from here, are you not?'

Stoner met her gaze. 'Of course. Yes.'

'I can't stop you, but there would be no point. I have no reason to lie about that.' She seemed nervous, suddenly. Watching the passers-by.

'You seem nervous,' Stoner remarked, solicitously.

'Surprise. You can pay. Thanks for breakfast.'

'That's fine. You're a cheap date.' She'd drunk four coffees and eaten nothing. Stoner placed a large note on the table and followed her out.

'You're following me. I'd prefer it if you didn't. You have nothing to gain by following me. I'll just lead you around in circles, call in interference and a block and lose you. Accept that and enjoy your day. Play the guitar, sing a song. Screw someone.'

'And you.' Stoner stood and watched as she walked to her car. Stood by its door, as if waiting for something. Then unlocked it, fired up and drove away.

32

PARK AND RIDE

Stoner drove. The skies leaked softly towards the end of the day and into the night's dark. The roads smeared beneath the wheels of the Transporter. He watched everything and he waited for anything. He varied his speed. He took alternate lefts and rights. He found a three-lane and he drove down the centre lane at twenty under the limit. Vehicles passed him on the left and on the right. He picked out his cell phones one by one, flicked them open in turn and read their displays. No one called.

The dirty blonde maintained her recent silence. He thumbed her a text message. One word. 'Dinner?' Dropped the phone into the dashtop tray and watched it. It failed to respond with the electronic delight of an incoming call. He steered the Transporter through the same series of road junctions in a creative and varied way. When being followed, it was Stoner's view that a chap should provide both challenge and entertainment for whoever was struggling with the tedious routine of following.

A phone buzzed. He swerved from one lane to another, then back, as he picked up the phone from the dashtop. It was mute. Another phone buzzed its irritation, or possibly its joy at being

368

a messenger. He replaced the silent device and flicked open the second. The Hard Man.

'Where are you?' Direct. To the point.

'On the road again. Being followed again.' Stoner could also produce oblique when it was needed.

'Do you have a report for me?'

'Yes. Of sorts.'

'Now is a bad time?'

'Is there urgency from your end? I'm driving in ever-increasing circles here. Should I be bringing someone to your office door? If we carry on waltzing around the city like this they are going to get dizzy soon. They'd probably appreciate a nice warm chat and a cup of that which refreshes in convivial company. Which is not me, not exactly, not at this moment.'

The Hard Man produced a competent impression of a man with nothing to say. Maybe he was thinking. Eventually, he spoke: 'Will it wait till tomorrow?'

'You called me, remember? Of course it will. When I reverse the tail, who knows what I'll discover. They're determined. Why are they following me? Do you know?'

A pause. 'How the hell would I know who's following you? Probably some half-stoned guitar groupie from that loud club of yours.'

'Wouldn't that be nice? I'm going to turn the tail. Do you have a time I should call?'

'I'll call you. I shall aim for maximum inconvenience, of course.'

'Of course.'

Stoner closed the phone. Swung the Transporter into an industrial development, accelerated as hard as the heavy engine would let him, which was very hard indeed, swept through the wide and empty night-time roads, cutting the corners and sweeping the bends, taking efficient racing lines and apexing, assuming there would be no oncoming traffic and uncaring if there was, then, as soon as he'd made enough distance to create invisibility in the eyes of his pursuers, he offed the lights, braked hard into a small service road between two dark warehouses and hand-brake-spun the Transporter to a stop; straightened it against the kerb.

Switched off. Silent in the night.

Climbed into the back. Swung into a black leather jacket, zipped it, unhooked a crash helmet from its shelf, hit the handlebar-mounted switch which motivated the hydraulic struts which lifted the rear door as high as it would lift, and carefully, near-silently, bounced the trailbike out into the night. Sat on it in silence as the van's door closed, and watched the moving patterns of head-lights as they approached, seeking the Transporter. Which sat, silent, one more anonymous van parked in a service road with at least another half dozen, their varied colours muted to mud beneath the industrial sodium yellow of the street lighting – what there was of it.

The followed becomes the follower. Prey becomes hunter. The conspicuous becomes hidden. Only one car had been following the heavy Transporter. Only one car was searching for it now. It cruised the roads, unlit. Stoner watched in dark silence. Until it moved slowly away. Stoner started the bike, it ticked over very quietly. No lights. Not even the instruments lit. He praised the military minds at NATO who had specified a bike for the battle-field. A bike which could run almost silently and without lighting. They even specified that particular and unusual ability along with the drab green paint, which was allegedly radar-fooling paint, and the large pannier boxes slung each side of the front wheel, making it look very unbikelike from many angles and particu-larly in the dark, an incomprehensible silhouette; they had specified a blackout switch, intended for those battlefield moments when being invisible would most certainly be an aid to survival.

Taking advantage of the studded off-road tyres and the long-travel off-road suspension, he pottered at walking pace along the neat grassy lawns of the industrial park. Keeping close to the buildings. Drifting from pool of shadow to dimly-lit corner to another shadow. So long as the car's engine was running, they'd not hear the bike's muted muttering. And they would be looking for a van or a man. Not the strange angular asymmetry which is an unlit motorcycle in the dark.

He could see the car. It was cruising towards the Transporter now, slowing to check out each of the parked vans as it passed them. Well driven, smoothly done. Quiet. No fuss. No histrionics. It drew level with the Transporter, passed it slowly, paused, passed on. No more pauses; the van had been identified. Stoner watched, silently. Wondering. Would the driver leave the car to take a closer look? That would be best; that way Stoner would have some chance of identifying his followers, could even intercept them if he felt like it.

The car reached the end of the road. And with a sudden explosion of noise and illumination, the driver spun it in a wheel-spinning tyre-shredding display of precision stunt driving which ended with the car, the dull saloon, facing the Transporter, which sat, mute, immobile and inscrutable in the full glare of the follower's headlights. A dark rabbit, caught in the hunter's beam.

Positions held for several minutes. Stoner watched his watchers, who watched the empty van. By now they would have worked out that the van was empty, this bird had flown.

The car door opened. A woman stepped out. Trim. Very blonde. Moved with an excellent and striking fluidity. Charity? That was not Charity's car. At least it was not the car she'd been driving earlier, and there was no reason for her to change it – it is difficult enough to spot a professional tail in the dark, it is impossible to identify make and model of pursuing vehicle from the brightness of its headlights, so she had no reason to swap, no reason at all.

371

Chastity, then. The killer sister. The dangerous sister. The deadly blonde sister. The extreme and increasingly disturbed sister. Apparently.

She walked smoothly to the Transporter. She moved easily. Fascinatingly fluidly. Her walk was nothing like her sister's walk. She prowled where Charity stalked. She walked soundless over the background music provided by the idling car's subdued engine. Leaned her back against the driver's door of the Transporter. Rocked the van a little. No alarms. Of course there were no alarms. What use are alarms? All they do is annoy the neighbours and awaken leashed dogs. She leaned there for perhaps a half minute, gazing around her, silently interrogating the darkness but evidently receiving few answers in return. She prowled to the front of the van, leaned her ass against the VW logo on the front, spread her lowered arms out to her sides, resting her hands on the edges of the front panels. And she laughed. Once. Not loud. Not soft. Not harsh. Neither with nor without humour. And she leaned back there, lit up like a lamp dancer on a stage, for a second half minute.

Then she was moving again. Was back inside the bland car and reversing it fast to the end of the road, to the junction. Reversed without pause across the bigger road, stopped, shifted gears and pulled away forward. No hurry, no racing, just a normal pace. Fast and fluid.

Stoner was ready. The bike was moving to intercept the car as it left the industrial park, as it headed off into the rural dark. Stoner was being led, of that he had no doubt, but he needed to be sure she was really leaving. She would know he was following her. He felt respect for that. A soldier, then. Another soldier. Fighting another war.

And she drove like the soldier she surely was. Steadily. No attention-seeking speeding. Well within the limits. All lights lit and clean. Perfect positioning and careful consideration for the few other users out in the evening. Stoner rode behind her, unlit.

The road led into the countryside, the air cooled. She was definitely leaving the scene. Stoner braked smoothly to a stop. He watched the car's lights fade into the gloom; when they had vanished he turned, headed back to the Transporter. Why follow further? He knew who she was.

He neared the Transporter, parked, dark and silent. Switched off everything. Lifted the visor of his helmet and listened to the night. The only audible engines were a way away, a steady drone. None under big throttle, none approaching fast. He fired up and rode to the van, flicked the button on the remote and watched the rear door open. A flip of the throttle wrist, a shift of his body mass to the rear of the seat and a haul on the handlebars; the front wheel rose just enough to ride over the van's low floor. Stoner leaned forward to avoid decapitation, rolled to a stop, killed the engine, and dismounted. Propped the bike, ratcheted it into the grip of a pair of restraining straps and flicked the remote again. Stripped off helmet and gloves, and slid between the two front seats and into bright – unexpected and unwelcome – light.

The drab saloon was back, face to face with the heavy Transporter. Stoner shook his head slowly, reached for the driver's door and stepping down into the road. She was standing away from her car, making the most of the disfiguring shadow. He started to walk towards her. She spoke.

'This is a gun. I dislike them myself, but this one would stop a man who, say, took one more step from . . . now.'

He stopped. Stood still. It was a night for surprises, not a night for heroics.

'Thank you.' Her voice was quite, quite different. Not like Charity's at all. A different pitch. Far, far less inflection. She droned her voice. Tight control then. She would fire without hesitation, of that he had no doubt at all.

373

'Gut shot?' He spoke with all the calm in the world. 'Leg?'

'Gut. Easier target. The light's not good enough for cowboy tricks.' No hostility. No emotion he could detect. 'You got an emergency kit in the lorry? Reckon you'd survive it?' She sounded genuinely interested. In a way. A remote way.

'Yes and yes, but it would be a considerable inconvenience. I would need to delegate. And I do not like to do that.'

'So I understand, Mr Stoner. That is your reputation. I admire your reputation, and I'm flattered that you've been set on me.' The gun was unwavering, held in her left hand. Pointed directly at his midriff. 'What should we talk about? We should provide the audience with some creative smalltalk, some badinage before the negotiation.'

'If you say so, Chastity. Is that really your name? Who names their daughters Chastity and Charity? And are you really left-handed? The men you destroyed were destroyed by a right-hander.' Stoner took a step back, leaned against the mute Transporter. If he needed to move suddenly he could gain traction from both arms as well as both legs. His options were increased.

Chastity leaned against the saloon's own front panels. The gun's dark eye wavered not at all.

'Right-handed, JJ. I'm right-handed. I'm keeping my preferred hand free in case it needs to perform duties of its own. I really do dislike guns. Nasty, noisy, clumsy, toys for boys. Is it OK to call you JJ, JJ?' There should have been a smile behind the words, but there was none. Just that gentle, smooth, purring and emotion-free voice. Educated. Very English.

'I prefer the intimacy of a blade.' Her right hand was suddenly and surprisingly lifting a matt black combat knife into a better light.

'That the one you used on the heads?' Stoner's voice was as steady as her own. No force, no stresses.

374

'Yes. Non-stick coating, y'know. The many wonders of science.'

'Saves on the washing up, I suppose,' Stoner spoke flatly.

'Many unexpected benefits. Easier on the wrists.' The knife had vanished again. The gun was steady. Both parties stood still.

'You any preferences, JJ?'

'About my weapons of choice or about the way I'm likely to die?'

'Good question. Well done. OK. Enough badinage. You've been employed to take me down.'

'Not so. I've been employed to find you. As I already told your sister. To find the whacko who chops accountants' heads off and poses them for the camera. That would be you?'

'Correct. I might have chosen a less dismissive expression than "whacko", but it really doesn't matter. You've found me. Well, let's be generous, we found each other. Charity helped. She's like that. She does like to supply a little kindness now and again. It's that big sister routine, I think.'

'She's older than you?'

'Indeed. Doesn't look it though, does she? It's the bathing in asses' milk I expect. I expect she spends her days doing that. And her nails.'

'Sibling rivalry, huh? Must be tough.'

'No. No rivalry. What's your plan, cowboy? You going to run me outta town? Turn me in to the law? Gun me down? Gunfight at the OK Diner?'

'Not so far. I'm simply reporting that you're identified and then either I or someone else will receive further instructions. Probably terminal, you know how it is, but you might get an offer of gainful employment. These are strange days. Dangerous days.'

'They are. Yes, they are. But you don't have a clue who I am. You don't know where to find me. You have no contact details at all. Ditto for Charity, sweet thing that she is, she isn't stupid. You know what I look like. What I look like at this moment, that is.

Girls can change their appearance, you know. It's all make-up. Scary stuff for you guys. We've met before. Did you know that?'

'Right.'

'And you don't get to do the James Bond thing with magnetic tracking devices stuck to the car, either. You try to fix one, I shoot you. That's not a game you can win.'

'Right.'

'And you can't follow me. That old van is too slow and the bike doesn't have the range. Neat touch, the bike, by the way. I like that. I should get one.'

'And the car's not listed in your name.'

'No idea. It could be. It'd almost certainly in someone's name, but the odds are long against it being mine. I don't think the number plates are altogether genuine. But I could be wrong.'

'So why are we here? Joyous conversation aside. Why are we talking? Are you working up to offing me as well?'

'No. You're not on the list. In any case it's entertaining to have you around.'

'You didn't find Dave Reve entertaining enough, then? You had to off him. He was OK.'

'He was OK. I tried to let him go. Had you worked that out? I . . .' There was a pause. An interruption in her flat tone. She looked down at the gun. 'I liked the guy. He was OK. He was funny. He sang stupid songs. He was supposed to make it. You killed him.' She looked up. Shadowy emotion had appeared around her eyes. It was a bleak emotion. Cold.

Stoner felt the familiar prickle, tickling of adrenaline building up.

'I killed him? How do you work that out? You sliced and diced with that machete of yours and you put his head on the net. I wasn't there. Remember? Is psychosis setting in? You altering realities now?' He kept his tone level, with maybe a light touch of mockery.

'You told Charity who he was. I'd taken out some other accounting twonk. They're mostly the same in the dark. Mostly.' The balance was restored to her tone. 'He died fast and easy. He didn't hurt. He didn't even see it coming.'

'How did you find him?' Stoner didn't expect a reply.

'You expect me to tell you? OK. Quality of intel. Our intel is excellent. Charity told me of my error. Our employer told me how to find him. Dave. He died.'

'So you just killed a guy you liked. Just like that. You feel good about that?'

'Don't go silly on me, Stoner. The world is filled with men. And women. None of them matters much more than any of the others. None has much value. Some have value to me only if they're dead. No real worries there. I'm sure you're fun, and I'm sure Chas . . . Charity likes you in her own way. But if I need to kill you I will kill you. She'd find some other guy soon enough. There's a lot of you around.'

'OK. Where to now? It's great to chat, so forth, but the night's drawing along, and I would like to understand what we're doing, where we're going.'

'Yes. You're going to leave. You're going to drive away. But before you do that, I'm going to supply you with a little information which may help you in the future.'

'If I have a future. Threats like that?'

'Nope. You can drive away from here untouched by me.' She shifted position, but only slightly. Comfort rather than weakness. 'You should step back from this investigation, such as it is. If not, you will get too close to us, to me or to Charity, and you will be instructed to take us out. You will claim to me at this point that you no longer do wetwork, but you're an operating psychotic – it takes one to know one, I guess – and when your buttons get pushed you will always go bang. And if you decline, then someone else will step up and take a shot. That's how these things work, as you know as well as I.'

'I can't stand back from this. I've accepted the job, and it's not the way I work.'

'OK. Fine. Charge me now, make your best move and get shot through the gut. That would be so stupid, so very stupid that I might make it nastier for you. There really is no need for this. You are not my target, I need not be yours.'

'Well thank you for today's great suggestion. Top idea. Why not save me all the tiresome rushing and just shoot me now? You sound like you want to.'

'Not even tempting. Don't bother with the provocation thing, it won't work.'

Stoner shifted, worked forearms and calves to boost the almost static blood flow.

'Your sister says you've gone mad. Insane. Is that true?'

Chastity paused a moment. Slowly and deliberately shifted the aim of her weapon until its single dead eye was staring at Stoner's crotch.

'It could be. It could just be.' She drew an audible breath. 'It surely feels that way. Feels ... good. Comfortable. You need to know that there are a few more names on the list. Just a couple. I don't know who they are and I don't know where they are. Not yet. Then when they're done we're gone. This is not our city. You should wander about in your own particular state of confusion and avoid getting killed. We intend to work with you in the future. That is what this is all about. In a way.'

Stoner stared, speechless.

'I'm speechless,' he muttered. 'What have you got against accountants, for the love of God? I mean ... accountants?'

'Until I met Dave Reve, I'd no idea we were targeting any profession in particular. It doesn't matter to me. All I care about is the who, the where, the when and the how, the how much.'

'You don't choose the how? The method?'

'No. If Chas. . . Charity is correct and I am losing it – which feels likely enough – it's the fucking bloodthirstiness of it which is doing it to me. You think I enjoy hacking some poor fuck's head off?'

'I have no idea. It never occurred to me.'

'Would you do it? Can you imagine how cracked it feels? Broken? Dislocated?'

Stoner raised his eyes to the heavens, to the darkness above. 'I take your point.'

Her shadow moved behind the twin glare of the headlights. Her voice was quite suddenly a different voice, some other person's. It snapped, 'What?' It was not a friendly interrogative. Stoner understood at once that she was no longer speaking to him. A cell phone. Both her hands were in obscure view; an earpiece. An opportunity. Chastity aimed the gun again, slightly higher; higher gut entry point, just as lethal. She could take a call and aim a gun at the same time, could possibly also walk, talk and chew gum simultaneously. Making a move at this point would be foolhardy or fatal, probably both. Stoner relaxed back against the Transporter, drawing no more comfort, feeling no less at risk . . . but no more, either. Had he had some gum to chew, he would have chewed it at this point. This was, he mused, a gum-chewing moment if there ever was one.

Chastity gazed at him with shadowed, expressionless eyes. Not blank eyes, there was nothing blank about them. She said 'OK,' and returned to listening in stillness, concentrating. Stoner lidded his own eyes, leaned his head back and stared upwards, away from the blaze of the lights. Chastity's one-sided conversation continued. And then it was over. As silently as it had begun. She was moving again, out of the lights and away from her car.

'You going to follow me again?' Her query sounded almost disinterested.

379

'You going anywhere interesting?' Stoner could do disinterest also.

'Would you believe me if I said no?'

'No. Probably not. Such is the world of grim suspicion in which we are fated to move.'

'Most poetic. You write songs, too, I gather. Talented. Must restrict your fighting skills, needing to watch out for those delicate guitarist's fingers.'

'Yup. Also fingernails. They do suffer in a struggle.'

'So shooting you through your hand would deter you from following me? You'd need to get it fixed pronto then?'

'No. Shoot me through the hand and I will kill you. Malice like that has no place here.'

'Oh you are clever, Mr Stoner. You are too clever. How did you know that? Do tell.'

'Elementary, my dear witless.'

'No no. Do tell. I insist.'

'Mercenaries always work for all sides. You know that. But steady your heaving bosom, I just guessed. And I have no idea what that strange soul wanted to tell you. I doubt it concerns me much; I pay them too much to be the target of serious betrayal.'

Chastity paused. Then spoke again, her tone amused, faintly questioning.

'It did in fact concern you. Completely. Mallis and Menace, our technomagicians, know we're talking and have issued an instruction concerning your future.' Her amusement was plain now. There was almost a smile in her voice.

'So they called me first.' Stoner forced a similar level of amusement into his own voice. 'They assumed that I'd be in command of the situation, as would any sane individual, and when they received no reply they worked out who had the whip hand. But issuing orders? Orders? Really? I've never known that. Not from them. Who are their real masters in this, I wonder? And if you were going to shoot me, you would have shot me by now, so can I relax and walk some blood into my legs again? My arse is getting numb from sitting on cold steel.'

'Stay right where you are. Exactly where you are. They have traces on both of us. Clever people. Clever, clever people.'

'You going to tell me why you're topping accountants, before you go? Apart from an attack of public-spirited social conscience?'

No answer.

'I'll catch your trail again at some point and I will reel you in. You know that, and I know that.'

The gun spat once, twice. Headlamp glass shattered and exploded into the air either side of Stoner. He hid his double flinch; he'd not seen the gun move, only a pair of dim muzzle flashes prevented his looking around for another shooter.

'Yeah. Go home. Go somewhere you call your own and relax with a friend. Or without one. It makes no difference. I'm avoiding you for forty-eight hours, it says here; a voice through the ethers, as you just observed. Maybe seventy-two. If we meet in that time it will be a bad result for you. So we won't meet. We'll leave that pleasure for another day, and maybe things will be different. Charity says you play a mean guitar. She says your club is good. If I catch you after me in the next three days I'll destroy your club.'

'Kind of you. So when I find you I'd better be better than you?'

'One of us is holding a big gun, Mr Stoner, and that person is not you. You may have a cannon in your pants, but I really don't think it's much of a threat to me.'

'Was that a joke?'

'Yes. Cool, huh? As cool as the three charges set in your club. They're funny, too. If I were you, I'd go and have a nice lie down and then I'd find them. They're not on a timer. They're just there to keep you busy while I get stuff done. A distraction. You can make like the headless chicken without actually losing your head. See? I do jokes. So I can't be mad. Not very. Mostly.'

Two more muffled muzzle flashes; the spotlights either side of Stoner destructed into splinters, the grains of glass flying glittering into the beams of the car opposite, raining down like an angry artificial hailstorm as the car reversed, swung into the road and accelerated away.

Stoner levered himself into the cab, fired up the engine, pulled his cell phones from their resting places. No missed call from Mallis. None from Menace. None from anyone. No friendly thoughts. Nobody loved him. He considered his drive through deserted streets under the bleak streetlighting and wondered whether he would just kill the first cop who pulled him over to book him for his lightless ways. Road safety is a serious concern.

As was the tap at his window. A face there in the night's light. Shard. He tapped again, some urgency this time. Stoner opened the door, stared the question.

'Come on. I bugged her wheels while you were doing the seduction routine; young lovers, you two, huh? Time to go. Time to see where she goes.' Shard was rarely a man who spoke volumes. But his own dull saloon car fled through the night while its satnav displayed the location of the car they pursued.

'Oxford?' Shard's tone revealed his incomprehension. Stoner considered, but did not enlighten him. The trace stopped, ceased its movement.

'Can you save those co-ordinates?' Stoner's question was a quick question. Shard nodded and did so. 'She'll move off again. Then she'll ditch your tracker. Fascinating. Tells me she'll kill me if I follow her, then sets a clear trail, to a place she wants me to see. Fascinating.'

'You said that. She can't have seen me.' Shard sounded affronted.

'She didn't. She just knew you'd be there – or if not you then someone just as effective. Why waste time chatting in the streetlights like that if she wasn't giving you time to stick on a bug or two? Neat. She's not very mad, is she? Clever. Subtle, too. She wants me to go where she's showing . . .'

Shard interrupted. 'She's on the move again.'

'Yes. Drop me where she waited. Then follow her. She wants me there on foot and she wants you away from there. Wheels within wheels; yours and hers. Very clever. I like this.'

'You know where she's leading you, then?'

Stoner's expression was bleak, bordering on grim. 'I believe so. But I don't know why. It's an address I've been to before. Do you know it?' Shard shook his head.

'No. Too posh for me. Businessman land.'

The car drew up. 'She's stopped again.'

Stoner opened the door and nodded. 'She'll leave your trackers there. If I'm correct in this wild goat chase, that's what she'll do. It's what I'd do. She's read me perfectly, matey. Fascinating really.'

'You want me to wait here? Cover your back?'

Stoner shook his head. 'No need. If she intended hurt, she'd have tried it back there. She had a better chance. She wants me to see something, and I – really – have no idea what it is. Must be important, at least to her. Get going. I'll catch up later.'

Shard hesitated, wound down a window, 'How you getting back?'

Stoner just smiled. 'Plenty of cars around here, I'd guess. I'll borrow one. Like I've borrowed your bins.'

He waved the binoculars in a gesture of thanks and headed off into the night, moving rapidly towards a large house he recognised too well, with a long gravelled drive, well-trimmed lawns and several well-lit and uncurtained windows. A night for observation, then. Maybe confrontation, too.

383

33

STEPPIN' OUT

'It was supposed to be a time without lies. No lies at all. Not one fucking lie. Just . . . just the truth. The truth between us.'

Stoner's face was flushed. Stubble glittered like frost in a field of burned wheat. His eyes stared without focus at nothing . . . into nothing.

'Her whole life had been a lie. No whore lives with the truth. No sane whore.' He looked around him, eyes apparently searching for something which would never be found. '"I do it for the money, just for the money," they say. Or "It's just for a short time, just to get me on my feet." Or "I enjoy sex, so it's not like it's really working. I just get paid to do something I'd do for free anyway, so it's like being paid just to do what you want to do, like playing in a rock 'n' roll band." But it is not like that. That is a lie. A crappy, tragic and utter lie. "It pays really well, so I don't need to do it because I need the money, and I get to choose anyway, so I don't have to screw guys I don't want to screw." That's just lies. That's just shit.'

Stoner glowered across the table at his companion. Gestured to an anonymous nobody behind the bar, a female nobody, for another drink. She gestured back with added vulgarity.

384

'We don't do table service.'

Stoner half-rose to his feet. The bartender watched his face closing, his eyes gaining an unwelcome focus, his limbs gaining a growing purpose, and she recognised the coming storm for what it was; she'd seen too many of them before, and she raised a bright and totally false smile. 'But in your case . . . what would you like? Same again?'

She brought double doubles. And two bottles of light beer, which had not been ordered but which seemed like a good idea.

'These seemed like a good idea . . .' her words trailed away into the hard atmosphere as Stoner locked her eyes. Their gazes held firm as his hand drifted into a pocket, emerged and presented her with a large denomination banknote.

'I don't need change. Keep them coming. An empty glass is just an excuse . . . for violence.' He sat down, dismissing her. Two paused seconds and she was gone. Money in one hand. Tray swinging like a defensive shield from the other. Her hips swayed as she left the two men, and before she'd reached the working side of her bar Stoner had re-seated himself and resumed his monologue.

'The truth was all of it. It was all that it was and it was all that we had together. She would not lie to me and I would not lie to her. Simple as that. I found peace in this. She did what she needed to do, whatever, and I did what I do. It was supposed to be no more than that. Is that too hard? Is that too difficult? Why does everyone lie to everyone? All the time. All the damned time. All she said she wanted was honesty. All I could offer was honesty. And the other way around. I could buy her out of the life. She knew that. She always knew that. The house she lives in, that flat of hers. That's my house. That's my flat, my apartment. It's yours, I told her, yours to live in. There's no fee. No need. I don't need that.

'But she needed to pay. I don't know why. She paid me rent.

After a year she paid more. I told her there was no need. None. She paid more. Money transfer. I told her, she wanted out of the life, then she'd get out of the life faster if she saved the money. Didn't waste it on me. Honest. Simple. I do not need the money. She did not need to work. She did not need to do anything. Unless she wanted to do it. Which is a different thing.

'But I trusted that, because she said it, so it was true. She needed that independence. She did not want ever to be dependent on me. She said that if I gave her the house I could always take it back again. It would always be mine. She wanted to be her own woman. I respect that. I still respect that. She was talking shit. She knew me better than that. Why would I give her something and then take it back? I'd just write it off. She decides she's out of my life? Well that is fine. I'd hurt, we all hurt when things go south, but I've known worse. I've watched friends bleed out in front of me. I've held their heads in my hands, told them more lies and watched the light and the life just fade away. I've popped enough people. Plenty of people. It's not hard. It's not easy but it gets more easy. Easier by the day. Easier with practice. She made me talk to her about it. There was no force. It was so damned good to talk about it. She'd seen a lot of killing. The deed caused her pain, not the words. Words, she'd say; words are the defence, the barrier between the unacceptable and insanity.

'The problem with the talking, though, is that the feeling returns when you talk out the numbness. When we were first a thing, a big thing, the biggest thing, y'know, then we'd talked about the honesty by then, it was as though I couldn't shut up. It just poured out like the gods' own toilet flushing. Poured out. It was brilliant. No nastiness. No shading black into a subtle very dark grey. None of it mattered to her. When I told her I was surprised she wasn't running away, when I told her about the pornographer – remember her? – when I told her about that I told her the full thing. What I did to her. Do you know what I did to her? Have you ever cut strips off someone's face while they stood and screamed and bled like a fountain? And as they faced themselves in the mirror and watched your hand do that thing? And felt good about it? Have you? Don't tell me. I don't care. This is all about me.

'When I told her that, and I asked why she was still there, still leaning back against me and being my friend, she said, "I fuck strange men for money. That's what I do. You kill strange men for money. That's what you do. There is no difference. Not to me. They're just flies. They're just not there. They don't matter. In my black Africa they have to fuck all the time so they can keep the population up, there are so many guys like you who kill so many guys. Just flies."

'Those tattoos on her cheeks? The tears? They're for her family. All dead. Every one. Killed by men like me. She didn't cry. She couldn't cry. But she believed that tears were called for, tears, her tears, were needed before anyone could get any rest. So she had her own tears stitched to her own cheeks.

'She told me; "I know that if I knew who had killed them all, and if I told you, then you would catch that plane to Africa. That you would be the hellhound I'd set on their trail and you would not return before you'd killed them all, and if you did not kill them all or if one of them got to you first then you would not come back."

'I agreed with her that this was so. That is who I am. That if she wound my spring and told me who these men were then I would fly me to Africa and they would die. All of them. Bad deaths. Pain-filled deaths. And I would return to her, all her debts would be paid, all my debts would be paid and we could start over.

'I would build up the club and I would set up a house band and we would be normal. As normal as fuck-ups like us can be.

The properties bring in the rent. I don't need more money than that. You know that. She knows that. I told her the truth. She told me the truth. Her life in Africa? Jesus holy god. And she came from a decent family, a family with enough money for her to get out and come here. I asked her to tell me who her family's killers were, but she didn't know. She knew why they were killed and when they were killed and how they were killed, and she worried a little that they would come here and kill her too, but she felt safe with me.

'She is safe with me.'

He drank more. Emptied both his glasses. Signalled for more. The bar was filling, but the drinks were prompt. He paid again with another large note. The tramp stamp on the girl's ass moved with her walk. He'd not noticed it before. An eagle gripping the Harley-Davidson logo. Biker chic by a biker's cheeks. He would have smiled. Another time.

'Drink up.' It was an instruction, not an invitation.

'It was good for a long time. Very good. She'd talk about the johns, the clubs, the fuck-ups she pleasured. Serviced. Fucked. Whatever. She'd ask me about the jobs I did. I'd tell her where I could, tell her when I wasn't able to, so I could be honest.

'I asked her to tell me when she'd saved enough to stop, maybe to buy me out of that house so she could call it home . . . hers . . . her home. She said she would. She would do that. We agreed that if she had the money there would be no need for her to spend it; she could simply consider the house to be hers, stop paying rent and simply pay me for it if and when we split up. Which we both felt was inevitable. It has to be honest. At this stage of my life I want nothing less than honesty and I want nothing more than honesty. With her. If we were honest together then everything else . . . everyone else could just go fuck themselves. Everyone else were just bit players in this dreamland, this stupid childish fuck-up of a fantasy.

'I don't believe in anyone, in anything but me. That's kept me alive and it's kept me sane. I like some people. They're OK. You. You're OK. Usually. But Lissa, my own dirty blonde Lissa? She is apart from that. She's my own noble whore, my very very own tragedy queen, she's my opposite number, the black to my white and a heart darker even than mine. But we could make it all work, redemption through honesty. Just us. No lies. Childish, isn't it? Dreamy hippy shit. Nonsense.'

Stoner sounded almost angry, the intensity of his mood shining through the words, although his delivery was quiet, his manner calm, his expression placid and flat. He drank. His hands did not shake. His fingers did not clench with the anguish of it all.

'The only thing we demanded of each other was truth. Honesty. Call it what you want. I was straight. I'm not monogamous. I suppose I could be. I suppose anyone could be. But why bother? Why construct some stupid fantasy world of two perfect people? It's not possible. I've never met a perfect person. I think they only exist in fables and bibles. She's the same. She gets paid to fuck. I hate that. Really hate it. Before her I would never have cared about it. I'd have cared about the diseases, the squalor of it, but not the fucking. Everyone fucks, anyone who doesn't gets fucked up by that. So why must everyone pretend? Why must everyone pretend?

'So it's great and it's groovy. She lives in one of my houses. She pays me a fair rent. She never takes her johns there. That would be too crap. It's my house; I turn up when I need to be there. It's my house; I do not make appointments. She's a decently high-class hooker, if you can believe in that thing. She charges enough to rent a good room in a good hotel. Most of her regulars have houses of their own, and when their wives are away – because they all have wives – the johns invite Lissa to stay there. How can they do that? That's bizarre. Doesn't bother her at all. She says she finds it fascinating, that she understands them a lot better when she sees where they live, how they live. It's not too easy to pretend to be a secret millionaire when you live in a two-room flat. But if you lived in a two-room, you couldn't afford Lissa. Oh no.

'She almost never comes to the club. Almost never listens to the music. Music comes from boxes, big boxes and little boxes, boxes filled with the stuff, all of it has no value because it's in a box. It has no life. None. None at all. Blue Cube is filled with real music, but she doesn't like it. I like that she doesn't like it. Reminds me that I do not know everything about music, that what is music for one guy need not be music for another.

'The crowd might love me for what I play and how I play it, but she loves me for what I am. Who I am. She is brilliant company. She is brilliant at many things. I long ago gave up asking her why she chose to whore rather than to work. She says it's the money. A lot more for a lot less effort. And she says she takes a lot less shit. OK. I can see that.'

The bar was filling, the noise level rising with the crowd. Big hotel, expensive rooms, expensive drinks, bargirl with an eagle tattooed to her ass cheeks. Stoner stood, waved her over. She came. Stood and waited. There was an unserved crowd waiting for her, waiting at her bar.

'Two bottles,' Stoner said. 'Two of the best; still capped, still sealed. Takeaway.'

She left silently, returned silently. Stoner gave her money; she pocketed it without even looking at it.

'I get off at one,' she said.

'That's nice.' Stoner walked away and headed for the stairs.

Led the way up the stairs to his room.

'Hold this.'

He passed the second bottle to his companion who took it, waited and watched while Stoner carded the lock and walked inside, stepped to one side and held the door for the other, who followed him in, walked to the table, reached down to steady the bottles against his inebriate unsteadiness, against the effort of climbing three floors on foot, turned to wonder why the climb when the lifts were easy and empty and stopped dead in his tracks as the long black blade entered his neck. Smoothly. Silently.

'Sit down.' Stoner motioned towards the bed.

'Sit down carefully. Do not touch the blade. If you move it, you'll slice the carotid and that would be that. Curtains. The goodnight call.'

The Hard Man sat, slowly, carefully. Placed a flat hand to steady himself against the mattress. Blood oozed from the wound. He raised his right hand to the handle at his neck, ran his fingers over it. Dropped the hand back to the mattress. His eyes, bright with fury, glared at Stoner.

A whisper. 'Just. Like. That.'

Stoner sat at the table, unscrewed the cap from the first bottle. Poured himself a generous measure.

'Best you ease off on the drink.' He smiled with no humour at all. 'This stuff can kill you. The demon drink.' He sank half the glass and turned his chair so its back was between himself and his guest; folded his arms along it. A second blade was visible now, longer and just as black, lying with muted threat on the table beside the half-filled glass.

'You're in no immediate danger. It's the short blade. Very clean. Not much chance of an infection. Move it and you'll die. A military medic will be able to remove it for you, no trouble. Triangular blade, three edges. Nasty things. You might be able to talk, but quietly, and I would consider how important it was before I started speaking, were I in yours. Think how much you need to tell me what you tell me. I'm going to ask a few questions, just a very few, and a little calm yes or no will be fine. No need to shout, and shaking your head would be a bad move.

'Try to jump me and you'll die. Fuck around and you'll die. Lie

391

to me and you'll die. If you would prefer to die now, just say so. It's not a problem.'

The voice was calm, quiet, polite.

'Like I said. All about honesty. That's what it was supposed to be. Honesty and respect. The two go together. The one grows from the other. Honesty comes first.'

The Hard Man gurgled, tried to cough, tried not to cough. Gurgled and wheezed. A thin red line straggled from his mouth. His eyes were filled with rage. Furious, staring rage.

'Ah. The tickly throat? Trachea's cut. That is one very sharp blade. It'll get hard to breathe. You could drown. Time is short. Time doesn't hang around, not even for you. Especially not for you. How long has this been going on?'

'Always.' A simple statement, made carefully. Another stifled cough. The sound of the echo of the rattle of death.

'She hates you.' Stoner made a statement. He wasn't asking a question. 'Always has. Right from the start.'

'Customer.' The Hard Man pushed against the firm orthopaedic mattress to maintain his upright posture, his balance. 'Good customer.' His eyes were watering. He blinked. 'Should have told you. Should have noticed. You ... should have. She ... should have told you. She ...'

He gasped carefully, breathing light, eyes weeping tears of frustration and rage.

'The country house. Yours?'

The Hard Man closed his eyes.

'Yes.'

'You told her you're a fucking member of fucking parliament?'

'Ex. Was.' Speaking was becoming difficult. The bubbling was more noticeable, the trickle of blood more pronounced, the red brighter, frothy.

Stoner propped himself in the corner of the room. Tapped the handle of the long black blade in his hand against the edge of the desk.

'OK. I see sense. Where do you work, Mr Man? Mr ex-MP? Where in Whitehall? You're more than a boss spook, then. More to you than ever I saw. How did you hide it? How did I fail to find it? What do you do? And who do you do it for?'

The Hard Man's gaze was focused, a grimace of concentration. Whispering . . .

'Procurement. Financial procurement. Cobra. As high . . .' he coughed finally, painfully, blood running, bubbling, from his mouth, pooling on the mattress between his legs. Slowly soaking. 'As high as it gets.'

Stoner levered himself with visible reluctance from the wall. Stalked slowly to, past and around the Hard Man who sat, transfixed, unmoving, staring. Reached inside his jacket, removing the wallet and the two cell phones he encountered. Patted down the other pockets, gently enough. Flicked open the phones, one after the other, read their displays. Unclipped the backs of the units, removed both SIM cards, replaced the backs and dropped them into a leg pocket of his own cargo pants. He walked around again until the two men faced each other, one standing, face expressionless, the other leaking his life away into a firm mattress. Stoner, a tired sigh marking the arrival of a decision, took another cell phone from the desk and placed it by his companion's right hand.

'Make your call. Make it fast. Never cross me again. Good luck.'

34

TIRED OF WAITING

One of the many appealing features of the Harley-Davidson motor-cycle is that the same basic design of machine has been in produc-tion for longer than anyone can remember without stooping to a work of reference. There was once a time when Harley-Davidson were not building large capacity twin-cylinder motorcycles, with those twin cylinders arranged in a vee layout . . . but few, if any folk alive could remember that time.

What this means is that all current models of Harley-Davidson motorcycle have been developed to a point close to perfection. At least, close to their builder's idea of perfection, and presum-ably close to the idea of perfection as perceived by their legions of loyal customers. It is maybe a small surprise that many of these customers, maybe a majority of them, prefer to improve upon the near-perfection upon which they have already spent their very many dollars, Harley-Davidsons being American motor-cycles, and the dollar being American currency.

Stoner sat on a stool, leaning into his own inevitably black Harley-Davidson. Not one of the 350cc semi off-road military machines which he sometimes transported in the rear of his heavy Transporters; this was his Sunday-best Harley-Davidson, his own permanently ongoing companion in his personal nonsensical quest for two-wheeled perfection. Every time he modified it, tuned it, altered its suspension settings, its seating, fuel capacity, engine capacity or riding position, he would head for the hills, ride for a few hundred miles then return it to the bench in his premises at Parkside, at the Transportation Station. Following this, he would, if he chose to ride a motorcycle rather than drive a car, habitually ride either one of his 350cc off-road Harley-Davidsons or something bland, possibly less conspicuous and certainly more efficient than his Sunday Harley. Such is an irony in the affluent motorcyclist's life.

Compared with earlier models from Harley-Davidson's Milwaukee plant, modern machines bearing that name boast excellent brakes, essential to handle the ever-increasing levels of performance demanded by the modern motorcyclist and crucial if that motorcyclist wishes to stay alive and kicking ass along the increasingly crowded highways of the world. Stoner always wanted better brakes. He was changing the front brakes of his Sunday Harley for probably the fourth or fifth time, reflecting silently to himself as he sat, relaxed and easy, measuring up the components he was replacing with the components with which he was replacing them. It was an absorbing task. It is possible that the task was so absorbing that he was unaware that he had company until that company spoke to him.

Then again, it is also possible, and in fact more likely, that he was entirely aware of the arrival and entry but was sufficiently relaxed about it that he appeared to have taken none of his customary precautions.

'Hartmann's dead.' Shard was careful to walk into Stoner's direct line of sight. 'Did you know that?'

Stoner laid his spanners down and looked straight ahead, at the motorcycle rather than at his visitor. Slow seconds ground past. A cell phone shook itself into a small electronic frenzy somewhere in the room. He looked up, met Shard's hard stare with a blank neutral gaze of his own. Pointed to a desk in the gap between two curtained dirty windows. The computer screen standing there displayed a pattern of shifting colours; a screensaver.

'Spacebar.' A single word. No stress, flat voiced and quiet. Shard walked to the computer, pressed the bar. The screen flicked to life, showing a severed head, revolving slowly. He turned back to Stoner, who had picked up a spanner, but was wiping it clean, not fixing fasteners with it.

'You know, then. Why are you here? Aren't you supposed to be looking for these guys? Shouldn't you be at the scene? Who told you, anyway?' Shard appeared concerned more than angry, bemused more than belligerent.

'Same as told you. Mallis. "Another head," he said; usual place, usual happy smiling face. In any case, SOC guys are there, forensics, experts littering the place, paddling through the blood, losing and confusing all those vital clues, misinterpreting evidence with their usual good humour. What's there for me?'

'He was ... fuck it, Stoner, he was your friend.' Shard's customary control seemed to be struggling.

'You're struggling with reality, Shard.' Stoner spoke evenly, almost gently. 'The guy's my employer – was my employer – not my lover. And now he's dead, I am unemployed. It's a good place to be, especially at the moment. I can recommend it.' He brandished a gleaming lump of metal. 'Look at these; six-pot Billet racing calipers. If these beauties don't haul down the speed, then there's no hope. No hope at all.'

Shard stared at him.

'Grief. It must be grief. I've heard it said that grief takes many strange forms.' His body posture suggested that he was taking stock of the situation; more care and caution than before.

'No grief. None here, at any rate. He was not a pleasant man.'

Stoner was giving the impression of being a very relaxed man, particularly relaxed, given the circumstances.

Shard however was far from relaxed. His agitation was visibly increasing, escalating along with his mystification at Stoner's obvious unconcern.

'Don't you want to know who killed him? You worked together for years. Years and fucking years. I can't remember how many years. Doesn't this matter to you? Are you off your head again? On the powder again?'

'Calm down. I know who killed him, give or take. So do you. I don't know why, exactly, but I can make several good guesses, and they're good enough for me. He will go unmourned. No grief-ripped widow, no known next of kin.'

'You have cracked. He used to be an MP. Mallis told me. Did you know that? Of course there'll be next of kin. There'll be the godmother of all investigations, inquiries, statements in Parliament. It will be hideous. Reporters. Heavy police. State spooks. Bad men with big guns and big budgets.'

'I doubt it. He'll probably turn out to have suffered a heart attack while climbing an alp, or something noble but nebulous. Betcha. I bet the body the plods have taken away will be an unknown John Doe, maybe an illegal drug-dealing immigrant from the Vatican or somewhere unlikely, and that our man was nowhere near the place at the time he was killed. Five and Six are good at that kind of thing when they turn their hands to it. Maybe a motoring accident. They can mince up a body pretty bad I believe. Possibilities are endless. You'll see.'

'And you don't care?'

'I don't care. I do not care. I care not at all. What's to care about?'

'He was your friend. Fuck it, JJ, sometimes you can be an utter cunt.'

'Life is tough and then you die. Everybody dies. Be grateful he beat you to it. He was not my friend, he was a professional friend. They are not the same thing. In theory we usually fought our little fights on the same side. He paid well and promptly, that's about as far as it goes. Coffee? Or is it too late in the day for coffee? Places to go? People to see?'

'Coffee's good. Make some decent stuff. The stuff I brought.' Shard was calming, as rapidly as his calm had deserted him, so it was returning. 'I worked for him too. He'd asked me to start working as your shadow, to watch your back. Did you know that?'

'I know that.'

'I was supposed to be meeting him tonight. When did you last see him? Had you told him about those blonde sisters?'

'Yes. I saw him last night. We had dinner.'

Shard's recently recovered composure was draining away again.

'Last night? You had dinner last night?'

'Uh-huh. And the autopsy will reveal how much we drank, too. Quite a night.'

'Was he OK?'

'Do you mean did he appear to have a premonition of his own sudden and bloody departure? I doubt it. I think he had a tickle in his throat, but it didn't seem fatal. Certainly not in the head falling off and landing in front of a convenient webcam stakes at any rate. But you never can tell, and you won't be able to ask him, either.'

'You are one cold fucker, JJ. You know that? Fucking cold.'

'Not so.' Stoner appeared absorbed by the rituals of fine coffee. 'I am simply reserving my sorrow for the appropriate moment, preferably when I am alone, when my sobs will be Shakespearian and I will be inconsolable. He was the cunt, Shard. A very bad man. My main concern is that an even more bad man will replace him. If he's replaced by a woman as bad as he was, we are all doomed. Doom would be inevitable. A woman so bad is an affront to nature and a sure sign of the coming of the end, amen.' Stoner appeared to be on the verge of bursting into song. He poured the coffee and the two men drank it, hot and black, while they watched each other. Carefully.

Shard interrupted the shared appreciation of Stoner's excellent coffee. 'I was to watch you. Not so much your back, more what you were doing. He seemed concerned at your lack of progress. I would have told you.'

'Of course you would.' Stoner sipped. 'Of course you wouldn't. That would have been stupid and unbelievable and unprofessional.'

'You're not angry?' Caution edged each word.

'No. Rarely. Almost never. Anger is simply unproductive. It wobbles the concentration, blunts the focus and clouds the thinking. Angry men make great fighters. They believe in causes, noble expensive stuff like that. And they always die. Angry men never grow old and die peacefully in their beds.'

'Crap. That's pure crap, JJ. I've seen you angry. Fucking furious in fact. Bouncing angry.'

'You are mistaken. You have mistaken angst for anger. I am a modern man. I have angst. I am a bluesman, my friend. I know depths of angst you could never even contemplate. If I wasn't also possibly the world's greatest unappreciated guitar player I could end up psychotic with the angst. Suicidal. Murderous is more likely, but you get the idea.'

'Killer angst?'

'You've got it. No one knows how tough is the struggle against the angst of a bluesman.'

'You're spouting nonsense again, JJ.'

'That is also true. More coffee?'

Coffee was poured, followed by a sipping silence. It was hot coffee. Also, it was good coffee, and strong.

'How come the good mood?' Shard's curiosity may have been

prompted by the politeness of enquiry. Or then again, it may not. 'Your . . . oh, I don't know . . . your colleague, your associate has been murdered. And you seem happy with this. How is that? I seem more affected, and I hardly knew him. I'd always understood that you two were thick as thieves. Thicker.'

'Long, long story. Too tedious for today.'

'OK. There is no easy way.' Shard stood, leaving Stoner sitting, relaxed. Calm. 'You admitted you had dinner with him yesterday. What did you do afterwards?'

Stoner smiled. An easy, relaxed smile.

'I went to the club. I played a song or two. Drank a drink. I had a lot to think about. You a policeman now? A bit of a comedown for a soldier. That lean, mean killing machine downgraded to a plodding officer of the law? Come on now. I said I didn't kill him, which means I didn't kill him. You should trust me, brother. I doubt you know many men more trustworthy than I am.'

'But you knew he was dead? Before I arrived?'

'Of course I did. I already said. I have reliable sources, as do you. As already agreed, matey, Mallis told us both. In the correct order, too. In fact, for your amusement, I instructed Mallis to let you know directly, rather than letting the knowledge dribble down through channels in the usual haphazard inaccurate way. Of course . . .'

He paused.

'Of course I was also making sure that the circle of those who know about his death is a wider circle than those who feel they need to know. Folk who feel a need to know too often employ folk like you to remove others who may know but who they feel should not. Did you follow that? Should I say it again, only slower? Is your thinking hat on? Time to throw away the dunce's cap, matey, and to understand that this is a risky time for you.'

'But not for you?'

'No. Not for me. I am retired. I have a pension fund and several

400

excellently endowed policies to support me in my retirement. I am quite suddenly delighted to be retired. I may actually ride my most excellent Harley-Davidson into several distant sunsets. I may go on a cruise. A long one. Around the world, maybe. It's hard to say at the moment. But I shall enjoy thinking, deciding what I should do.'

'And you'll take your tame tart with you, I suppose? Your strange black whore?'

Stoner paused a second, his eyes briefly distant.

'I think that retirement is a solitary adventure. You should be going. Time to leave.'

Shard stood his ground, as if uncertain.

'I should be taking you in, JJ. Some guys want to ask a few questions. You didn't kill him; that's OK. I believe that. But I think you need to tell them that. I don't think either of us wants them to send me to get you.' He almost shuffled his feet. Almost looked embarrassed.

'Heavy guys?' Stoner appeared more amused than alarmed. 'Real bad men?'

'Yeah. Real bad . . .'

Shard avoided a collision with the impressively engineered six-pot Billet brake caliper only by thrusting violently sideways as soon as he realised it was in fast flight towards his head. By the time he recovered his balance, which was almost no time at all, he being extremely fit, very well co-ordinated and almost perfectly balanced, a wave of pungent volatile organics splashed into his face, soaking it, freezing his eyes and running fast from his face into his clothing. He swiped the fuel from his eyes, feinted fast to his right, Stoner's left, and forced his better eye into as near to focus as he could manage. The eye attempted to focus upon a second shiny metallic object, this one stationary. This one, in fact, held out for him to see, as well as he could, in the circumstances.

'Do not be fooled by the badge.' Stoner appeared utterly calm, collected and cool. 'The badge may announce that this lighter is a Harley-Davidson lighter, in which case you might consider that it could be less than one hundred per cent reliable and may thus fail to ignite the fuel which is currently causing you some irritation. And I'm sorry about that, but I needed to make a small point here. The lighter is in fact a Zippo. Zippo lighters are beloved of our American cousins for their unfailing ability to produce a flame to light their cigarettes. Marlboro Man, for example, could have been burned-out man, smokeless man, without his trusty Zippo. One particular joy of the Zippo lighter is that once lit, it remains lit until a second physical act shuts down the flame. This makes it an ideal lighter to throw, should anyone actually wish throw a lit lighter. You can, I imagine, deduce the reason I have one to hand.

'The fuel is fuel. Motor fuel. It may smell of many volatiles other than the essential petroleum, because its constituent components have been the target for endless government inter-ference over the years, but it still burns reasonably well in a plentiful supply of oxygen, and were this Zippo lighter to ignite it, you would be in a hot place very quickly. I have no wish to do this, Shard, particularly not to you and certainly not here, but I will roast you without hesitation unless you sit down, catch the towel I'm going to throw to you, mop yourself a little and listen a whole lot. OK? Do we have understanding?'

Shard nodded, breathing carefully and slowly through his mouth, aiming to keep the amount of fuel in his lungs to the lowest possible level. Stone stepped away and threw him a towel.

'Shit, JJ. You planned all this.' A statement, not a question.

'Not a plan, my friend. A precaution. No wise man would even joke about taking me anywhere, particularly against my will, and particularly when I may be inconsolable due to the ravages of grief following the death of my close colleague and valued asso-ciate.'

402

'Hartmann?'

'How many others have I lost recently? Are there more I should be worrying about? Nervous tension is a terrible thing. It can be bad for the heart. And heart trouble would be unwelcome at the moment. Particularly at the moment.'

Stoner rolled the lighter between his fingers.

'That's enough of the amateur dramatics. I wanted to make a point. It's a simple point, so simple that it would be easy to mistake it for an unimportant point. But it is important. At delicate times like these it is crucial that we all know where we stand.'

Shard nodded, mostly dry, stinking of fuel, sitting and steady. Watching, waiting and listening. Red eyes slitting, pain-filled.

'So. The lesson is one lesson, but it will need some detailed emphases. That's the plural of emphasis.'

'I haven't gone stupid, Stoner, and neither have I lost my grasp of the English language.'

'But your noted sense of humour appears a little precarious. No need for that. There is humour in everything. You just need to know where to look and how to identify it.'

'Glad you think so. I can't see any at the moment.'

'Hartmann's death removes me from any investigations he may have been involved with. Any of them, all of them, express it as you will. I am removed. Detached. I have no interest in anything that man was doing. None. I hope that's clear?'

'I don't understand what you're saying, but I hear you loud and clear.'

Stoner shrugged.

'I don't care what you understand, although it's very important that you accept that any attempt ... by you or by anyone else ... to involve me further in any of that man's business will be unwelcome and unsuccessful. We would fight. You ... or whoever gets sent against me ... would lose that fight. I would feel a need to incapacitate anyone crossing me. It is important that I'm clear about this, and it is important to me that you tell me here and now that you accept this. If you arrive again uninvited I will treat you as an intruder.'

Shard bristled slightly, but his reply was measured enough.

'OK. If I'm asked to contact you I'll make an appointment.'

'That would be both welcome and wise.'

'But I thought we were both looking into finding out which maniac did that head-chopper's video show? I hear you, JJ, and I'll do what you say, but I don't understand how you can drop the thing like that. We both know it was that strange blonde woman . . . at least, she's connected to it somehow. Don't you want to see it through?'

'Through? I think it is through. I think it's over. I think that the man behind it is a dead man. I think that it's done. That's my best analysis. Mallis will do better, but he might not share his thoughts, findings, conclusions with you or your masters. He can be a challenge at times. But so can we all.

'I think there was a game in play. I think it's over. I think its result is not the result the players intended. But I do think it's done. If I'm wrong, if there are more of the headless in the future, then we can talk about it some more, but in any other circumstance than that one, it's done. No more dead heads, no more spookwork. And I want to get back to being off the books. Really off the books. Retired.

'Shard. Friend. I almost like you. I certainly don't dislike you. We go back a long way. I have no wish to do you harm. If any remaining players want to send someone against me for whatever reason then fine; don't let it be you. You want to learn more about motorcycles or increase your understanding of guitar music . . . then fine. Drop me a line, give me a call and we can get together. You want to talk about the spook world? Forget it. I'm through with it.

'And listen carefully. If someone, anyone decides that I need to be retired, actively retired, then I will defend myself one hundred per cent. And after that, assuming I survive it, I will work out who was responsible and I will move against them. One hundred per cent. Got it?'

Shard nodded.

'I want to say something, JJ, and I want you to listen. Any chance?'

'Go ahead.'

'Truth. I can't see a circ in which I'd take on a gig to take you down. But if I had to – if there was one of those unrefuseable offers – I would always use the long gun. You may be well past it and slow as a pensioner, but you might get lucky. Long gun. Clean head shot. Promise.'

Stoner smiled at him. Gently. 'What you're saying is the fact that you're here with me is confirmation that you never had any intent? OK. I can believe that. You always were a lazy fucker; long guns? Yeah. When I accept that last gig, the gig to take you down, y'know, the big ten dollar gig, I'll hire a helo or a drone or something. Sit in a bar somewhere and order an air strike.'

Both men smiled. A moment had passed, and they both recognised that.

Stoner broke the silence.

'I have an archive, a secure archive, and I know where many bodies are buried. I put a few of them away myself, way back. And I am not going to run away. I am not going to hide. But neither am I going to ponce about, thumbing my nose at anyone. Leave me alone; I leave everyone else alone.'

He walked over to the wall, retrieved the Billet brake caliper, inspected it for damage, shook his head sadly and returned to the bike.

'Take it easy, matey. When you feel the edge is losing you, then walk away. Don't try to be old and bold. You know what they say about that. OK?'

A long silence. Tension drained from it. Shard stood; Stoner turned to face him, both faces set in no expression at all. Shard broke the silence, finally.

'OK. More coffee? You up for another?'

Stoner turned to face his Harley-Davidson, his back to his companion.

'You know how to make it, and you know where everything is.'

35

BROKEN WING

After hours. The Blue Cube was quiet, dark, cooling. Echoes of the evening fading. Stoner walked alone, checking door locks, flushing, rinsing, stacking away all the dead soldiers into their crates. It's rare to find silence near a collection of instruments, and the piano's bass strings whispered as he passed by; cymbals on the drum kit hissed in conspiratorial reply, the valves on the last lit amplifier hummed their own monotonous melody. But it was quiet. The darkest hours; the longest hours. Always a time for reflections.

Chimp the barkeep would usually perform a basic clean around before setting out into his own later night, but Stoner had sent him away smiling, along with the last of the evening's customers. He'd not felt like playing himself, had left that with the house band, a guest musician moonlighting from the TV studio where she'd been recording a show and a couple of occasional players. But not Amanda the saxophonist. Not tonight. He wondered briefly where she was, where her own demons were driving her that night. But it was a brief moment; none of his concern. Not really.

Chairs stood around their tables, the houselights were shut

down, leaving the backlit bar and a single spotlight stage left, illuminating the tall stool he preferred to play from. His elderly Fender, the battered Stratocaster which had been more than a companion for a couple of decades, lay in its case, although the Marshall amplifier he mostly used was lit up and live, standing on stand-by alone in its own electronic world. The PA was down, as was everything else.

Stoner lifted the guitar from its case, slung its strap, an old webbing affair heavy with ancient buttons and badges from a faraway past, over his shoulder and collected the lead from its customary resting place under one of the amplifier's lifting handles. The jack plug crunched as he slid it into its socket. Even with the sound set low it crunched. A poor earth, he reckoned. Again. Old guitars are like old motorcycles; you think they're working well, that you are on top of maintaining everything which needs maintaining, and something wanders along to prick the perfection. Like having an old friend interrupt a quiet evening's reading. Not unwelcome, not exactly, but an interruption all the same.

Although he rarely played Hendrix when there was an audience to witness his attempts, apart from 'Red House', which he almost always played at great volume and at great length, Stoner relaxed his mind and limbered his fingers by attempting, once again, to play with the same effortless fluidity of style, the same massive understanding of the instrument always displayed by the late musical magician. The need to dig into depths of involvement as he struggled to play just-so always involved his conscious mind so completely that although it was always an effort – a genius like Hendrix he was not – the concentration allowed some unique opportunity for another part of his brain, maybe a more primitive part, to work its way through whatever was its current preoccupation. And anyway, he loved the sound; a Fender guitar played flat out through a Marshall. It does not get much better.

Not at the end of the day. Not at the end – the official end – of a long and dwindling relationship, a long and rewarding – if too often too painful – way of life.

The opening kick to the song 'Little Wing' is a delight to get right. Right, as in what feels right for the night. Hendrix played the song in several different ways, sometimes slowly, sometimes more rapidly, always with variations, embellishments and additions. The song was always instantly recognisable and always fresh as a new tune. Tonight, Stoner entertained the tables, chairs, the beer engines and optics, all the empty space of the place with a slow, meditative introduction, then paused, missing the point at which the first words would walk in through the clouds, and the audiences would typically applaud. Presumably they applauded themselves for recognising the tune, possibly not, but for this solo show to no one Stoner stopped, raised his eyes to inspect the ceiling and played the intro again.

He played it accurately enough, close enough not to the Hendrix original but close enough to the version – his own version – that he wanted to hear. But he decided to play it again, this time picking the notes with just the fingers of his right hand, dispensing with the abrasive accuracy of the flat pick in favour of thumb and fingernails. His right hand stalked the strings and he played it again, more slowly, using just the neck pick-up, the more bassy of the Fender's three pick-ups to provide a rich, full tone while allowing the opposed fingers and thumb of his wandering right hand to apply different weights, different emphases to the strings they picked.

He stopped again after the repeated intro. Picked up the discarded flat pick and held it loosely between the thumb and forefinger of that same right hand. Switched to the guitar's middle pick-up, introducing a little more treble and leaving out some of the bass. The flat pick could hit the bass strings harder than the nails of his middle and ring fingers, so the pick-up shift balanced that. And he moved the point at which his right hand played the strings further away from the bridge, removing some of the click-percussion from the contact between plucking finger and plucked string.

Stoner played the introduction again, declared himself pleased with it. The music suited the mood. He leaned into the stool's backrest, pushed back and sang the first verse to himself, inaudible over the Stratocaster's own amplified voice, then broke away from the song's original structure to allow himself a brief solo break. There was no audience to find fault and he was finding his own spaces between the clever chording and all the improvisational opportunities offered to the cunning player by the Hendrix original.

And after a full verse of part-chords and careful picking out of the melody while maintaining the basic beat in the background, Stoner drifted back the original and sang the second verse at the top of his tuneless voice, inaudible even to the audience of none above the Stratocaster's power shout.

Then, the final section, played all-too briefly on the original studio recording, but expanded and extended when played live by the maestro, and Stoner let rip. The guitar played itself, in that conjoined relationship – almost a coupling – between expert player and their familiar top-quality instrument. It felt that the Fender offered rarely trodden paths between the walls of notes, and Stoner walked those paths, lost in the self-indulgence which is probably unique to a confident instrumentalist.

Finally, after maybe twenty minutes of screaming, soaring, scheming and satisfying late-night guitar music, he pulled his song to its close, leaving the dying last chord to fade into the electronic stutter of the delay, reverb and chorus effect pedals he'd been using. He sat, drained but at peace.

A single pair of clapping hands. Applause where there should have been silence. Unexpected appreciation from the dark. A

410

female voice, almost lost in the hard silence which follows such loud music.

'That was so good, Mr Stoner. I can see why you look after your hands. "Broken Wings", was it?'

'"Little Wing", in fact. I wondered where we'd meet, Chastity, but you've done well getting in here.'

'Wrong girl, Mr Stoner; the wrong working girl. I've been here for some time. Your house band were good, although I do so enjoy listening to your girlie sax player, great set of lungs and lips on that one, so I missed her, but the others always seem a little . . . empty without your being there, kicking them up a gear. They were a little listless. Maybe they miss you. First time I've heard the piano guy sing, though. Nice voice. Bass player was drinking a lot. Always good to watch a band. You can pick up lots of stuff. Tonight? Like they were all waiting for someone, something? You? The second coming?

'And I borrowed your apartment upstairs for a little while, just to let everyone go their own ways. In their own time. No need to hurry them once you finally showed up.'

'You knew I'd be here? How?'

'I know you better than you think, Mr Stoner. Much better than you know me, for example. You were always going to come here, and I was always going to wait for you. The only mystery in this is how come you weren't expecting me?'

'Your sister, the crazy one, she killed Hartmann, right?'

'Wrong again, Mr Stoner. You're great on the guitar, less great at the deductive reasoning stuff, I think. But you will be tired. I can see that. Respect that.

'You killed him, Jean-Jacques. You.'

Charity's voice sounded completely calm. In complete control. Maybe it was. Stoner released the Stratocaster's strap from the rearmost of its two studs, held the instrument by its neck, close to the joint to the body, and swung it to his right, resting the silent device in its stand. He looked towards the sound of the voice. He could see a figure; dark coat or cloak or dress, bright hair shining in the dim of the bar lights.

'No need to get up, Mr Stoner. I'd prefer it if you stayed seated. More comfortable for the both of us. I mean you no harm ... I wouldn't be here were that not the case, but you are sometimes a little prone to an occasional rash act, so I'm told, and we could both of us do without that.'

Stoner sighed. He felt peculiarly exposed, alone on the stage, sitting in the centre of the beam of the only bright light in the building. A strange sensation, even for a musician of long standing.

'This feels dead strange, Charity. I can't see you well, and it's making me nervous. I do not enjoy the feeling. Can't we talk over a drink? There's plenty here to choose from. I did not kill Hartmann. From the vid I'd assumed it was Chastity, your flaky sis. Although what happened and how it happened is a bit of a mystery. Mysteries are good, though, so long as the truths they conceal deserve that concealment. Like the names thing; the thing with all your silly sisters using the same silly name. Chas. What's that about?'

Charity looked away, briefly. 'It's a game we played as kids. It was never my fault; it was always Chas. Chas did the bad thing. It's habit. And it confuses the innocent, so we sort of carry on with it. Pick up the phone and ask for Chas; you'll always get her.'

Stoner shrugged. 'OK. Drink?' He sounded calm enough, despite his suggestion of nervousness.

'A drink? OK. In a minute. Sit completely still. I'm going to land something with you. Between your feet. It's a difficult throw and I want to make a point without freaking you into some heroic male action hero kind of thing. OK?'

Stoner's face cracked into a smile.

'Oh, wow. I do enjoy a surprise. And you're full of them, lady. What do you want? I should maybe stand on one leg or something?'

'Think of the little boy with the apple on his head.' Charity's voice was calm. 'Think of the circus, where the big butch guy throws nasty sharp knives at the simpering girly, but always manages to just about miss her. But in reverse. And this isn't an easy target, and this isn't a good thing to throw. Frankly.'

Stoner spread his arms wide and shrugged. And a sudden crunch found his own knife, the three-inch black blade he'd left in the throat of the Hard Man, the three-edged killer's cutting blade with the blood gutters and the Teflon darkness and the composite moulded handle . . . that knife was standing almost exactly midway between his feet. He started to bend towards it, started to reach down.

'You can leave it there. I would prefer it if you did.' No threat in the female voice. None needed. It was not a throwing knife, and it was not an easy throw. She would of course also carry a blade of her own, or some other short-range weapon. That would be the only sensible option. In her place he would be well prepared and well armed. Maybe supported, too. Families were apparently close affairs, and he had met her sister . . . knew her better by reputation and result.

Charity rang a pair of bottles together. An invitation.

'Come down, if you like. Join me at my table. I brought drinks. You paid for them, you might as well enjoy drinking them. You can leave the blade where it is. You left it where it was, after all.' No tremor in the voice, just an open tone, an invitation.

Stoner jumped down from the stage. Carefully. This would be a poor moment to twist an ankle, strain a ligament, bruise a foot. Also embarrassing. She gestured to a seat facing her, stood for a second, fluid as a fitness freak, sat down again.

'You left the blade. Good move. I have another. A bigger one, though no more of an edge; that's one neat blade, and a clever use.'

'You're going to tell me how I killed him? Hartmann?' Stoner reached for a bottle, started to peel its paper label in single long strips, starting at the top.

Charity held his gaze, held her own hands out of his view. Viewed without the wall of the footlights between them, she was neatly turned out, white-blonde hair immaculate. A long, loose coat, dark material. An odd choice for an indoor encounter; better suited to the outdoor life.

'You called me, Jean-Jacques.'

'I did, did I?' Stoner held his tone as levelly non-committal as her own.

She lifted a hand into view; her left hand, he observed, presumably she was right-handed. The hand held a cell phone. Nothing flashy, not too smart. She slid it across the slick table, adding a spin so that it faced him when its motion ceased. Neat trick. Maybe she was left-handed, he wondered, and picked up the phone, flicked it open.

To view a text message, a simple message: 'Help me'.

The caller ID was his own name; 'Stoner'.

'Interesting. Thank you for that.'

'I did consider it a little strange that you would leave your cell there with him, but then I did consider it strange that you would ask Chas . . . Chastity for help. A strange choice for you to make, given that so far as I knew you were likely to be her next target. I did wonder when I got the call whether it was a trap. I expected that it would be, in fact.'

'OK. Excuse my slowness here. I asked Chastity for her help? For what? I needed no help. And in any case, you sisters swap phones?'

'No. Chas didn't pick up, so the call transferred to me. We

414

usually do that. Charm would've picked it up if I'd not answered. Answering machines are so . . . robotic, somehow. We like to offer a more personal service than that.'

'You can work it out then, Miss Personal Service? What happened?'

'Yeah . . .' she drawled her reply. Slowly, as though she was still considering it. 'You took his phones. You could trace his activities.' She paused. Stoner nodded his agreement. 'You'd done the fighting thing, whatever it was that you boys were fighting about, and you considered him neutralised, but had no reason to kill him yourself? You gave him your own phone so he could . . . so he could, what, exactly?' She paused again.

Stoner lifted the bottle to his lips, sipped. Held her gaze. 'Call for help. What else? My phone; I can watch who he calls. He called a number I didn't know. It could have been anyone. I expected a second call; one for a medic, one for a counter-attack.'

'He didn't make the second call?'

'No.'

'The short blade was perfectly placed, Jean-Jacques. He couldn't move, hardly at all, and his trachea was losing air. That is almost exactly how Chas likes to leave them, when she takes on the killing. Life leaking away. She enjoys watching it go. Watching the ebb of it. As they fade, she takes back her short blade. Sometimes she takes out the carotid with it, sometimes not. Sometimes she lets them linger. She can be very . . . cold. She says she feels loss, that the moment of death is a thing which can be shared if she's close enough. Like there's a moment when the dying soul touches her own. As it leaves. She says she lives for that moment. That it means something, something real in a life filled with lies, deceit . . .'

'What do *you* say, Charity? Hmmm?' Stoner was completely relaxed, focused on her. Both of his hands on the table before them. A deliberate no-threat indication, a sign that could not be missed.

She looked up, sipped a little from the bottle. 'She leaves them like that, Jean-Jacques. She leaves them as soon as she feels their passing. She is ... clinical. And sometimes they're not ... not dead. Their life has left them but the body, the biological machine is still running. I truly hate that. I hate that. I hate that!' Almost a shout, She was breathing loudly.

Stoner's voice was calm, his tone gentle.

'You clean the scene, then? Make it so confused that there's nothing for SOCO to hang on to? And you ...' he was smiling; she staring at him in reply to that smile, '... you take their heads and you set them in front of a laptop and you transmit the image to the website and then you just pack up and go?' If anything, his tone was admiring rather than revolted. She looked at him and nodded.

'Pretty much. That's pretty much how it goes. When it goes right it baffles the brilliant and when it goes wrong ...' She was visibly shaking now. Her customary cool seemed to have departed, although Stoner doubted that it was far away, she was far too experienced for that.

'There's more, isn't there? I'm missing something. I've been to ... four of your recent scenes and ...' His voice faded, then returned, loud with surprise. 'You fuck them. If they're not entirely dead you fuck them! Got it. Stone me. Twice.' He raised his bottle to her, saluted with a nod of his head and drained the bottle. 'Drink up. I'll get us another couple.' And he rose, walked to the bar and returned with four opened bottles swinging from his fingers, placed them on the table. Charity stared at him, wide-eyed, surprise writ large across her face. She lifted her right hand from its place at her side and raised the long, dark, flat, black cutting knife, the boning knife, to the table.

'Tell me one thing. Two things.' Stoner kicked his chair away from the table before sitting down again; he had anticipated the knife or something similar, but wanted no more worries about weapons.

She nodded. Took her hand from the long blade and raised her second bottle to her lips. Her eyes held a long focus; they were looking somewhere beyond the club, beyond that conversation, that moment.

'Whatever.'

'OK. Am I still your target? My interest in your headless chickens died with Hartmann; I have no . . .' he paused, a half-smile. 'I've no professional interest in you guys any more. If I'm still a target, your target . . .' he shrugged, lifted his shoulders in the Gallic way . . . 'I'll worry about it another night.'

Charity shook her head. 'I don't usually know the targets once we've agreed a contract, only Charm would know them all. She hands the details to Chastity one or two at a time. Chas sends me a text when her part's done and it's time for mine. So . . . so I finished Hartmann before I thought it through. It's not too easy. If I took time to think it through I probably couldn't go through with it at all.'

'But you know that I'm the next target? You sure? I would need to take steps, in that case. Or is this a truce? Do your truces apply to your sisters? To Chastity in particular?'

'You *were* the next target. I was waiting in your apartment upstairs for Chas to call. She felt that you would take two to take down.'

'I should feel flattered?'

'If you like. This is your home ground, you'll have hidden resources. We know that.'

'Chastity has devices hidden here, I believe.'

'She may. That didn't bother you? You wanted to play the guitar on your own rather than search out some . . . devices? That is

417

very cool. Very cool indeed. The Hartmann thing, then – a big thing for you?'

'We go back a very long way. I completely missed his dishonesty. Dishonesty with me. I am one paranoid bastard; it's not easy to see how I missed it all. I'm still . . . lost in that.'

'Oh come on!' Charity stared at him wide-eyed and incredulous. 'You didn't know about him and your tall black whore? You really didn't? You really needed Chas to show it to you? Love is blind, is it? Blinding? You were as good as the best and you missed that? We saw it as soon as you were involved in the operation. You must have known. At some level you must have been aware.'

Stoner shrugged. Ran fingers through his hair, then scraped their nails against the stubble on his cheeks. Looked up.

'So we sit and wait for your sister, is that it? Then we have a huge fight. Everybody dies. That's the most likely outcome. Or is she already here somehow?'

'You really don't see it yet, do you?' Charity made no move, but watched his face closely. He said nothing.

'Our contract was ultimately from Hartmann. Through cut-out and cut-out after cut-out. In fact, we weren't sure until you took him out . . . then all signals stopped. Chas . . . Charm is one great researcher. She was almost there, I think, before you topped Hartmann, but that confirmed it. She spoke with Chas; Chastity called me maybe an hour ago. And here we are. She's not coming for you. We can go in peace. You're shaking.'

'I'm fine. Tired. Never kill friends. It's tiring. Fuck.' He paused, reflecting. 'Do you know why he was doing it? The house for Lissa? All that?'

'Just winding up, is what Charm thinks. Winding up all his old networks and clearing out his contact book ready for his new job. He would have become a public figure, probably, and . . . are we to understand that you have a lot of dirt on him?'

Stoner nodded; smiled grimly. Shook his head. 'All I wanted was out. I just wanted to be out of it. I nearly was. He knew that . . . OK. He wanted Lissa. OK . . .' he paused again. 'It does make some sick sort of sense. He . . . they . . . *he* should just have told me.'

'You'd have killed him. He was never an operator. He couldn't take you. Not nearly. You'd have ripped him to pieces. You did that, Jean-Jacques; you did that. Destroyed men.'

'Did you fuck him?' Stoner was struggling to maintain any kind of level tone of voice, to avoid an emotional escalation to a level he couldn't manipulate.

'He was dressed. Chas's guys are usually stripped, ready for it. That's how she does them. How she gets them vulnerable. Disarmed. Distracted. Fatal distraction. No. No, I didn't. Dying . . . I don't know. Dying just gives some guys a hard-on, really. It's . . . I know it's weird, I know it's insane, I know how wrong it is, but it makes it easier for me. To end them. Kill them.' She was breathing loudly, panting almost. 'And they don't know, and they can't tell. They can't talk about it. To anyone. Important to me. Very. But,' her gaze quite suddenly locked focus with his, 'you're not to know that. Mr Stoner, every girl's best friend, every girl's dream.'

'Oh fuck off with that.' Stoner was dismissive, instantly, cruelly. 'If you want any amount of one-night stands, go play in a band. If you just want to work your way through an endless meat factory, then great. Fine. Get on stage. Put everything into it. The more of a strain it is for you, the more they flock around. That's all it is. Some impossible idea of some impossible reflected glory. There's no glory to it. They make it up. They pretend you're something special. But you're not. You're just some guy who's on stage. Do not go there with this "every girl loves a player" shite. It just isn't true. Half the time they're pissed and want to cop off with some guy to impress their sad buddies, the other

419

half of the time they have some romantic notion that, like, just because you can play the guitar or work the saxophone or kick a drum, that you somehow know the meaning of life and have the answer to everything at your fingertips.

'I don't mean to piss you off with this, especially as you have at least one fuck-off great blade nearby, but Christ on a bike, let's not trade Great Angst Moments I Have Known with each other. For fuck's sake, Charity, not only do you have a great name – a great name for a blues singer, hey! – but you're fitter than a flea on a fiddler's knee. So what's this shit – this fucking a dying man shit all about, hey?'

Stoner's usual preferred projection of a man under control was weeping with failure; he was shouting. Almost shouting. His voice was raised.

'Girls who whore get paid to be whores, you know? Guys like me get treated exactly the same but don't get paid. Do not give me all that poor little misunderstood woman shit. I have known far fucking far too many women to believe it.'

He paused. Reached for his bottle.

'I'm sorry. I'm sorry to shout. It's been another long day in a continuing sequence of long days. I'm fresh out of good manners. You going to slice me now? I might even be too tired to resist. Or are we really all friends together now? What is it with you and the poor little beautiful lady bit, anyway? You talk good and you surely do look good. From here. And we're damn nearly touching, so I could tell if you had terminal acne or halitosis or leprosy or something.'

'You can't see, Jean-Jacques. You simply don't see what's in front of you. You have become blind.'

Charity lifted her hands – both hands – behind her head, and lifted her hair away. Stoner became stationary before her. Turned to stone. Silent. He just stared. The entirely bald woman stared right back at him, her eyes black with intensity.

420

She pulled open her coat, her long dark coat. Nothing beneath it. A neuter's body sat facing him. Very fit, well-muscled, flat stomach below a perfectly defined six-pack below a set of pectoral muscles. No breasts. None. Small, near invisible scars. Thread-fine white lines and no nipples. Not a hair. Skin shining in the reflected stage lighting. Her eyes shone in defiance, challenge.

'Neat.' Stoner ran his eyes over her. Ran them down from her own eyes, past her mouth, over the length of her body to her pubis. No hair. 'Very neat.'

Charity rested the long black blade on her right thigh. Opened her legs. Wider, until the lips of her sex parted, audibly unfolding before Stoner's intensity. The blade was cutting into the taut skin of her thigh; tiny dark drops appearing at irregular intervals along its length.

Stoner leaned back in his chair, frankly staring. Said nothing. A strange tableau in the unnatural light and hard shadows of the silenced club. Neither moved for a stretched moment. Neither spoke. Then . . .

'And you're not lying to me. You're not being kind.' Charity's words added to the surreal silence, somehow. Stoner said nothing, shook his head slowly, gaze fixed, transfixed, a moth facing up to its candle.

Charity lifted the long black boning blade from her thigh, handling its balanced weight with ease, fluidity, practice and precision, and leaned into Stoner's silent space. Rested the tip of the blade on the crotch of his jeans. Unbidden and probably unwelcome, the denim shifted beneath the weight of the blade, which in turn twisted, slicing without effort into the material, which in turn parted. She rested her left hand on herself, ran a finger each side of her proud clitoris and met Stoner's gaze with a question. He nodded. Slowly, and with wonder.

She lifted the blade away and he unzipped and released himself, pulled his cock clear of his pants and rested it there. Charity moved the blade again until its point rested on the shaft of his cock, which grew, steadily, relentlessly beneath the pressure, gentle though that was. Stoner stared at her left hand. It worked her clit steadily and her fingers slid between her outer lips, moving easily on their slick wetness. He leaned towards her, reaching a hand to join with hers.

Charity looked up, shook her head, added pressure to the blade and ran it along the length of his cock, then turned it until the edge drew a thin red line between metal and skin. He took hold of himself and squeezed, the thin red line became a very slightly thicker red line as he did so. She removed the blade. He moved his own right hand on himself in time with her left hand on herself in the strangest dance of his life.

Without more than a lost beat in their shared rhythm, she slid the long blade into its sheath, spun it lengthwise and without taking her focus from Stoner's cock slid the black composite handle of the black steel blade into herself. It sank easily inside and she sighed. Stoner was lost in the dance; moving to her rapid rhythm, moving rapidly towards an inevitability.

Which arrived too soon. Charity shouted, sat rod-upright, removed both her hands, leaving the long blade hanging from her like an improbable ritualistic phallus and half rose from the chair, eyes staring, breath bursting. She shook and shouted something crude and loud. The blade flew from her and landed at Stoner's feet. He reflexed away from it, his chair tipped and the imbalance wrecked his moment. Lost in a short space of complete confusion, he stood up, stepped back and faced Charity, who had retrieved her blade with astonishing speed, closed her coat to his gaze and was shaking the shape back into the blonde wig. Her expression was timeless, tears stood unwelcome at the corners of both eyes, and a sheen of sweat glossed the skin of her face. The long blade lay on the table between them.

And quite suddenly and entirely unexpectedly she smiled. A radiant grin. Two teenagers with a shared secret. Stoner felt a reflection of her smile grow on his own lips as his cock sagged and leaked a little, strawberry and pearl jams mingling slowly; regret no doubt for its own lost moment. Charity had replaced her hair, was once again the conventionally beautiful blonde he had known before.

'You should probably put that away now. Chills can be quite bad news, I do believe. And you're leaking on your jeans.'

Silently, and with some reluctance, Stoner complied. The silence grew to maturity and bred a silent family of its own.

'I'm the bluesman,' Stoner announced, obliquely. 'I should leave now.'

'But this is your place, isn't it?'

Stoner agreed this was so.

'I should leave.' Charity decided. 'Leave you in whatever passes for peace in your world, Mr Stoner.'

Stoner nodded his agreement. Neither of them made a move. Neither wished to be the first to move.

'If I walked backwards to the door I would fall over a table,' Charity suggested, with a hint of humour, somewhere.

'I'm hardly royalty,' Stoner's smile was as cautious as her own, 'and I won't shoot you in the back.'

'Nor stab me there?'

'That neither. At no point, in fact.'

'I'm safe with you, then? Despite the business with Hartmann?'

Stoner paused for a beat, then nodded. 'Yes. No beef with you. You did what I could not, I think. And if that was the last of the dead heads, then we really are clear. I'll put that another way; if I'm not on your contract list, then we have no problems at all.'

'So far as I know.'

'Weasel words, those, Charity. Too many meanings. I've met your sister, remember.'

'If your name's on a list, I'll let you know. That suit you?'

'Yes.'

'Then I guess I'll be on my way.'

She turned, turned back again.

'Should I stay?'

'Probably not.'

'Probably best that way. Last couple of guys I fucked died inside me.'

'Tell me about it. Tell me about it some other time, hey?'

'There'll be another time?'

'Reckon it's likely, me. You?'

'Yeah,' she drawled her words through the strainer of her smile. 'Do I get a parting song? A tune, Mr Bluesman?'

Stoner bounced up to the stage, picked up the Stratocaster and sat his stool in the spotlight. 'A Beatles medley? A Beatles medley at midnight? The Beatles did songs for every occasion. "Nowhere Man"? "I Don't Want To Spoil The Party"? "Day Tripper"? "Paperback Writer"? "Girl"? "Norwegian Wood"? That's the one for now.'

'It's a book.' Charity looked at him in an angular way. 'And a movie of the book.'

'Before it was a book, and even further before it was a movie, it was a song. Here you go ...'

Thanks for reading right to the very end. We hope you enjoyed *A Last Act of Charity*. If you did, please take a few minutes to review it on Amazon or Goodreads. Your feedback would be very much appreciated.

If you'd like to stay in touch with Stoner, Shard and the Killing Sisters then you'll find Frank Westworth and news about the next book in the series at www.murdermayhemandmore.net